NO PLACE TO RUN

MARK EDWARDS

THOMAS & MERCER

Published by Thomas & Mercer, Seattle

www.apub.com

Amazon, the Amazon logo, and Thomas & Mercer are trademarks of Amazon.com, Inc., or its affiliates.

ISBN-13: 9781542027908
ISBN-10: 154202790X

Cover design by @blacksheep-uk.com

Printed and bound by CPI Group (UK) Ltd, Croydon CR0 4YY

NO
PLACE
TO
RUN

ALSO BY MARK EDWARDS

The Magpies

Kissing Games

What You Wish For

Because She Loves Me

Follow You Home

The Devil's Work

The Lucky Ones

The Retreat

A Murder of Magpies

In Her Shadow

Here to Stay

Last of the Magpies

The House Guest

The Hollows

WITH LOUISE VOSS

Forward Slash

Killing Cupid

Catch Your Death

All Fall Down

From the Cradle

The Blissfully Dead

NO PLACE TO RUN

Author's Note

I have taken some liberties with the geography of California in this novel. The town of Eaglewood is fictitious, as is Birches Rock.

Prologue

Francesca was six hundred miles into her journey home, and dawn was breaking over the forest, when she saw the woman come running out of the trees towards the tracks.

Francesca had finally given up trying to get back to sleep at five. The compartment was stuffy and claustrophobic, the bunk as stiff and narrow as an ironing board, and the train shook so much she could feel her insides coming loose. She had fantasised about flopping into her own bed in Seattle until she remembered she didn't have anyone to share it with. She had scattered Kenneth's last remains on a beach in Los Angeles. Seventy-five years old and she was all alone.

Francesca manoeuvred her aching body out of the bunk bed. She had gone to sleep fully dressed, just in case there was an emergency. She slipped her shoes on, the super-comfortable Nikes she used for running. Her son, Stephen, could hardly believe she still went out jogging, but she swore the day she gave up would be the day she dropped. In fact, she itched to stretch her legs and go for a run now. If only she weren't stuck on this stupid train.

It was all Kenneth's fault, God bless him. This journey had been part of his last will and testament. Once upon a time, an eighteen-year-old Angeleno had taken the train north to Seattle, where he had settled, and he had written in his will that he wanted his ashes transported to the city of his birth by the same method, along the same tracks. Which was all very romantic, in a self-loving kind of way – but had he thought about his poor wife having to endure a thirty-two-hour journey on Amtrak's *Coast Starlight*, and then another all the way home?

Like hell he had.

Opening and closing the door as quietly as she could, so as not to wake the passengers in the next compartment, Francesca made her way into the empty dining car and then into Business Class, which was hardly better than Coach. There were no beds here, just reclining seats – the passengers slumbering, eye masks on, ear plugs in. She wrinkled her nose at the sweet and sour odour of nocturnal gases and hurried through. She caught a glimpse of her own reflection in the window, glowing like a ghost of herself, and hurriedly averted her eyes. She was in no rush to join Kenneth.

The Sightseer Lounge had floor-to-ceiling windows which, during the day, gave the passengers a full view of the forests through which the train ran for much of its journey. There were a few sleeping bodies scattered around the car at this moment. A Japanese man – a railway enthusiast Francesca had chatted to earlier – was slumped over a table. Over in the corner, an American man with a beard and a baseball cap sat in the seat he'd occupied since they'd left LA, eyes closed. Beside him, his wife rested her head on his wide shoulder.

Francesca settled down at a table and wondered what time they would start to serve breakfast, and when she would get home. The train was moving slower than normal. Probably stuck behind a freight train. She turned to the window, expecting to see the washed-out phantom version of herself there again, but it was gone. The window was no longer a mirror. Without her noticing, the world outside had started to lighten. One moment, nothing to see, and then colours and shapes coming out of the blackness.

A strip of orange glowed on the horizon where the mountains rose. Dark blue brightened to purple, and pink-edged clouds drifted into focus. Francesca leaned closer to the glass, transfixed by the developing spectacle of the planet waking up.

Feeling the need to know where she was, she took out her phone and opened the Maps app – something a passenger she'd chatted to on the way down had shown her. They were passing through Northern California, not far from the border with Oregon. The nearest town was a place she'd never heard of: Eaglewood.

The train entered the forest.

Those trees they were passing looked like cedars, she thought, though she'd never been good with that kind of thing. But she didn't have time to study them, to figure it out, because in the next moment the train, still moving at about half its normal speed, entered a clearing of flat, yellow grass.

A girl was running towards the train.

Francesca sat upright.

She blinked twice, wondering if this was a hallucination. A trick of the mind or the light. But no, the girl – the young woman – was real. Francesca was certain of it. The woman also appeared to be wondering if she was seeing things, staring at the train as if it might be a mirage. She was white and youthful, with long legs like Bambi's and vivid auburn hair that bounced behind her as she sprinted across the uneven ground.

Then Francesca realised something else: the woman was not alone. There was a man running after her. He was white too, with a bald patch on top of his head. Francesca knew instantly he was chasing the woman, gaining on her, and Francesca wanted to yell, to tell her to hurry.

And then the woman stumbled.

Fell onto her hands and knees.

And as the spot on the train where Francesca stood passed the patch of ground where the woman had fallen, she looked up, straight at Francesca, and their eyes met through the glass. For a second, that was all. Because at that moment, the train picked up speed, and Francesca pressed her face against the window, her focus switching to the man. His face was down, so all she could see was that bald patch on top of his head, but as the train entered a thicket of trees, obscuring the clearing from view, Francesca saw the woman twist onto her back as the man reached down to grab hold of her.

Francesca sank back into her chair, a hand raised to her lips, unable to move or do anything else but breathe. And in her mind's eye she stared at the young woman with the red hair and the woman stared back, and it was as if she were speaking.

Saying, *You know me. You know who I am!*

Could it be? Could it really be?

She took out her phone and went onto Google. Maddeningly, the signal had dropped and she had to wait until they left the forest again before it returned. Then she searched for the name she remembered so well.

There it was on the screen. The face she had just seen. Staring back at her.

PART ONE

PART ONE

Chapter 1

Aidan Faith arrived at King Street Station an hour early. He'd been up since five, unable to sleep, his bag already packed.

If he disappeared and the police came to check his desktop computer's recent activity, they would find train timetables, the ticket purchase page, maps of Northern California. His history would show searches for Francesca Gilbert, Eaglewood and the name of his own sister. His Uber account would show that he had booked a car at 08.00, and that it had arrived at his address in Bellevue at 08.10. If the police had cause to speak to the driver, he would tell them his passenger had barely spoken, except to say 'Good morning', and that he had noted the man's British accent, and had attempted to start a conversation about soccer as they drove towards downtown Seattle. The staff in the coffee bar where Aidan had waited for the *Coast Starlight* would note that there was nothing particularly remarkable about the man in his late twenties who had sat at a corner table with an oat latte, except that he had appeared to be deep in thought, pale with what might have been nerves. One of them might remark that he had been tall and slim – good-looking if you liked the geeky type. Aidan's neighbours would tell them he'd said he'd be gone for two or three days, and had asked them to feed his cat, Frosty, while he was away.

But that would all be if Aidan disappeared – and he had no plans to do that.

One disappearance was enough for any family.

He took his seat on the left-hand side of the train in Coach. The train was half full. A man was roaming up and down the carriages complaining loudly to his companion about the unreliability of the Wi-Fi. A woman was on her phone, telling someone how she had chosen to take the train – despite the *great* personal inconvenience – because she had vowed to live a carbon-neutral life.

Aidan sat up straight and looked out of the window as the train rattled out of his adoptive city, passing the Starbucks headquarters, the mermaid peeking from above the central tower. Soon, they were passing through Tacoma, then out into the countryside.

Aidan put his noise-cancelling headphones on and, forcing himself to relax – he had a very long journey ahead of him – settled back to listen to a playlist he used when he was coding, when he needed to chill. He turned his face to the window again, and before long he found himself mesmerised by the view: lush green forests and the peaks of the Cascade Mountains. Later, after they'd passed through Portland, somebody spotted what might have been a bald eagle soaring high above the fir trees of the Willamette Valley, and half a dozen people leapt up and rushed to the windows, phones in hands. The *Coast Starlight* continued to speed through Oregon, past mountain peaks and shimmering lakes, through dense forests and one-horse towns, and Aidan got a sense of the country he had called home for the past five years. Its wildness. The great spaces between human settlements. It reminded him once again how hard it would be to find anyone in this vast, populous landmass – a country seemingly designed for those who wanted to vanish.

He picked up his phone and went to the website he had set up two years ago: FindScarlettFaith.com. There she was, his sister, gazing back at him. He'd taken the photo himself on the last day he'd seen her, the day she vanished. She was looking right at the camera, that slightly fake social-media smile on her lips, a few freckles visible on the bridge of her nose. As always, what stood out was her hair. That flame-orange hair that made her look like a Pre-Raphaelite princess with an Instagram filter. She had a little birthmark on her upper lip, which she hated, and a gap between her front teeth, which ran in the family.

Nobody had seen that face since 2017, two years ago.

Until this week.

ω

Yesterday's journey to Edmonds, which was about ten miles north of Seattle proper, had taken almost an hour from Aidan's office.

He'd seen the email while he was at work, grappling with a problem with a new app they were developing. Aidan had set up FindScarlettFaith.com so that any new emails that weren't deleted by the sophisticated junk filter were sent straight to his phone, with their own distinct chime. Hearing it, he immediately stopped what he was doing and grabbed his phone, just as he'd done a hundred times before, and read the email.

> *To the family of Scarlett Faith –*
>
> *This might sound like a strange story and I'm sure you've had a lot of false leads over the years, but please do not discard it. I am absolutely certain about what, and who, I saw. Yesterday, I was travelling home on the Coast Starlight from Los Angeles to my home in Seattle . . .*

As soon as he finished reading the email, Aidan phoned the number its sender had included. In the past, he'd been given phone

9

numbers that didn't exist or that connected him to lost-and-found offices or dog pounds. There were a lot of people out there who got their kicks in sick and peculiar ways. But this time, an older woman answered.

'Mrs Gilbert?' he said, and she sounded so relieved to hear from him that when he ended the call he knew that either she was a great liar or she believed everything she had told him. It was enough to merit a face-to-face meeting. He even managed to get his boss to let him leave early so he could beat the appalling rush-hour traffic.

Despite that, it was still slow-going, and as he waited at yet another stoplight he found himself scanning the sidewalks for a flash of auburn. It was impossible for Aidan to drive through Seattle without straining for a second look whenever he passed a red-headed woman. Impossible not to be thrown back two years, to be reminded of that awful lurching sensation, like going over a bump in the road, when he realised Scarlett was missing.

He found a parking spot close to the address Francesca Gilbert had given him, and got out of the electric hybrid he had started leasing a year before in an attempt to do his bit for the planet. It was overcast but warm. Puget Sound was a stone's throw from here, and above the soft drone of traffic Aidan could hear gulls in the distance.

He found Francesca's address easily. She lived in a blue clapboard house with a double garage, built on a corner lot with a neat, square lawn. Not dissimilar to the place he rented, though Aidan guessed property was considerably cheaper here than in Bellevue.

He took a deep breath and rang the doorbell.

To his surprise, a young woman answered.

'Hey,' she said. 'You must be Aidan, right? I'm Bethany. I'm Mrs Gilbert's housekeeper.'

Bethany was pretty, dressed casually in jeans and a white T-shirt, with a smile that revealed dimples in her cheeks.

The moment they stepped inside, a voice called out from somewhere in the house: 'Bethany? Is he here?'

Before Bethany could reply, a grey-haired woman appeared in the doorway of the nearest room. Aidan knew, from her email, that Francesca was seventy-five and that her husband of more than fifty years had died just a month ago.

'Would you like a cup of tea?' she said, then laughed. 'Why am I asking? You're English, of course you would. Bethany, I believe we have some breakfast tea somewhere.'

'I'd actually prefer coffee, if that's okay,' Aidan said. 'I've been fully converted.'

'Coffee I can do,' said Bethany, and she headed off to the kitchen while Francesca beckoned for Aidan to join her in the living room. She directed him to an armchair and sat opposite him. The room was bright and airy, a little chintzy, with floral patterns and several vases stuffed with flowers.

'You look like her,' Francesca said. 'Your hair's not as fiery as hers, but otherwise . . .'

'A lot of people say that.'

She gave him a sad smile. 'I can only imagine what it must have been like for your poor parents. I'm lucky. I've always known where Stephen, my son, is. Even if he's not particularly interested in what I'm doing these days.'

She went silent for a few long moments, apparently lost in a reverie about how she was neglected by her son. While Aidan waited, Bethany came into the room and handed him a mug of coffee.

Francesca snapped back to life. 'What were we talking about? Oh. Yes. Your poor parents. Your sister. It was the talk of Seattle at the time.'

'A *big* news story,' said Bethany. 'I think I saw you on TV.'

11

Aidan nodded. He'd been asked to do an appeal at a press conference. *Scarlett, if you're watching this, please know that no one is angry with you. We want you to come home.* Then, with a message aimed at an abductor: *If Scarlett is with you, please let her go. There are a lot of people who love and miss her.*

'A terrible business,' said Francesca. 'This city used to be so safe . . .'

Aidan noticed Bethany raise an eyebrow, as if this was something she was tired of hearing. How different things had been in the good old days.

'Can you tell me what you saw?' he said. 'I need to hear it again.'

'Of course.'

Francesca went ahead and told him the same story she'd told him in the email and on the phone.

'As soon as they were out of sight,' she said, after describing what had happened the previous morning, 'I went through the train, to see if anyone else had seen anything. But they were all asleep or glued to their phone screens. I thought about pulling the emergency brake, but Kenneth always said they were only to be used in a critical situation, like if someone was caught in the door. I really didn't think they'd take kindly to an old woman saying she'd seen something that had nothing at all to do with the train itself.'

'I don't suppose you got any photos? Or a video?'

'No. That's what Bethany said. But I'm not young like you. It didn't cross my mind until afterwards.'

'But you thought straight away that it was Scarlett?' This was the part of the story that most bothered him. How could Francesca be sure she had seen someone she had, presumably, never met?

'It's one of her superpowers,' Bethany interjected.

Aidan turned to her.

'When I first started to work for Mrs Gilbert, she kept saying she was sure we'd met before. Was insistent about it, even though I was certain it couldn't be true. Then one day, out of the blue, she said, "Where's your pink rabbit?"'

'Pink rabbit?' Aidan repeated.

'Yeah. I was shocked, because when I was a child I did have this pink rabbit that I carried everywhere. Anyways, I told my grandmother about it and it turned out she used to know Mrs Gilbert back in the day. My grandma was a waitress at a restaurant Mrs Gilbert used to go to, and sometimes I'd be there, sitting at a table in the corner with my crayons and my rabbit beside me. And Francesca recognised me, even though she hadn't seen me for twenty years, since I was a child.'

'Wow.'

'It's just something I've always been able to do,' Francesca said. 'I never forget a face. And I saw your sister's in all the TV coverage, in the papers, all over. There are still a few posters around the city, aren't there?'

'Yes. I put them there. I go around every couple of months and put up a fresh batch.'

Bethany looked at him, clearly impressed. 'I bet my brother wouldn't do the same for me if I went missing. He'd be hanging around my apartment helping himself to my stuff.'

'It's the least I could do,' Aidan said in a quiet voice. Addressing Francesca, he asked, 'You don't think you actually saw Scarlett in the flesh? Back then, I mean?'

'No. Yesterday was the first time I'd ever seen her in real life.'

Aidan took his phone out of his pocket and opened the web browser. He brought up the picture of Scarlett and handed the phone over for Francesca to look at.

'You don't need eyeglasses?' he asked.

'No. I still have twenty-twenty vision. And I'm certain this is the woman I saw.'

'You were really able to get a good look at her?'

'Yes – like I told you on the phone, the train was going slow, stuck behind a freight train, I imagine. I think maybe she'd been planning to cross the tracks, but of course there was a train in the way.' She sighed. 'If the *Coast Starlight* hadn't been going so goddamn slowly we would have already passed through that clearing and she would have made it. She might have gotten away from that man.'

'But then you would never have seen her,' Aidan said.

'True.'

Aidan sat back in his chair. Francesca seemed so convinced. But was it possible that this woman had really seen his sister? He tried to think clearly and rationally, to look past his desperation to believe her.

On the one hand, it seemed so unlikely, fantastical. Mrs Gilbert was an elderly woman. What were the chances that the only person on the train who had been awake and looking out the window recognised Scarlett? But then, Scarlett's face *would* be familiar to anyone living in Seattle; it really had been a huge news story, and Aidan had done everything he could over the past couple of years to ensure it didn't fade from the city's collective memory. The train had been on its way to Seattle, so was presumably full of locals. Perhaps if everyone on the train had been awake then lots of them would have recognised her. He might have had lots of messages. And Francesca had already proven, if Bethany could be believed, that she had a remarkable memory for faces – even recognising adults she had only seen as children, although he didn't think Scarlett's features would have changed enormously between fifteen and seventeen, the age she would be now.

He pictured the scene Francesca had described.

The man, chasing Scarlett. Bearing down on her. Catching her.

14

He tried not to picture what might have happened next, in the same way he had tried not to imagine all the terrible things that Scarlett might have endured since she disappeared.

'Please excuse me a moment,' Francesca said, and she got up and left the room, presumably to use the bathroom.

'What are you thinking?' Bethany asked after a moment.

He looked up at her. 'Do you think she really saw her?'

She shrugged. 'I honestly have no idea. But if that was my sister out there, being chased by some dude, I wouldn't hesitate.'

'You'd go and investigate?'

'I wouldn't be able to live with myself if I didn't.'

Aidan got up and went over to the window, thinking hard. From somewhere in the house a toilet flushed.

He turned back to face Bethany.

'I can't help but think this is going to be a wild goose chase.'

She rolled her eyes, then laughed when he looked offended. 'It seems pretty clear to me that you're going to go and check it out. I don't understand why you're hesitating.'

'I guess I don't want to get my hopes up.'

'Surely you'd rather that than spend the rest of your life wondering *what if?*'

She was right. Of course she was right. He thought about his parents back home – his parents who said they didn't blame him for what had happened, but how could they not? Scarlett had gone missing on his watch. She had been visiting him here in Seattle. He was supposed to have been looking after her. He pictured what it would be like if he was able to phone them and tell them he had found her, that she was alive.

And he pictured his sister. In danger. Scared. Waiting for someone to come and find her.

He wouldn't be able to live with himself if he didn't at least check it out.

15

Chapter 2

Aidan went into the Sightseer car. This was where Francesca had been sitting when she saw the woman run into the clearing. A lot of passengers had gone to the dining car for lunch, and Aidan found a couple of free seats at one of the tables. The car was filled with sunlight, so bright it almost hurt. He closed his eyes for a few seconds, and when he opened them he found that a young woman, aged around nineteen he guessed, had sat opposite him.

She was scribbling notes in a bullet journal, concentrating so hard the tip of her tongue poked out the side of her mouth. Her hair was dyed purple and black, there was a piercing in the side of her nose, and she looked nothing like Scarlett. But there was an energy about her that reminded him of how his sister had been when she was fifteen. She was wearing a T-shirt emblazoned with the peace symbol – rainbow colours against white. He was pretty sure Scarlett had owned the same T-shirt.

The young woman must have felt him staring at her because she looked up sharply, eyes boring into him, and although he looked away quickly, embarrassed, it seemed she had already decided he was a creep, because she got up and headed down the carriage, taking her journal with her.

A man who was sitting across the aisle – baseball cap, greying moustache – leaned towards him and winked.

'Looks like you went and invaded her safe space,' the man said with a smirk, shuffling across to sit opposite Aidan. He was holding a dog-eared novel called *One Second After*, the cover of which showed a man staring up at a flaming sky. 'Clyde,' he said, sticking out a hand.

Aidan, programmed to be polite, shook it and told the man his name.

'Young women today,' Clyde said, leaning forward conspiratorially. 'All you have to do is touch one of them in a friendly way and they run off, screaming "Me too! Me too!" I feel sorry for your generation, man. How are you supposed to get laid when you can't even hit on a girl without her screaming rape?'

Aidan cringed. He didn't want this guy to think he shared his opinions, but he also didn't want to spend the next few hours arguing with him.

Instead, he said, 'Nice to meet you', and moved to stand. But before he could get away, Clyde grabbed his wrist and held him still.

'When the end comes,' Clyde said, tapping the surface of his book, 'little bitches like that are gonna be grateful to have real men to look after them.'

Aidan pulled his hand free and stood upright.

Clyde grinned. 'You have a nice day.' He opened his book and sat back.

Aidan made his way back through the train, thinking of all the clever and devastating things he should have said. He went downstairs to the snack bar to buy some chocolate, thinking sugar would make him feel better. Then he went back to his seat, put his music on, tried to relax.

The *Coast Starlight* was due to arrive in Dunsmuir – the closest train station to the spot where Francesca had seen the woman she swore was Scarlett – just under fifteen hours after it left Seattle, at half past midnight.

Aidan wanted to experience it exactly as Francesca had. The forest at dawn. The sun rising behind the trees as the birds woke up. That meant travelling on the same train as Francesca, going north. The solution was to get off at Dunsmuir and spend a few hours at the station before taking the 4.56 a.m. train back the way he'd come, seeing what Francesca had seen, then getting off at the next stop, in Klamath Falls. From there, he'd head south again in a rental car to Eaglewood.

Aidan thought back to last night. After getting home from Francesca's, he had hesitated about calling his parents. Did he want to get their hopes up? But he had needed to talk to someone who cared about Scarlett as much as he did. His co-workers were, he sensed, tired of hearing about his missing sister. They never quite knew how to react when faced with his pain. The woman he'd been seeing had broken up with him six months ago – she'd said he always seemed distracted, like his mind was somewhere else, and he couldn't deny it – and his best friend in Seattle, another British ex-pat, Simon, was back home visiting his family in Kent.

Aidan didn't think his cat would be particularly interested, even if Frosty had enjoyed plenty of fuss from Scarlett when she visited.

So he had FaceTimed his parents from his kitchen, while Frosty weaved around his ankles, and filled them in on what Francesca and Bethany had said. His parents were in their kitchen in their house just outside Wolverhampton, where Aidan and Scarlett had grown up. They'd recently had a new kitchen fitted. Aidan's mum had developed a mania for home improvement since Scarlett's disappearance. Almost the whole house had been redecorated, the garden had been landscaped and they even had a new garage. The only room that hadn't been touched was Scarlett's room. It had been cleaned and tidied, her dirty laundry washed and hung in her wardrobe. Aidan's mum put fresh flowers on Scarlett's desk every week. She wanted it to be nice for when her daughter came home.

Aidan's dad, in the meantime, had two passions: Wolverhampton Wanderers and Lego. The latter was a new obsession, and Aidan's mum was constantly complaining about how the house was full of his dad's silly toys.

'Francesca seems genuine,' Aidan had said to them. 'I don't think this is a hoax. She's not after a reward and there's no sign that she's a crank who would get a kick out of misleading us. I totally believe she thinks she saw Scarlett.'

'Did she tell the police she'd seen her?' his dad asked. 'What was the nearest town called again?'

'Eaglewood. Francesca told me she called the police there as soon as she got home, but she wasn't sure if they took her seriously. Which isn't surprising, is it?'

'You should call Detective Heard,' his mum said. That was the name of the lead detective in Seattle who had handled the missing person investigation.

'There's no point doing that yet. Not until I've spoken to the local cops. Then I guess I can put them in touch.'

The more he spoke, the more it struck him that he had no idea what to do beyond checking out the area, talking to the local police and taking it from there. It wasn't much of a plan. Aidan wasn't a trained investigator and he wasn't a big fan of PIs anyway, not since he and his parents had given their combined savings to an agency in Seattle who had, as far as Aidan could tell, done very little despite being paid a hefty fee.

'Oh – what if it was really her?' his mum said, her voice catching as she spoke. 'Who was the man chasing her? Did the woman say she looked scared? She must have. She must have been terrified.'

Her shoulders shook with distress, and as the tears came Aidan's dad put his arms around her and Aidan watched them in despair, wishing he hadn't called, wishing he'd been a better big brother.

Wishing he hadn't let Scarlett out of his sight.

Chapter 3

2017

'Welcome to America!' Aidan said, the moment they got back to his apartment. 'And welcome to my humble abode.'

Scarlett rolled her eyes. 'You're so corny.'

After he had shown her the spare room where she would be sleeping, and given her the Wi-Fi password, he watched while she unpacked. He couldn't quite believe the size of the suitcase she had brought with her. As she filled the wardrobe with clothes and shoes, he tried to quiz her about the flight ('long'), school ('boring') and how their parents were ('fine'). She chucked the book she was reading onto the bedside table, and Aidan raised an eyebrow when he saw the title: *This Changes Everything: Capitalism vs the Climate*. When he was fifteen he'd been reading Dan Brown and graphic novels.

Frosty strolled into the room and Scarlett sprang to life. 'Oh my God, *hello!*'

He was a ragdoll cat, floppy and friendly and gorgeous. Aidan had inherited him from the previous tenants. According to Aidan's boss at Wonder, the tech business he had come out here three years ago to work for, Frosty came with the property, which belonged to the company. Scarlett scooped him up and, after cuddling him for a minute, laughed as he climbed into her now-empty suitcase.

'He wants to come home with me,' she said.

'Sorry, little sis. He's staying here.'

She pulled a face. 'Do you have to call me that? It's so condescending. I'm not little. I'm *fifteen*.'

'You're still my little sister.'

For most of Aidan's early life he had been an only child. Apparently, his parents had tried for another baby for years. They'd been to see fertility doctors, done IVF – spent a fortune trying to conceive a sibling for him. It was only when they gave up that Scarlett came along, when Aidan was twelve.

Suddenly having a baby in the house, one who took away most of his parents' attention, had been a shock. At first, it had irritated him, especially when she screamed through the night and when visiting adults went on and on about how much Scarlett looked like her big brother. How could that pink-faced, crying thing look like him? But Aidan was, by nature, an easy-going boy, and as Scarlett grew into a toddler and stopped screaming all the time, he'd had to admit she was cute and funny and it wasn't as if he was neglected. His parents were ecstatic to finally have this second child they'd always craved, and consequently their house became a happier home.

By the time Aidan headed off to university when Scarlett was six, he doted on his little sister. His friends thought she was sweet and he agreed, even if she did annoy him by constantly coming into his bedroom when he had his girlfriend there. Every time he went home after that, Scarlett was a little bit bigger, and he also found she was quite easy to mould. He played her his favourite music and showed her movies and recommended books he'd liked when he was her age, helping to shape her tastes.

'You're her hero,' his mum had said to him one day, when Scarlett was ten and Aidan was home from university, where he was studying computer programming.

'What do you mean?'

His mum had smiled. 'She really looks up to you. She's always telling her friends about her cool big brother and how amazing he is with computers and how he knows everything about music.'

'Wow. I guess I *am* pretty cool.' They'd laughed. 'Let's hope she never grows out of it.'

And now here she was, a teenager. In the three years that he'd lived in Seattle he'd only seen her twice, when he'd gone home for Christmas, and when he Skyped or FaceTimed his parents she would often be hanging around in the background but they rarely spoke. He often sent her links to things he thought she'd be interested in – new tracks by bands she liked, funny cat videos, petitions connected to the social causes he knew she cared about – but her responses recently had consisted of little more than a thumbs-up emoji, like she was too busy to chat with her brother.

'You must be exhausted after the flight,' he said. 'Do you want to take a nap?'

'No way. I'm wide awake. I want to go out and see Seattle.'

'I thought we could start doing that tomorrow.'

'Come on, *please*. I'm only here for a week and I'm not tired at all. I am the exact opposite of tired, in fact.'

She looked at him with those big eyes, just as she had when she was four and trying to persuade him to sneak her a bar of chocolate from the cupboard she was too short to reach.

He sighed. 'Okay, okay, you win. What do you want to do?'

'Yay!' She stroked Frosty, who was back in her lap, covering her clothes with white fur. 'I don't know. What about that big tower? The famous one.'

'The Space Needle? Yeah, we can do that. I've never been up it.'

22

'Wait, what?'

'There's also the Museum of Pop Culture around there.'

'Sounds kinda lame.'

'They've got a Nirvana exhibition.'

Her eyes lit up and she bounced off the bed, Frosty shooting across the room, startled by the sudden movement. Then she must have remembered that being overenthusiastic wasn't part of her personal brand.

'Sounds okay,' she said, sitting down and studying her nails. 'I guess.'

ϖ

Aidan didn't want to drive into the city and Scarlett turned her nose up at the idea of getting a bus – 'I've been travelling all day' – so they took an Uber. While they waited for it to arrive she fiddled with her phone, complaining that it hadn't connected to a local network yet. It wouldn't have surprised Aidan if their dad, who paid the bills, had asked the phone company to block roaming on her mobile.

'I'm not going to be able to take you the whole way,' said the middle-aged driver. 'There's some kind of big protest going on near Denny Park.'

'What are they protesting about?' Aidan asked.

'I don't know. Something to do with the planet, I think. Save the whales or whatever.'

Scarlett's ears pricked up. 'Really? That's exciting.'

'Huh.' The driver shook his head. 'People like that make me wanna take some nasty old truck and park up in the middle of their protest, handing out Big Macs.'

Scarlett narrowed her eyes and muttered something.

'What was that?' the driver asked.

Scarlett didn't repeat what she'd said, but the flesh around her collarbone had flushed pink and her eyes blazed with anger.

'Are you still vegan?' Aidan asked her. He'd had their mum on the phone recently, complaining about how annoying it was to have to cook two different dinners every night.

'Of *course* I am.'

'Man, I couldn't live without cheese,' said the driver. 'Why do that to yourself?'

Scarlett looked like she was too furious to speak. Aidan said, 'I think it's admirable. Believing in a cause. Doing something about it.'

They fell into an uncomfortable silence.

'I'm going to have to drop you here,' the driver said ten minutes later. 'I can't get any closer. The police have got all the streets blocked off.'

Aidan and Scarlett got out of the car and Aidan looked around to get his bearings. They were on Denny Way, which would take them to the pedestrianised area that housed the Space Needle and various other tourist attractions, including the museum. But as they started to walk west, the noise from the protest grew louder: car horns honking, chanting, the general hubbub of a crowd, and someone trying to deliver instructions through a loudspeaker.

'Maybe we should turn back, go round a different way,' Aidan said, but suddenly it was too late. A group of protestors came marching out of a side street, heading towards the little park where the main crowd was gathered, and Aidan and Scarlett found themselves swept along as dozens of men and women flowed down the centre of the road.

Two women around Aidan's age led the group, both waving loudspeakers. Behind them were protestors holding a large banner that read *THERE IS NO PLANET B*, and others at the rear waved placards with slogans like *OUR HOUSE IS ON FIRE* and *TIME TO PANIC*. The crowd were chanting 'We are unstoppable, another world is possible', which died down and became 'Climate action, climate action, climate action now!' Most of the protestors were young, including lots of kids who couldn't have been any older than Scarlett – some with their parents, others with groups of friends.

Aidan looked at Scarlett and saw that her eyes were stretched wide and her mouth was open, as she gaped at the people around her in amazement. A few years ago he'd taken her to see Katy Perry in Manchester – Scarlett's first pop concert – and the look on her face back then, when Katy bounded on stage, was similar to her expression now. Thrilled, excited, hardly able to take in what she was seeing. But there was also a hint of fear there, as the group of protestors pushed them and everyone else who had got caught up in this towards the park. Around them, police had appeared, lining the sidewalks – keeping an eye on what, so far, seemed to be a peaceful demonstration, but also blocking the side streets and entrances to the shops and other potential refuges along the way.

'Stay close to me, okay?' Aidan shouted over the din.

Scarlett stared up at him and nodded. Her face was shining. Her mouth moved but he couldn't hear what she was saying. From his limited lip-reading abilities it looked like she said something like, 'This is so cool.'

Aidan had no choice but to move in step with the protestors. As they neared the park, they found themselves heading towards the large crowd ahead, where the apparent leaders of the protest were standing on a makeshift stage, clutching loudspeakers and leading a call and response: 'You say climate, we say justice!' There were hundreds of people in the park, more signs and slogans raised above their heads, music blasting from a sound system, and police cars and vans were parked around the edge, along with a news crew and a smattering of hecklers yelling abuse, to the apparent amusement of the majority.

With nowhere to escape to, Aidan and Scarlett found themselves streaming into the park, shoulder to shoulder with various other bystanders who had been forced to go in the same direction. *Maybe*, Aidan thought, *we can cross the park and get out of here.* At least there was some space here, some room to stand still for a moment and breathe. Beside him, Scarlett was gazing around her as if she were a kid at Disneyland.

'We should head that way,' he said, pointing. He couldn't believe how many people were here. They were blocking all the paths, gathering beneath the trees, clusters of them sitting on the grass. It was like being at a music festival, with shouting and chanting drowning out the tunes.

'What?' She cupped her hand behind her ear.

'I said—'

But his words were cut off by a huge roar, then a cheer as yet another group of people reached the edge of the park. Among the bobbing heads of the crowd, he couldn't see what was going on, but suddenly this new group started to stream towards where they were standing.

It was like being hit by a wave. Aidan, who had been facing the street, was forced to turn around to stop himself from being knocked over. All around him he could see other people panicking as they were pushed along the path and across the grass, and the people who had been sitting down scrambled to their feet to avoid being trampled. When he turned his head to speak to Scarlett, to check she was okay, she wasn't there.

He looked left and right, and tried to turn back. 'Scarlett?' he shouted. The man behind him gave him a look, like, *No chance, buddy.* Aidan tried to spot her auburn hair, but there were numerous redheads in the crowd and none of them was his sister. He wanted to push his way back through the throng but it was impossible. There were too many people, moving too fast. He tried to look above the crowd, and called Scarlett's name again, but he was drowned out by a new chant that had risen from the makeshift stage and those gathered around it.

'What do we want?'

'*Change!*'

'When do we want it?'

'*Now!*'

He was never going to find Scarlett while he was stuck in this crowd. He managed to elbow his way through, forcing his way off the main path and trampling across a flower bed. The stampede was beginning to slow now, the protestors spreading out and finding personal space, some turning back to face the way they'd come. Aidan found a bench and climbed onto it, straining his neck to peer over the sea of heads and signs.

On the far side of the park he spotted a girl with vivid auburn hair, wearing a green T-shirt. *Scarlett!* He was sure it was her. He got his phone out, then remembered she didn't have roaming here yet.

Taking a deep breath, as if he were about to dive into deep water, he began to make his way through the crowd, not caring if he bumped into people or trod on anyone's toes. He tried to keep the spot where he'd seen her fixed in his mind. She'd been between two tall trees with upper branches that looked like arms reaching up to the sky. Finally, after skirting around a hedgerow and almost tripping over a couple who were sitting on the ground smoking a spliff, he made it.

'Scarlett!' he called, and there she was, turning towards him.

Thank God. He jogged up to her and she smiled, not worried or scared at all, the traces of fear that he'd noticed previously now completely gone.

'I thought I'd lost you,' he said, pulling her into a hug.

She wriggled out of his embrace, staring at him like he'd gone crazy. 'Gross,' she said. 'You're all sweaty.'

'That's not surprising. Oh my God, what a nightmare. I was so worried.'

'I'm fine. I know your address. If we got separated I could find my way back to yours. It's no biggie. And I knew if I found somewhere to stand you'd look around and find me.' She shrugged. 'And here you are.'

He let out a great breath. 'Here I am.'

'You keep forgetting: I'm not a kid anymore.'

All around them, the protest continued. A woman was giving a speech and the crowd were cheering. Scarlett looked towards the noise as if she wanted to stay, to take part, but Aidan had had enough. There was no way he was risking getting separated from her again.

'Come on,' he said. 'It's this way to the Space Needle.'

Chapter 4

When Aidan opened his eyes it was dark outside the train and he needed to pee.

Going down the stairs to the lower floor, where the restrooms were located, he heard voices. Or rather, one voice: a man, his gruff tones vaguely familiar.

It was Clyde. He was leaning against the wall, blocking the exit from the restrooms, his back to Aidan.

'Just one drink. I ain't gonna bite you.' A snicker. 'Unless you *want* me to.'

It took Aidan a moment to see who Clyde was addressing. It was the young woman in the peace-symbol T-shirt. She said something softly, her words drowned out by the rattle of the train.

'You know what that sounds like?' said Clyde. 'Sounds to me like you're thinking you're maybe a little too good for me.'

'She doesn't want to have a drink with you.'

Clyde whirled round and the woman seized the opportunity to slip past. She went by Aidan, head down so all he could see was her black and purple hair, and then ran up the stairs. Clyde, realising his quarry had escaped, called after her. 'Hey. Where you going?'

His eyes were watery. He was drunk. He focused, with some effort, on Aidan.

'I was only being friendly,' he said, slurring his words.

Aidan's heart was beating hard. 'Maybe you should go back to your seat, get some sleep,' he said, keeping his voice calm and neutral.

Clyde raised a hand and pointed it in Aidan's face. 'I was just having a little fun. We've gotta enjoy ourselves while we still can. Before the end comes.'

He came stumbling closer, fists clenched by his sides. He leaned towards Aidan until their faces were inches apart, and the stink of stale alcohol on his breath almost made Aidan retch.

Aidan pulled himself up to his full height – six foot two – and Clyde looked up at him, his bloodshot eyes widening a little as he realised Aidan had four or five inches on him, but he didn't unclench his fists. Aidan's heart pounded. He hadn't been in a fight since he was at school, and even then he had managed to talk the other boy down, using jokes to defuse the tension. But he didn't think Clyde would appreciate his jokes.

Then the train rounded a bend and Clyde staggered into the wall.

'Fuck this,' he said. 'You know what? People like you, like her, you're gonna be toast. There's a war coming, man. A reckoning! And you're—'

'Going to be toast? You said.'

'Asshole.'

With that, Clyde shoved past Aidan and made his fumbling way up the stairs and out of sight, muttering more expletives. A little later, Aidan walked through the train to check Clyde wasn't harassing the woman again. He found him lying with his seat reclined all the way back, fast asleep with his mouth open, drool on his chin.

ᵭ

The train pulled into Dunsmuir station at quarter to one in the morning, about twenty minutes behind schedule.

Aidan grabbed his backpack and got off, stepping into the warm night, struck by how tiny the station was and feeling like he had gone back in time to the Wild West. He half expected to see stagecoaches waiting to collect the passengers.

The train lingered for a while, a couple of passengers disembarking and dragging their luggage towards the parking lot, and Aidan made his way over to the small station building. He took a seat beneath the canopy and settled in, ready for the long wait for the train north.

The train pulled away and Aidan realised there was one other person still at the station. The young woman in the peace-symbol T-shirt with the black and purple hair. She was standing between the station building and the parking lot, staring at her phone, which illuminated her face. She seemed a little lost. Aidan saw her glance at him and hesitate before making up her mind.

'I don't suppose you vape, do you?' she asked, coming over.

'Sorry.'

'Damn.' She had a vape device, small like a USB stick, in her hand. 'I forgot to charge mine.'

'And you're in need of nicotine?'

'Huh. Yeah.' She glanced towards the car park. 'Guess I'll have to do it when I get there.' She went to walk away, then stopped. 'Thanks for earlier. With that asshole.'

'No problem.'

'Sorry I didn't hang around. I was just freaked out, you know. I hope he didn't give you any shit.'

'It was fine. We ended up exchanging addresses. He's going to invite me to this men's workshop he runs, where they go into the desert and scream at each other.'

'Sounds fun.' She hesitated. 'I'm Kristin.'

31

'Aidan.'

An awkward silence descended.

'Are you waiting for a ride?' he asked.

She pushed her hair out of her face. 'Yeah, and they're late. You waiting for someone too?'

'I'm waiting for the next train north.'

'Huh? Did you miss your stop or something?'

'It's a long story, but I'm looking for my sister.'

A white SUV with tinted windows and dirt-streaked doors pulled into the parking lot, keeping its lights on; the dazzle prevented Aidan from seeing who was driving but, on seeing Kristin, they honked the horn.

'Good luck,' Kristin said. 'I hope you find her. And thanks again.'

She walked over and climbed into the back seat, and the SUV pulled away with a crunch of its tyres, leaving him all alone.

ω

The world was silent. There weren't even any crickets or cicadas to keep him company. Bored, he wandered around the perimeter of the station and found a newspaper that was a few days old, open at the sports pages. It was a local paper and Aidan flicked through it, a story about Eaglewood catching his eye. The mayor had vowed to speed up the rebuilding of a substantial number of homes on the outskirts of town which had been destroyed by the wildfires that had swept through the area last year.

And that's just the start of it, Mayor Christopher Hood was quoted as saying. *We're going to continue investing in the whole town. Make it the best place to live in the whole state. We've teamed up with a private developer to ensure the swift creation of two new affordable housing districts.*

Skimming through the newspaper Aidan found numerous references to fires, including a mention of a memorial that was being built to remember a group of teenagers who'd got caught up in the terrible events, though the details in the paper were sketchy. He had watched the news reports last year as the Carr Fire burned its way through the forests not far south of where he sat now, leaving hundreds of people without homes. Another story in the paper told him the recent heatwave in the state had significantly increased the likelihood of it happening again this year.

Aidan looked across to the other side of the station, at the trees beyond and the forest surrounding him. Maybe it was Clyde's drunken words about a coming 'reckoning', or these reports about fires and the warning that it was going to happen again, but it was hard to resist the feeling that the world – especially here, where nature was untamed – was fragile . . . and dangerous. For a moment he even thought he could smell smoke, before persuading himself it was his imagination.

A few hours passed, and then the northbound train came clattering out of the darkness.

He boarded. It was five in the morning and almost everyone in Coach was asleep. He didn't try to find a seat. Instead, he headed through the train, taking care not to wake anyone, and made his way to the empty Sightseer Lounge with its observation windows. According to his calculations, which he'd made with the help of a website that told him when the sun rose on each day of the year, the train should pass the spot where Francesca had seen the incident, three days ago, a couple of minutes after first light. He had about fifty minutes to wait.

Aidan opened the Maps app on his phone so he could see exactly where the train was. The blue dot on the map told him they were heading at speed past Mount Shasta to the east. It was too dark to see anything except his own reflection in the glass, though if he leaned close enough to the window he could see the silhouettes of trees outside.

It happened quickly – the world emerging from blackness, like in a photo from the Polaroid camera his parents used to have. One moment, there was nothing to see. The next, colours and shapes. Buildings, some with their lights on. Mountains rising from the horizon, an orange stripe across the sky. Clouds streaked with pink.

The train entered the forest and he braced himself, seeing what Francesca had seen. A dark wall of trees. The light growing behind them. Any moment now . . .

And there it was: the clearing. The place where she had seen the woman who might have been Scarlett. He leaned closer to the window, picturing it like the scene was imprinted on the air. He imagined his sister, running, falling. The balding man catching her. Aidan's stomach clenched and he could hear himself breathing hard.

The clearing was empty now. Peaceful, almost eerily so. Unremarkable. Just another space in this great forest. Could something so important, so impactful on his life, really have happened here?

It struck Aidan again how hard this was going to be.

The proverbial needle. The proverbial haystack.

Chapter 5

'Hey, wake up.'

Kristin Fox opened her eyes and immediately closed them again. Harsh morning light streamed through the cracks in the roof, and the air had already started to heat up.

'Come on. No slacking,' said the man in the doorway. She peeked out from beneath the thin blanket. It was the man who'd picked her up from the station last night. His name was Jimmy; he was a guy around her dad's age, with deep crow's feet around his eyes. He wore a cowboy hat that cast a shadow over his face, but he still looked like he spent much of his life out in the sun.

Last night, he'd told her to sleep in here because it was too late to wake up the other recruits, and even though she had been exhausted from the long train journey it had taken hours to get to sleep. She'd been convinced there must be critters in here with her. Spiders. Scorpions. All creatures that deserved their share of the earth's bounty; she just didn't want to share a bedroom with them.

'You're in the army now, Kristin,' Jimmy said with a chuckle.

She pushed the blanket aside and was pretty sure Jimmy was disappointed to see she was fully dressed, wearing the same T-shirt she'd worn on the way here, the one with the peace symbol. She must stink.

'Can I take a shower?' she asked.

'I was about to suggest it. Follow me.'

She pulled some clean clothes from her backpack and he led her over to what he referred to as the shower block. The sun was so bright she had to put her forearm over her face to block the dazzle. The ground was hard and arid beneath her feet. Yeah, perfect conditions for scorpions. The shower block was a wooden structure with half a dozen stalls and the same number of basins inside.

She had her own toiletry bag, containing shower gel, shampoo and conditioner, her wooden toothbrush, and the Colgate toothpaste she preferred. Jimmy grabbed the bag from her and peered inside.

'None of this stuff, except the toothbrush, is allowed here,' he said, keeping hold of the bag and handing the toothbrush back to her. 'You'll find soap in the stalls and there's toothpaste in there too, plus towels. Once you're done, put your dirty laundry in that bin over there and I'll meet you in the mess room.' He pointed to another makeshift building across the way.

The water was frigid and the soap made her think of something she'd seen in a prison movie, but by the time she was done she didn't smell like a raccoon and she had to admit the cold water had slapped some life back into her. She felt excited again. After the long wait, the long journey, all the secrets she'd had to keep from her friends, she was finally here.

Jimmy was waiting in the mess. He had an empty plate in front of him and a mug of black coffee. There were a number of recruits sitting on benches eating, men and women, all young and, she noticed, attractive. Faces you'd swipe right on, not that she was interested in that kind of thing right now. She'd had enough of men.

The recruits turned to give the new arrival the once-over and Kristin smiled shyly. She might have gone over to talk to them and introduce herself, but Jimmy gestured impatiently for her to join him.

'Grab yourself some breakfast,' he said. 'All the eggs are from our own hens; everything else is locally sourced. The blueberries rock.'

Breakfast was laid out on a table along one wall, like in a hotel. She filled her plate. The food on the *Coast Starlight* had been gross, and she was starving.

Sitting opposite Jimmy, who was cleaning the corners of his mouth with a napkin, cowboy hat still on, she took her Juul out of her pocket and hesitated. She had a strong suspicion it would be confiscated like her other stuff, but surely it was best to be upfront and honest.

'Do you think I could charge my vape?' She held up the Juul. 'I'm dying for a nicotine hit.'

He grabbed it from her, and the disgust on his face made her instantly regret her decision. 'Those things aren't allowed here. You know about the waste trail they leave?'

'But . . .'

'It's all about treading lightly on the earth, Kirstin.'

'Kristin.'

He waved away the distinction. 'You need to rid yourself of your nicotine dependency. Now, hurry up and eat. Some of the recruits are shipping out today.'

She shovelled down scrambled eggs as quickly as she could, trying not to mourn the loss of her vape and her toiletries, reminding herself not to be selfish. Her needs were unimportant. It was all about the cause. The fight.

When she'd finished, Jimmy said, 'Let's go.'

She followed him out. Without looking over his shoulder, he said, 'You came from Seattle?'

'Actually, Spokane. I'm majoring in environmental studies at Gonzaga.'

'Great.'

'It's my passion.'

'And here you are. Doing something about it.'

He led her out into the open, the sun fierce above them, barely a cloud in sight to give the hope of respite. The land they trod on was dry and scrubby, all yellows and greens, until it gave way to the low mountains in the east. Just visible to the west was Goose Lake. They were in Modoc County in the north-east corner of California, close to the borders with Oregon and Nevada.

'We see wild horses sometimes.' Jimmy pointed towards the peaks in the distance. 'Mountain lions too. I watched one take down a mule deer last week. Quite a sight.'

'How long have you been here?' Kristin asked, trying not to picture the poor deer being mauled.

'Since the beginning,' he said, with deliberate mystery.

He showed Kristin to her quarters: a barn that had been turned into a dorm, divided along traditional gender lines with eight beds in each room.

'This is yours,' Jimmy said, indicating the bed closest to the door. 'You can leave your backpack here for now, but later you'll be required to hand over your personal possessions. That includes make-up and jewellery. I assume you've already done the wire transfer?'

'Yeah, of course. But what about my locket?' Kristin fingered a delicate gold heart that hung around her neck. 'My mom gave this to me before she died. It has her picture inside.' She never took it off.

'Like I said, it will be kept safe. You don't want it to get scratched or damaged, do you? I'll also need your phone.'

'My *phone*?' Her vape had been bad enough.

'Phones can be traced, Kristin,' he said. 'I hope you had it switched off on the way down, like we told you.'

'I did.'

'Good. You aren't going to need it here. And a phone is temptation. You get lonely, start missing your folks or your friends back home. Next thing we know we got your dad turning up.'

'I wouldn't . . .'

But she could see there was no point arguing. Reluctantly, she handed over her phone – it was a brand-new iPhone! – and took off her locket.

'Please look after it,' she said.

'As if it were my own.' He rubbed his palms together. 'Okay, I need to get going. Come with me.'

She followed him past a pair of large buildings – one of which was for training, Jimmy explained – and then the ranch house came into sight. This, Kristin thought with a little ping of excitement, was where Shannon Reinhardt lived.

For one moment, Kristin was sure Jimmy must be taking her to the house – for a face-to-face with Shannon herself? – but they walked past it towards the gate, where a small crowd had gathered around a white van, its back doors open.

Two women and a man, all in their late teens or early twenties, stood beside the van, exuding nervous but excited energy. A man in a trucker cap slouched against the driver's door, picking at his fingernails.

'You ready?' he said.

'Good to see you too, Frank,' said Jimmy. 'Yeah, I'm all set.' He addressed the three recruits, switching into dad mode. 'You all used the bathroom? We got a long drive ahead of us.'

'Yessir,' said the male recruit.

'They're shipping out?' Kristin asked, as the three recruits said their goodbyes to the others, hugging and bumping fists. There were even a few tears, but overall the mood was one of excitement. Envy, even.

'They sure are,' Jimmy said. He patted her shoulder. 'Your time will come. I have a feeling Shannon will have a special role for you.'

And then, before Kristin could ask what he meant – *a special role?* – a ripple of excitement ran through the little crowd.

'Shannon,' somebody whispered, and there she was, coming towards them from the ranch house. A woman with long brown hair tied back in a ponytail. She wore no make-up or jewellery, and her clothes were simple but elegant: a pair of well-fitting jeans, a white top, knee-high boots that Kristin assumed must be made from vegan leather. What struck Kristin was that Shannon looked so ordinary. Like a cool teacher, the kind who had a little gang of besotted students and was probably dating the football coach. But all the recruits turned to face her like they were flowers and she was the sun.

'It's a beautiful day,' she said, approaching the recruits who were leaving – the guy and the two girls. 'I know you're going to achieve great things out there.'

Shannon then faced the crowd. Kristin found herself enrapt, unable to tear her eyes away from this woman; not that she had any desire to.

'Last night, thousands of miles from here, deep in the rainforest, a kapok tree died. It had stood for three hundred years, beside its brothers and sisters. A home to animals and birds. Almost two hundred feet high. And now gone. Destroyed by the bulldozers that plunder the forest.'

Kristin felt a lump form in her throat.

'That tree cannot be resurrected. Its life and history were wiped out in moments. And nobody cares.'

'We care,' said a young woman.

Shannon smiled. 'That's right. *We* care. And here they are, our brave and beautiful soldiers, willing to risk everything to save trees like that kapok. To stop the world burning. To give this planet, and our children, a future.'

She approached the three 'soldiers' again and hugged each of them in turn.

'I'm so proud of—'

'Yep. Me too,' Jimmy said, cutting Shannon off.

Kristin could hardly believe it, and expected Shannon to look pissed, but instead she laughed and said, 'Apologies. I allow myself to get carried away. Jimmy, over to you.'

'Well, all right.' Jimmy thumped the side of the vehicle. 'We're good to go.'

The three recruits climbed in and Jimmy slammed the doors shut, then got into the passenger seat beside Frank. One of the other men opened the gate and the van pulled away.

Kristin stood watching as it disappeared into the distance, dust rising around its wheels. She didn't notice Shannon had come over to her until she heard a voice say, 'You're new.'

Kristin found for a moment that she couldn't speak. Finally, she was able to spit out her name. 'Kristin Fox. It's such an honour to meet you.'

Shannon touched Kristin's shoulder and Kristin realised that Shannon was looking her up and down, her eyes roaming her body, from head to toe then back again. But it wasn't sexual. It was more the way a farmer might inspect an animal at market. Weirdly, Kristin found she didn't mind. This was Shannon Reinhardt. She could do whatever she liked.

'Welcome to the Ranch,' Shannon said. 'Kristin, you have an exciting future ahead of you.'

And with that, Shannon walked away, back towards the ranch house, leaving Kristin feeling utterly star-struck. Who needed a vape or a phone or a hot shower? Shannon Reinhardt knew who she was. That was everything.

Chapter 6

It was midday by the time Aidan checked in to a two-star establishment called the Daybreak Inn and Suites. There were no hotels in Eaglewood – just this motel, located just off Main Street. Walking to his room, Aidan wondered if he was the only guest. The woman who'd checked him in seemed shocked to have something to do.

He had rented a car in Klamath Falls and driven down US-97, crossing back into California from Oregon. The roads were almost empty, the landscape alternately thick with pine trees and sparse and rocky, lined with stunted telephone poles. Mount Shasta loomed on the horizon like a mirage that shimmered in the morning heat, growing ever larger as he headed south. And there, as he got closer to his destination, was the evidence of the fires he'd read about: bare patches on the slopes of the hills close to the town. On the outskirts of Eaglewood, great chunks of forest were missing, a few blackened tree stumps standing on charred ground, and a few healthy trees remained – miraculous survivors of the devastation.

He'd driven past a feed store and an adjoining shop selling farm equipment, then entered Eaglewood proper, pausing to stare at what had once been a gas station. It had been destroyed by fire – nothing was left except some concrete plinths and the twisted remains of a Shell sign somehow still attached to its pole. Aidan could almost picture the balls of flame that must have erupted here. He slowed as he drove past what must have once been a small neighbourhood, now sealed off behind a chain-link fence with a sign that read *Paradise Park – Rebuilding Eaglewood in proud partnership with Shastina Spring Homes.* Beyond the fence, a hubbub of activity: bulldozers and men in hard hats and half-constructed buildings covered with scaffolding. It was heartening to see evidence of the town's determination to build back, to not surrender.

A little further on, there was no sign of the wildfires that had done so much damage to Eaglewood's outskirts. He headed down Main Street. There was a single diner on one side of the street; a Dollar General and a tavern called Cooper's Bar and Grill on the other. Just along the street from the tavern was a small police station, and he mentally noted its location. According to the GPS there was a lumber museum a few streets away and an elementary school to the south, and he guessed the town would be livelier when school wasn't out.

Here, at its centre, Eaglewood had a sleepy appeal. The sky was clear and bright and it was impossible not to marvel at that backdrop: Mount Shasta, its summit streaked with snow, dominating the horizon.

Now, he entered the motel room and chucked his backpack on the chair and collapsed onto the bed. The mattress was thin and the springs jabbed at his bones, but he was so tired he barely noticed. He was just happy to be horizontal.

ᐡ

He awoke just after four. Above him, the ceiling fan stirred the soupy air. Still lying on the bed, he sent a quick message to his parents to let them know he'd arrived, then took a shower before heading out.

He drove the rental car, a white Nissan Rogue, towards the spot he had marked on the map on his phone, a few miles from Eaglewood. The road pierced the forest. There was no sign of fire damage here. Half a mile in, his eye on the dot on the map, he realised this was as close as he would get to the clearing without going on foot.

He pulled over and parked on a rocky patch of ground on the edge of the trees. It was flat here, but just ahead the narrow road rose steeply as it went deeper into the forest.

He got out of the car and walked towards the woods, resting a palm briefly against the trunk of a tall tree. The ground at his feet was scrubby and dry. He went deeper into the shade. A bird sang an unfamiliar song and he tried to imagine what it would be like here in the dark, just before dawn, the moon still shining through the spaces between the cedars.

He kept his phone in his hand and threaded his way through the trees until he found himself approaching the dot on the screen. Here it was: the clearing. The rail track bisected it, almost concealed from view by the long, dry grass. Rocks and boulders were scattered across the ground, and he guessed it was one of these that had caused Scarlett – if it really had been her – to trip and fall.

He was looking for some sign that something had really happened here. A dropped earring or a torn shred of clothing. He spent thirty minutes walking slowly back and forth, staring down at the grass – there was nothing, not even any litter – then stood up and put his hands on his head. What was he doing? Did he really believe he might find something, some tangible sign that Scarlett had been here? It was fanciful, crazy. All he had was a tingle at the nape of his neck, the same sense he'd got when he looked out from the train, but that signified nothing.

A great feeling of hopelessness came over him. Birds sang in the trees. A pine cone fell nearby. The wind blew and the sun beat down.

The world didn't care, but he couldn't give up. He was here now. He was trying. He walked towards the train track and took a couple of photographs of the clearing. Relieved to find he had a strong signal here on the edge of civilisation, he texted the pictures to Francesca with the message: *Is this the spot where you saw her?*

The reply came almost instantly. *Yes! Have you found anything?*

He texted back: *Not yet.*

He spent another thirty minutes on his hands and knees, searching the grass – just in case, just in case – before accepting it was time to head back to the car.

When he reached the road he stood there for a little while, looking around. He couldn't see any buildings nearby. No houses or cabins; no places of business. He got back into the car and drove a little way up the hill, confirming that there was nothing here but road and forest and rocks. Beyond this point, the forest thickened. Up ahead, about twenty miles, was Mount Eddy and the Deadfall Lakes, with several campgrounds around them. Between here and there, the map was blank. No campgrounds. Nothing.

He popped a piece of chewing gum into his mouth and tried to focus his thoughts. He wasn't going to find any physical evidence. All he could do right now was speculate. Imagine.

He looked around him. The woman and the man chasing her must have come from a vehicle, possibly parked right on this spot. He tried to picture it, inventing a fictional young woman who wasn't Scarlett. A young couple who had driven into the forest. Perhaps they had come from an all-night party. Maybe they were returning home from a camping trip. What next? They'd had an argument. About what, it didn't matter. They yelled at each other.

45

Maybe he threatened her and she got out of the car and slammed the door. He called her a foul name. She told him he was a jerk.

It got nasty.

She must have been really scared of him to go into the trees in the dark. Desperate to get away.

Then Aidan conjured up another scenario. Perhaps they were strangers. Had he abducted her? And she'd managed to open the car door and throw herself out . . .

He was so deep in thought that he didn't hear the van that was racing up the hill until it was almost upon him. It shot past him, going so fast it made Aidan's car shudder.

About twenty feet along the empty road, the van screeched to a halt. It sat there, its engine rumbling. Aidan stared at it, a chill creeping up his spine. The van was streaked with dirt and the numbers and letters on the rear licence plate were half obscured with mud.

Aidan waited for the door to open but nothing happened. He could feel eyes watching him in the side mirror on the driver's side, but from this angle he couldn't see a face. He wondered if he should approach the van, though his brain – remembering all the horror movies he'd watched during his life – was screaming at him to get out of there.

Before he could make his mind up, the van lurched back into motion and sped away.

ϖ

Aidan parked on Main Street, outside the Tall Pines Diner, and walked up the street to the police station.

It was cool inside the small building. A male police officer stood behind the desk. His name badge read *Sanders*. He was very young, with a wispy moustache and acne-scarred cheeks.

'Can I help you?' he asked with a friendly smile.

'I hope so.'

Aidan told the officer his story, starting with Scarlett's disappearance from Seattle two years ago. As he spoke, the officer made some perfunctory notes. It was hard to tell if he was taking it seriously. From Sanders's bland expression, Aidan could have been telling him that he'd seen a fence that needed repairing on the outskirts of town.

Aidan had almost reached the end of his tale when the door behind the desk opened and a woman came out. She was older than Sanders, early forties, and stocky with short russet hair. Her name badge read *Giglio*.

'Mr Faith here is in town looking for his missing sister.' The young police officer consulted his notes. 'Scarlett Faith. It's kind of an unusual story.'

'Is that right?'

Sergeant Giglio was holding a coffee cup, which she put down on the counter. She took Sanders's place behind the desk. 'I'm a big fan of unusual stories.'

So Aidan told it again, with Giglio saying 'Uh-huh' and 'The *Coast Starlight*?' and even emitting a low whistle at one point.

Yes, she was more responsive than the other officer, but again he wasn't sure if he was being taken seriously. When he had finished, he said, 'I'm sure Mrs Gilbert saw someone. Even if it wasn't my sister, she witnessed a crime – I'm certain.'

'It sure sounds like it,' said Giglio. 'What time was this again?'

'Five fifty a.m. on June nineteenth. Three days ago.'

'If only all witnesses were as precise.'

'She's very reliable.'

'Hmm. And how exactly did she recognise your sister?'

'She remembered her from the news coverage. She looked her up immediately afterwards to check. I have a website.' He showed

Giglio his phone and she made a note of the URL. 'I've just been out to the clearing to take a look myself.'

'You mean you trampled over the crime scene?'

'I . . . Yeah, I guess. I shouldn't have done that, should I?' But he was pleased she was referring to it as a crime scene.

Giglio turned to Sanders. 'I guess we'd better go and take a look ourselves. We could speak to Amtrak too, just to check Mrs Gilbert got the time right.'

'Maybe we should get a K9,' Sanders suggested.

'Hmm. The nearest K9s are in Redding. But if we find some evidence a crime was committed that's certainly an avenue we can pursue. Do you have an item of Scarlett's? Something with her scent on it?'

'Shit. I don't.'

There were still some of Scarlett's clothes, packed away in her suitcase, in his spare room. The Seattle police had asked for the same two years ago, using their sniffer dogs around the lake, though they hadn't found anything.

'Not to worry,' said Giglio. 'If we get a dog in, perhaps you could get something sent down.'

She asked him to fill out a form with his contact details, including where he was staying.

'I'll be in touch,' she said.

He turned to leave. He felt both relieved, because she appeared to be taking him seriously, and deflated. What was he going to do now? Sit around and wait? He had a strong feeling the police would visit the clearing, find nothing and say there was nothing more they could do.

He went back to the desk. Giglio, who was about to make a phone call using her mobile, looked up. 'Yes?'

'I just wanted to ask . . . Do you have any issues on that road? With carjacking or women being attacked?'

Giglio seemed shocked by the question. 'This is a safe town, Mr Faith. Let me tell you, being a cop here ain't exactly a life of excitement. I don't think there's ever been a carjacking here.'

He thought about the van he'd seen. The weird way it had stopped, the driver looking at him. Like they were trying to intimidate him.

'You've had no reports of women being abducted?'

'Nope.'

'And what about domestic violence cases?'

'What about them?'

'I wondered if any woman had reported her partner recently. A boyfriend who wouldn't take no for an answer.'

She cocked her head a little. 'You think your sister's boyfriend might've been chasing her?'

'No no,' he said. 'Or, I don't know, maybe. I was just trying to rule *out* my sister. Figure out if perhaps Mrs Gilbert had seen some other, local woman.'

Giglio put her hands on her hips. 'My. You're really covering all the bases. Developing a whole investigation here. You trying to do my job for me?'

'No, I—'

'Hey, Sanders. I think Mr Faith here is after your job. Maybe mine too.'

Sanders said, 'Sure sounds like it.'

'I didn't mean to offend you,' Aidan said.

Giglio put her hands flat on the desk and leaned forward, smiling. 'I'm a very hard person to offend, Mr Faith. But leave us to do our jobs, okay? Sanders and I will go out to take a look first thing tomorrow. I'll call you.'

Chapter 7

Aidan left the police station. It was almost seven and the street was all but deserted. A pickup truck in need of a new muffler went by, and a harangued-looking mother herded a couple of small children into the Dollar General. Aidan's stomach growled and he realised he hadn't eaten all day. He headed down the road to the Tall Pines.

As he walked in, every head in the diner turned towards him as if he'd triggered an alarm. Eyes took him in, lingering for a few seconds before most of the diners went back to their conversations and food.

The place was surprisingly busy, with a mixture of elderly patrons, a few families and a couple of groups of construction workers, still dirty from a day of work. Over in the corner was a small group of teenage boys drinking milkshakes and sharing a couple of bowls of fries. Sitting at a table on her own beside them was a young woman with black hair, reading a Gabriel García Márquez novel.

Aidan slid into an empty booth in the corner and the waitress came over with a menu. She was around eighteen, willowy, with big eyes and long mousy hair tied in a ponytail. She took his order then returned a little later with his burger and beer.

He ate, wondering what to do next. Really, he knew he ought to wait until he'd heard from the police. He still felt a little shaken after his conversation with Giglio, even if she had been friendly in the end, as well as the strange encounter with the van. He was beginning to wonder if he had made a mistake coming here. He could have phoned the Eaglewood police from Seattle. He had found nothing of any consequence in the clearing, which was in no way surprising. He was certain the police weren't going to find anything tomorrow either, and then what would he do?

He was sending a text to his cat-sitter, checking Frosty was okay, when a female voice said, 'Sir?'

He looked up. The waitress was standing by his table. 'Sorry?'

'I asked if everything was okay with your meal.'

'Oh. Yes. It's wonderful, thank you.'

'Great. Let me know if I can get you anything else.'

She went to move away and he said, 'Hold on a second.' He reached into his pocket and she flinched, taking half a step backwards. 'Are you okay?' he said.

When she saw the phone, relief flooded her features. Had she thought he was going to pull out a gun or something? She still seemed nervous, even now she'd seen he was holding a phone rather than a weapon.

'Can I show you a photo of a girl and ask if you've seen her?'

It had struck him that if Scarlett had ever been in Eaglewood, there was a good chance she had visited the town's only diner. He had already decided that after this he would go to the Dollar General, the tavern, even the church. Speak to the staff at all the public buildings. Maybe one of them would recognise her. Or perhaps someone would say she reminded them of someone, a local red-headed woman, and Aidan would speak to her and she would tell him that, yes, she had been in the clearing on Wednesday morning, and he would be able to go home, no closer to finding Scarlett but knowing not to waste his time and hope.

The waitress's eyes widened as he held the screen out towards her.

He was sure he saw something there. A flicker of recognition. Something. But she shook her head and said, 'Sorry, I don't know her.'

'Are you sure? It looked like—'

'Elizabeth?' An older waitress over by the counter was gesturing to her. 'Can you take table fifteen's order?'

'Elizabeth,' Aidan said. 'Please. If you recognise her, I need to know. She disappeared two years ago and someone saw her near here, being chased.'

'Chased?'

'Hey, what's going on?' The older waitress had stomped across the diner. Everyone was looking.

'Can I show you this photo?' Aidan said, holding his phone up towards the older woman. She was unable to resist. Her eyes locked on the screen. 'Do you recognise her?'

'Nope. Sorry, never seen her. What are you, one of those private detectives? Is this another girl who came to Northern California looking for her fortune?'

What did that mean?

'She's my sister . . .' he started to explain, but she was already turning away. She vanished behind the counter, where she was joined by Elizabeth. Aidan was still being watched by half the customers in the diner but, one by one, they turned their attention back to their plates and their companions. All except the dark-haired woman with the Márquez novel. She had put the book down and was watching Aidan, frowning.

Suddenly, Aidan felt sick. Maybe it was the burger and beer, his tiredness, or all the emotions that had been stirred up by Francesca's call and the disappointment of not finding anything here but shakes of the head and mild hostility. Nausea swept up through him. He had to get out of here.

He threw down some money on the table and hurried out, gulping down air. It was growing dark outside now, and he could see his pale reflection in the diner's front window. Inside, he saw Elizabeth, behind the counter, her eyes on him.

ω

Aidan walked up the street, taking deep breaths until he began to feel more normal. He was sure he had seen recognition on Elizabeth's face. He should go back, talk to her again, maybe wait for her to finish her shift and approach her when she came out, although he was wary of frightening her, especially as he got the strong sense she was already scared. It was the way she had flinched when he reached into his pocket. Her whole demeanour had changed. Maybe she was a naturally nervous, on-edge person. Or maybe someone had made her like that.

He did as planned and went into the Dollar General and the tavern, showing Scarlett's photo. This time, the people he spoke to were convincing when they said they were sorry, but they didn't recognise her.

It was almost completely dark when he came out of the tavern. He had been tempted to stay for a drink or three. That was something he'd done a lot in the months following Scarlett's disappearance. Getting drunk helped him forget for a few hours. Took the edge off his pain. But then his co-workers had started to notice him turning up late; his performance at work had started to suffer and his boss had hauled him into his office to say that, while he sympathised with Aidan's situation, he couldn't afford for him to slack off. That, fortunately, had been enough to wake Aidan up – to push him off the path he was on before it became too difficult to change course. Now, though he still drank the odd beer – like the one he'd had with his dinner this evening – he forced himself to stop after one.

So instead he continued up Main Street, towards the church, not yet ready to go back to his depressing motel room. Then he spotted a poster attached to a streetlight, and stopped to examine it.

HAVE YOU SEEN OUR DAUGHTER? Paige Caldaralo, 19. Last seen 3/22/18. Much loved and sorely missed.

The poster had been bleached by the sun and come loose at one corner so it flapped in the breeze. It showed a smiling girl in a posed shot, possibly from a high school yearbook. Aidan wondered if she'd turned up safe and well, or if she was still sorely missed.

He kept walking and the church loomed out of the darkness, glowing white from its position at the end of the street on slightly raised ground. Aidan craned his neck to look up at the tall, pointed steeple and the cross that almost seemed to touch the sky. Mount Shasta was a hulking presence behind it, its white peak glowing beneath the star-rich sky. Aidan hesitated, wondering if there would be anyone inside, a priest or a pastor, until he heard a noise. Footsteps.

He looked back.

A woman stood beneath the streetlight.

It was the dark-haired woman from the diner. The one who'd been reading the Márquez book. She called out to him: 'I hear you're looking for someone.'

He walked back towards her, away from the church.

'That's right,' he said.

She glanced around her, apparently checking no one was watching them. Listening in.

'So am I,' she said.

Chapter 8

They went into the tavern and the woman asked Aidan what he was drinking, then went up to the bar while he found a table. He was tempted to ask her to get him a stiff drink, but forced himself to stick with Coke. He noticed that she didn't chat to anyone while she was waiting to be served. If anything, people appeared to be giving her a wide berth.

She came back with his soda and a bottle of Rolling Rock for herself.

'I know,' she said, nodding at the beer in her hand. 'The cheap stuff.' She shrugged. 'I acquired a taste for it when I was younger. My friends at college think it's hilarious.'

She was so immediately talkative that it disarmed him, and he found himself relaxing in her presence. 'You're at college?'

'Yeah. Well, I was. I just completed my master's.'

'What did you study?' he asked, sipping his Coke.

'English.'

'Did you write your thesis on magic realism?' He gestured to the book on the table. *One Hundred Years of Solitude.*

'Huh. Do I need to call you Sherlock Holmes? You've got the right accent.'

'Just call me Aidan. Aidan Faith.'

'And you can call me Lana Carrera.'

'You're from round here?' he asked.

'That's right. And I thought I'd escaped. I've been at college in DC – did I say that? – and I was getting ready to settle there when I got a call from my mother telling me my brother was dead.'

Aidan, whose drink was halfway to his lips, stopped and put the glass down. 'I'm sorry.'

'Except I don't believe that he's dead. Or, at least, that he didn't die in the way they said.'

She lifted the bottle and drank from it, swiftly, maintaining eye contact. She had very brown eyes, and even if she hadn't just told him about her master's he would have been able to tell she was fiercely intelligent. He guessed she was about twenty-six, a few years younger than him.

'What do you think happened?' he asked.

'First, tell me who you're looking for.'

He told her the whole story, up to his arrival in Eaglewood.

'Wow,' she said, her reaction seemingly genuine. 'And you think this Francesca actually saw your sister?'

'I don't know. She seems certain of it. But the closest I've come to getting any kind of confirmation that Scarlett has been around this area was a little earlier, when I showed her picture to a waitress at the diner.'

'Elizabeth. I was watching. What did she say?'

'Hardly anything. But there was something there. Something she didn't want to tell me, at least not in front of anyone.'

'Hmm. That's interesting.' Lana tapped the tip of her index finger against her chin. 'Really interesting.'

'Why?'

She leaned forward. 'Before I tell you, do you have some proof that you are who you say you are?'

'I can show you my driver's licence.'

56

'I mean proof that you're really Scarlett's brother. And that she really disappeared. I need to know I can trust you.'

'Of course. If you have proof that you're telling the truth too.'

She smiled wryly. 'Okay, Aidan. Let's trade. You first.'

He scrolled through the photos on his phone until he reached the pictures from that first day in Seattle, when they had gone up the Space Needle and visited the Museum of Pop Culture after they'd escaped the environmental protest. 'And this is my video appeal, when I asked Scarlett to come home.'

He showed her the news clip: Aidan, behind a long desk and flanked by detectives, camera flashes popping, pleading with Scarlett or her abductor.

Lana's demeanour immediately softened. 'Oh, that's awful. Jesus.'

'Yeah.'

'Okay, let me tell you about Samuel, my brother. This is him.' She handed Aidan her phone, which showed a picture of her with a boy in his late teens. 'But first I'm going to need another drink.' She held up the beer bottle. 'Are you sure you don't want one?'

Finally, he gave in. 'Just one,' he said.

'Good. It's your round.'

ϖ

'They said Samuel died in the fire,' Lana said, when Aidan came back from the bar.

'The wildfire?'

'One of them, yeah. It's become such a common thing in California but . . . yeah, the fire that reached Eaglewood last fall.'

She blinked a few times then went on. 'So, yeah, Samuel's my little brother, except our age gap isn't so big as the one between you and Scarlett. He's actually my half-brother by blood – we have different fathers – but I've never liked that term. He's a full brother to me.'

Aidan gestured to show he understood.

'So . . . last September he had just turned seventeen – going into his senior year of high school. And he was happy, excited about the future and totally in love with his girlfriend. Elizabeth.'

'Elizabeth from the diner?'

'Uh-huh. The very same. I mean, they were kind of a sickening couple, if you're not the romantic type. High school sweethearts. Talking about how they were going to be together forever and get married and all that stuff. I tried to tell him to slow down, that they were both too young for any sort of commitment, but he bought her a promise ring and she seemed as into it as he was – plus, she's a sweet girl – so I gave up. I mean, no boy wants dating advice from his big sister, right?'

'I guess not.'

'Well, Samuel certainly didn't.'

'So what happened?' Aidan asked. 'With the fire?'

He watched the muscles in her jaw flex a few times before she replied. 'The police said he was camping in the forest.' She opened the browser on her mobile and showed him a bookmarked news story: *Hikers, local boy killed in forest fire.* 'But it doesn't make any sense. Number one, he hadn't told Elizabeth or our mom about any plans to go camping. Number two, the other people he was supposedly with weren't even his friends. Number three, on top of all that, there's no way he would have gone into the forest that night.'

'Because of the risk of fire?'

'Yeah, of course. There were tons of fires already burning. Not right here, but further out. Everyone had been warned to shelter in place.'

'Hold on. You were in DC at the time, right?'

'Yeah. But I spoke to my mom after and she said the whole town had been told to stay put, to prepare to evacuate if necessary. My mom even had the car packed up ready, just in case. Samuel helped her do it! The police said maybe he didn't know how serious and dangerous it was, but that's bullshit.'

Aidan thought back to the article he'd read in the newspaper at Dunsmuir station. It had mentioned several deaths. Something about a planned memorial.

'Who were the other people who died?' he asked.

'They weren't from around here. Apparently they were back-packers, hiking the PCT.'

The Pacific Crest Trail. A hiking route that ran from the Mexican border up through California, Oregon and Washington.

'Samuel didn't even know them,' Lana said.

'Are you sure? Maybe he met up with them randomly and they invited him into the forest for a drink or a smoke.' Aidan was playing devil's advocate but he began to warm to the story. 'Were they female?'

'Two women. College students, a little older than him.'

'Maybe they came into town for supplies and he met them . . . and liked one of them.'

'That's exactly what the police said. But I told you, he was totally into Elizabeth. I can't believe he'd be unfaithful to her.'

Aidan tried not to let his scepticism show. Seventeen-year-old boys took risks, especially when girls were involved.

'Listen, I get it,' said Lana. 'People cheat. I understand temp-tation. But this behaviour was totally out of character.' She took a swig of beer. 'Plus, I never mentioned fact number four. They didn't find his body. The police said he must have been incinerated. The fire was so hot, they said his body would have . . . burned to ash and blown away. The only so-called proof he was there was that they apparently found his phone, all burned up but still identifiable.

Does that sound likely to you? Especially when they found the remains of the two hikers and there was enough left of them for the cops to ID them.'

The tavern had temporarily fallen quiet and Lana's voice cut through the silence. Aidan noticed a few people who were standing behind her shake their heads and roll their eyes.

'You still peddling that bullshit?' said a man with stringy blond hair, who was over by the bar. He was a tall, skinny guy, mid-twenties, apparently drinking on his own.

'Fuck you, Cody,' said Lana, without raising her voice or even looking at him.

He put down his beer and walked over to where Aidan and Lana sat. He barely glanced at Aidan, but swayed a little. He was drunk.

'Everybody knows your brother went into the forest chasing tail,' he said. 'Can't say I blame him. I've seen the photos of the two chicks he was out there with. They were smoking hot.' He smirked. 'Literally.'

'Leave me alone,' Lana said, still not looking at him.

But he wasn't going to. 'Folks around here are getting sick and tired of you trying to stir shit up. Trying to make out there's some kind of – what, conspiracy? I feel bad for your brother and your mom, but you need to let it go.'

Finally, she swivelled to face him. 'And who exactly asked you?'

He shrugged. 'I'm just speaking on behalf of the town. Folks here just wanna get on with things, live their lives, help put the damn town back together, and you going around peddling all this crap about the police and the mayor and God knows what ain't doing nothing but harm. You need to let it go.'

'Did I mention the mayor?'

'I'm pretty damn sure you have.'

That was presumably Mayor Christopher Hood, Aidan thought, who had been quoted in the paper.

'Makes sense, you defending him,' said Lana. 'You work for him now, right?'

'Most of Eaglewood works for him.'

'Well,' she said, 'you can tell your boss I know they're all lying. I don't know why. I don't know what's going on, exactly, what they're trying to cover up. But I will find out.'

Cody finally seemed to notice Aidan. 'Who's this?'

'That's none of your business,' Lana said.

'I'm here looking for my sister,' Aidan said, in the most pleasant voice he could manage.

Cody shifted from foot to foot. 'Another conspiracy nut, huh? I ought to warn you, Lana here might be pretty, but she's stone-cold crazy. I know some guys are into that sort of thing but—'

'Screw you, Cody,' Lana said, standing up at last and squaring up to her adversary.

Aidan stood too, though he had no idea of the history between these two. It was pretty clear there was bad blood between them. Were they exes? Surely not.

'You always were a bitch,' Cody said. 'Always thinking you were better than the rest of us. Acting so high and mighty, with your books and your perfect grades. Why don't you go back to Washington or wherever the hell you've been?' He leaned past her and picked up the Márquez book. 'What's this?' He flipped it over, stepping back and holding it up high so Lana couldn't reach it, though she tried. Cody twisted away and squinted at the cover. '*Magic realism*, huh? What the hell is that? Sounds like the kind of crazy bullshit story you been telling about your brother.'

'Give it back to her,' Aidan said.

Cody turned to him. 'You another college boy? Well—' He didn't finish his sentence because Lana jumped up and snatched the book from him, making him yell, 'Hey!'

'Let's go, Aidan,' she said.

'Gladly.'

But Cody blocked their path. 'Your brother is dead. Accept it and move on.'

'You know,' she said, 'maybe he is. But I won't accept it until I've got proof. And I'm certainly not going to take advice from a pencil-dicked loser like you.'

Cody gawped and a laugh rang out around the tavern.

'That's right,' Lana said. 'Maybe you forget I used to be friends with Kim. You know we *bitches* tell each other everything?'

'I'm going to fucking kill—'

Aidan was braced to step between them, even though Cody looked like he was a far more experienced fighter. In fact, anyone who'd ever been in more than one fight in their life had more experience than Aidan. But he didn't have to, because the tavern's beefy security guy had appeared and planted himself in front of Cody.

'Get out of here,' the security guy said to Lana.

'Don't worry, I'm going.'

She strode to the exit, with Aidan in her wake. Behind them, Cody called, 'Watch your back, bitch.'

'Shut up, pencil dick,' a woman shouted from the other side of the tavern, to another ripple of derisive laughter.

Aidan and Lana emerged onto the street and he followed her as she hurried away. She was laughing. 'Oh shit, I shouldn't have said that.'

'I think he deserved it.'

'Oh yeah, he definitely did. He's always been a creep.'

'How do you know him?'

'We were at school together. I do feel kind of bad. His home life sucked. His dad was an asshole. It's not surprising he turned out the way he did. But I couldn't take him saying that about Samuel.'

They were halfway down Main Street, outside the now-closed diner, and Aidan was relieved that Cody hadn't followed them.

They slowed down and Aidan recalled the question that had entered his head when Lana was arguing with Cody.

'You think the mayor has something to do with all this?' Whatever 'all this' was.

'I don't know. But I do know that Samuel was at the mayor's house the night before he supposedly died. The night before the wildfire.'

'What? Why?'

'Didn't I mention? Elizabeth is the mayor's daughter.'

'And what does she say about all this?' Aidan asked.

'I haven't been able to get near her since I got back. Her dad won't let her talk to me and whenever I try to speak to her here' – she gestured towards the diner, which was dark inside – 'she runs away to the kitchen. It's yet another thing that makes me suspicious. She is so obviously scared.'

'I'm sure when I showed her Scarlett's photo she acted like she knew something,' Aidan said. 'As if she recognised her.'

'Then we both need to speak to her.'

At that moment, a police cruiser slid up beside them, so quietly that it made Aidan jump when Sergeant Giglio leaned out of the window and said, 'Good evening.'

Lana glared at her and Giglio ignored her.

'Mr Faith,' the police officer said, addressing him, 'I'll be checking out that clearing first thing tomorrow.'

'Thank you.'

'I do hope you're not listening to Ms Carrera here. She's never been a big fan of the police around here, ever since I busted her for smoking weed when she fifteen.'

'That has nothing—'

Giglio didn't let her finish. 'Mr Faith, I'll be in touch in the morning.'

She drove away.

63

Chapter 9

2017

It was the third day of Scarlett's visit to Seattle. On day two, jet lag had caught up with her and she'd wanted to spend the day chilling at Aidan's place. She had brought her own laptop with her – a shiny little MacBook Air – and had passed the afternoon sunk into the sofa, tapping away at the keyboard, a look of rapt concentration on her face. Aidan had ordered in dinner via Uber Eats, and then asked her what she was doing.

'Homework,' had come the reply. 'Unfortunately I couldn't use the excuse of being in America to get out of it.'

Now they were doing something Aidan had been promising since they had started planning this trip, back when their parents had first suggested it might be good for Scarlett to get away, to visit her brother. They were going on a pilgrimage to Viretta Park.

The bus, which Aidan had insisted they take, dropped them on Lake Washington Boulevard, a short distance from the park. This was a rich area of the city, full of neat streets with grand detached houses, and Audis and Teslas and BMWs parked out front.

'How's school going?' Aidan asked as they walked up the hill.

'It's boring. I kind of like some of the subjects, like geography. Miss James is cool. But most of the teachers are annoying.'

Aidan smiled. 'Geography, huh? I wouldn't have thought that was your favourite subject.'

'Why not? We've been learning about how the ice caps are melting. Do you know what will happen if the Greenland Ice Sheet melts? What will happen to sea levels? The number of cities that will be underwater?'

'Climate change,' he said, slightly distracted as they prepared to cross the road.

'It's not climate *change*. It's a climate *emergency*. Jesus, this is why no one is doing anything. You make it sound so . . . benign. But our planet is being *destroyed*.'

Aidan was taken aback by the flash of anger. He resisted the urge to point out that she'd just taken a carbon-footprint-exploding plane across the Atlantic, in part because he knew she would only remind him it wasn't her idea to come.

'How are you getting along with Mum and Dad at the moment?' he asked, changing the subject.

'They hate me.'

'What? Don't be silly.'

'They do. All they do is nag me about how much time I spend "staring at a screen", complain about my friends, and go on about their golden boy and how you were always top of the class, not languishing near the bottom like me.'

'Oh.' Aidan hadn't been expecting that.

'And they're constantly talking about all the things they're going to be able to do when I leave home. Mum's already planning to turn my bedroom into a home gym. I know for a fact they wish they'd never had me.' Her eyes shone as she spoke.

'That's ridiculous.'

'No it's not. I know I was an accident.'

'That's absolute rubbish. They tried for years to have you. They were desperate for a second child.'

'Only because they thought they'd have another one as perfect as you. I'm just a massive disappointment to them.'

'You're not, Scarlett. But I'm sorry you feel like that.' He made a mental note to speak to their parents, to let them know how Scarlett felt and ask them to go easier on her. But right now he needed to lighten the mood. 'I'm also sorry I was so perfect and such a hard act to live up to.'

He grinned and she swiped at him. 'You're such a twat.'

'A golden twat.'

She laughed. 'That's a pretty gross image.'

'Oh, I don't know . . .'

'Aidan!'

They were still laughing when they reached Viretta Park, and Scarlett stopped, taking a breath to prepare herself.

Next to this minuscule park was the house where Kurt Cobain had killed himself. This was where fans came to pay tribute to their hero. And even though Scarlett had been born eight years after the Nirvana singer died, they were her favourite band. *Nevermind* was one of the albums Aidan had introduced her to shortly after she started secondary school. While her friends had been listening to One Direction, Scarlett had got into grunge.

As soon as they reached the park, which was so small it would barely have qualified as a garden for one of the enormous houses around here, Scarlett rushed over to one of two tatty wooden benches that were pretty much the only features of the space. At the foot of the park was the main road they had just walked up from. Traffic was sparse and the park was silent and still. The leaves on the trees were beginning to turn orange and brown, and there was a damp chill in the air.

Scarlett had made a beeline for the bench to the left, which was covered with graffiti. Kurt Cobain's lyrics, song titles, messages of grief and love. A knackered pair of black Converse sat on the wooden slats beside two bouquets of flowers.

Aidan stood with his hands in his pockets while Scarlett crouched in front of the bench like a worshipper before an altar, a sigh coming from deep inside her. She raised her phone and took a number of selfies with the bench in the background.

'He was so beautiful,' she said, getting to her feet.

'He was,' said Aidan with a smile. 'Don't forget talented. And tragic.'

'Tragic, yeah. He was prepared to sacrifice himself so his music would live on forever.'

'I'm not sure that's true, Scarlett. He was depressed.'

But she wasn't listening. 'Can you imagine what it must have been like to be him? To make such a difference to so many people? It'd be like . . . like living forever.' She produced a Sharpie from her pocket. 'I need to leave a message before I go home. I just can't decide what to write.'

'Just say how you feel,' said a male voice.

They had been facing the bench, and both Aidan and Scarlett turned around.

'It's what Kurt would want,' said the guy.

He was in his late twenties, Aidan estimated. Long hair. A little scrap of a beard on what was an indisputably handsome face. He looked not dissimilar to Kurt in his prime.

'You from around here?' the guy asked, ignoring Aidan and addressing Scarlett.

'No,' Scarlett said with a shy laugh. 'I'm from England.'

'Awesome. Kurt had some of his best times there. You know . . .'

He began to regale them with Nirvana facts and Scarlett nodded along, seemingly fascinated, even though she must have known most of the stuff this guy was mansplaining. Aidan kept an eye on Scarlett but drifted away, going over to the gate of the house where Kurt had lived and died, though trees blocked the view. He sat on the bench that wasn't a shrine and waited for his sister to stop chatting to the walking grunge encyclopedia. He was cold, and he wanted to get back.

'So listen,' Aidan heard the guy say, 'there's a Nirvana tribute act playing tonight at this bar in Capitol Hill. You should come check it out.'

'Sounds great,' Scarlett said.

'The band's called Penny Royal Tea.' He began to tell her where to find the venue and what time the band would be on.

Aidan had heard enough. He got up and went back over to the other bench. 'She's fifteen.'

The guy said, 'What? You're kidding me. You look totally mature. At least twenty-one.'

Aidan stared at him. Was he for real? But when he looked at his sister he saw that she was flattered.

The guy addressed Aidan. 'How old are you?'

'Twenty-seven.'

'Whoa, and you're hanging out with a fifteen-year-old?'

'She's my sister.'

The Kurt lookalike said, 'Ah. Well, *you* can get into the gig, dude. And I'm sure it wouldn't be too hard to get fake ID for . . . What's your name, babe?'

Aidan opened his mouth to tell her not to respond, but he was too late. 'Scarlett,' she said.

'Cool name. Red's my favourite colour. Listen, they're an awesome tribute band. And they're pretty lax with IDs at this place. I can get you in, no problemo.'

He actually said 'no problemo'.

Aidan was getting sick of this. He said to Scarlett, 'Come on, let's go.' When she resisted, he spoke to the guy. 'It's not a good look, hitting on a fifteen-year-old.'

'I'm not hitting on her. Jesus.'

'Do this a lot, do you? Hang around here trying to pick up impressionable young girls?'

'Fuck you, man. You think I'm some kind of paedophile?'

'I don't know. Maybe you are.'

Nobody said anything for a minute. The guy had one hand in his coat pocket and Aidan found his mouth drying, his heartbeat speeding up. This guy could be a psycho. He could have a knife. Jesus, he could have a gun. Aidan braced himself.

Nothing happened, except the guy shrugging, a faux-goofy smile replacing the anger. He spoke to Scarlett. 'If you change your mind, just google it. Penny Royal Tea. I'll get you in. Guaranteed. Your big brother can come along too. Maybe it'll help him loosen up.'

He slouched off towards the road, in the direction of the lake.

Aidan looked at Scarlett, expecting to see relief. He had saved her from a creepy weirdo with an obvious penchant for young girls.

'That was so embarrassing,' she said. 'So cringe.'

'Yeah, what a creep.'

'Not him. You. Treating me like I'm a baby.' He was shocked by the mortified expression on her face.

'Scarlett, you're fifteen. You're not going to a gig with some perv who tried to pick you up in a park. Jesus.'

She glowered at him. 'You're just like Mum and Dad. No wonder they think you're so perfect.'

She stomped away and he hurried to catch up. 'Listen . . .'

But she wouldn't. Hot tears spilled onto her cheeks. 'I was so looking forward to today. I've been looking forward to it for months. And you've ruined it! I hate you.'

He stood there for a moment, letting her march off down the hill. He should give her a few minutes to calm down. Keeping her in sight, he followed at a short distance, wondering if he could have handled things better.

Twenty-four hours later, he had convinced himself it was all his fault.

Chapter 10

Aidan left his motel room the next morning, intending to go to the diner to speak to Elizabeth Hood, and found Sergeant Giglio waiting in the parking lot. She was half sitting on the trunk of her car, scrolling through her phone. When she saw him coming towards her she straightened up and said, 'Sleep well?'

'Not bad.'

She looked over his shoulder. 'Sleep *alone*?'

He was sure his surprise must have shown on his face. 'I did. Not that it's really any of your business.'

'I guess it isn't. But you ought to be careful what company you keep.'

'Because Lana was once arrested for doing something that is now legal?'

Giglio shook her head. 'Approve of fifteen-year-olds smoking weed, do you?'

'No. Of course not.' He felt a little chastened.

She smirked. 'You wouldn't be the first person to be hoodwinked by that pretty face. But Lana Carrera is a loose cannon, Mr Faith. And what she says about her brother and this crazy conspiracy story is plain wrong. Samuel Carrera was a sweet kid. I know he treated Elizabeth right, at least until he went off with those hiker girls, and Mayor Hood was very fond of him. But he died in that fire. There is no police cover-up.'

You would say that, thought Aidan. But he said, 'Have you been out to the clearing?'

'I have. Went at first light. And I'm afraid I didn't find anything.'

That was hardly a surprise.

'Okay. So what are you going to do next?'

'Not much I can do, Mr Faith. We have no evidence of any crime taking place. I called Amtrak and nobody else reported seeing anything, including the conductors. So we're just left with the eyewitness account of an older lady who, according to what you told me, had only just woken up and who was recently bereaved, on her way home after an extremely emotional journey to scatter her husband's ashes.'

'You think she imagined it.'

'It must have crossed your mind, surely?'

'Yeah. Of course. But I believed her. And—' He stopped himself.

'What?'

Was there a police conspiracy? His instinct was to believe the idea was far-fetched, that Samuel Carrera had perished in the wildfire, no matter how much he had liked Lana. But he had seen that look of recognition on Elizabeth's face when he'd shown her Scarlett's photo, and she had been Samuel's girlfriend, which meant there might be some connection between Samuel and the woman in the forest – Scarlett or not. Until he had spoken to Elizabeth, he didn't want to reveal anything else to Sergeant Giglio.

'Just, she seemed like a reliable witness to me.'

That made Giglio laugh. 'You wouldn't believe how many seemingly reliable witnesses I've met in my job, Mr Faith. Witnesses who turned out to be nuts or liars or just plain human beings. Our brains and memories trick us in a hundred ways every day. If we're vulnerable or tired, make that a thousand.'

'So that's it?' he said. 'You're going to give up?'

Giglio lifted a hand to shield her eyes from the bright sun. The sky was clear and the thermometer was already creeping towards the mid-seventies; yesterday, Aidan had heard a couple in the diner complaining about how hot it was for June.

'I'll continue to ask around and will, of course, keep an eye out. If you have posters with Scarlett's face on them I can get some put up. But there's nothing else I can do right now. I've got your number. Go home to Seattle and I'll call you if anything turns up.' She checked her watch. 'I think you've missed today's *Coast Starlight* in K Falls, but if you call your car rental place, I'm sure they'll be happy for you to just drive it on back to Seattle.'

'I'm going to get breakfast and think about it.'

'Uh-huh. You do that. But believe me, there's no point in you sticking around here. And if you're planning to stay because of Lana Carrera, that's an even bigger waste of your time.'

ϖ

An hour later, Aidan emerged from the diner. Elizabeth hadn't been there – the waitress who'd served him hadn't been too friendly when he'd asked where she was – and he didn't know what to do next.

The thing was, he thought Giglio was most likely correct. Francesca probably had dreamed up the whole thing. He'd come here knowing his chances of finding Scarlett were somewhere between slim and infinitesimal. He could go back saying he'd tried, at least.

But he felt guilty even contemplating it – and how much more guilt could he take? He had come south because even the smallest chance of finding Scarlett was worth it. And he needed to talk to Elizabeth before he made a final decision.

He called Lana.

Thirty minutes later she pulled into the motel parking lot in a chocolate-brown Toyota. 'My mom's car,' she said as she got out. She was dressed for the hot weather in denim shorts and a loose-fitting T-shirt. Her hair was slightly damp, as if she'd recently got out of the shower. Aidan couldn't help but notice her long legs and he wondered if Giglio was right. Was he allowing himself to be swayed by her looks? He didn't know her and had no idea if he could trust her. A 'loose cannon', Giglio had called her.

'Why are you looking at me like that?' Lana asked. 'Having deep thoughts?'

He was momentarily flummoxed, worried she'd caught him looking at her legs.

'I'm just messing with you,' she said. 'Come on, let's take your car.'

'Where are we going?'

'You want to talk to Elizabeth, don't you?'

They left the town and Lana gave him directions, telling him to head towards the mountains.

'Turn right here,' she said, directing him off the highway into the foothills. They had passed the last dwelling a while back.

'You've been here before?'

'Yeah. Mayor Hood had a party here the summer before last, back when Samuel had just started dating Elizabeth. A pool party. It was fun. The house was kind of shabby then, though. Looks like he's had loads of work done on it.'

They climbed a hill, the road curving around a bend as they ascended, giving Aidan a view of Lake Shastina below. Ringed by low hills, it glowed metallic blue in the morning sun. They continued to climb until they rounded a final bend.

'Holy shit,' Aidan said. 'Elizabeth lives *here*?'

A mansion sat on the top of the hill. Pillars dominated its three-storey façade; there was a turreted tower at the rear and a crest above the front doors. It was like a castle, Aidan thought. A fortress.

He pulled up. Mount Shasta appeared to be right there beside the house, and the views in every direction took his breath from him.

'What does Elizabeth's dad do, apart from being mayor?'

'He runs a construction company. But he also owns Shastina Spring,' Lana said.

'What's that?'

'It's a mineral water company. They bottle water from the local springs and sell it to Japan, China, Europe. They used to charge the town to use the springs, but they've stopped doing that since Hood became mayor. It was one of his election pledges.'

'You mean he bought the election?'

'That's what Samuel said.'

'And his name's Hood?'

Lana nodded. 'Chris Hood.'

'No relation to Robin, obviously.'

This earned him a roll of her eyes.

'Why does Elizabeth work in a diner when her family is this rich?'

'I guess she doesn't want to be some vacuous trust-fund kid. Samuel said her dad hated her working there but that she wanted to earn her own money. She's supposed to be starting college this fall and she wanted to have some savings.'

'Good for her.'

Lana leaned forward to peer at the house. 'I'm hoping the mayor will be at work. Did I tell you Elizabeth's mom died when she was young, so it's just her and her dad?'

75

'If he's at work, what makes you think she'll talk to us? You said she's been avoiding you, and she wasn't exactly keen to speak to me yesterday.'

'I messaged her last night. Told her I'd found some jewellery that belongs to her in Samuel's bedroom – which is true, actually.' She reached into her shorts pockets and pulled out a pair of earrings. 'Pretty nice. She said I could drop them at the diner, but I'm going to say I wanted to make sure she got them.'

As soon as they got out of the car the great double doors opened and a man in his fifties came out. He was wearing jeans with a shirt tucked into them, and had thick salt-and-pepper hair, a matching beard and a smile that didn't reach his eyes. Mayor Hood, presumably.

'Shit,' Lana muttered.

'Lana,' said the mayor. 'This is a pleasant surprise.'

'I bet.'

'Who's your friend?' Hood asked, looking directly at Aidan, the fake smile clinging to his lips.

'My name's Aidan Faith.'

'Ah.'

It was obvious that Hood recognised Aidan's name. He guessed that Giglio had mentioned their encounter.

'This is a beautiful place,' Aidan said, gesturing at the view. 'You must feel like the king of the world.'

The fraudulent smile was still in place. 'Well, I don't know about that. But yes, we feel blessed. Tell me, to what do we owe the pleasure of your visit?'

'We want to see Elizabeth,' Lana said.

'Oh. I'm sorry, but she's sick in bed.'

'Really?' said Lana. 'She never mentioned that last night when I messaged her.'

'It came on suddenly. She's under the weather and needs to rest, that's all. I'm sure she'll be fine in a day or two. Want me to ask her to call you, Lana, when she's feeling up to it? I didn't actually know the two of you were still in touch, but I guess it's a comfort. To both of you, after Samuel's passing.' He cleared his throat. 'Again, I can't tell you how sorry I am about that. I still can't quite believe it. Terrible, tragic thing.'

'Thanks.' There was a frosting of ice in the word.

'And I'm sure Elizabeth will try to stay in touch when she goes to New Hampshire.'

'I'm sure I'll see her before that,' Lana said.

'Oh. She didn't tell you? She starts college in September, but she's actually going to head east tomorrow, assuming she's better.'

'*Tomorrow?*'

'That's right. My sister lives near there, so she's going to stay with her for a little while, get acclimated before the academic year starts. The sooner she gets away from this place and all the . . . memories, the better.'

'Convenient,' Lana said.

'I'd better get inside,' Hood said. 'Good to see you, Lana. Say hi to your mom from me. And I guess you'll be leaving town, Mr Faith? Sergeant Giglio filled me in on what happened to your sister. My heart goes out to you.'

He sounded genuine, but also – Aidan was sure of it – nervous. It was a hot morning, which might have accounted for it, but the mayor's brow was shiny with sweat. On top of that, why had Giglio bothered to tell the mayor about him and Scarlett?

Before Aidan could say anything else, Hood vanished inside and shut the door.

'Asshole,' said Lana. 'No way is she sick.'

'What are we going to do?'

'Come with me.'

77

She walked quickly towards the corner of the house, tapping at her phone with both thumbs.

'Are you messaging Elizabeth?'

'Yeah. I'm pretty much pleading with her to talk to us.' She showed Aidan what she'd written: *If you truly loved my brother, you'll come down and talk to me.* Emotional blackmail. It was hardly subtle.

As if she'd read his thoughts, she said, 'I'm done with being subtle. She owes me a conversation.' She looked up at the house. 'From what I remember from the party, that's Elizabeth's room.'

Lana was right. And Elizabeth must have heard them because her face appeared at the window. Lana gestured at her: *Come down.* But Elizabeth shook her head. She was pale. Maybe she really was sick. To Aidan, it looked more like fear.

Dots appeared on Lana's phone to indicate Elizabeth was sending a reply to Lana's message.

Dad has a meeting at 4. I'll see you 4.15 at the murder house.

Lana sent back a *Thank you.*

Back in the car, Aidan said, 'The *murder* house? What's that about?'

'There's a story to it, but it's pretty much what it sounds like. Jesus, I hate that place, and four fifteen is hours away.'

'But she's agreed to meet us.'

She looked at him. 'You're one of those glass-half-full kinda guys, aren't you?'

'Not usually. But when I meet a glass-half-empty girl, I feel the need to compensate.'

She laughed.

He started the car and headed down the hill.

There, waiting by the side of the road back into town, was a police cruiser. Sergeant Giglio sat behind the wheel.

'Looks like we've got ourselves an escort,' Aidan said, driving past the cruiser.

As he'd imagined she would, Giglio eased onto the road behind them.

'I think she's got the hots for you,' Lana said.

Aidan expected the cop to flash her lights, pull them over and ask what they'd been doing at the mayor's house. But she just stayed behind them.

'We don't want her following us around all day,' Lana said. 'Drop me at my house and I'll send you a pin so you can find the murder house. I think it might be a good idea if you pack up your stuff and drive your rental out of town. Make Giglio think you're heading home.'

'Really?'

She looked exasperated. 'Listen. Ask yourself: why is she tailing us? Why is the mayor making up stories about Elizabeth being sick? They're covering something up. Maybe it has something to do with your sister and maybe it doesn't, but Giglio clearly doesn't want you hanging around with me, does she?'

'She's definitely not your biggest fan,' he conceded.

'And she pretty much told you to get out of town, right?'

'She said there was no point in me staying.'

'Yeah. About as subtle as my message to Elizabeth. But I'm telling you, they want all this to go away. They want you to go home to Seattle and me to go back to DC, and now they're sending Elizabeth out of Eaglewood too. Why?'

She directed him to her place. Aidan was surprised when they arrived at a trailer park.

'Yeah. This is the shithole where Samuel and I grew up. You know the mayor's redevelopment plan involves tearing this place down? They'd have been tickled pink if the fire had ripped through it – burned it to the ground.'

He stopped and Giglio pulled up twenty yards behind them. Lana got out and turned towards the police car.

'Don't provoke her,' Aidan called through the open passenger window, convinced Lana was going to shout something or show Giglio her middle finger.

She leaned down and smiled darkly at him. 'I promise to be a good girl. I would invite you in for a cup of tea or something but my mom works nights and she'll be asleep. I'll send you that address and see you there at four fifteen. Okay? You're going to make it look like you're leaving town?'

'I will.'

'Good.' She paused, as if she'd thought of something. 'Hey, Aidan. You got a girlfriend waiting for you back in Seattle?'

'No.' He felt his cheeks grow a little warm. 'Why do you ask?'

'Just checking you're not going to leave some poor woman broken-hearted if something happens to you.'

'What?'

She looked like she was trying to grin, to indicate she was kidding, but the grin wouldn't materialise. 'Bad things happen at the murder house,' she said. And she walked away.

Chapter 11

'Okay, folks,' said Jimmy, adjusting the brim of his cowboy hat. 'Now I'm going to show you how to make vegan jello.'

Bemused noises came from the group of four assembled in the barn for the day's lesson. Another new recruit, a woman aged about nineteen, had turned up this morning, so Kristin Fox was no longer the newest person at the Ranch. The group in the barn also included a pair of young men who'd told her they'd been here a couple of weeks.

'You're gonna show us how to make dessert?' said one of the guys.

'It's an incendiary device,' said Kristin. 'That's right, isn't it, Jimmy?'

He grinned at her. 'I'm glad someone's done their homework. "Vegan jello" is what we used to call a mix of diesel fuel and glycerine soap. And, being an old fart, I still call it that.' Jimmy chuckled. 'It's used to start fires. We plant it, add an ignition device and . . . boom!'

Jimmy had already told them his backstory. In the nineties he'd been a member of the Animal Liberation Front. His proudest moment, he'd told them, was when he and a few of his fellow ALF members burned down the offices attached to a slaughterhouse that processed horse meat – many of the creatures former wild horses that had been rounded up by the Bureau of Land Management. A decade ago, he'd switched his attention to environmental issues and had spent time in Brazil, trying to slow the destruction of the rainforest.

He'd also talked to them about recent protests in London he'd read reports of, where young activists had, among other things, glued themselves to subway trains and blockaded parts of the city. 'Man, I wish I could've been there,' Jimmy had said, taking off his hat and smoothing the remains of his hair. 'The times they are a-changing. This generation, you give me hope. You actually give a shit.'

Now, Kristin watched as Jimmy showed them how to create the vegan jello. On that first morning, she'd thought he was an asshole, taking pleasure at her shock at the material deprivations at the Ranch. Then he'd taken the recruits to the drop-off point, wherever that was, and had only got back this morning. He must have been exhausted, but here he was, full of good humour and patience. She guessed the trip had been successful.

'Hey, Jimmy.' She turned to find Frank, the perpetually-trucker-hatted guy who had been on that trip with Jimmy, in the doorway. 'You're wanted at the big house,' he said.

ω

Shannon Reinhardt's office was dominated by a huge desk constructed from reclaimed wood. There was a vintage couch along one wall, on which Shannon reclined now. She had changed a hell of a lot since Jimmy first met her. Man, she'd been wet behind the ears back then. A new convert, keen to help, but without much of a clue as to how to go about it. When he'd waved her off – what, five, six years ago now – he hadn't expected to see her again, let alone for her to return with a sense of purpose and the zeal that had brought them all here. The new Shannon had fire in her eyes, and a vision that was clear and frightening enough to have convinced him to become her second in command. And Jimmy had never been anyone's second in command.

'Jimmy,' she said now. 'Take a seat.'

There were two other men in the room. One of them – Mayor Hood – Jimmy already knew. The other guy was much younger: mid-twenties, Jimmy guessed. He had the look of a tweaker. Skinny, with sharp cheekbones and blond hair that needed a good wash. He had his hands in his pockets and kept flicking glances at Shannon – the kind of look a well-trained dog would give a roast chicken.

'You know the mayor,' Shannon said. 'And this is one of his . . . assistants. Cody, is it?'

'That's right,' said the guy.

Assistant. That was funny. If the guy weren't so skinny and so clearly half a bubble off plumb, Jimmy would've pegged him as hired muscle or a bodyguard. He had to be here *because* he was such an unstable compound. Someone the mayor used to do his dirty work.

'The mayor is here to tell us about a potential problem,' Shannon said.

'A situation I thought you should be aware of,' said Hood.

'I didn't think you were delivering water yourself,' Jimmy said.

The mayor laughed like this was a great joke. 'Don't worry, your water will be here tomorrow.'

'Tell him what's happened, Mayor,' said Shannon, still seated on the couch. She was in a relaxed position, legs crossed, but Jimmy knew Shannon and could see tension there. A clenched fist. A tightness in her jaw.

'Sure, sure.' The mayor was sweating. Tension there too. Interesting. 'I've told you already about the young woman who refuses to believe Samuel Carrera died in last year's wildfire.'

'Yeah,' Jimmy said. 'The sister.'

'Lana,' Cody said. He spoke it like it was the filthiest cuss word he knew.

'I thought that was a non-issue,' said Jimmy. 'He did die in the fire, didn't he?'

The mayor scratched his head. 'He did. And no one else believes all the conspiracy theories Lana has been spouting. Folks in Eaglewood are sick of hearing about it.'

'So what's the problem?'

'She's made friends with a visitor to the town. A British guy who lives in Seattle. He's here looking for his missing sister. We didn't think this guy was going to be a problem at first. Sergeant Giglio has been dealing with him. But now he and Lana have teamed up and, well, I thought you ought to know about it.'

Jimmy turned to Shannon. 'This missing sister. Is she one of ours?'

Shannon had an iPad on the sofa beside her. She picked it up, opened it and handed it to Jimmy. A website was open on the screen.

'This is his website,' she said.

He took it in. 'Well, shit.'

'Exactly. He needs to be strongly discouraged. More effectively than Sergeant Giglio has managed so far. We can't afford to have any problems, especially right now. If this guy finds out about us and thinks his sister is here . . .'

'He'll call the Feds.' Jimmy clenched his fists.

'Or maybe he'll get the press involved. Or hire a competent private investigator.'

Mayor Hood mopped his brow with a handkerchief. Clearly he didn't like the idea of the Feds or journalists sniffing around either. 'Lana and this guy, Aidan Faith, have arranged to meet up with my daughter Elizabeth this afternoon. She doesn't know, but I have a piece of software installed on her phone so I can see all her activity. They're meeting at what the locals call "the murder house".'

'I know the place,' Jimmy said.

Hood was pouring with sweat. 'I'm absolutely certain my daughter doesn't know anything incriminating. But I thought it might be a good, um, *opportunity* for us to have a word with Lana Carrera and this Faith guy. Without any harm coming to Elizabeth.' He mopped his forehead again. 'It's absolutely vital that Elizabeth doesn't even see you guys. I thought you could wait for their little meeting to finish, and for Elizabeth to head home, and then you can intercept them.'

'Don't worry, Mayor. No harm will come to your little girl.'

'I'd like Cody to go with you,' the mayor said. 'He knows Elizabeth and—'

'He'll be able to watch out for her?'

The mayor swallowed, his Adam's apple bobbing. 'It's not that I don't trust you, but if anything happens to my daughter, I'll . . .'

'What?'

The mayor puffed his chest out. 'I'll no longer be able to work with you.'

Jimmy patted him on the shoulder. 'Like I said, she'll be fine.' He looked at Cody. 'I guess you can come along, if it's going to keep the mayor happy. But you follow my orders, okay?'

'Sure,' Cody said.

'You got any personal beef with Lana Carrera?'

The man shook his head. Jimmy knew this was bullshit, but maybe it wouldn't matter. He was more interested in the other guy. The Brit.

'You'd better set off now,' Shannon said, 'if you don't want to miss them. Mayor, I assume you're okay to drive yourself home?'

Mayor Hood left, having extracted more promises that not a single hair on Elizabeth's head would be harmed.

Jimmy found the keys to his truck and gestured for Cody to follow him.

'Hey,' Cody said to Shannon before they left. 'Do you actually know this girl?'

Shannon gave him her best Mona Lisa smile.

Chapter 12

Aidan did as Lana had suggested, packing up his stuff, which didn't take long, and getting into his car and driving towards the outskirts of town. Giglio, who had been parked in the motel parking lot, followed until he hit the highway. Then she took the first exit. Aidan took the next, and doubled back. He put the address Lana had given him into the satnav and took a circuitous route around the outskirts of Eaglewood. All these forest roads looked the same and he almost got lost a couple of times, but he eventually found it, barely in time for the meet-up. At just after four fifteen he drove onto a track that was hardly even a road, and there it was.

The house was tucked in the forest like an animal hiding in a burrow. Aidan pulled up outside a gate that was covered by snaking vines. Beyond, a long path led into the trees. Aidan killed the engine and saw that Lana's Toyota was parked a little way along the track, half concealed by vegetation.

Aidan greeted her. She had changed out of her shorts into jeans, perhaps because she had known it would be cooler here, inside the forest. It was still warm, though, and small black flies darted around, forcing both Aidan and Lana to swipe at them. Lana had a bag over her shoulder and her hair was tied back.

'So this is the murder house,' said Aidan.

'Not its official name.'

Lana pushed the gate, which opened with a low groan, some of the vines stretching then snapping in two. Lana went through. She was walking fast, and Aidan had to hurry to keep up.

'All right, I'll bite: why is it called the murder house?'

'Some survivalist guy went nuts fifteen years back and shot his wife and kids, then ended up in a siege with the cops. They said he was ranting about the Illuminati, that they were coming to take his children away.'

'Bloody hell. What happened to him?'

'What happened? The cops shot him, of course. And this place has been empty ever since. Nobody's ever been dumb enough to want to buy it.'

'And yet this is where the local kids hang out?' Aidan asked.

'Not these days. When I was fifteen or sixteen some of my friends used to come here to . . . you know, do what teenagers do when their parents aren't around, but I'm not sure if that happens anymore. This place has deteriorated a lot since I was at school. Rumour has it it's haunted. A couple of drug dealers used it as a base at one point, until some tweaker thought he saw a kid with a bullet hole in her head, telling him to get clean, and the story spread.' She shook her head. 'You know a place is seriously messed up if even addicts refuse to patronise it.'

'And yet, here we are,' Aidan said, a little hoarsely.

'Yup.'

They reached the house. A pair of chairs were still in place on the porch, either side of the front door, which stood ajar. Both of the ground-floor windows were boarded up and there was a rusty dog bowl at the foot of the front steps, half hidden by the overgrown grass. At night, this place would be creepy as hell. Actually, it was as creepy as hell *now*, with bright sunlight streaming through the trees.

Lana approached the front door. 'Elizabeth?'

No response.

She went to go inside but Aidan said, 'Hold up. Are you sure about this?'

'What do you mean?'

'What if the mayor followed Elizabeth here? Or there could still be drug dealers lurking around. Let me go first.'

'That's so sexist.' She peeked in through the dark doorway. 'But also an excellent idea. After you.'

He went through the door into a small hallway, with stairs straight ahead and doors either side. He was immediately hit by the stench of stale weed and something else: a ripe, cloying smell, like rotting meat. One door stood open, revealing a smashed-up kitchen with cupboards hanging off the walls and a jungle growing in the sink. There was no sign of human life. Something small darted across the floor and vanished into the shadows.

'Jesus,' said Lana, coming in and at once covering her nose with her hand.

'Elizabeth?' Aidan called, bracing himself in case anyone else appeared, ready to exit quickly but aware he had no weapon, no way to defend himself.

There was no reply.

'It's twenty past four,' Lana said. She called Elizabeth's name too, then checked her phone. 'Great. No signal.'

'I think we should go,' Aidan said.

'No. She might have been held up. Or what if she's here but injured? Look at these rotten—'

'Wait,' Aidan said. Lana stared at him. 'Listen. Can you hear that?'

In the silence of the house, he could just make it out. The soft sound of someone crying.

'It's coming from upstairs.'

They crept up the staircase, Aidan first, reaching an upstairs hallway. It was a mess. Filthy blankets on the floor. Piles of beer cans and fast-food cartons. Smashed crockery and pottery and books that had been ripped up and scattered across the floor. The rotten smell was less violent up here but Aidan caught sight of something equally offensive: discarded needles scattered in a corner. The walls were covered with graffiti. Someone had sprayed *YOU'RE NEXT* in thick red lines and beside it was a crude representation of a naked man with an outsized erection holding a shotgun, surrounded by stick figures in police hats, like a cave painting from hell.

The crying was coming from behind a door to their right.

Aidan opened it and found himself looking into what must have once been the master bedroom.

The young woman who'd served him in the diner stood there, looking out of a broken window. Behind her, on the floor, was a bare, filthy mattress with dark stains that Aidan hoped were mould. She had AirPods in her ears and was gazing into the distance, her cheeks damp with tears, apparently lost in her own world.

Lana entered the room and called, 'Elizabeth!'

Elizabeth jerked back, startled. 'I'm so sorry,' she said. 'I guess I was having a moment.' She removed the AirPods and stopped the music on her phone. 'I was listening to our song. Our album.'

'Yours and Samuel's?' Aidan asked.

She nodded.

'You didn't use to come to this place, did you?' Lana asked, incredulous, glancing at the mattress.

Elizabeth blinked at her. 'God, no. Not for *that*. This is actually only the second time I've been in this house. The first time I saw a rat after ten seconds and freaked out. But we used to come onto the property, when we wanted to get away and have some privacy.' She pointed out the window. 'I only came up here today to see that.'

Aidan and Lana stepped closer to see what Elizabeth was pointing at.

There was a tall tree a few metres away from the window. There were letters scratched into the bark. Aidan peered closer and realised it was Elizabeth and Samuel's initials: *EH* and *SC*.

'He climbed the tree . . . said he wanted to do it somewhere high, where it would be secret, private.' She laughed. 'I remember being down on the ground yelling at him to be careful. He was perched on that branch there and it was wobbling like crazy.'

Lana stared at the tree and smiled, clearly remembering what her brother had been like.

'I don't have very long,' Elizabeth said, glancing at the time on her phone. 'I'm not sure where Dad's gone for this meeting, but he's usually home by five thirty. If he gets back and I'm not there, he'll blame Yolanda.' She turned to Aidan. 'That's our housekeeper. I told her I was just going out for a bike ride.'

'Is that how you got here?' Aidan asked.

'Yeah. It's a thirty-minute ride. The path comes out close to the lake, near my house.' She looked at Aidan. 'I'm sorry I acted so weird when you came to the diner. I've been wary of strangers ever since Samuel disappeared. I thought you might be one of *them*.'

'Let's go downstairs,' Lana said.

Heading to the staircase, they passed what must have been the children's bedroom. There were piles of stuffed animals – teddy bears and cuddly rabbits – outside the closed door.

'I guess you've heard the stories about how this place is haunted by the kids who died here,' Elizabeth said. 'Some people say they've put a curse on Eaglewood. Kids bring stuffed animals to . . . I don't know. Appease them.'

Some of the toys were black with mould, their fur damp and pathetic. Aidan guessed this ritual had been going on for a long time.

'He killed them in their beds,' Elizabeth said. 'My dad says they were probably asleep. Or the first one was, anyway. Then their mom came running as soon as she heard the shots and he killed her too, right here, in this doorway.'

They all looked down at the floor. She would have died right here, where they were standing.

'Let's go down,' Aidan said.

The smell was so foul on the ground floor that Aidan suggested they go onto the porch. Elizabeth took the chair to the left of the door and Lana sat in the other. Aidan remained standing, his back against the rail, facing Elizabeth.

'So you're going to New Hampshire tomorrow?' Lana asked.

Elizabeth hung her head. 'Yeah. I don't have a choice. My dad's been super-agitated lately, even more than usual. Then this morning he sprang it on me. I'm going to stay with my aunt for the rest of the summer, before I start college.'

'Did he say why?'

'He has a long list of reasons, none of which make much sense. He says he's going to be working a lot this summer and won't have time to look after me – as if I need looking after. He says he's worried about fires. He says I look so sad all the time and that a change of scene will be good for me.' She exhaled. 'He's right about the last one.'

'Do you think he wants you out of town because he's scared?' Lana asked.

'Of what?'

'That the same thing is going to happen to you that happened to Samuel.'

Elizabeth twisted her hands together in her lap. Aidan noticed she was wearing what he assumed must be the promise ring from Samuel.

'He has been acting weird,' she said. 'Weird even for him. Jumpy. Drinking more than usual. And he has that creepy guy around all the time. Cody. I think he's there as extra security.'

Lana shook her head. 'I wouldn't employ that moron as security. He'd probably shoot his own foot off.'

Elizabeth gave a weak smile. 'Sergeant Giglio comes around a lot too. She and my dad are always going into his office and whispering about stuff in there.'

'Oh yeah? Interesting.'

'He suddenly told me I was going to New Hampshire,' Elizabeth said. 'Ordered me to go and pack my bag and that I wasn't allowed to go out, wasn't even allowed to say goodbye to my friends.' She was shaking now from the emotion of recounting the conversation. 'About half an hour after that, he came up and told me he'd booked my flight. I kept asking him what was going on, and that's when he started crying.'

'Crying?' Aidan said, hardly able to imagine the mayor being capable of such a thing.

'Yeah. It was horrible. He said that one day he'd tell me everything. And that he hoped I could forgive him.'

Chapter 13

'Did you ask your dad what he meant about forgiving him?' Aidan asked.

'Of course I did! But he went quiet and left the room. Locked himself in his office.'

'He must have been talking about Samuel,' said Lana, standing up and pacing across the porch. 'We need to grab your dad, make him tell us where Samuel is.'

'Lana, please, sit down,' Aidan said. 'We can't *grab* the mayor.'

Lana sat back down, clearly fuming. 'This is it. The proof we needed. Your dad is obviously involved in the cover-up.'

Aidan was far from sure this was proof. Not the kind you could take to the authorities, anyway. He could also see how uncomfortable this conversation was making Elizabeth, who was twisting her hands even faster now. And he was desperate to ask Elizabeth about Scarlett, about that flash of recognition in the diner, but Lana wasn't going to give him a chance.

'Tell me exactly what happened the night before Samuel supposedly died,' Lana said. 'You were together that evening, right?'

'Yes. We spent the evening together, watching a movie in my room.'

'And was your dad there?'

Elizabeth nodded. 'He made us keep my bedroom door open, like always.'

'And how did Samuel seem?'

'Totally normal. In a good mood, actually. The only time he seemed anything but happy was when he went onto my laptop to check the fire reports. Everyone in town was worried about it. I think it was, like, fifty-fifty at that point whether the fires would reach here. But that's why I'm so convinced Samuel wouldn't have gone into the forest on his own. There was a report about some people who'd gone camping close to where the fires were and Samuel said they were idiots.'

'You didn't have an argument or anything?' Aidan asked.

'No! I started to fall asleep and he kissed me goodbye and said he'd call me the next day.'

'But he never did?'

Elizabeth stared at the dirty floor. 'No. The next morning I texted Samuel a bunch of times but he didn't reply. It was like he'd turned his phone off, which is something he never did. To be honest, I didn't have time to be that worried. I had a shift at the diner and was busy. Even when we started to hear that the fire had reached the forest close to town, I wasn't too concerned about Samuel because I knew he would never go anywhere near it.' She shook her head. 'It was a crazy morning. There was this red tinge in the sky. Everyone was running around, going insane. They were talking about evacuating the town and there were all these arguments raging, these old guys saying they were going to stay put, that no one was going to make them leave their houses. We were all waiting, holding our breath. But it didn't stop people coming into the diner for breakfast and coffee. It wasn't until after I finished my shift and Samuel still wasn't answering his phone that I started to get really worried.'

Next she spoke to Lana. 'I went over to your house and your mom said she hadn't seen him at all that day. She'd assumed he was with me. That's when we called the police.'

Aidan had to ask the difficult question. 'Be honest, Elizabeth. Do you think there's any chance at all he might have . . . met up with those hikers, like the police said?'

She rubbed at her eyes. 'Everyone keeps saying to me that teen-age boys are, like, slaves to their hormones, that their brains aren't fully developed, that even the most saintly kid can be tempted into doing dumb things. But I know he loved me. And I can't believe he would have risked his life like that. He knew how dangerous it was in the forest. I can believe, even though I don't want to, that he might have cheated on me. But I can't believe he would have gone into the forest that day.'

'Of course he wouldn't,' Lana said. 'I think he heard or saw something at your house. Something he shouldn't have seen.'

Elizabeth blinked and a tear fell onto her cheek. 'I think that too.'

'But you have no idea what it could be? What your dad is mixed up in? You said he seems scared.'

'I honestly don't know. But . . .' She reached into the bag she was carrying and took out a little black notebook. 'There might be something in here.' She passed it to Lana. 'I've seen my dad lock that notebook away in his desk when he gets off the phone. It's after those calls that he seems most stressed and goes straight to the liquor cabinet. I've looked through it and can't see anything helpful, but maybe you'll spot something. I need to put it back in the drawer as soon as I get home, though.'

'*Call Giglio*,' Lana read aloud from the first page. 'With an exclamation point. She's in on all this. She has to be.'

Lana started to leaf through the book, taking photos of any potentially interesting pages with her phone. Aidan watched her, then realised this was his chance.

'Elizabeth, when I showed you Scarlett's photo in the diner, it seemed to me like you recognised her.'

'Oh God. I don't know. Can I see her picture again?'

Aidan brought up his website and handed Elizabeth his phone.

'I'm not sure,' Elizabeth said. 'But I think I saw her here.'

'*Here?*'

She nodded. 'It was last year. You know I told you Samuel and I used to hang out here sometimes – outside, in the yard? This must have been last summer, a month or two before the wildfire. We were just chilling out over there, on the grass, when we heard a vehicle pull up out front. We quickly went deeper into the trees, worried it might be drug dealers or something.'

Aidan was enrapt, down on his haunches in front of Elizabeth. He urged her to go on.

'We heard voices and then a few people came up the path. There were two men and three women. The men were walking behind, with the three women in front. One of the men, the older one, was wearing a cowboy hat. He was about my dad's age and I could hear him talking, telling them what had happened here, joking about it.'

Aidan nodded for her to continue.

'They all seemed quite happy. Excited, like they were out on a fun little outing. I could hear them talking about ghosts and one of them said something about preppers. Then one of the women, she was blonde, said something I couldn't make out and the redhead said, "That's rubbish."'

'"Rubbish"? She was British?'

'I think so,' Elizabeth replied. 'I haven't heard many Americans use that word. And she had red hair. I mean, ginger hair. Auburn. Like your sister. They went into the house and Samuel and I headed home.'

Aidan's heart was beating hard. 'Did you get a look at her face?'

'Only in profile, which is why I can't be sure. That picture is face-on.'

'Hold on.' Aidan got his phone out and scrolled through his photos of Scarlett. There were very few that showed her side-on but, finally, he found one that had been taken on Scarlett's visit to Seattle. She was in Viretta Park, near the Kurt Cobain bench. Aidan had taken it shortly before that creepy guy had shown up.

'Yeah,' Elizabeth said. 'I think that's her. I called her a woman, didn't I, but she's only a girl. Younger than me.'

'She's always looked older. Elizabeth, how sure are you?'

She looked at the photo again. 'About eighty per cent.'

'Oh my God.'

He had to walk away for a moment, to compose himself. He walked a little way down the path towards the gate, stopping in the shade beneath a tall cedar. Scarlett had been here. Francesca hadn't been mistaken. But what had she been doing here? Where was she now? And was it linked in some way to whatever had happened to Samuel?

He needed to figure out what to do next. Maybe it was time to get the Seattle police involved. Ask them to talk to Francesca and Elizabeth, or approach the local cops to do it. Maybe that would force Giglio to take it seriously.

He left the shade and stepped onto the path. In the same instant, he heard an engine out on the main road, coming closer.

He ducked behind a tree and looked out.

A police car pulled up outside the gate.

Chapter 14

Aidan ran back up the path towards the house.

'Where's your bike?' he said to Elizabeth.

'Behind the house. Why?'

'Because you need to go. Now. Sergeant Giglio's here.'

In the near distance, he heard a car door slam shut.

'Come on, quick. You don't want Giglio finding you here and telling your dad, do you?'

She shook her head. 'But what about you guys?'

Aidan looked at Lana, who had come down from the porch. She still had her bag over her shoulder and a look on her face he didn't like. Aidan said, 'We should get out of here too.'

'No. I want to talk to Giglio.' Lana's blood was up and, although he had only known her for less than twenty-four hours, he knew there was little point trying to argue with her.

'Elizabeth, go,' Aidan said. 'And thank you.'

The gate groaned, just as it had when they'd come through it earlier.

Elizabeth jogged round the side of the house, which was presumably where she'd left her bike. She had already told them that the forest path led to the lake near her house.

For a moment, all was silent. Then Giglio came into view, heading up the path towards them. She wasn't surprised to see them; of course, she must have seen their cars parked out front.

Aidan took a deep breath.

'Sergeant Giglio,' he said, resting his hands on top of the porch railing in an attempt to keep them still. Adrenaline had flooded his system, sending a tremor through him, from his guts to his limbs. 'How good to see you. I thought I'd check out some of the local real estate. What do you think? It's a fixer-upper, isn't it? I mean, I might need to get an exorcist in, but it's definitely got potential.'

'Where's Elizabeth Hood?' she asked.

'I have no idea,' Aidan replied.

'Don't bullshit me.'

'You knew she was coming here to meet us?' Lana said. 'What, is her dad spying on her messages?'

Giglio didn't deny it.

'She's gone home,' Aidan said.

Giglio looked genuinely relieved. She looked over her shoulder.

'Wait. What's going on?' Aidan asked.

The police sergeant had a little smirk on her lips. 'You'll find out soon enough.'

The sound of another engine came from out on the track. Car doors opened and closed and Aidan heard male voices. He exchanged a look with Lana, whose anger had turned into something else: fear.

'Let's get out of here,' he said.

'You stay right where you are,' Giglio said. She had her hand down by her side, resting lightly on the grip of her gun. 'There are a couple of guys who want a word with you. I would advise you to listen to them better than you listened to me.'

The gate opened and two men appeared, walking quickly down the path. One of them was wearing a cowboy hat. The man who had been here with Scarlett last year? The other one was Cody, eyes giving off sparks.

'Oh Jesus,' said Lana.

The cowboy-hat guy looked at Aidan. 'Aidan Faith, right? And you must be Lana.'

'Who the hell are you?'

'My name's Jimmy,' he said. His voice was calm, pleasant. Beside him, Cody glowered at Lana like she'd just stolen his lunch.

'I wasn't expecting to see you here, Sergeant Giglio,' Jimmy said.

'I'm just here to make sure everyone is civil. And stays within the law.'

That made Cody snicker, his eyes still on Lana. She returned his look of contempt.

'So what is this?' Lana said. There was the slightest quiver in her voice. A touch of breathiness. 'You've come here to tell us to back off, to stop asking questions about Samuel?'

'And Scarlett,' Aidan said.

Jimmy's face didn't reveal anything.

'I know she was here, with you,' Aidan said. 'It was you, another guy, and three women, one of them blonde. About a year ago.'

Now Jimmy looked surprised.

'There was a witness.'

'Who?'

Aidan didn't reply.

'Wait,' Giglio said. 'His sister really is in Eaglewood?'

'Not anymore.'

'Then where the hell is she?' Aidan demanded. 'What did you do to her?'

'And where's Samuel?' Lana added.

'Now that one is easy to answer. He's dead.'

Lana's face turned a shade paler. 'You killed him.'

'Nope. He died in the wildfire. Way I heard it, he hooked up with a couple of hikers and—'

'That's bullshit!' The colour had returned to Lana's face and she jabbed her finger towards Jimmy. 'I know you're lying.'

Jimmy took a step closer to her. He was still calm, hardly showing any emotion except the slightest hint that he was getting pissed off with her. Cody was still sneering at Lana, and Aidan remembered how she had humiliated him in the tavern the night before. The other patrons laughing and jeering.

'Cross my heart,' Jimmy said. 'Your brother died in that fire.'

Giglio, who had been watching all of this with the impassiveness of a referee, said, 'It's time to let it go, Lana. Move on with your life.'

'Cody here tells me you're an academic,' said Jimmy. 'Just got your master's, right? Bright future ahead of you – as far as any of us have a bright future on this fucked-up planet, anyway. You don't want to throw all that away, do you, sweetheart?'

'Don't fucking call me sweetheart.'

That made Jimmy laugh. 'I apologise. I'm old-fashioned.'

'You're a prick,' said Lana.

Jimmy sighed and then tutted. He threw in a shake of the head to complete the set. 'I really was hoping we could talk this out in a friendly way. But you're clearly not willing to listen, and now we have the issue with Mr Faith's witness. Who was it? Elizabeth Hood?'

'It was me,' Lana said.

Everyone's attention snapped to her.

'I was out here trying to score. That's why I've been helping Aidan. As soon as he showed me her photo, I recognised her.'

Aidan guessed Elizabeth must have recounted what she'd told Aidan, while he'd been wandering around. And now Lana was trying to protect the other girl. He couldn't decide if it was brave or foolhardy.

'I see,' said Jimmy. And he pulled a gun, a black revolver, from the back of the waistband of his jeans. Cody did the same, though his gun was smaller. Grey.

'Hold on,' said Giglio.

Jimmy ignored her. He pointed his gun at Aidan, and Cody trained his on Lana. 'Get in the house.'

'What the hell are you doing?' Giglio asked. 'I was told you were just going to talk to them.'

'Shut it, pig,' said Cody.

Giglio reacted as if he'd slapped her.

'Take her gun,' Jimmy said to him, and Cody, whose eyes were back to glittering with excitement, approached the police sergeant and held out a hand.

Giglio backed away and Jimmy pointed his revolver at her. 'Give it to him.'

'You wouldn't dare,' she said.

Jimmy shrugged. 'Darling, I've been fighting the Man my whole life. You'd be amazed by the things I dare to do.'

Giglio glanced towards the track where her car was parked. Where her radio was. Slowly, she withdrew her gun from its holster and passed it handle first to Cody. 'This is not something you want to be doing,' she said to them.

Cody looked at the gun, then smacked Giglio with the side of it, striking her temple. She crumpled into the long grass.

'Jesus, man,' said Jimmy.

Cody tucked Giglio's gun into his waistband and returned his focus to Lana.

'What are you going to do to us?' Aidan asked. He could hardly believe he was still able to speak. A few days ago he'd been behind his desk, dealing with a tricky coding problem, and now here he was in the middle of the woods with two men pointing guns at him. And he knew that Scarlett was alive. Or, at least, she had been earlier this week, when Francesca had seen her.

'It's a simple but sad story,' Jimmy said. 'You guys came out here to look at the famous murder house, sparked up a joint and burned the whole house down with you still inside it.' He looked down at Giglio. 'And there's a twist. Brave Sergeant Giglio turned up, tried to rescue you, and got trapped in the blazing building.'

'They'll give her a medal, I bet,' added Cody.

Aidan met Lana's eye. She was clearly scared, but there was still that defiant air about her.

'If you're going to kill us,' she said, 'why don't you just tell me the truth about Samuel?'

Jimmy made an exasperated noise. 'Get in the house.'

'You're going to have to carry me in.'

'I'll do it,' said Cody, stepping towards her.

'Don't you dare touch me,' she said.

Aidan tried to figure out if there was any chance they could escape into the woods, but he was pretty sure Jimmy or Cody would shoot them after they had only taken a few steps. His brain raced. There had to be a way out of this. He just couldn't see what it was.

'I actually do have some weed for you,' Jimmy said. 'The finest shit from Humboldt County. It'll take the edge off. Or we can make this really hurt.'

'I'm going to haunt you,' Lana said, and she turned to walk towards the house. Aidan saw Jimmy's eyes stray to her butt, getting a good look, and Aidan wished he had a gun. But all he could do was follow Lana. The men walked behind them and then Lana whispered, 'Follow me', and broke into a run. It took Aidan a second to react, to sprint after her: up the porch steps and right behind Lana into the house.

'Hey!' Jimmy shouted, but it was too late. Aidan had slammed the door shut behind them. There were bolts at the top and the bottom of the door frame, a little rusty but still functional. Aidan quickly jammed them into place.

Lana ran into the back hall. Aidan had started to ask what they were going to do when she unfastened her bag, then threw it onto the floor and stood there holding a gun. A little black pistol.

'It's my mom's,' she said. 'Home security. I brought it along just in case.'

From outside the door, Jimmy said, 'If you don't open this door now I'm going to go all Big Bad Wolf on your asses.'

'We're not going to defeat them in a shoot-out,' Aidan said quietly.

'I know,' Lana hissed. 'But we have surprise on our side. They don't know we have a gun.' She nodded at the windows, which were boarded up, so Jimmy and Cody couldn't see in.

'Do you know how to use that thing?'

'I've practised a few times.'

'Jesus Christ.'

'If I open the door,' she called out to them, 'will you tell me what really happened to my brother?'

A pause. 'Sure.'

'Do you swear?'

'On my mother's life,' said Jimmy.

Lana hesitated.

'I'm going to count to three, and then I'm going to kick this door in,' Jimmy said. 'And then you'll never find out what really happened to your brother.'

'Okay. I'm going to open the door now. Don't forget your promise.'

'I won't.'

Lana whispered to Aidan: 'Open the door, then immediately duck behind it. Okay?'

He felt sick. 'Okay.'

He went to the door and quickly, before he could change his mind, slid the bottom bolt back, then the top. He turned the handle and pulled the door open, ducking behind it.

Lana fired.

There was a yell, then a bellow. Jimmy's voice, crying out in pain. Aidan stared at Lana, who had the gun out in front of her, frozen to the spot. Aidan poked his head out from behind the door so he could see. Jimmy was on the porch, on the ground, clutching his right hand – his gun hand. Aidan couldn't see properly but there was a lot of blood. The surface of the porch was slick with it, and there was no sign of Jimmy's revolver.

Lana stepped closer to the door and pointed the gun at Jimmy. 'Tell Cody to unload his gun and toss it in here or I'll kill you.'

'Do it,' Jimmy said, his voice thick with pain. He was looking around him as he spoke, apparently searching for his gun, which must have skidded across the porch and through the railings to the ground below. He held his injured hand out before him to assess the damage. Blood gushed from the stumps where two of his fingers had been.

'Giglio's gun too,' Lana shouted.

Nothing happened. Aidan couldn't see where Cody was. Was he heading around the back of the house, looking for another way in?

'Now, or he's dead,' Lana screamed, her pistol still trained on Jimmy.

No movement. Jimmy tried to say something, and then his head hit the wooden floor of the porch. He had passed out.

Lana scooted behind the door, panting hard, her back pressed up tight to Aidan. Where the hell was Cody? It was silent outside.

A peaceful day in the country; the birds who had been scared away by the gunshot already returning to the trees. Aidan was convinced Cody was going to burst in through a back door. The gun trembled in Lana's hands.

She crouched, looking around her. Her shoulder bag lay on the other side of the doorway. 'Do you have your phone?' she whispered to Aidan.

He nodded.

'We need to call 911. Tell them what's happening.'

'Okay.'

He took his phone from his pocket and, as he hit the nine key, there were footsteps outside, on the porch steps. Lana sprang from her crouched position into the doorway, holding the pistol with both hands, and fired twice.

'Oh Jesus,' she said, lowering the gun. 'Oh God.'

Aidan stopped dialling and peered out around the door.

Giglio lay there, twisted on the steps, the front of her uniform wet with blood.

Lana slowly went out through the door, looking down at the cop. Aidan ran out after her, half crouched, waiting for Cody to start shooting at them, but there was no sign of him. Aidan spotted Jimmy's revolver lying in the grass and scooped it up while Lana knelt beside Giglio, checking her wrist for a pulse. Aidan had never seen a dead body before, but it was pretty clear that was what he was looking at.

A noise came from the rear of the house. A door crashing open.

'We need to get out of here,' Aidan said, picking up Lana's bag.

Lana didn't move.

He tugged at her arm. 'Lana!'

She snapped back to life, just as Cody appeared in the hallway behind them, raising his gun.

Aidan slammed the front door shut and heard the bullet strike it. He ran, sprinting towards the gate, Lana at his shoulder. As they reached the gate, the door of the house opened and another gunshot rang out. Aidan would never know how close the bullet came to hitting one of them – or the bullet after that. They flew through the open gate, Aidan scrambling in his pocket for the car key, pressing the button to open the doors. He could hear Cody running after them. Lana hesitated for a second, perhaps thinking of returning fire, but Aidan was already behind the wheel, yelling, 'Get in!' and she did as he said, slamming the door shut as Aidan screeched away onto the track, passing the parked Jeep and police car. Cody appeared in the rear-view mirror, firing once, missing, and then they were on the road, Aidan driving blindly, not knowing what direction he was going.

Beside him, Lana sat with her head in her hands, shaking.

'I killed a cop,' she said, turning her face to Aidan with tears on her cheeks. 'Aidan, I killed a cop.'

PART TWO

Chapter 15

Aidan drove without thinking, aware only that he was heading deeper into the forest, the fear that Cody would appear in the rear-view mirror compelling him to put his foot down. Beside him, Lana was silent and still, almost catatonic.

'There should be some bottles of Dew in the bag on the back seat,' he said. 'Drink some. Sugar is meant to be good for shock.'

He had no idea if this was actually true or not but, like a robot, she reached behind her and found the bottles of soda. She opened one and took a deep drink. It seemed to bring her back to life.

'Where are we going?' she asked.

'I don't know. Maybe we should go to the police.'

'No! I just killed one of them, Aidan.'

'By mistake.'

'You think they're going to care? They'll match the bullets to my gun and it won't matter what I say, I'll go to jail.'

'Not if—'

She cut him off. 'Give me a minute. I can't think straight.'

He wondered what was going on back at the murder house. Jimmy had passed out, presumably from loss of blood. Would he die too? Aidan didn't think there was much chance that Cody would call the police or an ambulance. He would probably take Jimmy to wherever it was they had come from. There had been numerous gunshots. People might think it was hunters but, surely, sooner or later, someone would come looking or stumble across Giglio's body.

And what about Elizabeth? The mayor knew she'd gone to the murder house to meet Aidan and Lana.

It was a mess. And Lana was right: they needed to figure things out before they went to the cops.

Lana had put her gun, along with the one Aidan had found in the grass near the prone Jimmy, in the glovebox. Maybe they should get rid of them. Find a lake to throw them into.

No, Aidan decided. It might be better to keep hold of them. Because the police weren't the only people who were going to be looking for him and Lana.

He kept driving. A little later, the trees thinned out and the sky came into view for the first time since they'd left the murder house.

'We should stop and fill up,' Aidan said, nodding at the gas station up ahead. 'Do you think it's safe?'

Lana looked over her shoulder at the road they'd come down. 'I don't know.'

'I think Cody must have stayed behind to help Jimmy,' he said. 'And we really need gas. I need to eat something too, and so should you.'

They pulled over. There was no one else around except the guy working behind the counter. After filling the car, Aidan went round the gas station's store with a basket, loading it with snacks and junk food, which was pretty much all this place sold. He paid the young man behind the counter, who barely looked up from the phone he was playing a game on. Aidan could feel a great energy flowing through him and was aware that he was bouncing from foot to foot while he stood at the counter. Scarlett *had* been here. Despite the chaos and the violence and the danger they were in, that fact kept popping into his mind, blotting out everything else.

When he got back to the car, he found Lana standing beside it.

'There's a little picnic area over there,' she said, nodding to the side of the gas station. 'Maybe we should stop for ten minutes, talk things through.'

Aidan followed her gaze. 'That *is* a lovely spot for a picnic.' His voice sounded odd to him, as if he were underwater.

He moved the car around the back of the building, so it would be harder to spot from the road, while Lana went over to the picnic area and deposited the bag of snacks on a half-rotted picnic table. She descended on them like a starving wolf, tearing open a family-sized bag of Doritos like she hadn't eaten for a week. Even though they were meant to be talking, they sat and ate in silence. Lana looked like she was deep inside her head, trying to process what had just happened.

'I'm going to use the loo,' Aidan said.

When he came out of the filthy restroom set into the back of the gas station, sure the smell would linger in his nostrils for days, he found Lana waiting for him, holding two paper cups of coffee that she'd got from the vending machine inside.

'I don't think the bears shit in the woods around here,' Aidan said. 'They use these facilities.'

'Probably don't even wash their paws,' she said, and they exchanged stunted, hoarse laughs.

'We shouldn't be laughing,' he said.

'Would crying be better?'

She handed him his coffee and they walked a little way from the bathrooms. Lana perched on a tree stump and Aidan sat on the ground beside her. The coffee was foul but caffeine was caffeine, whatever the delivery mechanism. Aidan kept an eye on the road, prepared to run if he saw the Jeep that had been parked outside the murder house pull in to the gas station.

'Let's run through what we know,' Aidan said, massaging the back of his neck in an attempt to remove some of the tension there.

'First, your sister was here. That's amazing. I've gotta say, I didn't see that one coming, but you kept the faith.'

'Excuse the pun.'

'Ha. Yeah. What did they say? They used to know her?'

'They said she wasn't here anymore. But we know that's not true. Francesca saw her in that clearing just a few days ago.' He thought back to what Elizabeth had told him. Scarlett had been joking around with Jimmy and the rest of the group. 'It didn't sound like they were holding her prisoner,' Aidan said. 'Or like they were coercing her to go along with them.'

'Maybe. But we don't know what's going on, do we? I mean, who is this Jimmy guy? Where the hell is he from? I've never seen him around Eaglewood.'

Had Jimmy been the one chasing Scarlett through the clearing? It was a shame Aidan didn't have a photo of him or know his surname so he could try to find him online. He could have sent his picture to Francesca to see if she recognised him.

Lana put her coffee cup down. 'They're still sticking to their bullshit story about Samuel, though. About him being dead.'

Aidan searched for the right words.

'I know what you're thinking,' Lana said. 'Why would they bother to lie when they thought they were about to kill us? I know he's probably dead. Fuck it, he's almost certainly dead, isn't he?' She sighed audibly and hung her head.

'I'm sorry,' said Aidan. 'Although we don't know for certain . . .'

'He's dead,' Lana said. 'I think I've always known it. But I also know that I've always been right: he didn't go camping with those hikers. Why else would everyone be so desperate to stop me asking questions? The mayor, the police, Jimmy – whoever he is – are all mixed up in it. They murdered him, for whatever bullshit reason.'

114

She looked Aidan square in the eye. 'Giglio was part of it. I'm not sorry she's dead.'

He nodded.

'But if there is a conspiracy with the mayor and the Eaglewood cops and whoever this Jimmy guy is, handing ourselves over to them would be the stupidest thing we could do. I can see it now, how they'd dismiss everything I said as the paranoid ramblings of a bereaved sister. Shit, everyone in Eaglewood thinks I'm a pain in the ass. They'll say I came out here with the plan to kill Giglio, or maybe I shot her in a rage because she wasn't telling me what I wanted to hear.'

'But what about me? I'm a witness.'

'They won't listen to you. They'll say you're a liar, that you're in love with me or something. Another crazy bereaved person who's lost their sibling. You'll be thrown in jail too, for helping me and fleeing the scene.'

'And if we're in jail . . .'

'We'll never find Scarlett. And we'll never find out why they killed Samuel. What we need to do is find proof of what's going on. Evidence that the mayor and the people he's tangled up with murdered my brother.'

'And find Scarlett too.'

His excitement about Scarlett being here was dying down now. Because what if the same thing had happened to her? He had to face it: there was a very good chance that after Jimmy, or whoever it was, had caught her, he'd killed her. That's why he'd said she wasn't around anymore.

Whether she was alive or not, this was all connected. And he and Lana were the only people who could do something about it. The only ones who could expose the truth.

'Are we on the same page?' Lana asked.

'We are.'

'Good. Right now, I think the most important thing is to put as many miles between us and the scene of the crime as we can. Because the moment the police find Giglio's body, they're going to be looking for us. And they're not the only ones. The mayor, Cody, Jimmy – assuming he survived – they're going to be after us too.'

They gathered up the empty wrappers and coffee cups and put them into a trash can, then headed back to the car.

Lana paused. 'Wait here,' she said.

She headed into the building and Aidan watched her speak to the young guy inside. She handed him something, then came back out.

'What were you doing?'

'Encouraging him to keep quiet,' she said.

They pulled away, leaving the gas station behind, and headed deeper into the forest.

Chapter 16

'Tell me again,' Shannon said to Jimmy through clenched teeth. They were in her office and Shannon was finding it very hard to hold on to her inner peace. 'Tell me everything that was said.'

Jimmy sat on the couch, pumped full of painkillers and cradling his bandaged hand. He'd lost his pinkie and half his ring finger when this Lana person had shot him, and the Ranch doctor had done his best to patch him up, to ensure it didn't get infected, although he'd kept on about how Jimmy needed to go to a hospital – until Shannon had told him to shut his mouth, that no one was going to any hospital, not now, not ever. Jimmy was just going to have to learn to fire a gun with his left hand.

Cody, who had raced across California with a groaning Jimmy in the back seat, stood in the corner, occasionally brushing his lank hair away from his eyes. He stank of stale sweat and cigarettes. But he had done well.

Jimmy ran through it for the third time while Shannon did breathing exercises to keep herself calm.

'You're a moron,' she said, once he'd finished and the true horror of what he'd told her had sunk in. 'Repeat after me: *I'm a moron.*'

Jimmy stared at the floor but he didn't repeat her words. Instead he said, 'I'm going to make amends.'

She took half a step closer to the couch. Jesus, he stank too. Dirt and blood and pain. He was polluted. Like everyone out there, all the doomed hordes, he was impure, sullied, dirty.

But he looked so pitiful, and he had done so much to help her get to where she was. She knew she ought to forgive him. After all, she was a good person, wasn't she? Everything she did was for the forces of good. She blessed him with a smile then turned to Cody.

'Have you spoken to Mayor Hood?' she asked.

'Uh-huh.'

'And?'

'He's not happy. He's pissed about Giglio getting offed. I always thought she was a stuck-up bitch, but he sounded genuinely upset. I don't know. Maybe they were fucking.'

'Maybe they were. But Cody, don't say "bitch".'

'Huh?'

'Do you think I'm a bitch? Perhaps you think all women are. Bitches and whores and sluts. Is that right?'

'Uh, no. I mean, some are . . .'

She got right up in his face and he shrank from her, shocked.

'We don't allow misogyny here. Do you know what that is?'

He nodded.

'Good. I think you could play an important role here, Cody. Especially now, with Jimmy not fully functional. Would you like that?'

'Uh, I guess.'

She laughed. 'And I guess you don't actually know what we're doing out here, do you? What our mission is?'

'You're, like, trying to save the planet and shit, right?'

She laughed again, though there wasn't much warmth or humour in it. 'You're on the right track.'

'Sorry, Shannon, but this guy's a jerk,' said Jimmy from the couch. 'He's not one of us.'

Shannon turned back to him. 'Did he get half his hand blown off by a young woman who has probably never even used a gun before?'

'I guess not.'

'There's a lot of guessing going on around here today.' She returned her focus to Cody. 'I'll explain everything to you, Cody. And I think when you understand how urgent what we're doing is, you'll realise how privileged you are to be joining us.'

She sat down at her desk and opened her iPad.

'Show me on the map exactly where all of this went down.'

Cody did as she asked and Shannon said, 'Okay, this is what's going to happen. First, I'll call Mayor Hood and tell him to deal with the dead cop situation. I'm going to offer to pay for Giglio's funeral, so he can give her a big send-off. He'll like that.'

'He will,' Cody said.

'I also need to talk to him about his daughter,' Shannon continued.

'He's already put her on a plane to the East Coast. He drove her to the airport the minute she got home. And he said to tell you, if we send anyone to talk to her, if we get within sniffing distance, he'll – what did he say? – "blow the whole thing wide open". Said he won't have anything to lose.'

Shannon rolled her eyes. 'We're going to have to deal with him, but it's not a high priority right now. He's not going to talk.'

She swivelled her chair to face Jimmy. 'The second thing we need to do is decamp from the Ranch.'

He stopped examining his bandage. 'What, *now*?'

'It's time,' she said, with a tremor of excitement in her voice.

She and Jimmy locked eyes and she was aware of Cody watching them, probably wondering what the hell they were talking about.

'Are you . . . sure?' Jimmy asked. 'It's really about to go down?'

She nodded. They had told her while she was meditating, while all the shit was taking place at that so-called murder house. It was sooner than expected, but there was no mistake. 'It's time to move. You know the plan, so I want you to stay here and take care of it. Move everyone out. Organise supplies and weapons. Can I trust you with that?'

'Of course you can. But what are *you* going to do?'

'I haven't finished what I was saying yet. Moving out is the second thing. Third, we need to get the word out to everyone we know in this area. All our friendly contacts. We've got photos of Faith and Carrera, yes?'

'They're all right there on social media.'

'Ah, of course.'

Shannon opened Instagram and found Lana's account. Open to the public. She scrolled through it. There were a lot of pictures of her posing with her student friends, nights out in Washington. Photos of her brother too. Among all that were some political posts, including more than a few about the climate emergency and the need for action. Perhaps, if things had taken a different turn, Lana could have been one of them.

'Jimmy, you can delegate that to one of the others. Get these pictures out there.'

'What about you?' he asked. 'You still haven't told me.'

She looked out the window. The sun was beginning to dip, clouds taking on a pink hue. It seemed so beautiful out there. So peaceful. But she knew better. When she concentrated, she could feel the heat of the coming fires. Could smell the smoke.

'Cody and I are going to find Faith and Carrera,' she said.

Jimmy grunted. 'You oughta head to the Moses place. He'll be able to help.'

She thought about it. Moses was an asshole, but he knew the area and he had men. 'Good idea.'

'But you'll have to take him something. A gift.'

Shannon didn't like the sound of that. A gift from *her* for that psychopath? But she listened to Jimmy, and when he'd finished she said, 'All right. What do you think he would like?'

Chapter 17

It was dark by the time they got to Fortuna, having taken a detour off the 36 onto Route 101. They found a cheap motel between the highway and the Eel River and checked in, giving false names, after parking their car in the most hidden spot they could find. As they were about to leave the office, Lana turned back to the receptionist and said, 'Can I ask you a favour?'

The woman looked up from her keyboard.

'If anyone calls asking about us, it's really important you don't say anything. It's my husband. I'm trying to get away from him, and if he finds me . . .' She grimaced and trailed off, letting the receptionist fill in the gaps. A violent husband. A scared wife.

'Sure,' the woman said. 'I haven't seen you.'

Lana's voice cracked a little as she said thanks. The receptionist's reaction suggested this was not a rare occurrence. She flicked a glance at Aidan, possibly wondering if he was the new boyfriend and wondering why they'd booked separate rooms. Just for a moment, Aidan allowed himself to entertain the fantasy that they were lovers on the run, scared but excited, together at last . . .

'You okay?' Lana asked as they walked to their rooms. 'You looked like you were having deep thoughts again. Oh God, now you're blushing. You're sweet, Aidan.'

Sweet. Of all the adjectives that had ever been used to describe him, it was possibly his least favourite.

'I was just thinking about how impressive you are,' he said.

'Ha. Yeah, so impressive that I've probably just totally fucked up my life and dragged you into the shit in the process.'

'I'm pretty sure I was headed towards it anyway.'

She had been quiet on the drive down, drifting off into her own head. He wondered if she was replaying what had happened at the murder house, or if she was able to stop herself thinking about it. He hoped he would never know what it felt like to kill someone, but he expected Lana would see it when she went to bed and closed her eyes – probably for a long time to come.

Lana told him she was going to rest and Aidan went into his room, which was adjacent to Lana's. It smelled of air freshener and cigarette smoke and had twin single beds. He was glad he'd packed up the car before heading out this afternoon, but he'd already worn most of the clothes he'd brought with him. He turned on the shower and took his dirty underwear and socks in with him, scrubbing them with soap before washing himself. He stood under the hot water for a long time, letting it cascade over his face, trying to cleanse himself of the day he'd just had. He tried not to think about the police and Jimmy's people, out on the road looking for them. He tried not to picture Giglio lying there on the porch steps with her eyes frozen forever in surprise.

He hung his wet clothes over the shower rail. It was so warm in the room he didn't think they'd take long to dry. He put his jeans back on and his one remaining clean T-shirt. Moments later there was a soft rap at the door.

He stiffened – had they been found already? – but Lana's voice came through the door and he opened it, trying not to let her see that he'd been scared. She had tied her black hair into a ponytail and her face was free of make-up. Her eyes were pink and he guessed she'd been crying for her brother.

'We should talk,' she said. 'Also, I could murder a drink.' She grimaced. 'Bad choice of words.' She looked around at their low-rent surroundings. 'You think this place has room service?'

'Maybe if you're after meth or a hooker.'

She smiled. 'I saw a 7-Eleven down the block. Why don't I check that out and I'll see you back here in fifteen?'

Aidan waited outside his door, needing some air. It was a warm, still night, and there was nothing much to hear except the distant passing traffic. He kept seeing flashes of Giglio's body, then forcing himself to push them away. Seeing someone die. It was something he was going to have to process later.

Lana came walking back towards the motel, carrying a brown paper bag, and when she looked up and met his eye, a little smile on her lips, he caught his breath. She was stunning.

Jesus, Aidan, he told himself. *This is really not the time or place. Focus.*

'Ta-dah! I have wine,' she said when she reached him, holding up a bottle of red. 'My place or yours?'

'I'm easy.'

'Do you have that on your Tinder profile?' she said, unlocking the door of her room.

'I don't use dating apps,' he said. 'I find them awkward and depressing.'

'That's funny, because awkward and depressing is exactly how I describe myself on *my* Tinder profile.'

He laughed and tried not to wonder if she really was a user of dating apps; nearly everyone he knew was. He had actually tried it when he'd first come to Seattle, but after a couple of hook-ups that left him feeling empty, he'd deleted the app.

'Let me just find the cut-crystal glasses,' Lana said.

She was bantering, being funny, but he could tell her heart wasn't in it. It was as if she were a fire that someone had doused with water. If she wasn't thinking about Giglio, she was definitely thinking about Samuel. Accepting that he had been murdered.

She grabbed two tumblers from the grubby bathroom and poured wine into them. This room also had twin beds, and Lana sat on one while Aidan took the other. Their knees were inches apart in the narrow gap between the beds.

'Cheers,' he said.

'Cheers.' She said it in a faux-British accent. 'Listen, don't take this the wrong way, but can I have a hug? I really need one.'

He was taken aback, but said, 'Of course.'

She stood and he got to his feet too, then he put his arms around her, feeling the side of her face pressing against his shoulder. She was trembling. He thought she might be crying, but when she eventually pulled away his T-shirt was dry.

'Thank you,' she said. 'That was a nice hug. I feel a bit better now.'

'Glad to be of service.'

She sat back down on her bed and he did the same on the other. 'So . . .' she said.

'So.'

'How are we going to find Scarlett? And how are we going to get evidence that will keep us out of jail?'

'What about the notebook Elizabeth gave you? The one that belongs to her dad. Was there anything in it?'

'I didn't spot anything.'

'You took photos of some of the pages, didn't you?'

'Yup.' She took her phone out of her bag. 'I'm going to need to borrow your charger, if that's okay, before I go to bed.'

She crossed the gap between the beds and sat beside him, opening the photos app and holding the phone so they could both look at it.

'Most of this stuff seems to be about some big building project,' Lana said. 'I told you Hood runs a construction company, right? They're doing most of the rebuilding work in Eaglewood. There are just lists of materials. Concrete, steel. There's a note here about air purifiers. And fish tanks. What, is he building an aquarium or something?'

'Water pumps too,' Aidan said.

'Maybe that's his big plan for revitalising the town. An aquarium, miles from the ocean. I mean, there were pages of notes with names of electricians, builders, et cetera, et cetera. I didn't bother taking photos of them because it seemed pointless. I really don't think Samuel was killed because he found out Hood and his men were violating building regulations.'

She flicked through to the next picture.

'His handwriting is like a five-year-old's,' Aidan said.

'I know, right? This is slightly more interesting. It looks like a record of payments. Or maybe costs?'

There was a list of dates, stretching back a couple of years. There were some large sums next to them: *4/23/17 $9,345. 5/11/17 $13,050*. As the dates got closer to the present, the sums got considerably bigger: *2/10/18 $90,000. 11/13/18 $65,000*.

'When was the wildfire?' Aidan asked after thinking for a minute.

'September fourteenth last year.'

'Hmm. I wonder if it's a coincidence that the sums increased so much after that?'

'It makes sense, I guess,' Lana said. 'If these numbers are related to rebuilding the section of the town that burned down, and building all the other new stuff they've been working on. Anyway, none of this is useful.'

Lana flicked through a few more of the photos she'd taken, which were mostly of more columns of numbers.

'What's this?' Aidan asked, getting Lana to stop.

The page had caught Aidan's eye because, while it looked like yet another jumble of numbers, there was some heavy doodling around the edges. Dark, scratchy lines. Spirals that looped and crossed over each other. From the photo it looked like the pen had been pressed down so hard it had torn the paper. Aidan knew from experience that when he was stressed or feeling under pressure in a work meeting, he would mindlessly draw patterns like this. The heavier the lines, the more unhappy he was.

'I reckon Hood was tense as hell when he was making these notes,' he said, indicating the doodles.

The page mostly consisted of a column of large numbers, some of which were crossed out. At the bottom of the page, almost illegibly, Hood had written a string of numbers and, in a sloping scrawl that went right to the edge of the page, *S L Caldar*.

'Any ideas?' Aidan asked. *S L Caldar*. It rang the faintest bell.

'Not a clue.'

Lana flicked to the next photo. 'This was the last page I managed to photograph before Butch Cody and Jimmy the Kid showed up.'

There were more doodles and thickly etched lines. Jagged arrows and crosses. In the top corner of the page, Mayor Hood had drawn a skull, viewed from the top down, with more jagged lines cutting across it diagonally, like a lightning bolt. Again, this rang the faintest bell. Beneath it, Hood had written: *7am Lorenzo. Dogwood B*.

'Dogwood B?' Aidan said. 'Does that mean anything to you?'

'Nope. I mean, dogwood is a type of shrub, but I have no idea what the *B* might stand for.'

They scrolled back through the photos, and again Aidan tried to remember why 'Caldar' was ringing a bell, but it was just out of reach. And maybe it meant nothing at all. He suddenly felt very tired, all the adrenaline that had kept him going draining away. Lana, though, still seemed wired, and he sensed she didn't want him to go yet. Didn't want to be left alone with the contents of her brain.

'Did you think you'd ever find out what happened to Scarlett?' she asked.

'I haven't found her yet.'

'I know. But at least you know she's alive. Or was alive, a few days ago.' She grimaced. 'Sorry. I'm sure she's still out there . . .'

'It's okay,' he said. 'I think . . . I think I always believed she was still alive. I'm not going to stop believing that now.'

She stared into her wine glass, no doubt thinking about Samuel.

'Tell me what happened,' she said, meeting his eye again. 'When she disappeared. Did the police think she might have come this way? Was it ever put forward as a possibility?'

She leaned towards him and it struck him how long it had been since someone had actually asked him about Scarlett and seemed genuinely interested in the answers.

He took a deep breath and told her about that morning.

That terrible morning.

Chapter 18

2017

Aidan went into the kitchen, fresh from the shower, and made coffee. It was ten thirty and he couldn't remember the last time he'd stayed in bed so late. Scarlett was still asleep, although that was to be expected. She was fifteen. It was what teenagers did.

He would have to wake her up soon, though, because they were supposed to be going on a trip out of town later that day. He'd promised to take her to Bellevue Square, the massive, upscale mall at the heart of the city, even though it wasn't his idea of fun. Scarlett had never been to an American mall before and he had tried to persuade her that even this one was not too different from the big shopping centres in the UK, like Merry Hill, but she didn't listen. Going to a mall, having a slushie and spending her savings on clothes for herself and presents for her friends back home was high on her vacation wish list.

He made scrambled eggs and thought the smell might wake her, bring her into the kitchen, but there was no sign of her. No sounds coming from the spare room where she slept. Then he slapped his own head. Of course she wouldn't be drawn by the smell of eggs. She was a vegan. He put a bagel in the toaster and went to her door, knocking on it lightly.

'Scarlett?'

No answer. He knocked again and, when there was no response, he pushed down the handle and slowly opened the door.

Some lives have a rip in them. A moment when everything changes. Not a prepared-for moment, like the birth of a child or the death of an aged parent, but something unexpected: a lottery win, or a paralysing accident.

Life tore in that moment. There was the before, an alternate universe he could only return to in dreams, in which Scarlett was still in bed, complaining that it was too early and that she wasn't hungry.

And there was the after. The real world. The nightmare.

ω

Aidan tried to call Scarlett first. When it went straight to voicemail and the text he sent wasn't delivered, he called the police. They asked some basic questions then told him to come down to the station. Aidan didn't want to leave the apartment in case Scarlett came back. And how long would it take for them to actually do anything?

He called his boss at Wonder, whose brother-in-law was something high up in Seattle PD, and begged him to pull some strings. Two hours later, the police turned up at Aidan's door. By that point Aidan had searched the apartment – as if she'd be hiding in a closet – then scoured the spare room for Scarlett's phone. There was no sign of it. Frosty, who had been curled up on the bed when Aidan came into the room, watched him, and Aidan wished the cat could speak. Had he watched Scarlett leave the apartment? Had she whispered something to him as she'd gone?

There were two detectives: Richelle Heard, who Aidan guessed to be in her thirties, and her partner, Tom Stretton, a stocky man who was Aidan's parents' age. Stretton took the lead, asking questions while Heard watched Aidan and made notes. Every now and then, Aidan would feel her eyes on him, but whenever he looked directly at her she would be concentrating on her notepad.

'Can you tell me everything that's missing?' Stretton said.

Aidan was so panicked that he was finding it hard to think straight. 'Her phone. Well, I mean, that's maybe not missing, exactly. She'd have it with her in any case. I'm not sure about clothes because I didn't do an inventory of everything she brought with her. My mum might know what she packed.'

'Have you spoken to your parents yet? Asked them if they've heard from her?'

'No.' He hadn't been able to face it yet. Scarlett might walk through the door at any moment and he didn't want to panic them unnecessarily, especially when they were on the other side of the Atlantic, unable to do anything. He pictured his mum going frantic; she panicked when the cat went missing for a few hours. His dad would pace the kitchen, trying to persuade her that everything would be okay, that Scarlett had probably just gone off for a wander.

'Okay, you should do that in a minute. They might have heard from her. We're going to want to speak to everyone she's in regular contact with, so a list would be helpful.'

'You can check phone records, right?'

'If it comes to it. The chances are we'll find her quickly, or she'll find us. Just walk in. But you were right to call us. Just in case.'

Aidan clung to their words. 'Her laptop is still here,' he said. 'It's password-protected but I'm sure I could get into it.'

'Leave that with us. Again, if necessary.'

'You can track cell phones too, can't you?' Aidan said.

'As long as they're turned on,' said Heard. 'Mr Faith, we're doing everything we can. I've got a team coming who are going to start talking to your neighbours. But first, talk me through the events of last night.'

'We got home at seven, had dinner, watched a film. Then Scarlett said she was tired and went to bed. I did the same shortly after.'

'What time was that?'

'She went to bed at about eleven. I think I turned in at about half past. I listened to a sleep story for a while and then drifted off at around midnight, I guess.'

Heard cocked her head. 'A sleep story?'

'On one of those apps?' Stretton said. 'My wife listens to those. Damn things keep me awake.'

'But listen,' Aidan said. 'I have an idea where she might have gone. We met this guy yesterday, in Denny-Blaine.'

And he told them about the Kurt Cobain fan in Viretta Park.

Heard immediately looked it up on her computer. 'Penny Royal Tea. They played the Vampire Bar last night. That's downtown.'

Stretton went over to her and checked the screen. 'It's over-twenty-ones only. Could Scarlett pass as an adult? Do you know if she had fake ID?'

'I don't know. I mean, to me she's my little sister, but she does look older than fifteen. The guy in the park made a big deal about how mature she looked and said the bar is lax with IDs. He was a creep. I had to tell him to back off. Told him her age.'

'Did Scarlett seem interested?'

'Yeah. I mean, I thought she would be pleased I'd got rid of this guy, who was obviously a total perv chatting up an underage girl. But she was angry. Said I was treating her like a baby. She didn't talk to me for about an hour afterwards, was tapping away on her phone, presumably messaging her friends to tell them what a killjoy I am.' Scarlett's roaming data had finally kicked in yesterday. 'She had calmed down by the time we got back here, though.'

'So you didn't get his name? Did he give Scarlett his contact details? A phone number?'

'No. I didn't give him the chance. But he told her about the gig. It wouldn't have been hard for her to find out the details and go looking for him.'

Heard made another note. 'And do you think it's the kind of thing your sister would do?'

'I don't know. Maybe. Mum and Dad were having some problems with her. Staying out past her curfew, hanging around with "undesirables". I thought they were being overprotective but it's one of the reasons they suggested she come here. They were hoping I'd be able to set a good example, show her if you work hard at school and concentrate on your studies . . . Oh God, I think I might throw up.'

Detective Heard fetched him a glass of water and advised him to sit down.

'This guy, this place, is an excellent lead,' Stretton said. 'If Scarlett went to this bar last night, we'll find her. Try not to worry, Mr Faith. I have every confidence she'll be back here by sundown.'

ϖ

A week later, sick of being stuck in his apartment waiting for the phone to ring, Aidan drove back to Denny-Blaine.

Scarlett's disappearance had, for a few days, been the biggest news story in Seattle. A white British teenager disappearing on vacation, with a possible Kurt Cobain connection: it was media catnip. There had been reporters camped out outside Aidan's

133

apartment. His parents had appeared on TV, via Skype, appealing to whoever had taken their little girl. Aidan had been on TV too, at the press conference, but now the media frenzy had quietened. Another big story had come along, and as the chances of a happy resolution diminished and no body was found, the reporters had packed up their things and moved on.

His parents had wanted to come over but he had persuaded them to stay in England, knowing that having them here wouldn't do any good. They phoned him what felt like every ten minutes, asking if there was any news. It was agonising. He'd found himself avoiding them, because he was sure he could hear recrimination in their voices whenever he spoke to them.

The unspoken blame. *You were meant to be looking after her.*

It tortured him.

Now, it was raining, his windscreen wipers swishing back and forth on their fastest setting but still unable to cope with the downpour. He parked and waited for the rain to ease a little, then walked down the hill to Viretta Park. Various news crews had been here over the past week, pointing out the bench where tributes to Kurt Cobain were left, showing the house where the rock singer had killed himself, describing how Scarlett was reported to have spoken to a long-haired stranger here the day before she vanished. The artist's sketch, which had been produced from Aidan's description, was everywhere too, even though Aidan knew it wasn't a fully accurate depiction of what the man had looked like. The sketch just looked like a crappy cartoon of Cobain. He wished some technology existed that could extract the picture of the man from his brain so the Nirvana fan's true likeness could be shown to the world. And, to make things worse, no matter how much Aidan tried to hold on to his own memory of what the stranger looked like, it was fading, and he would lie awake at night panicking that he wouldn't even recognise the man if he saw him.

He needed Scarlett to come back. Her return was the only thing that would wash him clean of the guilt that tormented him. Everyone else, including the police, told him he shouldn't blame himself, but he couldn't help it. She had vanished on his watch.

The park was empty, the rain keeping visitors away, and Aidan realised he didn't want to stay here either. Hunched against the wind, he made his way down Lake Washington Boulevard until he reached another small park that had a view over the lake.

He stopped and looked out at the churning grey water.

One of the first things the police had done was attempt to trace Scarlett through her phone. Using GPS, they had been able to tell that Scarlett had been at Aidan's apartment at eleven fifty, but then the signal had gone dead. Either her phone had died at that point or she had turned it off. Aidan wondered briefly if someone had broken into the apartment while he lay listening to his sleep story, but there was no evidence of it. The police believed Scarlett had done it herself. They had asked the phone company to retrieve her messages and call records from the couple of days before she disappeared, but there was nothing that shed any light on where she'd gone.

'If she was using WhatsApp, it's all secure and impossible to access or recover,' the police reminded Aidan, who already knew that fact – and that Scarlett frequently used the app to message her friends.

They had searched her laptop too and discovered that she had wiped her search history. Using special data tools they had been able to recover it, but hadn't found anything interesting. She had mostly been on social media and YouTube, where she had watched a couple of make-up tutorials, various clips by her favourite content creators, and a video about the climate protest she and Aidan had got mixed up in. Aidan speculated that she had been looking to see if she could spot herself. There was nothing to indicate why she had felt the need to delete her history. Maybe it was something she did regularly, out of habit.

On day three, someone had come forward to say he had seen a red-headed woman or girl on Lake Washington Boulevard in the early hours after Scarlett disappeared. Apparently, she had been walking down the hill, which made the police wonder if she'd gone back to Viretta Park. Over the next couple of days there had been a lot of activity on the lake. The police had gone out with boats. Divers had plunged beneath the surface and scoured the area close to where Aidan stood now. They'd found nothing.

CCTV hadn't turned up any sightings of her either. No credible witnesses had come forward.

Most importantly, no one at the club where the Nirvana tribute act were playing had seen her. Over and over, on the news and online, people kept repeating the same two clichéd phrases: 'It's as if she disappeared into thin air'; 'It's like she vanished from the face of the earth.'

Now, Aidan stood in Howell Park, hardly aware of the rain that flattened his hair and soaked his skin, until his eyes could no longer focus on the lake. He wished Scarlett had never come to America. Wished she'd stayed at home. He almost wished he'd never come here either.

Most of all, he felt scared. And guilty.

And he vowed never to stop looking.

Never to give up.

ω

'You're a good brother,' said Lana.

'You think?'

136

'Of course. You never did give up, did you? And you're going to find her. I feel certain of it.'

'And you never gave up on Samuel.'

'It's not in my nature.'

'I wish I shared your certainty about Scarlett,' Aidan said. 'We have no idea what to do next or where to go. We've got the police and at least one homicidal criminal on our tail. Our faces are probably going to be all over the media and the internet by the morning. Wanted for murdering a police officer. I'd say the chances of finding Scarlett right now are pretty slim.'

They both fell silent. Lana excused herself for a moment and went into the bathroom. He watched her go, knowing he ought to go back to his room but not wanting to. Wondering what she was thinking. He poured out the remains of the wine, a quarter of a glass each, and knocked his back, setting the glass aside.

Lana came out of the bathroom and sat back down on the bed opposite him. She held her hand out flat. 'Look. No trembling. It was shaking earlier.'

He smiled. 'It still looks like it's shaking a tiny bit.'

'What? No – feel it.'

She held her hand closer and he took it in both of his. It was warm, the skin soft. He was suddenly very aware of his body, of his heart beating, the blood in his veins.

'Well?' she said.

'I think it might be me . . .' he began.

'What?'

'Nothing. I . . .'

She looked at him, a little smile at the corner of her lips. For a second, a tantalising moment, he thought she might lean forward and kiss him. He realised he was holding his breath.

She yawned. 'Oh God. I'm sorry.'

He let go of her hand. The moment slipped away.

She yawned again. 'Okay, that's it. I'm going to bed.'

He stood up. 'Yes. Me too.'

'Aidan,' she said, as he moved towards the door. He turned back. 'If she's still out there – if Scarlett's around here somewhere – we'll find her.'

Chapter 19

It was cold in the back of the Jeep, the AC cranked high and the forest dark beyond the tinted glass. Shannon had instructed Cody not to disturb her while she meditated in the back seat. She closed her eyes and concentrated on her breathing, her palms spread out either side of her on the leather upholstery.

She let the pictures come. Let them fill her up, until she could smell it. The smoke. The burning flesh. Could hear the screams of animals and the cries of birds: panicked; doomed. A chorus of despair.

When the meditation was over, when she felt replenished and reassured – because it was important to remind herself, every so often, of why she was doing all this – Shannon opened her eyes and found Cody watching her in the rear-view mirror.

'Eyes on the road,' she said.

There was a long pause. 'You were making sounds,' he said.

'Was I?' That was news to her. She had thought she was silent. 'What kind of sounds?'

'I don't know. Like you were kinda . . . in pain.'

That was interesting.

'The whole world is in pain,' she said.

Cody nodded. 'You really believe it all, don't you?'

She leaned forward between the seats. The road, lit by the headlights, rushed beneath them. The trees shrank back from their approach, and her heart ached for them.

On the way here from the Ranch she had filled him in on everything – or, at least, told him everything he needed to know. She didn't want him to think none of this mattered. It was still important to find Faith and Carrera, remove the risk of them going to the authorities or the newspapers. And there was the simple of matter of justice too, wasn't there? They had humiliated her people and had to pay the price for that, with Shannon as the agent of karma.

'What do you see?' Cody asked. 'When you close your eyes.'

'I see the fire. I see the coming flames. And they're close now, Cody. It's happening even sooner than I expected.'

Her phone rang. It was Jimmy.

'What is it?'

'Wanted to let you know, the cop's body has been dealt with.'

'What kind of accident did she have?' Shannon asked.

'We went with suicide in the end. Her niece found her an hour ago, sitting in her own bed, surrounded by photos of her ex.'

This was a piece of info the mayor had given them. Giglio had been heartbroken six months earlier, when her boyfriend had walked out on her and moved to Montana.

'What about the coroner? Won't they question the time of death?'

'No, because as far as they know, she shot herself this evening. We had some issues with blood on the sheets. Would've been a lot better if she'd been shot in the head, not the chest. But the symbolism works. Her heart was broken so she shot herself there. We typed out a suicide note to say that's what she was going to do. Anyway, it's taken care of.'

'And the mayor's being a good boy?'

'He is. As long as we don't go near that little girl of his, he'll play along.'

'And there's no sign of any visitors to the Ranch?' she asked. 'Aidan and Lana haven't shown up, hoping to find Scarlett?'

'Nope. How would they know where to find us? They don't even know the Ranch exists.' He coughed. 'It's as quiet as the surface of the moon out here tonight. We'll be ready to head out in the morning.'

'What's the matter? You sound upset.'

'Do I? I guess I'm still pretty pissed about what happened earlier. Turns out I was kind of attached to those fingers. And I'm going to miss this place.'

'Me too,' she said. 'But think of where we're going, what we've created. It's beautiful.'

'Beautiful?' He sounded shocked. 'I don't know if that's the word I'd use.'

'I didn't mean aesthetically. The world won't be pretty for a long time. I meant, what we're doing.'

'Yeah, yeah. Of course.' He paused. 'Shannon, are you absolutely sure now is the time?'

'You're doubting me?'

'No. I mean . . . it just feels like it's all happened so suddenly.'

She made an impatient noise. 'Didn't I always tell you that's exactly how it would happen, once the dominoes started falling? That's why we've spent so long preparing. So we're ready. Are you really doubting me?'

'No. I've never doubted you, Shannon. Not since the day you came back.'

'Good.'

A beat of silence.

'Can you promise me something?' he said.

'It depends.'

'When you find them? Hurt them.'

ϖ

They pulled into the gas station and killed the engine and lights. Cody filled the tank while Shannon went into the building. There was no one else around. She checked the coolers and grabbed a couple of bottles of water. Picked up an apple and quietly despaired at the sight of all the junk food around her. Looters were certain to swarm places like this after the first wave, desperate for food and sustenance. Apart from the apples and water, there wasn't a single healthy thing here.

That included the slack-jawed moron behind the counter.

The dude, who was maybe twenty-one, still pimply and with hair dyed the colour of a blueberry Slurpee, barely looked up from his phone as he rang up the water and fruit.

'What pump?' he asked, still not looking up.

'One.'

She paid cash. At the same time, Cody came inside and began wandering around the aisles, checking out the candy.

Finally, the attendant, aware that Shannon hadn't moved away, looked at her.

'Um. Can I help you?'

'You could try paying a customer some attention.'

He blinked.

'You supposed to be playing video games when you're serving customers?' She squinted at the guy's name badge. 'You going to answer me, Kevin?'

Kevin blinked, but he still didn't put his phone down. 'I'm . . . sorry?'

Shannon laughed. 'I'm just messing with you.'

Relief mixed with confusion on his face.

'Maybe you can help me,' she said. 'I'm looking for some friends. A woman, black hair, Latina, mid-twenties, and a man, white, British, reddish-brown hair. I think they might have stopped here to get gas this evening.'

'Nope,' he said, the tiniest tremor in his voice. He didn't meet her eye. 'No one's been by for hours.'

'Oh. That's a shame.' She glanced up at the CCTV camera on the wall, which pointed straight at both of them. 'So if I took a look at the recording, I wouldn't see them.'

Kevin hesitated a beat too long. 'I told you, no one's been here.'

He lifted his phone, intending to go back to his game, clearly hoping she would leave. She noticed his hand was shaking.

Shannon reached across the counter and snatched the phone from his grasp.

'Hey!'

'I don't like it when people lie to me, Kevin.'

He swallowed. Cody was standing behind her shoulder now. She could hear him breathing heavily, excited like a wolf that had smelled blood.

'Let me ask you again,' Shannon said. 'A woman and a British dude. Driving a white Nissan. They were here, weren't they?'

He stared at her.

'Just fucking answer,' said Cody.

'No. I swear.'

There was probably a panic button beneath the counter. Kevin's hand slipped out of sight, no doubt wavering close to it. There was the CCTV camera too, though this gas station wasn't part of a chain and she guessed the recording was only local, probably stored on a hard drive that got overwritten every few days.

'I'll give you five hundred bucks if you tell me,' she said.

He blinked at her. 'You're kidding, right?'

'No, Kevin. I'm not kidding. I've got the money right here.' She wasn't lying. She took out her wallet and opened it, showing him the thick wad of bills within. 'All I need to know is when they were here and what they said. Then you can have the cash and your phone, and you'll never see us again.' She gave Kevin her most pleasant smile. 'I'm sure this is a lot of money for someone like you.'

He exhaled. 'Okay. Yeah. They were here.'

'What time?'

'Around six.'

'And did you overhear them say where they were heading?'

He shook his head.

'Which way did they go?'

With a trembling arm, he pointed west.

'Anything else you can tell me?'

He glanced at her wallet. The tip of his tongue flickered out, wetting his lips. Never underestimate a person's greed.

'You want more, huh? Okay, how about this? You tell me something good, I'll make it a thousand.'

Behind her, Cody puffed out air.

Kevin spoke in a high voice, like his balls hadn't dropped yet. 'The woman. She told me if anyone came by and asked, I hadn't seen you.'

'How much did she give you?'

'Fifty bucks.'

'You were gonna protect her for *fifty bucks*?' Shannon laughed. 'Oh Kevin, if I'd known you were so cheap.'

She placed his phone on the floor. She put the stack of twenty-dollar bills beside it.

'There you go,' she said. 'I'm a woman of my word. I won't even deduct the fifty Lana already gave you.' She nudged Cody. 'Come on, let's go.'

She walked towards the door, Cody at her heels. He hissed in her ear, 'You're really gonna give this asshole a thousand bucks?'

'No,' she said, as Kevin scurried out from behind the counter. 'But I needed to get him away from that panic button.'

As Kevin bent to pick up his phone and the cash, Shannon signalled and Cody rushed back towards him. Kevin looked up, just in time to see Cody's boot swinging towards his face.

There was a crunch. Kevin flipped hard onto his back, clutching his nose and making a horrible keening noise. He tried to get to his feet, to get back to the counter, to the button. Cody kicked him in the ribs and Kevin went down flat on his belly. He tried to get up but slipped on the blood that had sprayed from his nose.

Cody put his foot on his back. 'What do you want me to do?' he asked.

Shannon looked down at the kid. He had been rude, and greedy. He was a worm. A plastic bottle floating in the ocean. Trash choking the planet. He was nothing.

And he would be dead soon anyway.

'Let off some steam,' she said, and she walked away, fanning the dirty money, pocketing the phone.

ϖ

Afterwards, they sat in the car, Shannon in the passenger seat, beside Cody. The CCTV hard drive was in the footwell and the SIM card had been removed from the boy's phone and destroyed. Cody reeked of blood and sweat and violence.

'I guess you'd like to do that to Lana when we find her,' Shannon said. 'Did you leave some anger in the tank?'

He nodded.

'You know, I'm gonna need someone by my side. To protect me. If you prove yourself on this trip, show me that today's fuck-up at the murder house was an aberration . . .'

He was still breathing a little heavily. 'I'm not a fuck-up,' he said.

'And you understand loyalty too, don't you? But if we don't find them . . .'

'We'll find them.'

She nodded. 'I think it's time to visit Moses. Take him his gift before it expires.'

As they drove into the dark, she told him to put the radio on.

'. . . a growing number of wildfires breaking out across Southern California are moving north, with local fire crews struggling to contain them, and warnings that strong winds and dry weather conditions have greatly increased the risk in northern parts of the state . . .'

Shannon sat back and closed her eyes. Now it was even more important that they find and deal with Lana and Faith quickly.

A ripple of excitement ran through her.

It was happening.

Chapter 20

Aidan woke up with a name in his head.

He jumped out of bed and pulled his clothes on, not bothering to wash or to brush his teeth. It was still early, just 7 a.m., but the sun was already pouring through the window of the motel room, and when he opened the door he saw it was going to be another hot day.

He banged on Lana's door.

She must have been awake too because she opened it almost immediately, wearing a long T-shirt that came down to her knees and tugging at her unruly bed hair.

'Is the motel on fire?' she asked. 'Shit, is it Jimmy and Cody? They're here?' She tried to peer past him.

'It's all good,' he said. 'I need to look at your phone.'

'It's dead. I forgot to ask you for your charger.'

'Damn.'

He turned to go back to his room to fetch it.

'While you're there,' she called after him, 'you should brush your teeth.'

He did as she suggested. Normally, he would have been embarrassed, but he was too excited to care. His subconscious had done its work overnight, as he'd hoped it would.

When he got back to Lana's room she had pulled on her jeans and was sitting on the bed she'd slept in. He plugged in the charger, attached the phone and waited for it to boot up.

'Did you sleep okay?' he asked.

'Not really. You?'

'I think I passed out more than slept.'

'Me too. I had a dream about a construction worker trying to get through my window. Then he turned into a cop, and then a cowboy. I'm not sure if my brain was stringing together all the people we met or talked about yesterday, or if I was dreaming about the Village People.'

'Was there a leatherman?'

'That was a different dream.'

The phone finally woke up and Lana unlocked it. Aidan went straight to the photos and navigated to the second-to-last one. He pointed to the word at the bottom of the page. *Caldar.*

'I think when you photographed this page you cut off the edge,' he said. 'It should say *Caldaralo.*'

Lana said, 'Yeah?'

'I saw that name on a missing poster in Eaglewood. Paige Caldaralo. It said she went missing last year. The format of American dates confuses me because you write the day and month the wrong way round—'

'No, you put them the wrong way around.'

'—but it definitely said 2018. I know what these numbers are too, next to her name. It's a bank account number.'

'Shit, so it is.'

'I'm assuming S L Caldaralo is one of her parents. Maybe the mayor was paying them off. Trying to get them to stop asking questions. Perhaps she's someone else who needed to be kept quiet.'

Lana took the phone back from Aidan. 'I don't know. That's quite a leap. The payment could be for anything.'

'I know. But think about it. This situation already involves two missing teenagers: my sister and your brother. I know Samuel is officially meant to be dead but his body was never recovered. Really, he's a missing person. I bet you this S L Caldaralo is one of Paige Caldaralo's parents.'

He opened Google on his phone and typed in *Paige Caldaralo Eaglewood*. The first result was a short news story from the local newspaper, the same paper he'd found at the station.

'*Parents appeal for missing daughter to come home*,' Aidan read aloud. '*Eaglewood residents Maddy and Simon Caldaralo . . .* That's her dad . . . *have put out an urgent appeal for their nineteen-year-old daughter, Paige Caldaralo, to come home. Paige, who last year graduated high school and is currently unemployed, was last seen on the evening of March twenty-second, when she told her parents she was going out to meet a girlfriend . . .*'

Aidan skim-read the rest. It was mostly an account of what a good student Paige had been, as well as a regular churchgoer and a keen environmentalist who had taken part in a campaign to clean up the nearby Eel River.

'Oh hell, there's a quote from Sergeant Giglio,' Lana said, with a pained expression. '*We have no reason at present to suspect foul play. If anyone has seen or heard from Paige, can they please contact Eaglewood Police Department.* I wonder if there are any follow-up stories.' She searched but nothing else appeared. 'I guess a nineteen-year-old disappearing isn't big news.' She handed her phone back to Aidan. 'So what have we got? Three teenagers going missing, one of them in Seattle but ending up around here.'

They both sat in silence, thinking.

'My brain doesn't work properly without coffee,' Lana said. 'We drove past a coffee shop on the way in. Let's go and get breakfast.'

ϖ

There was no one else in the coffee shop when they got there except a group of men and women in walking gear. Hikers. Aidan didn't think the PCT ran through this town, but it was still excellent hiking country. They'd seen a number of signs for trails on their way in, and Aidan heard the group say something about redwood groves.

They sat in the furthest corner from the door and ordered coffee. Lana declared herself ravenous and ordered a huge stack of pancakes, which prompted Aidan to do the same. He had gone off eggs. The smell of them reminded him of the morning Scarlett had disappeared.

'Look,' Aidan said, pointing at the noticeboard. Among the signs advertising local mother-and-baby classes and fishing trips was a missing poster. This time it was a young man: Jack Draper from San Diego. Missing since April, last seen on a Greyhound bus to Eureka via Fortuna.

'It's an epidemic,' Lana said.

The waiter, a forty-something guy with sleepy eyes and a five o'clock shadow, came over with their food, which Lana attacked immediately. Before the guy could step away, Aidan asked him about the poster.

'Do you know if Jack was ever found?'

The waiter looked towards the poster as if he'd never noticed it before. 'I got no idea. We get a new one of those every week. We could plaster all the walls with them, but the manager doesn't like there to be more than one up at a time. Says it's too depressing.'

'A new one every week?'

'Yeah. Okay, maybe that's an exaggeration, but we get a lot.'

'Any idea why?'

The waiter checked over his shoulder. The hikers were on their way out the door, and a few other people, locals presumably, had come in. 'I can tell you're not from around here, but you know where we are, right?'

'Enlighten us.'

'This is the Emerald Triangle, man. Mendocino. Trinity. And Humboldt County, which is where we are right now.'

Aidan had heard of it – the area of Northern California that produced most of the country's cannabis.

'It's been going on for years,' the waiter said. 'All these kids, they turn up on the Greyhound planning to work on the weed farms, maybe even start their own grow. They think it's cool, think they're going to make their fortune and get a load of free pot to smoke. Even legalisation hasn't stopped it, because there are still tons of farms supplying the black market. And the gangs are here waiting for them.'

'Gangs?' asked Aidan.

'Traffickers. They're like spiders, waiting in a web for all these silly little insects to come flying to their doom.'

Lana appeared to be deep in thought, leaving Aidan to ask, 'These trafficked kids . . . Are they being forced to work in the drug trade?'

The waiter pursed his lips. 'That's part of it. But sex trafficking too. Either around here – I've heard about these secret brothels deep in the woods – or they're being shipped off to other parts of the state. I guess a lot of them are taken south to LA, or north to Portland.'

Aidan and Lana stared at each other, and the waiter went off to serve a man who'd just come in.

'Do you think that's it?' Lana asked.

'Drugs?'

'Or human trafficking?'

'Both?' they said at the same time.

Lana had put down her fork. 'If that's what the mayor's mixed up in, and Samuel overheard him talking about it or found out some other way . . .' She didn't need to complete the sentence.

'Maybe Paige Caldaralo found out about it too. And her parents were paid off so they stopped asking questions.'

'Or she was trafficked.'

Aidan had lost his appetite too. 'Do you really think this is what this is all about? Human trafficking? Drugs are one thing but *that* . . .' He knew that people were trafficked for several reasons – all grim, all demonstrative of how evil men could be. Forced labour. Sex. Even organ harvesting, though he believed that was far rarer. He had imagined all these fates for Scarlett. Had to force himself not to dwell on it each time, though it was impossible to stop the dark whispers from creeping in at four in the morning – the shadowy, horrific images that compelled him to sit up and turn the light on, driving them away like they were cockroaches scurrying to the edges of the room.

Now he had to face the dreadful possibility that this really was what had happened to her.

He thought back to the scene Elizabeth had described at the murder house. Two men, including Jimmy, and three women, one of them Scarlett. Were the girls flies who had ended up in the spider's web?

He had so many questions. Had Scarlett met Jimmy in Seattle? Had the guy from Viretta Park brought her here, or introduced her to someone else? Had he sweet-talked her into joining them, or just abducted her and brought her here? None of the scenarios he could come up with quite made sense. All he knew was that she was here, a victim of traffickers or drug dealers, or both. Francesca had seen a man, very possibly Jimmy, chasing her across that clearing. Had they been keeping her prisoner and she'd tried to get away? Had she just discovered who they really were?

He thought back again to the encounter at the murder house. Giglio had been surprised, hadn't she? Said something like, 'So his sister really is in Eaglewood?' And Jimmy had replied, 'Not anymore.'

Why – because she had been taken somewhere else after they caught her?

Or because she was dead?

'Aidan. Aidan.'

He looked up. He had been so deep in thought he hadn't heard Lana speaking to him.

'Look at this.' She was holding her phone out to him. 'I went onto the local news site for Humboldt County to see if I could find any more stories about missing people or trafficking in this area. Look at this this headline.'

Aidan read the words on the screen: *Eaglewood Police Sergeant in Tragic Suicide.*

'Suicide? What the hell?'

Aidan started to read the story. *Sergeant Michaela Giglio of Eaglewood Police was found dead at her home this morning.* He skimmed the rest. *Found by niece . . . recently broke up with her boyfriend . . . suicide note . . . survived by her mother and brother . . . Eaglewood's mayor Christopher Hood said, 'Sergeant Giglio was a great servant of and friend to this community. She was committed to helping to rebuild the town after the terrible fires last year. She will be missed by everyone who knew and worked with her.'*

'They're covering it up,' Lana said. She seemed stunned.

'You know what this means, right? It means the police aren't looking for us. We can go to the authorities.'

'Are you crazy?' she hissed. Across the coffee shop, the man who had been sitting closest to the door got up and left. He looked back over at them as he went. 'What are we going to do? Walk into a police station and say, *Hey, that cop in the paper didn't kill herself. It was me. I shot her.*'

'Okay. Good point. But it's good news, right? The police aren't—'

'Aidan.'

'What?'

'That guy. The guy who just left. He took a photo of us through the window.'

Aidan spun around. There was no one outside the window now. 'Are you sure?'

'I'm positive.'

She stood up, chucking some money onto the table to pay for their barely started breakfast, and Aidan followed her out onto the road.

'That's him.'

The man, who was wearing a checked shirt and baseball cap, was about fifty yards up the road, standing beside a black SUV. He was looking back at Lana and Aidan, his phone in his hand.

'We need to get out of here,' Aidan said.

They jogged across to the car and got in, slamming the doors, with Aidan in the driver's seat. The man in the checked shirt was still standing by his SUV, watching them. He held his phone up, presumably taking another picture.

'Wait,' Lana said. 'We're not wanted by the police. So why is he taking our photo?'

'I don't know.'

'Well, we need to find out. This guy might be one of them. He might know what happened to Samuel.'

'Lana!' But it was too late. She had taken her gun out of the glovebox and was out of the car, running up the street towards the SUV, holding the pistol down against her hip. Aidan couldn't believe it. What if this guy was armed? He braced himself for a shot, but it didn't come. The man tried to open the door of his vehicle but he must have left it locked, because then he was groping in his

154

pocket. Aidan got out of the car and ran in the same direction as Lana.

The man in the checked shirt managed to get his keys out of his pocket and put his hand on the door of his vehicle, but he was too slow.

Lana reached him and stuck the gun in his side. He looked around, but there was nobody else on the road.

'Get in and slide across,' she said. She jabbed the gun into his side and said something else that Aidan couldn't hear.

The man nodded once, then did as she asked, getting into the SUV and sliding across to the passenger side. Lana got in after him and sat in the driver's seat. Aidan reached the SUV and opened the back door. There was a child seat in the way on this side, so he jogged round and got in the other side so that he was sitting behind the man. He could see the nose of the gun pressing into the flesh of the man's flank.

The woman who'd been deeply shaken after shooting a cop was temporarily missing. Here was the Lana he'd met two nights ago, trading insults with Cody, willing to do anything to find out what had happened to Samuel. No, scrap that. She was even more desperate now. More determined. Because any residual doubts, any shades of grey, were gone. It was black and white now.

'Do not do anything with your hands. Okay?'

'Okay.'

'What's your name?'

'Zach. Zach Van Beekum.' He swallowed. He had a thick beard and it was hard to tell his age, though Aidan thought he was probably in his late thirties. Aidan noticed the footwells of the car were littered with a dozen empty cans of Red Bull.

'Why were you taking our photo?'

He opened his mouth then closed it again.

'Tell her, Zach,' said Aidan.

'I got a bulletin with your photos. There's a reward. Fifty thousand dollars.'

'Bloody hell,' said Aidan.

'Who was this bulletin from? Mayor Hood?'

He glanced at her, surprised. 'The Shastina Spring dude? No.'

'Then who?'

His Adam's apple bobbed. 'Do you have to grind that gun barrel into me? You're gonna bruise my kidneys.'

Lana ignored him. 'Who was the bulletin from?'

'A guy named Jimmy Marson. He's a customer of mine.'

Jimmy.

'What do you sell him, Zach?' Lana asked. 'Drugs? Or are you in the human trafficking business too?'

'What?' Again, Zach looked shocked. 'No! I sell him beer.'

'Beer?' Aidan repeated.

'Yeah. I run a microbrewery. The Redwood Brewing Company. Look in the back and you'll see I'm not lying.'

Aidan peered over the back seat into the storage area. There were half a dozen crates of beer stacked there, a mixture of lagers and IPAs.

'You sell Jimmy beer?' said Lana.

'Yeah. I told you. He buys quite a lot of it too. He's a good customer. The bulletin said that you two had stolen from him and that you were armed and dangerous. The reward was for locating you and telling Jimmy where you were.'

'Fuck,' said Aidan. 'They're going to be on their way here.'

'No,' Zach said. 'I didn't send it yet. I've got no signal on this road. Not enough to text a photo anyway.'

His voice was shaky and it sounded to Aidan like he was telling the truth.

'Give me your phone,' Lana said.

'It's in my pocket. I'm going to have to reach in to get it.'

'Aidan, you do it.'

He leaned between the seats and slid the phone out of Zach's shirt pocket. 'What's the code?'

Zach told him and he opened it, going to the Messages app. It looked like Zach was indeed telling the truth. Aidan opened the Photos app and deleted the photos, which showed him and Lana in the coffee shop and in the front of their car. Then he went to the deleted photos folder and removed them from there too. It was true that Zach's phone signal was extremely weak here, so Aidan was confident the pictures wouldn't have been uploaded to the cloud.

Aidan powered the phone down and dropped it on the back seat beside him. Then he took out his own phone and found Scarlett's photo. He held it in front of Zach. 'Do you recognise her?'

'Nuh-uh.'

'Where is Jimmy based?' Lana asked.

'Somewhere near the Nevada border, I think. I don't know his address. He always comes to the brewery himself, or sends someone. I asked him why he comes so far for beer and he said he's in the area all the time.'

'And you don't know what he does?'

'It never came up. He said something about heading back to the ranch once, and with that and the way he dresses, I assumed he was a ranch hand or a farmer or something.'

'What do you talk about?' Lana said.

'Nothing. Brewing beer. He wanted to know the whole process, the ingredients and whatnot. We laughed about it because I said I couldn't tell him in case I lost a customer.'

'Lana, we should hurry,' Aidan said. 'Someone could come by at any moment.'

'I don't know. The minute we leave, he's going to be on the phone to his great pal and loyal customer Jimmy.'

'I won't. I promise!'

'Do you want to know who Jimmy really is? He's a human trafficker. He was involved in the murder of my brother. Yesterday, he tried to kill us, and he's after us because he wants to finish the job.'

Zach didn't say anything. Aidan didn't think he'd be persuaded to take the side of this woman, who was digging the barrel of a gun into him, against his charming regular customer. On top of that, $50,000 was a hell of a lot of money. He had little doubt Zach would call Jimmy as soon as he was able to. They were going to have to get as far away from here as they could.

'I think we should go,' Aidan said.

'Wait.' With the hand that wasn't holding the gun, she opened her phone and navigated her way to the photos of the notebook. 'One more thing. You know this area well, do you? Do you know someone called Lorenzo?'

It took Aidan a beat to recall who this was. The name written in the mayor's notebook, next to the *S L Caldaralo* notation.

'I don't think so. There was one guy at school, but I don't know—'

'Lana,' Aidan said. 'This isn't getting us anywhere.'

'You a fan of the Dead?' Zach said to Lana.

'Huh?'

'That logo, in the picture.' He nodded at her phone. 'The skull with the lightning bolt. It's the Grateful Dead logo.'

'I guess the mayor's a Deadhead,' Aidan said, surprised. If the mayor had been a hippie once, he'd done a good job of reinventing himself. 'That doesn't help us. Lana, we really have to go.'

'Dogwood B,' Zach said, still looking at the notebook page on the screen. 'That must be Dogwood Bluff Road.'

'Where's that?'

Aidan figured that Zach just wanted Lana to stop pressing that gun into him. He wanted them to stop asking questions and get out of his car.

'It's in Birches Rock.'

'Of course it is,' said Lana. 'Okay, Zach. My friend is going to get out of the car first. Aidan, take his phone with you.'

'What?' said Zach. 'That phone cost—'

'Shut up. Give me your car keys too.'

'But how am I supposed to get home?'

'I'm sure you'll figure it out. I also want you to stay sitting here for ten minutes after we go. Listen, Zach. What I'm about to tell you is the truth. You might choose not to believe it. I'm sure you don't have a high opinion of me right now. But Jimmy is a criminal. A murderer. If you tell him you spoke to us, he'll know we told you what he really is. I don't care how much he likes your beer – he'll kill you.'

Aidan got out of the car, and Lana followed. On the way back to the Nissan she dropped Zach's keys into a drain.

'Where are we going now?' Aidan asked. 'What's Birches Rock?'

'Somewhere I didn't think I'd ever have to go,' said Lana.

Chapter 21

'How much longer?' Shannon asked, talking to herself, to the sky, the trees. She was in the back seat again, lying on her back, staring at the underside of the Jeep's roof.

'He said they'll be here soon, didn't he?' Cody replied.

'They'd better be.'

They were parked at the foot of a low mountain, just outside Birches Rock. Shannon had called Darryl Moses last night but had only managed to speak to one of his minions, who'd told her that Darryl was away 'on business' but would be back first thing tomorrow. Shannon had never had any direct dealings with Moses before – she usually left that to Jimmy – though she had a good idea what he would look like: beard, baseball cap, stinking of pot, dirty fingernails. Like the guys who were always trying to feel her up back in high school.

She felt dirty herself, being stuck in the car with its increasingly fetid air. The Eel River was nearby; maybe she should go down there for a swim, except the water was filthy with pesticides from the illegal pot farms that had operated here for so long, endangering what remained of the fish population. It sickened her how few people respected this ancient land, choking it with garbage and chemicals, and she had to remind herself that soon it wouldn't matter anymore. One day, the water would be clean. The wild salmon would return.

The trees whispered it to her.

Sometimes at the Ranch, far from the forest, she had doubted everything. Was she doing the right thing? Were they really so close to the end? But now that she was back among the trees, she felt strong and certain again. She guessed it happened to all great leaders and visionaries. It would have been strange if she didn't doubt herself. But the trees told her she was right. And they reinforced her conviction: the end was coming. It was almost upon them. The final chapter. The last throes of a dying world.

There was something beautiful about it.

After talking to Darryl's minion, she had asked Cody to find a spot to pull over.

'We ought to rest,' she said. 'Get some sleep.'

'A motel?'

'Screw that, Cody. We're going to sleep among the trees. With nature. While we still have the chance to.'

Cody tried hard to mask his disappointment. What, did he think she was going to invite him to share a motel room with her? She'd noticed him checking her out when he thought she wasn't looking, just like they all did, and she guessed he was popular with the trailer-park girls of Eaglewood. But to think he stood a chance with *her*? Not even if he ended up being the last man on earth.

She was above all that.

Beyond it.

After pulling over by the side of the road, Cody went into the trees to take a leak and she called Jimmy.

He answered immediately.

'How's everything proceeding?' she asked.

'Good. We're all packed up. We'll be ready to ship out at first light.'

'Excellent.'

There was a pause, and she was sure he was waiting for her to ask how his hand was, how he was *feeling*. Another man-baby seeking comfort from his mommy. Her estimation of Jimmy had plummeted in the last twenty-four hours. He was another one who had tried to get into her pants, back when they first met. Sometimes, in moments of clarity, she wondered if that was why he had followed her so readily, because he thought they would form some kind of power couple, an Adam and Eve for the new world. To Jimmy's credit, though, he had never tried it on. And he had thrown himself into the work at the Ranch like only a true believer could.

'Let me ask you a question,' she said.

'Sure.'

'That day. In the clearing. What exactly happened?'

He sighed. 'I told you all this earlier. I fucked up, I know. Do we need to go over this again? She realised where we were taking her and tried to run. We caught her. We dealt with her. That's all there is to it.'

'But how did she figure it out?'

'I don't know. I guess she must have overheard something.'

'Hmm.'

'You want me to apologise again? Because I will.' He was irritated now. The snarl had returned to his voice. 'But like I said, we dealt with her.'

Shannon hung up, but not before telling him to keep her posted. She had been on the phone too long and was worried about what the radiation was doing to her brain. At least this wasn't a 5G area. Never would be. This whole forest would be burned down before the government got the chance to extend that network here and enslave them.

Cody had climbed back into the Jeep, stinking of cigarettes. Something else that would soon be eradicated.

After a while, unable to sleep, she was so bored she said, 'What's your story, Cody? You've always lived in Eaglewood?'

'Uh-huh.'

'How well do you know Lana Carrera?'

She couldn't see his face in the darkness but imagined his curled lip, the snarl of contempt. 'I grew up with her.'

'You were at school together?'

'Yeah. We lived in the same trailer park. She always thought she was too good for the place, though. Always reading.' He said 'reading' like some people might have said 'skinning cats'.

'You ever screw her?'

'Fuck, no. I wouldn't touch that . . .' He stopped himself from saying the B word. 'I wouldn't touch her.'

This was obviously a lie.

'I get it,' Shannon said. 'There were girls like her at my school too. A lot of them were rich, but there were girls who were just as dirt-poor as me. The pretty girls, the ones who were good at sports. The teachers' pets. I remember the way they used to look at me, like I was a cockroach. The things they used to say . . .'

She trailed off. All that was a long, long time ago, but she still didn't like to remember it.

'Lana should never have come back,' Cody said. Then he muttered something that sounded like 'pencil dick' and Shannon understood.

Lana had humiliated him.

In other circumstances, Shannon might have talked to him. Told him that he owned the humiliation. That you could only be humiliated if you gave the other person the power to do so. An adult would let it go. But she wasn't going to do that. Cody's anger towards Lana was a tool that Shannon fully intended to use.

ϖ

The sun had been up for three hours and Shannon was about to tell Cody to drive up the hill, demand an audience with Darryl Moses, when – at last – two quad bikes came rumbling down the dirt track towards them.

Shannon stood straight. She watched Cody tuck the Glock she'd given him into the waistband of his jeans so it nestled against the small of his back. She raised a hand in greeting as the quad bikes came to a halt before them, kicking up a cloud of dust from the dry road.

Both men were clad in camouflage gear, with baseball caps pulled low, sunglasses covering their eyes and bandanas tied across their mouths. Only their noses and a strip of flesh across the centre of their faces were visible.

The first man got off his bike and walked slowly over to them, pulling his mask down to expose a pair of dry, cracked lips. He grinned, revealing a gold tooth in the front of his mouth.

'Well, shit,' he said, brazenly looking her up and down. 'You're Shannon Reinhardt?'

'I am.'

'The boss lady, in all her glory. Gotta admit, I didn't know what to expect. The way Jimmy talks about you, I guess I figured you'd be older. A wise old woman who came down from the mountain.' He grinned again.

'You're late,' she said, squaring up to him, hands on hips.

Darryl looked Shannon up and down again, a twist of amusement on his lips, then turned his attention to Cody. 'Who's this?'

'It doesn't matter who he is,' said Shannon. 'He's with me.'

Darryl didn't seem able to keep still. He walked around them in a circle, then went over to the Jeep, peering through the windows. It had been a long time since anyone had treated Shannon with so little respect. She was used to people staring at her in awe, kowtowing to her, acting like they'd throw their coats onto a rain puddle for her. Darry's silent companion, who still had his bandana over his face, stood beside his quad bike, watching with flat eyes.

'Where's Jimmy?' Darryl asked.

'Not here,' said Cody.

Darryl rolled his eyes and said, 'More importantly, where's my merchandise?'

'We're not doing that anymore,' Shannon said.

He stared at her. 'I hope you're kidding. You are kidding, right?'

'I'm sure you can find other sources.' She didn't tell him that he wasn't going to have any need for merchandise after the fires swept through here. He probably thought he was safe, up on his mountain. Didn't know that nowhere was safe.

'Well, that is not the kind of news I was expecting to hear today,' Darryl said. 'I thought the arrangement was working well for both of us. I get the bodies I need, you get paid. Everyone wins. So what the fuck is going on?'

'We're changing our model,' Shannon said.

He laughed without humour. 'So what *are* you doing here?'

'We're looking for someone. Two people, actually.'

'Yeah, I got the email. Haven't seen them.'

Shannon walked up to him. 'I need your help looking for them.'

Another laugh. 'Wait. You just told me our business arrangement is coming to an end and now you're asking for my *help*?'

'It's for your benefit too,' she said. 'These people haven't been to the police or the Feds yet, but it won't be long. There was a witness . . . It got a bit messy.'

'Jesus Christ,' Darryl muttered.

'I brought you a gift,' Shannon said. 'As an offering. An attempt to make it up to you for the inconvenience.'

Darryl and his sidekick exchanged a look. 'A gift?'

'Cody, show him,' Shannon said.

Cody strolled over to the Jeep and opened the back. Darryl wandered over to take a look, with Shannon just behind him.

There, between the back seat and the swing gate, was the gift. She lay on her side with one wrist handcuffed to one of the metal bars to the left of the back seat, eyes half closed. They had left her other hand free so she could drink from the water bottle she'd been given. Her hair was stuck to her face with sweat, but the ketamine and tranqs they'd given her had kept her quiet. She would have no idea how much time had passed since they'd put her in here. Shannon had hardly known she was there.

'Her name's Kristin,' she said.

Darryl snapped his fingers in front of the girl's face and Kristin stirred and blinked at him. 'Who are you?' she asked. 'Is this my mission?'

'What did you give her?' Darryl asked, stepping away from the Jeep.

Shannon told him. 'It should be almost worn off now. Cody, help her out.'

Cody unlocked the cuffs and, with surprising gentleness, helped Kristin out. She wobbled and just about managed to stay upright. Her pupils were still pinpricks and she could hardly keep her eyes open in the bright sunlight.

'She's strong, fit and healthy,' Shannon said. 'One of our newest recruits.'

Darryl barked out a laugh. 'I'll grant you, she's in better shape than the last little bitch Jimmy brought me. I assume she was the one involved in your fuck-up, huh?'

'One of them.'

A slimy grin crept onto Darryl's lips. 'Well, we found suitable work for that one. Special work, if you know what I mean. But this one looks like she'll be versatile. Now, what else have you got for me?'

'This is it.'

'Huh. One lousy chick. You really think that's enough to get my help? I knew you lived in cloud fucking cuckoo land . . .'

The guy in the bandana snickered and Shannon glared at him.

'Maybe *you'd* like to come and work for us,' Darryl said, licking his top lip. 'That little bitch you brought us is almost worn out and we need a replacement. You'd be a big hit at the joy house.'

'What the hell is the joy house?'

'It's where all the girls go once they're not strong enough to work on their feet anymore.'

Shannon stared at him. 'A brothel?'

'We just call it the joy house. A place for the men to let off steam after a hard day's work. Yeah, you'd be a *big* hit.'

He took a step towards her, looking her over. He was tall and broad and, although it had been a long time since she'd allowed any man to intimidate her, she found herself taking a step back.

'You think you're really special, don't you?' he said. 'You come here making all these demands, looking at me like I'm some kind of dumbass hillbilly. You're nothing but a stuck-up bitch, and I am sick of people like *you* looking down on people like *me*.'

Shannon turned to Cody. 'Are you going to let him talk to me like that?'

Cody reached behind him. Immediately, Darryl and the guy in the bandana had guns pointed at him.

'I wouldn't,' said Darryl. He nodded at Bandana Guy, who walked behind Cody and plucked the gun from the waistband of his jeans.

Darryl pointed his gun at Shannon while the other man kept his trained on Cody.

'We could put both of you to work. Cody here on his feet and you on your back. Actually, maybe Cody here could work in the joy house too. I'm a liberal guy, and I know we got some men who aren't into girls or who like both.'

Cody went to grab Darryl's gun and Bandana Guy stepped between them, shoving the nose of the Glock he'd taken from Cody into his belly.

'I'd rather die,' said Shannon.

Darryl giggled. 'Shit. Really?' He released the safety.

Shannon was almost overwhelmed by shock. This wasn't supposed to happen. This wasn't her destiny.

But then Darryl let the nose of the pistol dip. 'I guess if I kill you, it will lead to all sorts of pains in my ass,' he said. 'Plus I got a lot of respect for Jimmy. So I'm going to let you go.'

He grinned, showing off his gold tooth again.

'But you're gonna have to walk. I'm keeping your ride. Call it compensation to go along with this *gift*.' He returned to the Jeep and put his arm around the dazed-looking Kristin's shoulders, then turned to smile at them. 'Now, I'm going to give you two five minutes, and if you're not out of my sight by then, you'll be joining Kristin here.'

Chapter 22

'What's the deal with Birches Rock?' Aidan asked as he drove out of Fortuna.

'It's the kind of place my mother warned me about. You know what that waiter said about the Emerald Triangle? The weed farming? Birches Rock is the most notorious part of it. The way my mom went on about it, it's like the Wild West.'

'This is California. Cannabis has been legal for, what, three years? It can't be that bad, surely?'

'I guess we're going to find out.'

They were headed south on the 101. Just after they passed the town of Rio Dell, Lana took the guns out of the glovebox and checked them over. They were both loaded.

'You ever used one of these things?' she asked.

'You must be joking.'

She sighed and put the guns away. 'You Brits.'

'You were pretty badass back there,' he said.

She laughed. 'Aidan, I feel like I'm right on the edge. Do you know what I mean? Right. On. The. *Edge*.'

'Well, try not to tip over it.' He concentrated on the road for a minute. 'Would you really have shot Zach?'

'If I'd thought he was involved in Samuel's death, yeah. Maybe.' Her voice cracked on the final word.

'You don't know for sure that he's dead.'

She had her face turned towards the window so he couldn't see her expression. 'I don't think there's much point torturing myself with hope right now.'

'I've been torturing myself with hope for the last two years.'

'Yeah? And how's that been working out for you?'

'It's better than the alternative.'

They drove by the entrance to the Avenue of the Giants, with its mighty redwoods.

'You know,' Lana said, 'some of these trees are almost two thousand years old.'

'Wow.'

'These are the last of their species. All it would take is one intense wildfire and *boom*. Gone forever.'

Living in a city, even one as close to the water as Seattle, made Aidan feel cut adrift from nature and the plight of the planet. But here, so close to the redwoods, he could feel it. Their fragility. The responsibility of the people who lived here now to protect the parts of the earth they hadn't yet destroyed.

'What is it?' Lana said.

'Huh?'

'You were smiling to yourself.'

'Oh, I was just thinking about how Scarlett's had an influence on me. She's really into green issues. We got sucked into this big eco-protest the first day she was in Seattle and she loved it. I had to drag her away.'

'It is pretty terrifying,' Lana said. 'I had a friend at college from Houston and she was there when Hurricane Harvey hit. Her house was destroyed. She said a third of the city was flooded at some point.'

'Shit.'

'Here, it's fire. I mean, California's always had a wildfire season, but now it's two months longer than it used to be, and twice as much burns now than fifty years ago. You heard about the Thomas Fire a couple of years back? It burned something like fifty thousand square feet in one day. And that happened in December, when it's supposed to be the rainy season.' She gazed out at the passing redwoods and Aidan thought he saw her shudder. 'And after the fire came the mudslides. You know, because the vegetation that usually stops them was all gone? It gave me nightmares for a while. I kept dreaming about being buried alive or burning to death.'

The ground they were driving on was growing rockier now. For a while, the forest was less dense, and then the GPS announced that they'd reached their destination: the tiny town of Birches Rock, where there was little except a smattering of houses, a post office and a general store. The place had an empty, forbidding atmosphere. An old sunburnt woman squinted at them from her front stoop as they went by. Aidan thought Lana's mother almost certainly had a point about this town.

They passed a sign that read *Trespassers Will Be Shot*.

Lana fiddled with her seat belt. 'I feel like someone could shoot you here, bury you on the mountain and no one would ever know or care.'

'Me specifically?'

She patted his knee. 'I'd care.'

Was it Aidan's imagination, or did she keep her hand there, on his knee, for a second longer than she needed to? It sparked an image of her leaning across to kiss him, then pulling over by the side of the road and climbing into the back seat; the danger they were in, these creepy surroundings, adding heat and urgency and—

'We're looking for Dogwood Bluff Road,' Lana said.

'Huh?' Snapped out of his fantasy, he felt simultaneously a little ridiculous and annoyed that he couldn't have lived in it a little longer. She had that amused look in her eyes that told him she'd noticed; had been able to see into his mind. He cleared his throat. 'I assume you're waiting till we find it before you unveil your brilliant plan?'

'Wait. I thought you were the one with a brilliant plan?'

They crossed a bridge, and soon they were climbing a hill.

'I feel like I'm in that movie,' Aidan said.

'*The Blair Witch Project*?'

'No, *Deliverance*.'

'Wrong state. That was Georgia.' She started to hum the duelling banjos tune.

'Hang on, what's that?' Aidan said.

They were halfway up a steep hill that led into thick trees. There was a quad bike parked at an angle on the side of the road. Abandoned. There, just up the slope, was another sign: *Private Property. Turn Back Now.*

Aidan slowed and wound down the window to get a better look at the quad bike, a gnawing sensation in his belly. There were fresh tracks in the dust beside it. As he wondered what it was doing here, he heard an engine somewhere in the distance. A car engine.

'There's someone behind us,' he said.

Lana tilted her head, then nodded. The noise grew louder. Whoever was behind them was catching up. They were driving fast, the engine snarling like there was something wrong with the exhaust.

'Don't slow down,' said Lana, craning her neck to look out the back window. Aidan noticed her glance at the glovebox, where the guns were.

'It could be anyone,' he said. 'Maybe someone who could help us. Someone who knows where Scarlett is.'

He looked in the rear-view mirror as Lana turned back to face the front.

'Look out!' she yelled.

There was a car parked sideways across the road ahead of them. Aidan stamped on the brake and slammed to a halt a foot away from the car, a brown Chevrolet. If they'd been going downhill instead of up they would have smashed into it. There were two men in the car, and the one who was closest, in the passenger seat, stared straight into Aidan's eyes.

Aidan immediately tried to reverse, but Lana touched his arm and nodded at the mirror. The car they'd heard before, which was actually a white pickup truck, was coming up the hill behind them. It pulled to a halt, blocking their retreat.

'Too late,' she said.

A man with a head as smooth as a hard-boiled egg got out of the car in front, and another man got out of the pickup truck. The bald man from the Chevy strode towards Aidan and Lana's car.

Aidan's hand went towards the glovebox but Lana stopped him.

'Not a good idea,' she said, nodding towards the bald man. He stood there with his legs planted apart and his arms folded.

Lana wound down the window and put on her most winning smile. 'Hi.'

The man from the pickup truck, who was wearing a red plaid shirt, was walking around the back of their car, looking at it like it was the saddest vehicle he'd ever seen.

The bald man said, 'What are you doing here? Are you lost?'

'Looking for a friend,' Aidan replied.

'Oh yeah?' He scratched behind his ear. 'What friend?'

'His name's Lorenzo.'

The two men looked at each other.

'What do you want with Lorenzo?' said the bald guy.

'We have a message for him,' Aidan said. 'From Mayor Hood.'

The bald man came a little closer. 'Christopher Hood? Go on, then, what is it?'

'We need to deliver it directly to Lorenzo.'

'Well, here I am,' said the bald man.

During this exchange, Aidan noticed that the man in the plaid shirt was studying Lana closely. Then, in the silent moment after Lorenzo told them his name, Plaid Shirt whispered in his colleague's ear.

Now they were both staring at Lana.

'Tell you what,' Lorenzo said. 'Why don't you come with us. Leave your car here and we'll give you a ride.'

Lana glanced at the glovebox, like she was regretting not getting the guns out before. Then she sighed and opened her door, getting out. Aidan did the same.

As Plaid Shirt escorted them to the back seat of the Chevy, Lorenzo nodded at the quad bike and said, 'Bring that too.'

Aidan watched as Plaid Shirt and the third man, who'd got out of the truck to help, strained to lift the quad bike onto the back of the pickup.

This is it, Aidan thought. *I'm never going to find Scarlett. And they're never going to find me.* All his bravado from earlier seemed very foolish now.

Beside him, Lana had gone pale and quiet, staring straight ahead. She looked as sick as he felt. Catching him watching her, she reached out and took his hand.

ʊ

The road narrowed to a single track as they climbed. Every so often there was a gap in the trees that gave Aidan a full view of the valley below, the Eel River snaking through the forest, the neighbouring mountains so crowded with vegetation they looked like they were made not from rock but from trees. The sky was sheer blue and as cloudless as he'd ever seen it. But he was too scared to find anything beautiful right now. In the driver's seat, Lorenzo barely spoke. The pickup truck trundled up the hill behind them.

They reached a chain-link fence, guarded by a man with a dog, a German shepherd, that came bounding towards the car as it pulled to a stop, jumping up excitedly. Then it spotted the strangers on the back seat and barked, sinking low to the ground and baring its teeth.

The gate – above which was a sign that read *Sugar Magnolia Farm* – was opened, and both vehicles drove through, leaving the dog and its handler behind, and when they rounded another bend, Aidan gasped.

Stretched out before them, in a clearing between the trees, was an area as big as three football pitches which contained row upon row of huge, arched greenhouses. Aidan couldn't see inside the greenhouses as they were fully covered with white plastic sheeting, but he knew what they contained.

'Marijuana,' he said, not realising he'd spoken aloud until Lorenzo chuckled.

'What did you think we grew up here? Roses?' He turned in his seat and spoke with obvious pride. 'Welcome to Sugar Magnolia. Biggest weed farm in Humboldt County.'

Lorenzo got out of the car.

'Wait here,' he said through the open door. In the meantime the pickup truck had pulled up behind them and Plaid Shirt had got out, standing by the Chevy with his arms folded. Aidan watched Lorenzo stride across the farm, between the huge greenhouses, until he disappeared from view.

When he reappeared, he had someone with him. A young man. But they were too far away for Aidan to make out his features.

Lana had been staring into her lap, but when Lorenzo reappeared, Aidan nudged her and she looked up to see the two men coming towards them.

She was in tears before she got the door open. She half fell out of the car in her haste, one knee hitting the dirt, but she was back on her feet in seconds and then she was running, arms stretched out before her, and the young man was running towards her too.

Lorenzo smiled at Aidan through the window.

'I thought I recognised her,' he said. 'He's got her photo in his wallet. Her, his mom and his girlfriend.'

But Aidan was hardly listening.

He was watching Lana embrace her brother.

Chapter 23

'I'm gonna tie him to a chair – no, I'm gonna *nail* him to a chair – and then I'll take the sharpest blade I can find and cut off his—'

Shannon paused to take a breath. She was soaked with sweat, smeared with grime, and thirstier than she'd ever been in her life. They'd found a little brook a while back and she'd lapped at the water from her cupped hands, trying not to think about the animals that might have crapped and pissed in it, the bacteria. Oh, how she longed for a chilled bottle of Shastina Spring, fresh from the cooler, streaked with condensation. There had been a time when she had been violently opposed to plastic bottles, but since she'd realised it didn't matter – recycling wasn't going to save the planet – she had relaxed and bought a truckload from Mayor Hood; crates of the stuff were stored in a barn back at the Ranch.

Cody walked a step behind her. He'd hardly spoken since Darryl Moses had taken the Jeep and told them to walk. He had his phone in his hand.

'You got a signal yet?' she asked. Both their phones had lost all bars as soon as they'd come off the mountain. Even the GPS wasn't working, so they couldn't check Google Maps, but Cody said he was confident they were heading east. He remembered driving past a store on their way here. A place that would sell water and have a landline so they could call Jimmy.

He checked his cell. 'Nope.'

'Me either. Jesus. I'm going to—' And she launched into another satisfying revenge fantasy involving nipples and scrotums and clamps and razors. It spurred her on. Made her feel a tiny bit better as they trudged along the hot road.

'The joy house,' she said under her breath.

'I heard they had cathouses hidden away around here,' Cody said.

She stepped into his path. 'Visited them, have you?'

'Shit, no.' He puffed his chest out. 'I don't need to pay for it.'

'Oh, I'm sure, Cody. You're a big man, aren't you? But not as big a man as Darryl Moses.'

'There were two of them with guns . . .'

Shannon wasn't listening. 'Darryl Moses is going to learn. When the fire peels the skin from his bones and the smoke blocks his lungs. They're all going to burn, Cody. *All* the big men. *All* the swinging dicks who've ruled this planet for so long, with their big cars and their big plans and their big appetites. Well, their time has run out!' Spittle flew from her lips. 'They're the ones who are going to be ravaged and burned! And do you know what fire leaves, Cody?'

'I don't—'

'Ashes, that's what fire leaves! And do you know what rises from the ashes?'

He blinked at her, sweat dripping into his eyes, and she turned away, disgusted by his stupidity, returning to her fantasies about revenge. Thinking about men. For some reason, her thoughts turned to her childhood. To her stepfather.

Derrick had been kind of a dick. Not mean, not a big man, but weak. Full of bitterness and regret, always spouting off about immigrants and liberals and all the people he imagined spent their lives trying to figure out how to make his life more miserable. He was easy to manipulate, though. As a child, Shannon had figured out how to twist him around her little finger, and he often came home from his shift as a blackjack dealer in Reno bearing gifts for her and her mom. Their trailer had been full of stuffed animals and dolls and cheap necklaces and trinkets.

A few years back, after she got the call saying her mom and Derrick were dead, after that truck hit them driving home from Reno one night, Shannon had gone back to Sun Valley to clear out the trailer. All those old toys were still there, crammed into a cupboard, cascading onto her when she opened the door. And Derrick had left her another surprise: a life insurance payout. Not a fortune, but enough to change the direction of her life.

'Come on,' she snapped at Cody. 'We've got a long way to go.'

An hour passed. Then two. The sun continued to beat down and the thirst got worse. Her feet hurt, her sneakers rubbing at her heel so that every step was agony. Despite the yoga and the clean eating and the Peloton bike she rode every day in her private gym in the Ranch house, she was not as fit as she'd thought, and that only added to her fury.

She went back to plotting revenge.

Nobody fucked with her like Darryl Moses had.

Like a cloud passing in front of the sun, her hatred of him blotted out the fury she felt towards Lana Carrera and Aidan Faith. They could wait. Right now, all that mattered was wiping that smirk off Darryl's hick face.

'How much further?' she demanded.

'I don't know. I'm sorry.'

'I'm going to die of thirst,' she said. 'You're going to have to go look for a stream or something. I can't—'

She broke off. He was grinning at her.

'What is it?' she asked, barely daring to hope.

He held up his phone like he'd just won the state lottery.

'I got a signal,' he said.

Chapter 24

Samuel was alive. All Aidan could do was stand and stare as Lana hugged him so hard Aidan feared she might break one of his ribs, tears streaming down her face. Finally, she let go of him and stepped back, still holding on to his arm, not wanting to break contact with him. She kept saying his name, and Samuel was smiling, tears in his own eyes.

Lorenzo stood watching too, with a goofy grin on his face. The other man, the one in the plaid shirt, had wandered off.

Aidan had to fight back the urge to ask a million questions. What was Samuel doing here? Why hadn't he been in touch with his family? And the big one: did any of these men know where Scarlett was?

Lana had already started asking Samuel most of these questions herself, firing them at him even as she clung to him.

'Hey, Samuel,' said Lorenzo. 'Why don't we go up to the house, pour some lemonade, and we can all sit down and answer your sister's questions.'

Lana had stepped away from her brother, giving Aidan a good look at him. He was over six feet tall, lanky and handsome with short black hair. The resemblance to his sister was striking – they had the same eyes, identical lips – but Samuel seemed softer and calmer.

'Can I freshen up first?' he asked. He gestured at the white scrubs he was wearing, which were damp and stained green.

'Sure,' said Lorenzo. 'We'll meet you at the house in ten, okay?'

They watched him hurry away, heading towards a barn beyond the greenhouses. 'I don't want to let him out of my sight,' Lana said.

'While we're waiting, why don't I give you the tour?' Lorenzo said. He was keen to show off the farm, like a father wanting to introduce everyone to his new baby, and Aidan and Lana allowed him to lead them across the dirt and onto a path between the greenhouses.

'Jesus,' Lana said, putting her hand to her nose.

Lorenzo giggled. 'Stinks, don't it? Except I'm so used to it I can hardly smell it. Only when the crop's in full bloom.' He opened the door of the nearest greenhouse and beckoned them inside, shutting the door behind him. 'A sight to behold, isn't it?'

And Aidan had to admit, it was. The greenhouse was packed with vivid green cannabis plants. There must have been a thousand of them, probably more. The smell and the heat were almost unbearable. Within moments of stepping into the greenhouse, sweat had soaked through Aidan's T-shirt. Lana was drenched too, dark patches blooming beneath her armpits.

Lorenzo went deeper into the greenhouse, gesturing for them to follow. A couple of workers, wearing white protective scrubs like Samuel's, drifted between the plants, including a young woman with dirty blonde hair that was covered with a plastic hairnet, who was taking cuttings and dropping them into a plastic bin. She nodded a greeting before returning to her work.

'How many greenhouses do you have?' Aidan asked. They stretched as far as the eye could see.

'They're actually called hoop houses,' said Lorenzo.

The sound of a car engine came from outside.

'Nancy's back,' said Lorenzo.

'Nancy?'

'The boss lady.'

He sauntered back out into the blinding sunlight, Aidan and Lana following.

The car that had come through the gate was a black Range Rover. The driver's door opened and a woman got out – presumably Nancy. She was in her sixties, Aidan guessed, with long chestnut-coloured hair streaked with grey. She looked over at them, a hand shading her eyes.

'Hey, Nancy,' Lorenzo called.

'Who do we have here?' she said, looking them up and down. She was slim and fit-looking, in a pair of jeans and a Grateful Dead T-shirt. The same logo that Mayor Hood had doodled in his notebook. Lorenzo whispered something in her ear and she looked surprised, then concerned.

'So you're Lana,' she said. 'Samuel talks about you all the time. His awesomely clever college-student sister, the one his mom is so proud of, who helped protect him from bullies when he was a kid. He told us some story about when he was in fourth grade and these little assholes started hitting him with all these vile racist slurs and you fixed it. Scared 'em so bad they never went near him again.'

'I remember that. Those kids still live on our trailer park. They're still assholes.'

'You're his hero,' said Nancy, and Lana looked simultaneously thrilled and embarrassed. 'Come with me.' Nancy walked away towards a wooden house on the east side of the property. They followed, with Lorenzo coming too.

They entered the house – blissfully air-conditioned – and Nancy led them into the kitchen. It smelled like someone had been making jam in here recently, sweet and mouth-watering. Lana kept looking towards the door, like someone in a restaurant waiting for their date to turn up. Nancy told them to sit down at the large

183

dining table, and Lorenzo went to the fridge and took out a large jug of what looked like homemade lemonade. He poured a glass for each of them.

'You're honoured to meet Nancy,' he said. 'This woman was instrumental in getting cannabis legalised in this state.'

'And what a mistake that was,' said Nancy.

'A mistake? How come?' Lana asked, dragging her attention away from the door.

Nancy sighed. 'We've been doing this a long time. We weren't quite in the first wave of growers, but we came here in the seventies.'

'"We"?'

'My husband, Trent, and me.' She indicated a framed photo on the wall which showed a younger Nancy, in full hippie garb, with her arms around a shirtless man with shoulder-length hair and a straggly beard. 'That was taken at Woodstock,' she said. 'First time I saw the Dead play live.'

'You were beautiful,' said Lana. 'I mean, you still are, but . . .'

'It's okay. We *were* beautiful, weren't we?' Nancy's eyes misted over as she looked at the photograph, a sad smile on her lips. 'We came here shortly after that. Dropped out.'

'I don't think I've ever met any real hippies before,' said Aidan. 'There was a kid at my school whose mum smoked pot and kept a goat in their back garden, and she was always trying to get us to listen to Pink Floyd, but the closest she got to Woodstock was watching documentaries about it.'

'So you dropped out and came to Birches Rock,' Lana said, with another glance at the door. 'Why here? I mean, it's got a bad rep.'

Nancy smiled. 'This was a wonderful place back then. A real community. And it wasn't all about money. It was about freedom and liberation and not being beholden to the Man.' She looked out of the kitchen window and Aidan followed her gaze towards the hoop houses, resisting the urge to start asking questions about Samuel. 'It wasn't industrial like it is now.'

'So why did you campaign for legalisation?' Lana asked.

'Because we were tired of constantly being busted. Of having our crops destroyed. And we thought if it was legalised it would drive out the people who'd taken over most of the growing. Most of that first wave – those who truly believed in the positive power of the herb – gave up a long time ago. There's only a few of us old-timers left now.'

Aidan had drained his glass of lemonade while he listened – it was the best lemonade he'd ever tasted – and Nancy gestured for him to go ahead and refill.

'And these . . . gangsters,' Nancy went on, spitting out the word. 'They don't care about anything but getting rich. Unfortunately, legalisation has hardly improved the situation at all. We legal growers now have a million goddamn rules and regulations to follow – and a lot of taxes to pay – while the criminals have moved their grows onto public land or underground. We got the county sheriff saying the amount of illegal pot in this area is dwindling, and they're sending in the National Guard and using all this fancy satellite technology to spot grows, but . . .' She stopped. 'Sorry, you got me riding my hobby horse. I could go on and on for hours. Ah, here's the man of the hour.'

Samuel came into the kitchen, a sheepish grin on his face. Lana got up and went over to him, unable to resist another hug.

'I keep thinking I'm hallucinating you,' she said. 'Though the hallucination smells a lot better now you've washed up.'

Aidan thought he might burst if he didn't find out the answers to his questions soon. As Samuel took a seat next to Lana at the table, Aidan said, 'You need to tell us everything. What are you doing here?'

Samuel glanced at his sister.

'It's cool,' she said. 'This is Aidan. He's a friend. He's in California looking for his sister.'

'Her name's Scarlett Faith,' Aidan said, looking from face to face, hoping one of them would say, *Oh, Scarlett! She works here too!* But, of course, they all returned blank looks.

He got his phone out and showed them her photo. More blank looks.

'Sorry,' said Nancy, although Aidan noticed her and Lorenzo exchanging a concerned look. 'What happened to her?'

He told her the short version of the story.

'Oh, honey.' To his surprise, she gestured for him to stand and pulled him into a hug. He resisted for a second – he hardly knew her and he wasn't the kind of person who felt comfortable hugging strangers – but he found himself surrendering, melting into the moment. She smelled faintly of lavender, the scent his mother always wore. He closed his eyes and imagined this *was* his mum; his mum, who hadn't embraced him in a very long time. For the millionth time, he pictured himself delivering good news to her. Telling her he'd found Scarlett.

Then they all turned to look at Samuel. And he told them why he was here.

ϖ

'The night before all the shit went down, I was at Elizabeth's house. We were studying in her room. Watching a movie too.' He looked slightly sheepish saying this, although Elizabeth had told them her dad had made them keep the door open. 'Wait, is Elizabeth safe?'

'We think so,' Lana replied. 'The mayor's sent her to the East Coast, to settle there before she starts college. But we saw her yesterday. She misses you like crazy.'

His eyes filled with tears. 'I miss her too.'

'But back to your story,' Aidan coaxed.

Samuel cleared his throat. 'Sorry. So, Elizabeth fell asleep after the movie ended, and I knew that was it, she was out for the night, so I went to let myself out of the house. When I got downstairs I could hear Mayor Hood in his study, talking to a woman. Except it wasn't *talking*. It sounded like they were fighting, you know? So I stopped to listen.'

'Why did you do that?' Lana asked.

'I don't know. Shit, I regret it now but . . . I was curious. I thought maybe it was a business thing, something to do with Shastina Spring. Elizabeth knew I had a problem with how her dad makes money – bottled water is one of the most wasteful, polluting products in the world – and, I don't know, I thought maybe I'd overhear something useful.'

Aidan opened his mouth to ask a question but Nancy raised a hand, indicating for him to wait. Samuel went on.

'Like I said, they were arguing. I guess I was kind of paralysed, and then suddenly the door opened and there was this woman I'd never seen before, standing in the doorway, staring at me. I guess I must have mumbled something – something dumb like "I didn't hear anything" – and then I got out of there as fast as I could.'

Lorenzo poured him a glass of lemonade and he took a long drink.

'I got in my car and started driving home, and five minutes down the road I got a call from the mayor telling me he needed to talk to me. Urgently. He told me to meet him in the park first thing in the morning and that I shouldn't tell anyone where I was going or what I was doing.'

'So you met up with him,' Aidan prompted. He thought back over what Elizabeth had already told them. That morning the wild-fires had been close to Eaglewood, but hadn't yet reached the out-skirts of the town.

'Yeah. It was real early. I heard Mom come in from her night shift and go straight to bed. And Mayor Hood was freaking out. Like, super-angry with me for eavesdropping. I told him I hadn't actually heard anything but he said it didn't matter. All that mattered was the woman he'd been with thought I might have.'

'Who was the woman?' Lana asked. Aidan guessed she was as surprised as him to discover the mayor had been talking to a woman and not Jimmy.

'He said her name was Shannon Reinhardt.'

Aidan looked at Lana, who shrugged to indicate she'd never heard of her.

Samuel went on. 'The mayor said she was bad news. That she was part of this crazy organisation that didn't want anyone to know of its existence, and that she would kill me to keep me quiet – along with anyone she thought I might have told. That included Elizabeth. Even Mom, if they thought I'd said anything to her.'

'What the *hell*?' Lana said.

Samuel sniffed, his eyes brimming with tears. 'We had this big fight about whether or not I'd heard anything, and he said it again: it didn't matter. Like I said, he was mad, but he seemed scared too.'

'Because of the threat to Elizabeth?'

'Yeah. But more than that. He seemed . . . I don't know, like, in way over his head. Like a guy who's made a deal with the Devil and now he regrets it.'

The room was silent. All Aidan could hear was the faint hum of the refrigerator.

'I really thought he was going to hand me over to them, but then he said, "You love my daughter, don't you? And I know she loves you." He told me again that it wasn't safe for me in Eaglewood anymore, and that's when he called Nancy.'

'We've known each other a long time,' Nancy said. 'Believe it or not, Chris Hood's something of an old hippie too. Another Deadhead. I met him at one of their gigs.'

Samuel went on. 'The mayor drove me into the forest. He had the radio on and everyone on there was talking about the wildfires, about how they were getting closer to the town. By the time we got to Humboldt County, the reporters were saying the fires were almost sure to hit Eaglewood. The mayor was thumping the wheel and cursing and muttering about how he didn't have time for all this, that maybe he should just hand me over to Shannon and be done with it.'

He blinked at Lana, close to tears again, and she put her arm around his shoulders.

'It's okay, honey, I can take over from here,' said Nancy. 'Chris had already called me, told me Elizabeth's boyfriend was in danger, and we'd figured out a plan. The wildfire gave us the perfect cover story. Samuel took some persuading, but I told him he'd be safe here. That he just needed to lie low for a while, work here on the farm until this Shannon, whoever the hell she is, and her people had forgotten about him. Then we heard about the missing hikers and that helped our cover story. Chris just had to have a word with the cops and spread the rumour that Samuel had met up with them – suffered the same fate.'

Aidan turned to Samuel. 'So what *did* you hear? You said they were talking in raised voices.'

Samuel looked pained. 'It was confusing. I couldn't make all of it out. But at one point the mayor said, "But it's slavery."'

'*Slavery?*'

'Yeah. And she, Shannon, said something like, "Where do you think the money comes from?"'

Aidan and Lana stared at each other. 'Holy shit,' Lana said. 'We were right. They're trafficking people.'

'There was something else too,' Samuel said. 'On the way here, I admitted to the mayor that I'd overheard something about slavery. He went quiet for a minute, and then he said, "That's only the half of it. The other place is even worse."'

'What did he mean by that?'

'I don't know. He didn't say anything else to me. But he went pale and started muttering to himself.'

'Could you make out what he was saying?'

Samuel nodded. 'He said, "Forgive me, God. Please forgive me."'

Chapter 25

When Shannon left her with the men, Kristin had still been trying to emerge from the fog of confusion. Who were these men? How were they connected to her mission? Jimmy had come to her room, given her a drink and told her she was being taken into the field, that they had been so impressed by her that she was being fast-tracked. He'd told her they were going to rendezvous with some allies who would take her to the next point and explain the details of her mission. She had been thrilled and excited, if a little nervous. But, waking up with a guy snapping his fingers in front of her face, she'd realised she had no memory of anything after her conversation with Jimmy. These men didn't look like environmental activists. Why was she in the back of a vehicle? And why did her head hurt and the world look so fuzzy?

The argument between the men with the quad bikes and Shannon and the blond man had been like listening to dogs bark. Then Shannon and the man were walking away and rough hands had lifted Kristin back into the Jeep and the door had slammed shut again. Her head had throbbed and she'd wanted to sleep, but the bumping of the vehicle had made it impossible.

After a shuddering journey, the trunk had been opened again and the same rough hands had pulled Kristin out and thrown her to the ground. A man in a baseball cap had given her tepid water to drink, then he'd said, 'Put her to work.'

'In the joy house?'

'No, you idiot. Not yet. Let's get some actual work out of her first.'

Now, hours later, sweltering beneath the glass of the hoop house, her arms and legs and back aching, her head still throbbing, Kristin realised she'd been betrayed, and she wished she'd never come to California, never heard of Shannon Reinhardt, never left her dorm in Spokane. She missed her college friends. Missed her mom and dad. She wanted to rewind time. Go back. Change every decision she'd made since she'd been invited to join that secret WhatsApp group.

She was too deep in thought and regret to see the man come up behind her. A hand slapped her hard on the back of the head.

'Quit daydreaming,' said the man. He picked up some of the buds Kristin had already trimmed. 'Look at this! Jesus, man. Darryl is gonna go fucking postal if he sees this. Hey, you. Yeah, you.' The man called over a younger guy who was working on a table across the way. 'Come and show the noob how to do it right.'

The man stalked away and the younger guy, who Kristin guessed was in his early twenties but who looked much older thanks to his scruffy beard and sallow skin, came over. Like everyone here, he wore scant protective gear. A pair of plastic gloves with holes in the fingers. A mask that looked like it had been fashioned out of an old handkerchief. His hair was long and dirty, and his eyes were pink and bloodshot but kind.

He told her his name was Cameron.

'Here,' he said, sitting beside Kristin and taking the scissors from her hand. His sleeves were rolled up and she noticed he had *NO PLANET B* tattooed on his forearm. He took a bud out of the bucket in the centre of the table and showed her how to carefully

192

trim it. 'You need to snip away the leaves, like this. Didn't anyone show you?'

'Kind of,' Kristin said. 'But I was so freaked out I didn't really take it in. Plus the people who brought me here gave me ket or something.'

'You were at the Ranch?'

She stared at him. 'You too?'

'Most of us were. Feel pretty bloody dumb now.'

'Are you British?' she asked, noticing his accent.

'Australian,' he said with a smile. 'I won't take offence.'

'Hey, quit gossiping!' yelled the guard.

Cameron flinched like someone who was used to being beaten. 'Here, you take a turn.' He passed Kristin the scissors and told her to give it a try.

'That's a lot better,' he said as Kristin trimmed the plant. 'You're getting the hang of it already.'

'How many do I have to do?'

'You just sit here and do as many as you can. Just don't do less than fifty an hour or they'll punish you.'

Kristin swallowed. She felt sick and dizzy from the stench of the cannabis. She had already decided she was never, ever going to smoke weed again, no matter how long she lived. And trimming the cannabis buds was already proving to be hard, fiddly work. 'Punish?'

'Sorry. Don't want to scare you. It's your first day.'

But even as Cameron said it, Kristin heard a shout from outside, and a cry of pain. Somebody shouted, 'Please, I didn't mean—' and then there was a cracking sound, a scream.

Cameron tried to give her a reassuring look. 'Keep your head down, don't screw up, you'll be fine.'

'What if I need water? Or the bathroom?'

193

'You'll get a five-minute bathroom break every couple of hours. Though I wouldn't exactly call it a bathroom. It's more of a bucket. And the water . . . It'll make you sick at first, but you don't have a choice. You'll die if you don't drink it. And pray they don't send you to work in the meth lab. Or the fucking joy house.'

'I heard them mention that. Is it . . . ?'

He nodded grimly. 'It's where a lot of the women end up once they're too worn out to do anything else. A few of the guys too.'

The guard was coming back towards them between the rows of plants. He carried a rifle and looked like his hobby was beating dogs for fun.

'You'd think they'd look after us better,' Cameron said. 'They paid for us, after all.'

'They didn't pay for me,' Kristin said, wondering if this made her even more disposable. 'The asshole who brought me here said I was a gift.'

Cameron gave her a look of pity. 'I'd better get back to my table,' he said. 'Remember, shoot for at least fifty an hour. And no more than sixty. You won't get any reward for it. And don't try to suck up to the guards. You're better off staying under their radar. Keep your head down and you'll survive.'

The guard was almost back now.

Cameron moved to go back to his table but paused for a second. 'You know all that stuff Shannon used to say about the world burning? How everything was gonna end soon? That's why I came here. I'd seen the bush fires back home. Felt the world heating up. The apocalypse, happening in our lifetime.' He traced the letters of his tattoo with a grimy finger. 'After a few days here, you'll start to hope she was right.'

Chapter 26

The trucks came rumbling into the clearing, sending up a cloud of dust. Shannon struggled to her feet. Every muscle in her legs ached, her blisters screamed, and her mouth was so dry that when Jimmy hopped down from the front truck and she tried to speak to him, to ask for water, nothing came out but a rasping croak.

Thankfully, he understood what she was getting at.

'Sorry it took us a little longer to get here than we anticipated.' He seemed better today. More himself. 'We had to detour around a fire outside Redding and it's even worse down south. They're evacuating north of the Bay. There are fires in Tahoe too. And San Luis Obispo. Monterey. There's even one out near Sacramento. A sand fire.'

Their eyes met.

'It's happening,' he said. 'Just like you said it would.'

'Never doubt me, Jimmy.'

The water in the bottle of Shastina Spring that Jimmy gave her was the sweetest, most delicious liquid she had ever tasted. Somewhere in the back of her head, as she drank, she thought about Mayor Chris Hood and wondered what was going on in Eaglewood right now. The mayor knew more than Shannon was comfortable with. Now, with the end approaching more quickly than she had ever anticipated, there were going to be loose ends to tie up. People who knew about the other place. Who might, in their desperation to escape the coming flames, come knocking.

That couldn't be allowed to happen. But first she had to deal with Darryl Moses.

'Any news about Faith and Carrera?' Shannon asked.

'Oh yeah. I meant to tell you. A guy I buy beer from called me. Seems he had an encounter with them. Guess where they were heading?'

'Here?'

'Nailed it.'

She walked over to the trucks. In the backs of both trucks were all the remaining recruits from the Ranch. Her army.

They were about to be tested.

She strolled back to Jimmy, who was talking to Cody and smoking a cigarette. The stumps of Jimmy's missing fingers were bandaged and he was holding the cigarette between the forefinger and thumb of his right hand. She decided, just this once, not to chide him for smoking.

'You should rest,' he said. 'Have some food and take a nap.'

'I don't need a *nap*. But yes, I should rest.'

She climbed into the cab of one of the trucks and one of the recruits brought her some food: a protein bar and a banana. She put the radio on and listened to the updates about the spreading fires. There was a debate about whether they were caused by climate change, with some nut claiming it was all part of the cycle of nature, that the climate emergency was a hoax. Shannon hoped he'd be sorry when he watched his house burn down, saw his family choke to death on the smoke.

ϖ

On Christmas Day 2012, when she was twenty-seven years old, Shannon woke up on the cold floor of a strange apartment, half-dressed and covered in her own vomit. She had no idea where she was or how she had got there. There was a naked man on the couch. An empty bottle of vodka lay by her head, beside an ashtray, cigarette butts strewn all around. She went into the bathroom, where she found a used needle in the filthy basin. A baby was crying through the wall of the next apartment.

Shannon gulped down water straight from the faucet and threw up into the toilet. She was shaking and couldn't remember the last time she'd eaten, but glimpses of the night before were coming back to her. The bar, the club, the dance floor, a man, an alleyway, a blonde girl with an angry face and sharp fists, another man, smoke rising from silver paper, cigarettes. She saw herself on her hands and knees on a dirty rug, bottles and pills and the sound of breaking glass.

Shannon sank to her haunches and sobbed.

Still sobbing, she stripped and got under the shower, expecting a lukewarm dribble but surprised by the heat and ferocity of the water. She found a bar of soap, tried not to think about who'd used it before her, and scrubbed herself clean.

She left her filthy, puke-stained clothes in a bundle in the bathtub, found a pair of men's skinny jeans and a Guns N' Roses T-shirt in a drawer, and left the snoring man on the couch behind. In a daze, she staggered home to her tiny apartment in north-west Reno. There was no one around. Christmas morning – everyone was with their family. For maybe the first time, she missed her mom and Derrick.

She couldn't face her empty apartment. Instead, she got into her car and drove out to Lake Tahoe, acting without thinking, as if God were whispering instructions to her. She pulled into an empty public parking lot near Kings Beach and walked down the trail to the lookout. The cold breeze that blew in from the lake made her shiver but woke her up. Her head throbbed and she was sore in her stomach and between her legs. The inside of her mouth felt like she'd been chewing fur. For once, her body recoiled from thoughts of alcohol and drugs and sex.

What had she done with her life?

What had happened to the little girl she once was?

She couldn't even blame her current screwed-up state on the truck that had killed her mom and stepdad. She'd gone off the rails even before she graduated high school. Smoking weed with all the boys who did whatever she told them to. The months she spent hanging out with that biker gang. The menial jobs that came and went. The men who gave her drugs and paid for her drinks.

For years, she had been telling anyone who listened that she was having fun. But she was numb. So numb that when she found out Derrick and her mom were dead, she couldn't even cry. She'd hardly even smiled when she found out about the life insurance payout.

Suddenly – and maybe it was because it was Christmas and an image of herself as a child, sitting by the tree, giddy with joy as she unwrapped gifts, kept flickering in her mind's eye – the numbness was gone. The anaesthetic had worn off.

Suddenly, she could feel everything.

All the pain. It was as if she'd been flayed. Skin stripped, nerves exposed.

She screamed.

Kept screaming.

Next thing she knew she was on her hands and knees beside the path, her throat raw, head ringing. She looked up, tentatively, as if there might be a crowd gathered around, gawking at her distress. But there was no one around.

Except for a small bird, black with a yellow head. It landed on the path beside her, and Shannon was struck hard by a crazy notion. One of the men she'd hung out with was into yoga and spiritual shit and he was always going on about reincarnation, about how everybody came back, again and again, in different bodies, as cats or rats, tigers or roaches, until they found enlightenment.

'Mom?' Shannon whispered to the bird. 'Is that you?'

The bird tilted its head and regarded her.

'Do you have a message for me?' She was aware that she was being crazy. But screw it. There was nobody around to hear her. 'What . . . what should I do?'

The bird took off.

It flew towards the lake. South.

It took her a week to make preparations. She visited a sexual health clinic and got herself tested, and was amazed and relieved to find everything was negative. She found someone to take over her apartment. She sold her car and everything else she owned, all except her backpack and some clothes and shoes. And with that money, plus the little she had left over from the life insurance payout, she bought herself a plane ticket.

Then she did what the little bird had done.

ω

Shannon lifted her head. Shit, she had dozed off, the radio still blaring with more reports about wildfires and evacuations. She drank some more water and got out of the truck, going over to where Jimmy and Cody stood talking. While she'd been resting, many of the recruits had got out of the trucks and were milling around, chatting, stretching their legs. They reminded Shannon of children on a field trip.

Jimmy was saying something to Cody. '. . . like the fires are spreading north. We ought to get on our way.'

'But Shannon wants—' Cody fell silent the moment he realised Shannon was standing there beside them.

'Shannon wants what?' she asked.

'The same as me,' Cody replied.

'What are you two talking about?' asked Jimmy.

'Moses.'

'Darryl?' said Jimmy. 'I really don't think that's a good idea. We don't know how many men he's got. Plus, it's his land. His turf.'

Shannon jabbed a finger in his direction. 'You think it's okay to let him threaten me? Do you? To steal our Jeep and leave us stranded? I know he's your buddy . . .'

'He's not my buddy. I can't stand the guy. We do business with him, that's all.'

'Did you know they've got a brothel up there?'

'I didn't.' He hardly seemed surprised, though.

'It's vile. Those women, they came from the Ranch.'

'I didn't think you cared what happened to them,' Jimmy said.

Her blood was hot beneath her skin. 'I thought they were being sent there to work on the farm. Not . . . do that.'

'Shannon, with all due respect—'

She cut him off. 'I want them back.'

'What?'

'The recruits who are working on the farm. I want them back with us. Everything has happened so much faster than we anticipated.' She gestured at the trucks. 'There's way too few of us. We're going to need a lot more bodies or we may as well just wait here and die with everyone else.'

'You really want to go in there?' Jimmy asked.

'You want me to keep repeating myself until you understand me?'

200

Cody smirked and Shannon watched the anger flash across Jimmy's face.

'We've got thirty soldiers here, right? Plus you, Cody, Frank . . . That's enough to bring Moses down.'

'Except half of them are women,' said Jimmy.

Shannon looked at him with disgust. 'Haven't you been training them to fight?'

'Yeah . . . I guess.'

'What about guns? How many?'

He did a quick calculation in his head. 'Enough.'

'That's what I thought.' She smiled. She felt a lot better. Almost as good as she'd felt the day she'd left America and flown south to begin her new life, seven years ago.

Jimmy said, 'You really want to do this? You want to risk the lives of the thirty soldiers we got here so we can bring back a couple dozen workers from Darryl's farm, all of whom are going to be in a bad way? Not to mention they know we sold them out. They're not exactly going to be eager to re-join us.'

Shannon glared at him, and she saw his Adam's apple bob. She knew, deep down, that he was talking sense. But they did need more bodies, she was confident they could keep casualties on their side to a minimum, and – most important of all – she wanted Darryl's blood.

'All right,' Jimmy said with a sigh. 'You're the boss. You've got us this far. But we should wait till it gets dark. Agreed?'

'Of course.'

'I guess I'd better put together a plan,' Jimmy said. 'I know the layout of the farm. And I need to brief the recruits.'

'You do that,' Shannon said.

She watched him go, and was left standing with Cody. She smiled at him.

'Do me a favour,' she said. 'When we're there, stick with me. And when we find Moses, I want to be the one who puts a bullet between his eyes.'

'Sure. But can I ask a favour too? If Lana's there . . .'

Shannon patted his shoulder. 'She's all yours.'

Chapter 27

Nancy and Lorenzo made lunch and, as soon as it was over, Samuel left the house to go back to the converted barn where he and the other workers slept. Lana went with him. They had a lot to catch up on. Aidan stayed behind to help clear up. As he removed dirty plates from the table, Nancy said, 'I haven't told you everything yet. Samuel's not the only stray we've taken in recently.'

'Really?'

'About a month back, all our security lights were triggered in the middle of the night. We thought it was thieves. Bandits. We have a lot of problems with people trying to sneak onto our property to steal the merchandise. But this wasn't a thief.'

Lorenzo nodded. 'We found a young, terrified woman down by the hoop houses, begging us not to hurt her.'

Nancy continued before Aidan could ask any questions. 'We took her in. She was in a terrible state. Malnourished. Covered with bruises and cuts from where she'd climbed over a barbed-wire fence. Filthy too. I put her in the bath, gave her a drink and a hot meal—'

'What was her name?' Aidan asked, unable to stop himself from interrupting.

'Emira,' she said.

'Is she still here? Can I talk to her?'

Maybe, if she was one of the people who had been trafficked, she might know something about Scarlett.

Nancy shook her head sadly. 'I'm sorry. But the morning after we found her, she left a note to thank us and snuck off. Said she needed to get as far away from here as possible. She was afraid the men who'd been holding her would find her, seeing as they're so close.'

'Close?'

'Yep,' Lorenzo said. 'The farm next to ours.'

'The Moses Farm,' said Nancy, her lip curled with contempt. 'Run by a bastard by the name of Darryl Moses.'

'Did you call the police?' Aidan asked.

'We're not exactly on good terms with the cops round here,' Lorenzo said. 'Even though we've gone legit. I guess it's been hard to get out of that mindset. We don't like them and they don't like us.'

Nancy shook her head. 'That poor girl. We were planning to let her rest up for a couple of days, then take her somewhere safe so she could get home.'

'But she panicked and bolted.'

'Did she tell you anything?' Aidan asked. 'Like, what kind of stuff they made her do?'

'It was mostly working on the farm,' Lorenzo said, his voice grim. 'But I got the impression there was other stuff she didn't want to talk about.'

'The truth is, we don't know what's going on over there,' said Nancy. 'It used to be a good farm. We've known the Moses family a long time. They've been growing pot in this part of Humboldt even longer than we have. But then Bobby and Nora both passed away and their son took over.'

'So this Darryl guy – he's still growing cannabis illegally?' Aidan asked.

'Nope,' said Lorenzo, smiling at the surprise on Aidan's face. 'They got a permit, just like us. It would be almost impossible for them to get away with it otherwise, being on privately owned land. Especially here. Birches Rock is the first place they're always going to look.'

'But we don't know what else they're up to over there,' said Nancy. 'There are rumours they're producing meth. Other stuff too. We've heard they have a brothel on the site; Lorenzo ran into some guys out on the road who were looking for it. They might have all the permits and licences to grow pot, but we think that might be a smokescreen. And we know from what Emira told us, the workers they've got . . . they don't want to be there. None of them.'

'Did Emira mention Shannon Reinhardt?' Aidan asked.

'She didn't use that name,' Nancy replied. 'But when I asked her where she'd come from and how she'd ended up on the farm, she said they'd all been betrayed.'

Aidan felt it bubble up through his blood. A weird kind of elation. They had found Samuel. And the people who were being trafficked: at least some of them were right there. Next door.

Could Scarlett be there?

Aidan got his phone out. He only had a little charge left.

'What are you doing?' Nancy asked.

'Calling the police. Don't worry, I won't mention you. I'll—'

Lorenzo snatched the phone from his hand.

'What the hell?'

'I'm sorry,' Nancy said. 'But we can't allow you to do that.'

'What, because you don't get along with the local cops?'

'You think they don't already know what's going on? You think it's different here than it's been down in Eaglewood? Darryl Moses and the local chief of police are best buddies. You call the police, they won't be heading to the Moses Farm. They'll be coming here,

205

for you – and taking you straight to the people who are after you. Shannon and this Jimmy guy.'

'Then we go to the FBI,' Aidan said. 'Or the DEA. Tell them about the meth dealing and the people trafficking.'

'The *DEA*?' Lorenzo acted like Aidan had suggested they call the Ku Klux Klan. 'We don't want those bastards, or any goddamn Feds, sniffing around here.'

'Why not?' asked Aidan. 'You're legal, aren't you?'

Lorenzo and Nancy exchanged a look. 'Mostly,' said Nancy.

'Oh, for God's sake. I don't even want to know. But my sister might be on that farm. Or someone who knows where she is.'

Aidan sensed a presence behind him. It was Lana.

'Samuel needed to rest,' she said.

'Did you hear what we were talking about?' Aidan asked.

'Some of it.' She came over and stood next to Aidan, putting a hand on his arm. 'How do we get onto Darryl Moses's farm?'

Lorenzo hesitated for a moment. 'That's not a good idea.'

'Well, if you're not going to let us call the cops, we don't have any other choice,' said Aidan angrily. 'I'm not leaving until I know whether Scarlett is there.'

'Okay, okay, I get it.' Lorenzo held up his hands in a gesture of surrender. 'You get in the same way Emira got out.'

Chapter 28

They waited till after the sun set and then they waited some more, wanting to be sure that most of the people on the neighbouring farm would be asleep. It was a clear night and the sky, so vast up here on the mountain, was festooned with stars. The temperature had dropped dramatically, though, and Aidan felt goosebumps ripple across his arms as Lorenzo – who Nancy had persuaded to show them the way – walked ahead of them, flashlight in hand as he led them to the border between the two farms.

Samuel had begged Lana not to go, pleading that it was too dangerous. Aidan had been in the next room, trying not to listen in but unable to help himself.

'We need to see if Scarlett is there,' Lana had replied. 'He helped me find you. I owe it to him.'

There had been a pause. 'Are you and this guy . . . ?'

'We're just friends,' Lana had replied. 'Barely even that. We're just helping each other.'

Aidan had stopped listening at that point, going into the bathroom and finding himself looking into a mirror. His hair was messed up and he had several days of stubble. He looked and felt like he'd aged five years since coming to California.

'You're an idiot,' he'd said to his reflection. Nothing else mattered except finding Scarlett. So why had Lana's words stung so much?

He had splashed his face with cold water and gone back into the kitchen, where he asked Lorenzo if he had a razor he could borrow.

Now, they entered a heavily wooded area on a steep slope. 'Mind where you walk,' said Lorenzo, after almost tripping over a tree root. 'You might want to turn your own flashlights on now too. But keep them dipped, okay?'

Lana and the clean-shaven Aidan did as he suggested and followed him up the incline, flashlight beams dancing low among the trees. Aidan used his free hand to push aside low branches, glad the earth beneath their feet was dry and relatively easy to traverse. He was aware of the hard, uncomfortable bulk of the pistol tucked into the waistband of his jeans, pressing against his lower back. That evening, while it was still light, Lana had given him a quick lesson. He had slain a number of pine cones.

'We could be going home tomorrow,' she had said when they finished.

'Or we might be dead.'

'That's what I like about you, Aidan. Your optimism.'

Lorenzo stopped now and shone his flashlight back towards them. 'We're here.' He shone his light at a chain-link fence that ran through the trees in front of them, dividing the two properties.

'Be thankful this isn't electrified,' Lorenzo said, taking out a pair of wire cutters. With some effort, he snipped through the wire in two places, creating a gap big enough for them to crawl through. 'There you go,' he said. 'Good luck.' Then he sighed. 'It's not too late to pull the plug on this nonsense. Come back with me. That's the smart play.'

'We'll be fine,' said Lana. 'We can handle ourselves.'

'You should have seen her in Fortuna,' Aidan said, trying to ignore the wave of sickness that was making his legs go weak. 'She was totally badass.'

'Is that right? I heard about how you blew this Jimmy guy's fingers off too. And accidentally shot a cop. Then you stumbled into Birches Rock like two little pigs strolling into an abattoir. Sounds to me like it's a miracle you two are still alive.'

'Well,' Aidan said, 'be that as it may . . .'

The two of them stepped towards the fence.

'Just hold it.' When they looked back, Lorenzo was wiping one meaty hand hard down his face. 'God help me, but I can't let you go in there on your own.'

Neither of them argued. It was all Aidan could do to stop himself from hugging the man.

'I must be goddamn crazy,' Lorenzo said. 'But you're Samuel's sister. You know how much the kid has talked about you since he got here? I don't think I could live with myself if something happened to you now.'

'Thank you,' Lana said.

'But just to be clear, first sign of trouble and I'll be back through the hole in this fence like a jackrabbit fleeing a fox. I got no intention of dying on this mountain tonight. Now, let's go before I come to my fucking senses.'

Aidan squeezed through the gap, following Lorenzo and Lana, and stood up. This was it. They were on Darryl Moses's farm. He touched his chest and felt his heart pounding beneath his palm.

'Follow me and keep quiet,' Lorenzo said in a low voice.

The forested slope finally began to level out and the trees thinned. Lorenzo pointed his flashlight to the left, revealing nothing but empty space. 'You don't want to go that way. It's a sheer cliff.'

'Noted,' said Lana.

They followed Lorenzo until they reached flat ground that was dotted with tall trees, then paused. In the moonlight, Aidan could see the outlines of a cluster of buildings in the distance, including what looked like a large barn and a couple of smaller outbuildings close by. Beyond that, rows of hoop houses and, on the far side of the property, a house that appeared to be a similar size to Nancy's.

'Emira told us they kept the workers in a kind of bunkhouse,' Lorenzo whispered.

'So we should head to the barn?'

'Uh-huh. But keep low. Use the trees for cover.'

One by one, they moved forward, Lorenzo leading, Aidan going last. Aidan noticed that Lorenzo now had his gun in his hand. Eventually, they reached a small copse of trees that had a rusty, abandoned pickup parked beside it. The three of them stopped about fifty feet away from the barn.

Close to the barn, a shadow moved. Aidan's heart leaped in his chest.

'Security,' Lorenzo whispered. 'Looks like two of them.'

Peering into the gloom, Aidan saw the shadow break in half. Lorenzo was right. There were two figures, presumably men, standing close together near the side of the barn. In the silence, if he listened hard, he could just about make out the low rumble of voices. He could see something tiny and orange, like a firefly, between them.

'They're smoking,' said Lana.

'Hopefully weed,' said Lorenzo. 'Getting high on their own supply. People are always easier to deal with when they're baked.'

'What are we going to do?' Aidan asked.

'We watch and wait. There's no way we're getting to that barn unless these two move.'

So they waited. Nothing happened. The two security guards stood close together, chatting and smoking. Behind them, all was quiet and still. Aidan could just make out a couple of lights on in the window of the farmhouse, and he wondered where the meth lab was – if indeed there was one here. He wondered how Moses explained the presence of all the trafficked workers on his farm if they were inspected, which must surely happen. Aidan guessed he must have legit labourers there too, to act as a kind of cloak. Finally, he wondered how many men Darryl Moses had working for him and how many guns they had, but then he did all he could to shut down that line of thought before it sent him fleeing back to Sugar Magnolia.

And he hadn't forgotten that Cody and Jimmy, and presumably Shannon, must still be out there somewhere, looking for them. At the very least, Moses would have got the same memo that Zach the microbrewer had got. They'd be keeping an eye out.

Lorenzo tapped Lana's arm and pointed towards the barn. One of the shadows was peeling away from the other. Lorenzo put a finger to his lips.

One of the two security guards was walking towards them. Aidan experienced a heart-in-mouth moment – had they been spotted? But as he came closer, Aidan could see the security guy was ambling, his head down. He was no longer smoking, though there was something about the way he loped towards them that made Aidan think Lorenzo's wish might have come true: the guard might well be high.

Aidan, his back pressed against a tree, was sure the guard must be able to hear his heart, it was beating so loud, but as the guard's face came into view – he was young, early twenties, with a nose that had been broken at least once – he showed no awareness that they were there.

The guard reached the copse, just a few feet from them, and stopped walking. He undid his zipper and lifted his face towards the sky.

As the sound of urine hitting the base of the tree filled the air, steam rising, Aidan watched Lorenzo sneak out from the trees, in a low crouch, silently making his way behind the man.

The guard had just begun to tuck himself away when Lorenzo rose from his crouch, clamped his forearm around the man's throat and pressed his gun to his temple.

'Don't make a noise,' Lorenzo hissed.

The guard instinctively put his hands up to grab Lorenzo's arm. Lorenzo doubled his pressure on the man's windpipe and the guard began to thrash against him, kicking and convulsing for what seemed like a long time before suddenly slumping.

Lorenzo lowered him to the ground.

'Keep your gun on him,' he said to Lana.

This didn't feel real to Aidan. It was as if he were in one of the video games he'd used to distract himself in the months following Scarlett's disappearance. Stealth games, where the aim was to creep up on your enemies and subdue them. In those games, Aidan would die many times before getting it right.

Lorenzo nudged the incapacitated guard with his foot, checking he was still out for the count. 'Now we wait till his buddy comes to investigate.'

'I thought you were going to make like a jackrabbit at the first sign of trouble,' Aidan said.

'I guess I just remembered how much I hate all these assholes,' Lorenzo replied. 'But don't tempt me.'

The guard wasn't unconscious for long. He stirred and went to rise but Lorenzo sunk to his haunches and showed the man the gun. 'Stay quiet and everything will be okay.'

The guard lay still, apparently accepting his fate. Aidan figured he wasn't paid enough to risk getting shot in the head.

'Maybe we could take the other guard out, now there's only one?' Aidan said. 'Or create a diversion?'

'Okay. Why don't you run off over there by the cliff edge waving your pants above your head and yelling "God save the Queen"?'

'What?'

'We do it my way, James Bond. We wait. The other guard will come over to investigate. Just wait and see.'

'Okay. But if that guard shows any signs of going to the house to get help, I think we should retreat.'

'Now you're talking,' Lorenzo said. 'Retreat! Hell yeah. Stick a sock in this guy's mouth, tie him up tight and get the hell out of here.'

'We're not going anywhere,' Lana said. 'We're too close.'

'Right,' Aidan said quickly.

Lorenzo grunted in disgust and peered off into the dark.

Of course Lana was right. Where had that impulse to retreat come from? From the hot, roiling ball of panic in his gut, Aidan supposed. He was learning he could feel any number of ways at once. Terror-stricken and ready to gnaw the nearest tree with frustration, for instance. If he wanted to be able to live with himself when this was all over, he needed to choose which impulses to ignore and which to follow. That choice was simple here: the barn was fifty feet away. Scarlett could be in there. After all this time, all these months, he might be *this* close to finding her.

But the remaining guard wasn't moving. In fact, he had gone closer to the barn door, seemingly unbothered by his colleague's absence. Perhaps this was a regular occurrence. Maybe he was too stoned to have a sense of how much time was passing.

'What is he doing?' Aidan whispered. 'Surely he should have come looking by now?'

'Patience,' said Lorenzo. And as he said it, the guard by the barn moved, apparently looking in their direction. 'He's finally noticed his friend's taking an unusually long time. Now, come on, man. Take the bait. That's it. Come over here.'

The guard slowly but surely made his way towards them, his face still shrouded by darkness. Aidan could see that he had a gun in his hand. This guard wasn't going to be as easy to take down as the first one.

'Come on, little fish,' Lorenzo whispered. 'Come see where your buddy's got to . . .'

The guard began to walk a little faster towards them. Then, all of a sudden, he stopped, like he'd heard something. And in the next instant, Aidan heard it too. A car engine in the near distance. Maybe more than one.

The guard turned towards the house, and hesitated. Lorenzo and Lana looked at each other, concerned. The engine noise grew louder, then stopped.

All was silent for a moment. No one moved.

Then, from somewhere near the house, came a shout.

And the unmistakeable sound of gunshots.

Chapter 29

Shannon waited in the cab of the truck, the tang of blood on her tongue, the sweet buzz of anticipation in her belly. If she were Darryl Moses, if earlier that day *she* had screwed with Shannon Reinhardt, she would have had half an army out front, ready for war. But maybe that was because she'd had to fight or work for everything she had. When you started out with nothing, you were always prepared for your something to be taken from you, and you learned to defend it. You guarded it with your life.

From what Jimmy had told her of Darryl, he was an arrogant, privileged dick, raised with the belief that the world owed him a living. He had never experienced a serious setback. He was soft.

Just like the world was soft: a turtle rolled onto its back, belly exposed, mistaking the coming conflagration for the kiss of sunshine.

Cody was waiting by the side of the cab, gun in hand.

As soon as they heard the rattle of automatic gunfire from inside the Moses Farm, Cody opened the door for her and she jumped down.

Double-checking the path was clear, they hurried through the gates, the sounds of gunshots and yells and cries of pain growing louder. Shannon pulled herself to her full height. She felt powerful. Invincible. A god come to this mountain to inspect the pathetic efforts of mortal men, striding through the summer darkness, powerful in the bright moonlight, ready to mete out the kind of justice the ancient Greeks would approve of.

Most of the shooting was coming from inside the large house to the right of the gate. Glass shattered. A woman screamed. As Shannon watched, a man came running out wearing nothing but a pair of boxer shorts. Jimmy stepped out of the front door behind the man and shot him in the back of the thigh. The man went down and rolled onto his back.

Jimmy saw Shannon watching and gestured to her, a question.

She nodded and Jimmy stepped forward, the Glock trained on the man's face.

'Please,' the man said. Blood seeped into the dusty ground beneath him, blooming in the dirt. 'I didn't do nothing.'

'Where's the joy house?' Shannon asked.

He stretched out an arm and pointed. 'Behind the barn. The cottage. Please, I can help you. I can—'

At Shannon's signal, Jimmy shot the man in the head.

Shannon and Jimmy stood over the body, with Cody beside them. 'Is Darryl dead yet?' she asked.

'Nope. No sign of him.'

'His wife?'

'Yeah, we got her. She took out two recruits before we ended her.' He said it pointedly, like he was keeping track of the balance sheet. Bodies lost versus bodies gained. 'But everyone in the house has been dealt with. Just a few of them left in there.' He nodded towards the barn. It was a scene of chaos, with shadowy bodies surrounding it, shouts coming from within, bullets popping as the men inside tried to defend themselves. A recruit who Shannon vaguely recognised – a woman with a buzz cut – took shelter behind a power generator, sticking her head out every thirty seconds to shoot at the barn windows.

'You can handle this?' Shannon asked.

Jimmy nodded. 'Uh-huh. We're gonna smoke the fuckers out.' He glanced down at his gun. 'Who knew I could shoot just as well with my left hand?'

'Come on,' she said to Cody.

'Wait,' Jimmy said. He handed her a pistol. 'Take this.'

Shannon had never shot anyone. It was a matter of pride. Let others do that kind of dirty work. But then she pictured herself ending Darryl Moses, and accepted Jimmy's offer.

They gave the barn a wide berth to avoid getting caught by a stray bullet. Out of the dimness loomed a cottage: a white, wooden structure with an awning over a pretty little decking area. There were no lights coming from inside.

'What do you think?' she asked Cody.

'I think you need to take shelter while I check it out.'

She considered objecting to his sexist condescension, then thought better of it. There was a black car parked out front of the cottage. She crouched behind it and watched as Cody fetched a couple of recruits: a skinny woman with cropped hair, and a guy with the girth of a linebacker. He gave them instructions and they approached the cottage with Cody behind them. They opened fire, a hail of bullets shattering the front windows, and there was a cry from inside. One of Darryl's men popped his head up from below the shattered window and Cody took him down.

'Go check inside,' Cody said to Linebacker Guy. 'Make sure it's clear.'

The young man went in and returned a minute later.

'All seems quiet.'

Cody nodded to Shannon. As they walked towards the cottage, the air around them suddenly grew lighter. Somebody must have finally triggered the security lights. Feeling exposed, Shannon hurried through the door of the cottage, Cody right behind her.

There were four rooms. The first contained two young women who sat huddled together on a double bed, shards of glass all over the floor along with the body of the guard. One of the women looked familiar. When she saw Shannon, she blinked like she thought she might be hallucinating. Shannon guessed the other woman had been procured elsewhere. One of the teenagers who came looking for a lucrative job in the weed industry. They were both undernourished, their eyes haunted. The second one opened her mouth to reveal that most of her teeth were missing.

'I've come to set you free,' Shannon said. 'It's going to be okay.'

She took no pleasure in this lie. Having to deliver it only increased her anger with Darryl Moses. He had ruined these women. Just looking at them it was obvious they had been fed meth, and probably a cocktail of other drugs too, to keep them compliant and quiet. They would be no good to her. She would have to get Jimmy or Cody to remove them. It would, she supposed, be a kind of freedom for them.

'Have you seen Darryl Moses?' she asked.

They both shook their heads.

Shannon and Cody moved on to the next room. This one contained two young men. In the room beyond that, a trio of women. All of them had the same tweaker look, the same wrecked bodies. One of the three women leapt up when she saw Shannon and tried to attack her, but she was so weak it was like fighting off a kitten. Cody shoved her back onto the bed and slammed the door.

There was one more room to check.

Shannon stood back while Cody and Linebacker Guy stood either side of the door. Cody reached across and turned the handle, flicking his wrist to pull the door open.

A bullet thudded into the wall inches from where Cody stood.

'Shit,' he whispered.

'Darryl,' Shannon called. 'That you?'

'Fuck you.'

Shannon grinned. She'd been afraid he'd slipped away from her.

'All your men are dead, Darryl. Throw out your gun and I might let you live.'

'Bullshit,' came his reply.

'You alone in there?'

'There are three of us. And we've got a bomb. You try to come in and I'll blow the whole place to the sky.'

Cody, who was able to see through the crack between the door and the frame, shook his head and whispered, 'It's just him with a single gun. There's a girl on the bed too.'

'I know you're lying,' called Shannon. 'I've got over thirty soldiers here. I'll say it again: throw out your weapon and, out of respect for all the business we've done, I'll let you live. I just want to hear you say sorry, Darryl.'

'Screw you,' he called.

'You shouldn't have disrespected me.'

'Fuck you, bitch.'

Movement in her periphery turned out to be the young men and women from the rooms they'd already cleared. They were crowded together in the hallway, watching Shannon and Cody. Shannon gestured for one of the two men, a wraith with a single tooth remaining, to come to her. He dutifully crept closer and she tossed him the gun Jimmy had given her.

'This is your chance,' she whispered to the young man. She recognised him. He'd come from the Ranch. What was his name? Jeffrey? Jordan? Jordan. That was it.

Jordan looked down at the gun that he held in his trembling hand. From inside the room, Shannon could hear Darryl panting with fear.

'Go on,' Shannon whispered. 'Kill the piece of shit who did this to you.'

Jordan nodded like an automaton, raised the gun and pointed it at Shannon.

'No!' yelled Cody. He shot Jordan in the chest. The man crashed to the floor, and behind him the other young man cried out. At the same time, a series of shots blasted out from inside the room.

Darryl had panicked.

Now his gun's firing mechanism just clicked as he pulled the trigger.

Before he could reload, Cody stepped into the doorway and trained the Glock on him.

'Put it down.'

When Shannon stepped forward to look past Cody, she found Darryl sitting on the floor, the gun limp in his hand, dressed in just his underwear. He spat out a stream of cuss words – just the kind of misogynistic filth Shannon expected from him. He was crying too, and there was a puddle beneath him. The big man had pissed himself.

She picked up the gun that the zombified Jordan had tried to kill her with and shot Darryl in the chest. Then she shot him again, in the forehead.

Her ears whistled but she didn't care. She turned to the young woman on the bed, who had pulled the sheet up to her chin. Her pale shoulders shook.

'You,' Shannon said. 'You've caused us a hell of a lot of trouble.' She shook her head. 'You should never have tried to run.'

Chapter 30

Aidan stood by the barn door. From inside came the sound of a commotion. Confused voices. Someone banged at the inside of the door, which was padlocked from the outside.

As soon as the gunfire had started, the security guard who'd been closest to the barn had taken off, sprinting towards the house, and Lorenzo had given Aidan a shove, telling him this was his chance. The three of them had jogged across to the barn while shouts came out of the darkness, cries of pain. Halfway to the barn, security lights had popped on all around them.

Lorenzo had announced he was going to see what was going on.

'No.' Aidan had grabbed the other man's arm. 'We need to stick together.'

'I have to see if there's any danger to Nancy and our farm. You concentrate on getting this barn door open. I'll be back in two minutes.'

Aidan had looked around for something he could use to break the padlock but had come up empty-handed. More than two minutes had passed and Lorenzo hadn't returned. Somewhere up near the house, a man was screaming in pain.

'We're going to have to shoot it off,' Aidan said. He'd been reluctant to use his gun because he didn't want to attract attention.

'Okay. Stand back.' Lana aimed at the padlock, then hesitated. 'I have to say something. Just in case we don't survive this.'

Aidan opened his mouth to speak but she said, 'Shut up. Don't say anything. I know you overheard me talking to Samuel, about us barely being friends. I just want you to know I didn't mean it, okay? I like you a lot, Aidan. Now, let's get this fucking barn open.'

Her first shot went several inches wide. Aidan noticed that she was sweating and was about to offer to try himself, when she fired again and the lock was blown apart.

Aidan yanked the door open.

A crowd of faces stared at him from within.

'I'll keep watch,' Lana said.

Hurriedly, he stepped inside. The barn had been done up like a dorm room, with two rows of bunk beds with thin mattresses. The room stank of body odour and worse, presumably coming from a row of buckets on the far side of the barn, half concealed behind a tatty sheet that had been strung from a beam above them. There were no windows, just a few bulbs that emitted a sickly light. He squinted into the gloom. Scarlett. Was she here?

'Scarlett?' he called, scanning the faces staring at him. 'Scarlett?'

A white man with copious facial hair stepped forward. 'Are you the police?' He had an Australian accent. 'Have you come to get us out?' A murmur of barely contained desperation came from behind him. So much hope. It was almost too much to bear, and Aidan felt anger rise up inside him. Fury at the way these people had been treated.

'I'm from the next farm over,' he said.

No one had answered when he'd shouted his sister's name. His hopes had sunk. What was important now was getting these people out of here. To safety.

'Come on,' he shouted. 'Let's go.'

They all started talking over each other, asking questions, demanding answers. He had half expected a stampede towards the exit, but no one moved. He guessed most of them had been kept like this for so long that they were afraid to act, like sheep cowering before the open gate of their pen.

He put up both hands, appealing for quiet. As soon as he could make himself heard he said, 'I don't know what the situation is up at the house. But this is what's going to happen. When we leave here, we're going to head down towards the trees. Are you all from the Ranch? From Shannon Reinhardt's place?'

'Why all the questions? Can't we just get the fuck out?' said the Australian.

Aidan handed him his flashlight, which he'd need to find his way through the trees. 'You lead the way.'

He and Lana stood back, with Lana focusing on the path up towards the house, while everyone filed out from inside the barn. Then, to his shock, Aidan found himself staring at a familiar face.

The young woman from the train. The one in the peace-symbol T-shirt who'd got off the train when he did. She had the expression of someone who had been through a lot since he'd last seen her. Shit, hadn't they both.

He remembered her name: Kristin.

'You,' she said, her eyes wide.

Aidan held up both arms to the group as a whole. 'Let's go. And everyone, keep quiet.'

They were surprisingly disciplined – another result, he guessed, of being kept prisoner and being ordered around. The Australian went first, followed by Kristin, then the others.

Aidan stood by the open barn door, studying the faces of every woman who came out. No Scarlett. No one who could have been mistaken for her. Could she be elsewhere on this farm? Nancy had said something about a brothel. A cold wave washed over him.

'I need to look for Scarlett,' he said to Lana.

'Let's get these people out of here first.'

'No. You do that. I have to find the brothel.'

She rubbed her face. 'Jesus, Aidan. I don't know.'

But he couldn't leave the farm without searching the whole place for his sister. He ran down the slope until he caught up with Kristin and the Australian guy.

'There's a brothel here, right?' he shouted. 'Where is it?'

Kristin looked blank but the Australian clearly knew what he was talking about.

'I think my sister might be there,' Aidan continued.

'There's a cottage. Up behind the barn, that way.'

Aidan looked up towards where the Australian was pointing. The gunshots and shouting had ceased, but somehow the silence seemed more ominous than the sounds of mayhem and violence that had come before.

'Your sister. What's her name? She's the Scarlett you were yelling for?'

Aidan nodded.

'I haven't run into any Scarletts. But a lot of the people who came to the Ranch changed their names before they got there. This whole place, it's full of people running from something. My name's Cameron, by the way. My real name.'

'She's British,' Aidan said. 'Red hair.'

Cameron shook his head, then stopped talking, hearing the footsteps a moment before Aidan. He turned his head towards the sound. Someone was sprinting towards them from the direction of the big house. Aidan whirled around.

It was Lana. Lorenzo was beside her.

Lana saw him and gestured and yelled at the same time. 'Run!'

There were three people chasing her and Lorenzo. Two men and a woman, all carrying guns. Aidan froze for a second, just long enough to see that one of the men was familiar. Jimmy.

Gunfire exploded out of the darkness, so close Aidan could smell it, and then he was running too, Lana beside him. Aidan yelled, 'That way!' – pointing towards the trees – and Cameron and Kristin sprinted to catch up with the others from the barn.

Aidan stole a glance over his shoulder. Their pursuers weren't gaining ground, but neither were they falling behind.

'They're like a goddamn army,' Lorenzo shouted. 'It's carnage up there. Bodies everywhere. Total freaking carnage.'

More gunfire rattled behind them. Up ahead, the escapees, including Kristin and Cameron, were disappearing into the trees that led down to the chain-link fence. There was no way they would find the gap quickly enough. They were going to be trapped.

Lana must have realised the same thing.

She veered off to the right, yelling, 'Follow me.'

Both Aidan and Lorenzo hesitated for a second, and a shot cracked behind them.

Lorenzo went down.

Aidan froze to the spot, staring at Lorenzo, at the blood soaking the back of his shirt.

'Aidan!' Lana screamed.

He managed to get his legs to move, following her, running blind in the near-darkness. He stumbled on the uneven ground. His lungs burned, but adrenaline and fear kept him going. Down among the trees he could hear the men and women he'd released from the barn calling out to each other.

Lana stopped and said, 'Oh . . .'

They had reached the cliff edge that Lorenzo had warned them about. All Aidan could see beyond were shadows, greys and blacks, but he could sense it. The drop. The empty space.

Jimmy and the two soldiers he was with – Lorenzo's description of them as an army had lodged in Aidan's head – pulled to a halt a few metres in front of them.

'Put down your guns,' Jimmy said, that grin still on his face.

Lana replied, panting, 'And then what?'

'I'm going to let Shannon decide that.'

And then, out of the darkness, they appeared. Cody, with a woman beside him. Half a dozen soldiers behind them.

Aidan and Lana dropped their guns, and one of the soldiers scooted forward to grab them.

The woman – it had to be Shannon – stepped forward. A manic energy seemed to radiate from her. More people were coming down the hill and Shannon pointed towards the trees and shouted, 'Round them up. If they resist, kill them.' The soldiers jogged off in that direction.

She turned to Cody.

'She's all yours.'

Cody took a step forward. His eyes glittered with hatred.

'Found yourself a girlfriend at last, have you?' Lana said to him. 'Or are you her pet dog?'

He grinned, showing her his teeth, and took another step closer. Raised his gun.

Aidan tried to get between them, but someone – Jimmy – sprang forward and grabbed him, pulling him backwards. Aidan went down and his head bounced against the hard ground. Everything went white, an explosion of pain blotting out the world, and when he could see and feel again he was on his back, Jimmy on top of him, pinning him down, his gun in Aidan's face.

Aidan managed to turn his head to look at Lana. She was backed up at the cliff edge. Cody stood before her, his weapon trained on her. Lana had her palms raised. But it was as if she didn't care. She had found her brother, made sure he was safe. Or maybe she just didn't want Cody to see her fear.

'What are you doing?' Jimmy said to Cody. 'If you don't shoot her, I will.'

'I've got a better idea,' Cody said.

He marched forward and, before Lana could react, Cody shoved her over the edge of the cliff. She cried out as she vanished, and then there was a bang and a scraping noise – the sound of her body hitting the slope, bouncing off the rocks as she fell – followed seconds later by a sickening crash, far below.

Aidan yelled Lana's name, the word getting stuck in his throat, almost a sob, and he felt Jimmy's left hand around his neck, pinning him down, choking him.

He looked up through the tears in his eyes and saw a face looking down at him. Shannon. She was smiling curiously.

'Aidan Faith,' she said.

Jimmy's one-handed grip on Aidan's throat stopped him from speaking. From yelling at her.

She crouched beside him, still wearing that strange smile. She cocked her head.

'You look just like her. Doesn't he, Jimmy?'

'I guess.'

He tried to say Scarlett's name. To ask where she was. If she was still alive. But he couldn't speak. He tried to wriggle free, kicking out at Jimmy, who swore and loosened his grip for a second. Aidan managed to roll slightly and push himself up, but someone else – Cody? – grabbed his shoulders. Aidan swung his head back, connecting with something hard, a chin maybe, and then Jimmy was in his face again. A blur of motion, the butt of a pistol arcing down.

Then nothing.

PART THREE

Chapter 31

Aidan awoke from a dream about Scarlett – she was telling him that she had decided not to come to Seattle after all, that she was going to stay home with Mum and Dad – with no idea where he was or what was happening. He was in some kind of moving vehicle, the back of his head banging against metal, a pain inside his skull that spiked with every thump. He could smell gasoline and sweat and he could hear people all around him, breathing and shuffling in the dark.

The vehicle he was in went over a pothole and someone cried out. A woman. And then it came to him.

Cody, shoving Lana off the edge of that cliff.

Aidan took a moment to gather himself, to fight down the panic and the grief. He breathed. Counted backwards from ten. He was in the back of a large van. There were around a dozen or so other people in here with him, all in the same position: seated on the floor, being jostled and shaken as the van sped along bumpy roads.

'You're awake,' said a female voice.

He recognised it and, for a wonderful moment, he thought it was Lana, that she had somehow survived, or that maybe he had only imagined her plummeting into empty air, but then he realised it was a voice he'd first encountered right at the beginning of all this.

'Kristin?' he said.

'Yeah.'

All remaining hope sank. 'They caught you.'

Her silence said everything.

'All of you?'

She spoke softly. 'Yeah. Except . . . they didn't take all of us alive. A few people got through the fence but they went after them. I heard shooting . . .'

This was too much. Too much. He felt something inside him threatening to break.

He had to hold it together.

'I'm sorry I didn't get you out of there,' he managed to say. He was felled again by the image of Lana falling, and seconds passed before he was able to speak again. 'Do you know what's happening now? Where we're going?'

'They're taking us to the other place,' said a male Australian voice.

'Cameron?' said Aidan. So he was still alive too.

The echo of Mayor Hood's words came to Aidan. *Forgive me, God.* 'Do you know what this other place is?'

Cameron grunted. Aidan could see him now. He sat opposite, beside Kristin, leaning out of the gloom.

'There are rumours,' he said. 'Jimmy said something to a couple of people just before he handed them over to Darryl Moses. That we should be grateful we wouldn't end up at the other place. I assume that's where we're going now.'

'But you have no idea where that is? Or what it is?'

'All I know is that it's not a freaking theme park. And that it's worse than the farm. Or the brothel.'

Aidan could hardly imagine what could be worse than that.

Then, with a start, he remembered what Shannon had said before Jimmy knocked him out. *You look just like her.* Surely that was the final confirmation that Scarlett was, or had been, with Shannon.

'The Ranch,' he asked. 'What is it?'

'It's a training camp,' Kristin said. 'That's what they told us, anyway. We were told we were being prepared to go out into the field, to fight and protest and agitate.'

'All bullshit,' Cameron said.

'Protest against what?' Aidan asked.

They all looked at him like they were stunned by his ignorance. 'The destruction of the earth,' Kristin said.

'You mean you're environmentalists? Shannon Reinhardt is some kind of eco-warrior?'

'She pretends to be,' said Cameron.

'I think she really believes,' said Kristin. 'The way she talks . . . the look she gets. She can't be faking it.'

They all began to argue, Cameron and Kristin and some of the others, talking over each other, until Aidan said, 'Please!'

Over the next ten minutes he got the full story. How each of them had been committed to green issues from a young age and how this had progressed to activism. Joining marches and strikes. Teaming up with local groups of fellow believers. How they had all come to believe that greater, more extreme action needed to be taken, because time was running out and politicians weren't doing anything. They had got involved in direct action: helping to block-ade roads, flying drones over airports, standing by deli counters in supermarkets handing out leaflets that described exactly how the meat had got there.

'After this one airport protest,' Kristin said, 'I got invited to join a private WhatsApp group. A more hardcore group. And shortly after that I got the invitation. A train ticket and instructions were

233

emailed to me. They don't believe in flying, so I had to get the train all the way across the country.'

The others had had similar experiences.

'Before we got to the Ranch they told us we would be trained and sent into the field to take part in covert operations,' said Cameron. 'We were shown how to make explosives and how to glue ourselves to trains; how to avoid arrest, and how to act if we were interrogated. Every three or four weeks, several people were told it was their time. I remember when I was told. I was so excited. Nervous, but thrilled. That's what I was there for.'

'Where did they say they were taking you?' Aidan asked.

'No one at the Ranch is told where they're going. All we're told is that we are going to rendezvous with the people who will take us to the next place.'

'That sounds crazy.'

Cameron shrugged. 'It's standard practice for this kind of group. We were told not to ask questions in case we got intercepted. The less you know, the less chance there is that you can be coerced into giving out sensitive information that will damage the cause.'

'It sounds like a terrorist group,' said Aidan, not caring if he offended them.

Kristin bristled. 'That's what they call us. Eco-terrorists. But drastic, serious action is required *now*. I was prepared to do anything.'

'And that was drilled into us at the Ranch,' Cameron said. 'By any means necessary. We had to be prepared to sacrifice ourselves for the cause.'

'But it was all a lie,' said Kristin.

Aidan thought about what they'd told him. It didn't make sense. He understood that it was clever, persuading these people, who were barely older than kids, to be secretive, cut themselves off from their families, even change their names. To get them to voluntarily travel across America to a place where they were cut adrift and vulnerable. But why go to all the trouble of training them up if they were just going to be trafficked? Why bother keeping them at the Ranch? It would be easier and more efficient to sell them straight away.

There had to be more to it. Aidan had seen for himself that some of the recruits were being used as soldiers. Were they being tested at the Ranch? Was it only the rejects who were trafficked? He decided not to voice this theory now.

Because another question had crept into his head, and expanded so it was suddenly all he could think about.

The eco-protest in Seattle. Scarlett's clear excitement. For years, they'd been looking for the Kurt Cobain lookalike, but Aidan was starting to think that was a red herring. A false trail.

He remembered how Scarlett had temporarily vanished during the protest, going missing for five minutes before he found her.

Had she spoken to someone in those missing minutes?

Been told that she could be part of something like this? That she could make a difference?

Was that where all this had started?

Opposite him, Cameron's eyes were dark. He gestured towards the other people in the back of the van, sitting quietly on the floor. 'Look at us. You'd think we'd all be freaking out, banging on the door, knowing they're just taking us away to kill us. But we're just sitting here. We're just done. When you let us out of the barn, we managed to rouse ourselves, to think maybe we might get away. But we were wrong, weren't we? We never stood a chance. We don't stand a chance, wherever they take us. Wherever this other place is.'

'You can't give up,' Aidan said. '*I'm* not giving up.'

He crawled towards the back of the van, between a dozen pairs of legs, a dozen pairs of eyes staring down at him, until he reached the back doors. He pressed his palms against the metal and felt for the handle. The van was moving fast and he knew that throwing himself out of it would likely be suicide. But surely they would have to pause at some point, at a junction or a stop sign, or at least slow down. He wanted to be ready.

He tested the handle but it wouldn't budge. It must have been locked, or jammed, from the outside. He cursed.

'I told you, man,' called Cameron. 'We're not getting out of here.'

And then the van began to slow down. Aidan grabbed the handle again, holding on to it with both hands, and pushed it with every ounce of his might. But it was no good.

The van slowed further, then stopped.

Everyone in the back appeared to cease breathing. Up front, they heard doors open then slam shut. Aidan pressed his ear against the metal, sure he could hear footsteps.

The door rattled and opened.

Chapter 32

Aidan found himself looking at two men. Cody, with his stringy blond hair, and Jimmy. At the farm he hadn't been wearing his cowboy hat, but here it was again, perched atop his head.

Aidan turned back to his fellow captives. 'Come on,' he said in a hushed voice. 'There are thirteen of us. We can overpower them.'

Nobody moved.

'Kristin?' Aidan said. 'Cameron?'

Cameron scowled at him but Kristin wouldn't meet his eye. Nor would anyone else. Cameron had been right. They were beaten. Resigned to their fate, whatever that was.

'What's this?'

Aidan swivelled towards the voice. Cody was standing by the doors.

'You trying to start a . . .' He looked over his shoulder. 'What's it called? A revolution?'

'Insurrection,' said Jimmy.

'Yeah, that's it.' Cody reached behind him and pulled out a Glock, levelling it at Aidan. Behind him, Aidan heard people scrambling out of the way. Cody called back to Jimmy: 'Can I shoot him?'

Aidan stared at the gaping black muzzle of the gun and felt something go loose inside him.

'Shannon says not,' Jimmy said, in a bored tone.

'Kick his ass a little?'

'For crying out loud, Cody. Just get on with it.'

'Crap.' Cody lowered the gun. 'You. Faith. Get your ass out here.'

Aidan hesitated.

'*Now.*'

Aidan got out, the bright sunlight screwing his eyes shut. His head throbbed and his legs felt shaky, but he was determined not to let the two men see this. Squinting against the glare, he forced himself to stand erect and toe to toe with Cody, who just laughed and grabbed his arm, dragging him around the side of the van. Aidan knew he wouldn't be able to fight them, not two of them with guns.

There was a large plastic bucket on the ground. It was filled with bottles of water. Shastina Spring, of course. Seeing the brand made him think about Mayor Hood hiding Samuel at Nancy's farm. Where was Samuel now? Was he safe? And what about Nancy and everyone else who worked there? Aidan felt a stab of guilt as he pictured Lorenzo's death. It had been his fault.

'See? We're good guys,' Jimmy said. 'One bottle each. We've still got a long drive ahead of us.'

'We don't want any of you dying in there,' said Cody. 'Stinking the place out. Drag that bucket around and water the stock, Faith. And if you or any of you try to run – if you try anything at all – I'll not only gun you down, I'll start pulling people out and shooting them.' He grinned, showing his crooked teeth.

Stepping over towards the bucket, Aidan took a look around. They weren't in the forest anymore. They were on open land, parked beside a quiet road, an immense wind farm in the distance, the sails of forty or fifty turbines turning almost imperceptibly slowly. On the horizon, a hazy mountain ridge, the sun blazing low in a merciless sky. There was no sign of any other trucks or vans, apart from

Cody's black Jeep, the one Aidan had first seen outside the murder house. Aidan figured Jimmy must have been driving the van, with Cody following behind in the Jeep. Shannon and the others from the Ranch were nowhere to be seen.

'Beautiful, ain't it?' said Jimmy. 'God's own country. Take those goddamn turbines away and this is what it was like before we all came over here and started fucking it all up. Listen.' He cupped his ear with his hand.

Despite himself, Aidan stopped and found himself doing what Jimmy asked.

'Hear that? Silence. Blissful, beautiful silence. This is what it's going to be like everywhere, soon enough. Back the way it was always meant to be.' He turned his face towards the sun. 'God's had enough of us. Nature's had enough of us too. And together . . .'

He slammed a fist against an open palm.

'What?' said Aidan. 'Extinction? The end of the world?' He couldn't keep the mockery out of his voice.

Jimmy glowered at him. He adjusted his hat. 'Get moving with that water. Your friends are thirsty.'

Jimmy and Cody smoked cigarettes while they watched Aidan drag the bucket across the rocky ground and begin handing the bottles to the people inside the van.

Then he turned back to the two men with guns.

'What happened at the other farm? Did you kill them too? What did you do to Nancy?'

Jimmy shrugged. 'We couldn't leave witnesses.'

Aidan's stomach plummeted. Samuel too? He didn't dare ask.

'It doesn't matter anyway,' Jimmy said. 'I told you. We're nearing the end.'

Cody had spent this whole exchange staring at Aidan like he was waiting for something.

Finally, Aidan could bear it no longer and met Cody's eye. '*What?*'

'Just wondering if you're missing your girlfriend.'

'Fuck you, pencil dick,' said Aidan.

Cody went for him, swinging a fist that caught Aidan on the cheek.

'Cut it out!' Jimmy pulled Cody away and held on to him. 'This isn't the schoolyard. Jesus.'

Cody stepped away, still glaring at Aidan.

Jimmy ground out his cigarette beneath the toe of his boot, and looked down the road towards the shimmering horizon. 'You think the cops or the Feds are gonna come save you, don't you? Well, I got news for you. No one's going to find us, Faith. Not where we're going. Man, I cannot wait for you to see it.'

The other place. 'See what?'

But Jimmy just grinned.

ϖ

They drove on. Hours passed; how many, Aidan couldn't tell, but it grew hotter and hotter inside the van until it must have been close to a hundred Fahrenheit in there. They just sat there, stupefied by the heat, dripping sweat onto the filthy floor.

His water was all gone and he had slipped into a semi-conscious state, trying to remember how long it took to die from dehydration.

He came to with a start. The van had stopped moving. A grinding noise came from outside, something slow and mechanical, and then the van moved forward, just for a few seconds before coming to a halt. Shortly after that, the grinding sound came again.

Kristin and Cameron were asleep, or unconscious, slumped against each other, her head on his shoulder. Aidan leaned forward and, with a sweat-slick hand, shook them both awake. Kristin blinked at him with pink eyes.

Then came another noise, the sound of the back doors being opened, and the interior of the van was once again flooded with light – but not sunlight this time. Artificial light.

Jimmy peered inside at them. 'Come out, come out,' he called.

'Water,' one of the men closest to the doors said.

'Don't worry, we've got water for you. Food and fresh clothes for you all too.' He wrinkled his nose. 'Goddamn, it stinks like a high school locker room in here.'

Aidan blinked the sweat from his eyes and stared past Jimmy. All he could see was a grey wall. Faint voices, with an echoey quality. The air that entered the van smelled dry, metallic.

'Where are we?' Aidan asked.

Jimmy smiled. 'The last place on earth,' he said.

Chapter 33

Jimmy and Cody told them to get out, handing them each a bottle of water as their feet touched concrete. Most of the people in the van were too weak to stand, and they slumped to the ground, cradling their bottles. Kristin retched, bringing up stringy bile, and Cody made a disgusted sound. As Aidan got out of the van, just behind Kristin and Cameron, he heard Jimmy mutter, 'They're not gonna be any use if they can't even stand up. What the hell was she thinking?'

'Huh?' Cody said. He was staring around him like a kid who'd just wandered into Santa's grotto. 'Holy fuck. Look at this place. It's goddamn *huge*.'

Aidan forced himself to stay standing, sipping the water slowly and taking deep breaths. He looked around too. They were inside a large industrial space, the size of an aircraft hangar, with a concrete floor and walls, illuminated by fluorescent lights. The grinding noise had come from the set of huge metal doors they'd driven through. Cody's Jeep was parked beside the van and crates were stacked against a wall, along with various pieces of equipment that Aidan couldn't identify, though one of them emitted a series of clicking noises. The air was stale, with a faint smell of oil and metal. Just beyond where the huddled men and women from the van sat was another, smaller set of doors, a keypad beside them.

Aidan watched Cody walk around the perimeter of the hangar, tapping the walls and shaking his head, like a surveyor inspecting a property and making a mental list of all the things that were wrong with it. He inspected the machine that was making the clicking noise, then called over to Jimmy: 'What's this?'

'How the hell should I know? I left the construction of this place to Shannon and Hood.'

Cody peered at it more closely. 'Maybe it's for keeping birds out or something. Huh.' He wandered back over. He and Jimmy took no notice of the men and women they'd transported here in the van, who were mostly slumped on the floor, only one or two of them other than Aidan standing. One of them was Kristin, who looked like she'd woken up from a nightmare and found herself in hell.

'Where's Shannon?' Cody asked. 'Has she texted?'

Jimmy checked his phone. 'No reception. But she should be here any minute.'

And as if he had uttered a magic spell, the sound of an engine came from outside and the metal doors opened. A truck – like an army truck, but painted black, with two benches at the rear on which about a dozen people sat – drove through, followed by another, also carrying a dozen young men and women. A pair of men jumped down from the front of the second truck and headed for the doors, but a woman's voice came from the cabin of the first truck: 'Leave them open.'

Shannon climbed down from the passenger side of the truck.

She looked straight at Aidan and smiled, then beckoned Cody and Jimmy to stand by her side. Behind them, the new arrivals in the back of the trucks were climbing out, gazing about them with a mixture of confusion and awe. Aidan scanned their faces. No Scarlett. At the same time, on the other side of the hangar, an inner door opened and a pair of men came through. They had semi-automatic weapons slung over their backs. One of them stepped forward and saluted Shannon.

Shannon raised her arms and waited for everyone to fall quiet, the two guards handling their semi-automatics as if to suggest that anyone who didn't stop talking and pay attention would be on the wrong end of a hail of bullets.

'I think we all need a shower and a hot meal,' Shannon said in a raised voice, like a teacher at the front of a class. 'If you would form two lines and prepare to follow these gentlemen.' She indicated the guards. Jimmy said something in her ear. She nodded impatiently and said, 'All of you from the farm, line up to the left. Everyone else, line up on the right. No speaking.'

So they were keeping the two groups separated. The men and women who'd been in the trucks with Shannon immediately began to form a line. Aidan wondered what Shannon had told the recruits who'd been in the trucks about the people from the farm. They didn't appear to want the two groups talking to one another, because when one of the newly arrived women tried to speak to Cameron, exclaiming about how happy she was to see him, how pleased she was that he'd been rescued, Cody told her to shut up.

Rescued. So that was the story that had been fed to the recruits who'd arrived with Shannon from the Ranch: Cameron and the others from Moses's farm had all been liberated. Aidan wondered what would happen if he yelled out the truth. How many words he'd get out before he was shot.

Aidan noticed that some of the people from Shannon's trucks were limping and bruised. One woman was having to be half carried by two of her colleagues. Had they all been injured in the battle at the weed farm? He also noticed Jimmy watching, shaking his head slightly.

The people who'd been in the van with Aidan, the former farm workers, were struggling to their feet, forming an uneven line. It struck him again that Cameron had been right. These people were beaten, their spirits crushed by mistreatment and terror at the hands of Moses and his men. Aidan went to join them and Shannon said, 'Not you, Faith. You stay here.'

It took them five minutes to stagger into line while Shannon tapped her foot impatiently.

Finally, only one woman from the van had yet to do what she was told.

'Hey, Kristin!' Jimmy barked at her. 'Get in line.'

She hesitated.

'I said, get in line.'

Still Kristin didn't move.

Aidan noticed the guards watching, alert, and the faces of most of the people in the two lines turned towards Kristin and Jimmy, who now cursed darkly under his breath and strode to her, gripping her arm.

Kristin ripped herself free and glared at him. 'Get your damn hands off of me.'

'What the hell's going on?' Shannon demanded, coming over.

Kristin squared up to her. 'You betrayed us. You *sold* all these people to that stinking farm. Gave me as some kind of gift to that creep.'

Shannon smiled and shook her head sadly. 'Oh Kristin, you know that's not true. They kidnapped you.' She raised her voice. 'You were there less than a day before we came back and rescued you.'

'You're lying,' Kristin said.

Aidan moved towards her, ready to back her up, but Cody stepped into his path and put his hand on the grip of his gun.

Shannon turned to face the group from the farm, speaking clearly and loudly.

'As I've already told those that arrived here with me, there *was* a terrible betrayal here. Darryl Moses betrayed all of us,' she said. 'We had a deal with him: that he would shelter you at his farm before he took you to the coast, to the rendezvous point, from where you would be taken to your separate missions. He assured us it would be a safe place, that he was a believer like us. As soon as I discovered what was happening, we went in there and liberated you. We got you out so we can all be together, here. And Moses is dead. He and all his men – everyone who tormented and mistreated you. They have been punished.'

Aidan could see that the people from the farm were shaking their heads, looking at her with contempt or disbelief. But the others, the recruits who had still been at the Ranch with her, seemed to believe her.

'She's lying!' Kristin called out. 'She was trafficking us. *Selling* us.'

Jimmy whispered in Shannon's ear. Aidan was sure he caught the words 'take her outside', but Shannon gave Jimmy a sharp look and went to Kristin. She wore a soft smile and put her arm around Kristin's shoulders. Kristin tried to shake her off but Shannon held on.

'I'm sorry you've lost your faith in us,' Shannon said. 'And I feel foolish. I am *sickened*. I should have realised what was happening, that Moses couldn't be trusted.' She let go of Kristin and faced them all. 'But I promise you, all of you, that I'm telling the truth.'

'What is this place?' called out one of the recruits, a man who'd arrived on the trucks with Shannon.

'I promise you,' Shannon said, 'everything will be explained. But first, like I said, you all need a shower and a hot meal, some rest. Then, once you're yourselves again, I'll take you all through it. It's a lot to take in.'

She nodded at the guards, who began to shepherd the two lines through the inner doors.

Soon, only Shannon, Cody and Jimmy remained, along with Aidan and Kristin.

As soon as the inner doors closed, Jimmy said to Shannon, 'You sure you don't want me to take her outside?'

Kristin had gone white. All the anger had drained from her and she looked as defeated as the others from the van.

'Please,' she said. 'I'm sorry. I just didn't understand. I won't—'

Shannon shushed her. 'It's okay. We're not going to hurt you.' She glared at Jimmy. 'He was only talking about taking you out for some air.'

Aidan forced himself to stay quiet. Cody still had his hand on the grip of his gun.

Shannon took hold of Kristin's hand. 'You've been through a terrible experience. Don't you remember? You were travelling with us, and Darryl Moses stole our Jeep with you in it. Cody and I had to walk miles to get help. Then we came straight back to save you and all the others.'

Now Kristin looked utterly lost. 'But,' she said, 'I was drugged . . .'

'You were carsick. We gave you a travel sickness pill. Maybe you're allergic to them? But it's all going to be fine now, Kristin. We have a very special role for you here.'

Jimmy seemed surprised. 'Are you sure?'

'Of course. Look at her.' She smiled at Kristin. 'She's fit, young, healthy. With some rest, some food, she'll meet all the criteria. Cody, why don't you take Kristin to the ninth level? One of the guards here will show you the way.'

'Sure. Come on.'

He gently led Kristin away, through the doors that must lead into the belly of this place, and Aidan felt a cold drip of anxiety in his own belly. He alone had been left behind. Was this it? The end?

He glanced towards the outer doors. From this angle he could see outside. There was an expanse of nothingness. Yellows and pale browns. Fierce sun. He thought he could see a tall fence in the near distance, shimmering in a haze of heat.

They were in the desert.

'What about him?' Jimmy said, nodding at Aidan, who shot another look at the outer doors. Could he run?

Shannon's fake smile had vanished. 'Take him to floor fourteen.'

Jimmy grabbed Aidan by the crook of his elbow. 'Let's go.'

'Wait.' Aidan resisted and spoke to Shannon. 'What is this place?'

She smiled.

'It's the Cradle.'

He wasn't sure if he'd heard her correctly. 'The what?'

Her expression changed. Her eyes darkened, and it was as if he could see flames dancing in her pupils. It was the look of a believer. A zealot. Of someone who had not just drunk the Kool-Aid, but mixed it and served it up.

'This is where life begins again,' she said.

Chapter 34

Shannon had started her journey of self-discovery in Mexico, in Tulum on the Caribbean coast, where she took yoga classes until her money ran out and it was time to move on to the next destination.

She kept heading south, taking whatever work she could find. Guatemala. Colombia. Down through Peru and into Brazil, where she spent six months on the edge of the rainforest. There she met a group of people – a mix of locals and Westerners – who had dedicated their lives to the fight against deforestation. They marched. They blockaded the highways that ran along the outskirts of the Amazon. They sabotaged loggers' equipment. It was insanely dangerous but also exciting, and for a while Shannon believed she had found her calling. She met an American man called Jimmy, who told her she should stay with them and fight. But although she felt a deep affinity with the forest – sometimes she thought she could hear the trees crying – she knew she hadn't found herself yet. She wasn't ready. Reluctantly, she exchanged numbers with Jimmy and moved on.

For a while, she teamed up with another American called Lucy, who had spent her entire adult life backpacking and knew where was safe, what was worth seeing. They kept going south. Bolivia. Paraguay. She and Lucy worked on a horse ranch in Argentina – she loved the vast open spaces of Patagonia, the animals, the physicality of the work – but when Lucy decided to stay, after falling for one of the ranch hands, Shannon struck out on her own again, searching, always searching, until she reached the southern tip of the continent, and skipped back into Chile. She stayed for a while in Puerto Williams, working for a company that operated boat trips to Antarctica. A small town that would later be given city status so it could claim to be the southernmost city in the world, Puerto Williams was a sleepy, friendly place that drew few travellers. She thought she might settle there, in this cold town on the edge of the earth, but she was still dissatisfied. She hung out with hippies and amateur philosophers, earnest young men who were keen to share their deep thoughts and get her into bed. She smoked weed and skim-read Nietzsche and Kant and Coelho. She meditated. She thought about heading back to Brazil to see if Jimmy and the other protestors were still there.

And then, at the loosest of loose ends, she met a woman who had come to Puerto Williams to spot dolphins and whales, and who told her she should go to Peru and try ayahuasca.

'It changed my life,' the woman said, laying a bony hand on Shannon's arm. The woman had the eyes of someone who had seen many things. 'I promise you. It will change yours too.'

ω

Shannon gave all her remaining money to a company that organised trips to take ayahuasca.

'It will open all the channels in your mind,' that proselytising woman had said that night in Puerto Williams. 'It will allow you to find the truth you're looking for, about who you want to be. You won't find that truth in books. It's all in there. In your head. In your heart.'

'It's what, like acid?' Shannon asked.

'Oh, it's much more than that. And it's completely natural, not something that was created in a lab. There are tribes in the Amazon who have used it for centuries. *Ayahuasca* means "vine of the soul".' The woman whispered this as if she were invoking the name of a god.

A week later, Shannon landed at Iquitos and was transported first by bus and then by boat downriver to a remote spot in the jungle. The retreat. There were five other people: two Americans, two Brits and a Canadian. One of the Americans was a medic who was there to observe and help anyone who got into trouble. Shannon tried not to think about what this trouble might be.

The ceremony was due to take place on the second night, and by the time it arrived Shannon had worked herself into a state of dread. Why was she doing this? She had sworn off drugs when she left Reno. The one time she'd tried acid she'd imagined beetles crawling all over her and had sworn never to touch it again. In the days before she left for Peru she had read numerous accounts of what it was really like to take this 'medicine', most of which mentioned copious vomiting and diarrhoea. She feared she'd made a terrible mistake. But it was too late to back out now.

The sky turned pink, then darkness fell over the jungle. Shannon and the others were led to a hut high above the river, where the shaman awaited them. He was a small man, with black cropped hair, and he spoke no English so a translator passed on his instructions. They had been told to eat very little and to go into the ceremony without fear and with an open heart. Shannon paused at the door, staring behind her at the dark rainforest, listening to the sounds of the river below, and took a long, deep breath. She told herself not to be scared, and went inside.

The five participants sat on thick mats in a line on the wooden floor, with the shaman facing them. They were each given a bucket. The shaman said something.

'Are you ready?' the translator asked, and they all looked at each other with various degrees of nervousness, and nodded. After that, the shaman came to them one by one and held out a small cup containing a dark, hot liquid. Before handing it to them he blew onto the liquid's surface, lifting a plume of steam into the humid air.

Shannon drank.

She sat cross-legged on the mat, wearing a tank top and loose pants. She had a bottle of water and her hair was tied back. The shaman began to chant, words Shannon would never know the meaning of, and he shook a handful of large dried leaves in time with his chant.

Shannon lay back and waited. This was it. Whatever happened tonight – and part of her hoped it wouldn't work, that she would somehow turn out to be immune to the drug's powers – she knew this was the end of her journey. After this, she would go home to America. She would find a job. Perhaps she would meet someone, get hitched, have kids. Grow up and grow old. She would live an ordinary life and tell her bored grandchildren about her South American adventure, about the horses she rode in Argentina, the trees she tried to save in Brazil.

At first, it was like being stoned. Like she'd smoked the strongest weed. The inside of her head burned, and it felt like her brain was trying to push its way out of her skull. The heat spread to her limbs; they didn't feel like they belonged to her. When she moved, the walls of the hut shifted and swayed. Lights expanded and retracted. The shaman chanted on, the rhythm of it connecting directly with her spine, and part of her wanted to dance but all she could do was lie there, immobile.

It was awful, terrible; it felt like she had been possessed by a dark spirit. The woman beside her kept saying, 'Oh Jesus, oh Jesus', over and over, and the man next to her was crying, pleading for it to stop. He vomited into his bucket and then they were all vomiting, except Shannon. The translator seemed slightly panicked, as if she'd never witnessed such negative reactions before. Had they been given an extra-potent batch? But the shaman chanted on and Shannon latched on to it, riding on the waves of sound, holding on like it was a rope connecting her to the real world. Gradually, she began to feel lighter. Before long, she was euphoric.

She put her hand on the wooden floor beside her mat and it felt like it was breathing. More than that, it was imparting its wisdom: everything it had seen when it had been a tree flowed up through her palm and into her head. And once she had opened herself up, she heard the jungle beyond the hut, she heard all the trees whispering to her, the river joining in too, all of them talking over each other in a babble, not using words but pictures, images that floated straight into her consciousness – except they were out of focus, unclear.

She grabbed the bucket and vomited. It felt like her insides were coming out, like she was expelling pieces of her own body, all the parts that contained bad memories, memories with faces. It hurt, it was too intense – she needed it to stop, stop the roller-coaster, let her off – but it was wonderful too, somewhere between the worst pain and the most exquisite pleasure.

And then it happened.

It was as if she'd been catapulted into the future, through a hole in time and space, and here she was, spinning, floating, looking down upon the world to come.

She saw the earth splitting open, buildings crumbling into the chasm, mouths opening in screams as bodies tumbled down, down into the belly of the world.

She saw waves as high as skyscrapers, rushing like wild horses towards the shore, carrying the wrath of the pillaged oceans on their backs. Rivers boiled and turned black, spewing forth dead fish and a dark, thick chemical sludge.

Hurricanes lifted trees and houses, tearing them to pieces, ripping apart whole cities. The surfaces of the desert cracked.

And then the wildfires came, roaring through the forests, devouring the jungles, tearing through woods and obliterating arboretums. Tribes who had never had contact with the rest of the world ran for their lives. The mighty redwoods fell, and smoke as dense as tar poured into the sky. She could hear animals and birds screaming. She watched the continents turn orange and the oceans go black.

She vomited again, then plummeted back onto her mat in the hut and was back in her own body, her own time, sobbing from fear and wonder and hatred and love. She might have screamed, because the translator came over and spoke to her, though the words didn't make sense. She tried to rub some kind of oil on Shannon's feet, which made her curl into a ball. And all the while the trees kept whispering, the river kept calling. The woman beside her paced around, talking about how she needed to call her mother, because she'd seen it, she'd realised that her mother really loved her, and the shaman chanted on. A man on the other side of the hut was crying, keening. And all the while the trees whispered to her, soothing her, calming her down.

Slowly, slowly, the physical sickness faded. Even more slowly, her newly purged body began to feel like hers again. Her cheeks were slick with tears and she was filled with the most enormous sense of responsibility. She wanted to tell the others, to share the news, but at the same time she felt as if nature had shared its secrets, its visions, and she knew with her whole being that it was not a hallucination. It was not her imagination.

It was real. She knew it with absolute certainty.

The world was going to end. They only had years left.

And she was the only person who knew it.

Chapter 35

Jimmy led Aidan along a dimly lit corridor. The overhead light flickered like the bulb was about to die. There was a strange smell, as if someone had tried to conceal the stink of damp with bleach. They found themselves in front of an ancient-looking elevator with a dent in its aluminium door. The light kept flickering. From somewhere nearby came a voice, echoing as if coming from a vast, empty room: 'Everybody into the showers. Men on the left, women on the right. You'll find fresh outfits on the benches.'

The elevator arrived and Jimmy pushed Aidan inside. The doors slid shut behind them, muting the barked commands. Jimmy hit the button marked *14* and took a step away from Aidan, keeping his gun trained on him.

They descended.

'Where are we?' Aidan asked.

Jimmy ignored him.

'I'm going to hazard a guess. The Mojave, right? And this is a bunker. What is it, a converted missile silo or something?'

Aidan had read about billionaires building luxury bunkers. Bill Gates was rumoured to have one in Seattle, though Aidan didn't believe that was true. He had a memory of watching something on YouTube about luxury underground developments, fully stocked, waiting for rich families to move in when the apocalypse came. A lot of them were in New Zealand, but they were all over America too, on the empty plains of Kansas and South Dakota, and out in the desert.

'It's like an inverted skyscraper, right?' Aidan said. 'A tower block dug into the earth.'

Jimmy was silent for a moment. 'It's called a geoscraper,' he said eventually.

'And this is the construction project Mayor Hood has been working on?'

Jimmy didn't reply. He was inspecting the bandage on his hand. It was dirty and needed changing. Aidan imagined the wounds must itch like hell.

'Come on, I know it is. So was it a missile silo?'

Jimmy looked irritated. 'An Atlas F missile silo. Built in the sixties, strong enough to withstand nuclear attack. It's got filters to keep out radiation and chemicals and all that shit.' He was warming to the subject in spite of himself, eager to geek out, show off his knowledge. 'Those front doors weigh seven tonnes.'

'And do you know how deep it goes?'

'Three hundred feet.'

Aidan did a quick calculation. That was about ninety metres.

Shannon's fabled 'other place' was a bunker, except this was hardly one of the luxury bunkers Aidan had heard about. It seemed half finished. The elevator juddered as it descended, and Aidan could hear the metal cables above grinding in the shaft. Jimmy flicked his gaze upwards, hearing it too. For the first time since arriving he seemed a little nervous, and Aidan thought he was as relieved as Aidan when they bumped to a halt and the doors opened.

'Shannon mentioned a cradle,' Aidan said, not moving. 'Life beginning again. She thinks the world is ending, right? And this is her shelter. That's why she's been selling people to Darryl Moses.

To fund this place. Except it looks like she ran out of time or money. I mean, converting this place must have cost millions. Surely Shannon couldn't have made that much trafficking recruits to Moses?'

'Shut up and walk,' Jimmy said.

'Come on. Where did the rest of the money come from? Look, we both know Shannon's going to kill me. I just want to get the whole picture before it happens.'

Jimmy sighed. 'Shannon makes her recruits sign over all their money so it can go towards the cause. We sell their possessions too. Phones, jewellery, everything they hand over when they join us. We deliberately targeted a bunch of rich kids when we were starting out. Trust-fund brats, wealthy orphans. Some young guy who'd made some crazy-ass amount of dough selling his website to Google or some shit like that. Dumb, rich assholes. The world is full of them.'

Aidan nodded. He knew from working in the tech industry that there were a lot of rich young people around. In the time he'd been in the States, he'd met a dozen or more twenty-somethings who'd created some app or website in their bedrooms and made a fortune. Mini Mark Zuckerbergs. And a lot of them – especially in Southern California, he'd heard – were looking for meaning, for some higher calling. What greater cause was there in the twenty-first century than saving the planet?

Aidan wondered what had happened to this first wave of 'investors'. They were probably buried somewhere.

They went along another badly lit corridor that smelled of metal and oil. It was an ordinary corridor, but Aidan was aware they were deep underground, of the weight of all that earth above them, and he had to push away an image of the ceiling collapsing, crushing them. On top of that, the air tasted stale and thin. And what were those brown stains on the walls and ceiling?

They turned a corner and it was even worse. Here, a section of the ceiling had fallen in and a girder had been wedged in place to keep the whole thing from collapsing. Rubble was strewn across the floor. As Aidan watched, a shadow darted between the piles of broken concrete. A rat? If so, an enormous one.

'Good God,' Aidan said. 'Hood really did run out of time.'

He looked around. Jimmy had just told him about the filters to keep out nasty particles. He assumed they kept the inside air clean too. Aidan also knew that Hood owned a company with expertise in tapping into natural water supplies. Presumably there was a source here, further beneath the ground. What Aidan didn't understand was why Hood had told Samuel that this place was even worse than the farm.

One thing was certain. Shannon hadn't ever really intended to try to save the planet. She believed they had already passed that point. She was preparing to shelter.

'Do you believe it too?' Aidan asked. 'That the world's going to end?'

'Not just going to,' Jimmy replied flatly. 'It's already ending.'

'And this is going to be your new home? This hole in the ground? What are you going to eat?'

Jimmy sneered. 'We got enough canned and freeze-dried shit to last us five years. We're going to be growing our own food too. Fruit and vegetables, herbs. Plus we got chickens, and I heard something about fish tanks. Tilapia.'

'What do you use to grow vegetables? Heat lamps?' Aidan was fascinated, despite the situation he was in. 'Don't tell me you're growing cannabis too?'

Jimmy's thin lips spread into a smile. 'Well, you gotta keep the people relaxed, don't you? Plus, CBD – that's good medicine.'

'Do you have doctors?'

'We got one. And everyone who has been through the Ranch has a degree of medical field training.'

Aidan looked up at the fluorescent lights that were doing such a bad job of illuminating the corridor. 'How are you powering everything? You have your own generators, I assume?'

'What do you think?'

They stopped outside a door and Jimmy shoved him into a small, empty room with a thin mattress on the floor and a bucket in the corner. It looked like a storage room that had been turned into a makeshift cell. A bare bulb hung from the ceiling.

Jimmy pointed at the mattress and said, 'Sit.'

He turned to go, his uninjured hand on the door handle.

'Is she here? My sister.'

Jimmy smiled, then backed out of the cell and slammed the door. A key turned in the lock. Aidan heard Jimmy's footsteps retreat.

Aidan sat on the mattress.

Something scuttled up the wall.

It was a spider. A huge freaking spider, not much smaller than a tarantula, with fat legs and a hairy body. It squeezed through a crack in the wall and vanished.

'Jesus wept,' Aidan muttered. Did the spider have a family behind the wall? Had it just gone back there to tell the rest of them that supper had arrived?

It was hard, down here, not to let his imagination get the better of him.

He leaned back against the wall, trying not to think about the spiders. Tried to concentrate on this place, to solve the mystery of what exactly was going on here. He was gripped by the urge to turn to Lana, who had been by his side through all of this, but of course she wasn't here. Wasn't here to talk this through with, to help him figure it out. To trade jokes with to lighten the horror. She was gone, and the world was poorer for it.

'Oh Lana,' he said out loud, and he let the tears come. The release of pressure, of grief. The exhaustion and frustration and anger. He sat like that for a few minutes, shoulders quaking, letting it all out, and then he stopped.

He stood and paced the cell.

Why did Mayor Hood think this place was so bad? Because they were all going to be stuck down here, believing the world was ending? Because Shannon's recruits were going to be kept prisoner in this subterranean prison? It had to be more than that.

It came back to him. What Shannon had said about Kristin. *She's fit, young, healthy . . . She'll meet all the criteria.*

'Oh my God,' he said aloud.

Of course. Shannon had already given him the answer.

This is where life begins again, she had said.

Aidan knew what this cradle was intended for.

Chapter 36

Shannon followed Jimmy into the elevator and pressed the button for the ninth level. Her stomach fluttered as they started to descend. Halfway down, the floor beneath her lurched and she threw herself against the wall, bracing herself. Was this it? Had she come all this way to die, because Hood's men had screwed up and failed to fix the elevator? She sucked in a breath and, thank God, the elevator stabilised and continued its descent.

She exhaled.

'You all right?' Jimmy asked. 'You look pale. Tired.'

'I'm fine,' she snapped. 'Though I'm starting to wonder if we made a mistake bringing the people from the farm.'

'We didn't have much choice. The other recruits had already seen them. Plus, we need the bodies, right? Especially since we lost a few at the Moses place.'

'Are you still going on about that?'

He didn't respond.

She wished she could push away the anxiety that had begun to creep through her veins. She had expected to feel elated to be here. She had been planning for this, building up to this moment, for years.

'Why don't you go and get some rest?' Jimmy suggested. 'When did you last sleep, huh? I can take care of things. I'll talk to the recruits, make sure they're all okay, check none of them believe all that stuff about us selling their friends to Darryl Moses.'

'We never did that,' Shannon said.

Jimmy blinked at her, then smiled. 'Sure. It never happened.'

She didn't like that sly smile. Sooner or later, she thought, Jimmy was going to cause her problems. She had a feeling that, at the first sign of trouble, the first hint of dissatisfaction, he would see her gender and relative youth as a problem. He had never quite accepted her authority, still saw her as the young backpacker who'd turned up in Brazil all those years ago.

'Did you talk to Faith when you were escorting him to his cell?' she asked when the elevator reached its destination. They stepped out.

'A little. He's still asking whether Scarlett is here.'

She stopped walking. 'And what did you tell him?'

'Nothing. But he'll find out soon enough, I assume. Have you told her he's here?'

'Not yet. Jesus, look at these walls. They look like they're going to fall down.'

It had been months since Shannon had last been here. She had come to inspect the work Hood and his men had been doing, back when this place was empty, before they began to send the first guinea pigs out here. And all the reports that had come back from the doctor and the psychologist had been optimistic. The psychologist had recommended a few changes to the environment, advising her to put in screens that acted as fake windows, showing a landscape that shifted from light to dark between dawn and dusk. The psychologist had worked for a while for the Navy, and had been involved in keeping men and women sane on submarines.

'Except no submariner has ever spent anywhere near five years beneath the surface,' the psychologist had said. 'You need to mimic the patterns of natural light as much as possible. Keep people active, make sure they exercise.'

Most of it, as far as Shannon was concerned, seemed to be common sense.

They'd had big plans. The whole place was going to be converted into a luxury subterranean community, like a hotel but completely self-sufficient. There'd been plans to build an underground swimming pool. A gym. A movie theatre. But the money they'd earned from the Moses arrangement had fallen way short of expectations and, once construction began in earnest, wouldn't have been remotely sufficient in any case. And as it became increasingly difficult for her to get out into the field herself, recruitment began to lag, especially the work of ferreting out rich kids willing to sign it all over to the cause. Still, they'd been making progress. They'd thought they'd have years to finish the work.

It would still be fine, Shannon assured herself. They didn't need pools and exercise bikes. They had food and light and water. They had enough bodies . . . just. It was all they required.

As long as the whole place didn't collapse around their ears.

As she thought this, her stomach lurched and she had a sensation, just for a moment, of the walls closing in on her. Shadows crowding in from the corners of her vision.

'Are you sure you're okay?' Jimmy said. 'You look a little sweaty.'

She flapped a hand. Snapped out of it.

'I've been thinking about Mayor Hood,' Shannon said. They were still standing outside the elevator.

'You think he might turn up on our doorstep, begging us to take him in?'

'I think he will. When the fires start burning through the forests, when he realises what's happening, where else will he go? He'll turn up with his daughter, banging on the door.'

Jimmy nodded. 'And you know how much he loves the people of his glorious little town. He'll tell them about it too. Shit, we'll have most of Eaglewood trying to get in. Plus all their cousins and friends, and all their idiotic internet chat-buddies, radiating out to infinity. You want me to go and deal with him?'

She thought about it.

'Send Cody,' she said. 'Hood trusts him. He'll let him in.'

'Good thinking. Okay, I'll see you later. Get some rest.'

He got back into the elevator and saluted her with his bandaged hand before the doors slid shut.

ϖ

It was mostly quiet in the corridor, except for the sound of sobbing coming from one of the rooms. Shannon paused outside the door, just as a woman in a white outfit came out of one of the other rooms. She already looked harried, her features pinched and stressed, but her expression changed to alarm when she saw Shannon.

'You,' Shannon said. 'Come here.'

The woman came closer. Shannon struggled to remember her name. Miranda. That was it.

Shannon gestured to the door. The sobbing was growing to a hysterical pitch. 'What's wrong with her? Is this one of the new arrivals?'

Miranda, whose pallor matched her clothes, shook her head. 'No. That's Cindy. She was one of the first to arrive.'

Cindy. Shannon remembered her. A pretty twenty-year-old from Texas. Perky and cheerful, with freckles and long brown hair. A former cheerleader.

'How long has she been like this?'

'A while.'

264

'And what have you done to deal with it? Have you tried giving her camomile tea?'

Miranda looked at Shannon like she'd suggested feeding Cindy arsenic.

'What about yoga classes?'

'She refuses to take part. We keep telling her that this is a gift, an honour, but she keeps screaming about her human rights.'

Shannon rolled her eyes.

'That's not all,' Miranda said.

'What else?'

'Some of the women here are thrilled. Looking forward enormously to fulfilling their roles. But a few of the others have been complaining about nightmares.'

'What kind of nightmares?'

Miranda hesitated. 'Being buried underground, that kind of thing. One of the women keeps having this recurring dream about giving birth to a monster. A blind monster with teeth. Half mole, half jackal, that's what she said. She told the others and the dream seems to have spread.'

Shannon felt herself shudder. She could picture the creature the women had dreamed about. Black and eyeless, with smooth fur and jagged teeth . . .

Why was she standing here listening to this nonsense?

'A couple of the girls have been resisting sleep because they're so scared of the nightmares,' Miranda said.

Shannon held up a hand. 'Okay. I'll talk to them. Remind them that it's a wonderful thing that they're doing. That we don't have a choice.'

'Thank you.'

'In the meantime, camomile tea. Now, I came down here to see—'

They were interrupted by someone banging on the inside of one of the doors and yelling, 'Hello? *Hello?*'

Miranda consulted a notepad she produced from her pocket. 'That's one of the new arrivals. Kristin.'

Shannon sighed. 'Let me talk to her.'

ω

Kristin took a step back as Shannon entered the room. The room was painted in warm, neutral shades, with a soft carpet. Hood's men had worked on these quarters first and had done an excellent job. There was a TV hooked up to a hard drive which contained thousands of movies and TV series. There were books to read – *What to Expect When You're Expecting, Eating for Two*, along with numerous classic novels – and even a video games console. Shannon had picked out the mattresses and bedding herself. There was also a refrigerator containing fruit juice and snacks, and an en suite containing a small bathtub and toilet.

It was much nicer than Shannon's own room, which was half finished, the walls plastered but not painted, the floor bare. Shannon's first horrified thought when she'd stepped inside was that it was little better than a cell. But she was prepared to make sacrifices.

Kristin and the others should count themselves lucky to have such comfortable rooms in which to look after their new babies.

'How are you settling in?' Shannon asked.

Kristin had crossed to the other side of the room, like she couldn't bear to be near Shannon. But the fear that had cowed her before had swapped places with the emotions she'd displayed when they'd first got here. Outrage. Anger.

'What is this place?' she demanded. 'Why was I brought here? Where are the others?'

'The people from the farm, you mean? They're upstairs. They'll be settling in to their quarters now.'

'So why have I been separated from them?'

'Because you're special, Kristin. I told you that.'

'So special that you handed me over to a weed farm? You tried to confuse me before, but I remember. You locked me in a trunk and *drugged* me.'

Shannon tutted. 'Oh Kristin, you know that didn't happen.'

Kristin goggled at her. 'Do you actually believe your own lies?' She stalked over to the bookshelf and pulled down a copy of *What to Expect When You're Expecting*. 'What is this?'

'It's a very useful book.'

Kristin leafed through the book, then threw it to the floor. With a sudden movement, she swept half a dozen other books from the shelf and gazed down at them, at the soft-focus pictures of glowing new mothers and cute newborns. 'You want us to . . . you want us to *breed*. Don't you?'

'That's such an ugly word.'

'But isn't that what you want us to do?' She sat down on the bed. 'I keep thinking I bumped my head trying to get off the farm and I'm actually in a coma, having the weirdest freaking dream of my life. A dream where some crazy-ass bitch has brought me and a load of other women to an underground bunker and told us the world is ending.'

'It is ending.'

'Wow. Wow wow wow. And what? It's up to you to repopulate the planet? Like this is Noah's freaking Ark or some bullshit?'

'The Cradle,' Shannon said.

'Oh my God.' Kristin put her head in her hands.

Shannon waited patiently.

'So, how long have we got?' Kristin asked when she looked up, unable to keep the sarcasm out of her voice. 'Before the world ends?'

'It's okay, Kristin. I know you think I'm insane. But you haven't seen what I've seen.'

'Which is? Don't tell me – you had a vision.'

Shannon smiled and ignored the incredulous look on Kristin's face.

'We have days,' Shannon said, sounding to herself as though she were speaking from far away. She gazed into the middle distance. 'Maybe a week. Or two. They haven't told me exactly how long. But the fires are coming.'

'*They* haven't told you? Who are *they*? Aliens? The Illuminati?'

'The trees,' Shannon replied.

Kristin laughed. Not just a chuckle but a full belly laugh, bent double across the bed. She began thumping the mattress helplessly. She tried to speak but started laughing again.

Shannon had to fight back the urge to slap her. She should have let Jimmy take her into the desert. Shannon should do it herself. That would stop her laughing.

But that was out of the question, she had to remind herself. They needed every one of these young women. After the casualties at the farm, they couldn't afford to lose anyone else.

'This is amazing,' said Kristin when she'd gathered herself. 'So, where's the sperm coming from?'

'The chosen ones aren't just women,' said Shannon.

'You have, what – studs?' Kristin asked with horror in her voice. For a moment, Shannon thought the girl might leap up and attack her, but instead she shook her head and said, 'This isn't real. It can't be real. I'm in a coma.'

'I didn't want to do this,' Shannon said. 'But I don't have a choice. This is our chance, don't you see? Our chance to start again.'

But Kristin was no longer listening. She had her head in her hands again, saying, 'I'm in a coma', over and over, and from the next room came another, even more terrible sound. Screaming.

Someone pounding on the walls, her voice pitched high like a siren as she cried: 'They're coming! They're coming!'

Shannon banged on the door to be let out. 'Miranda! Open up.'

It had come on suddenly, along with Kristin's intoning and the other woman's screaming. The walls were closing in, the room shrinking. The earth pressing down on her from above, and now from the sides too. She banged on the door again and screamed for Miranda to let her out. When at last the witless woman released her, she leaned against the corridor wall, lights dancing before her eyes, sheathed in a second skin of cold sweat.

'Are you okay?' Miranda's voice seemed to be coming from a long way off.

Shannon staggered down the corridor. Was this what a panic attack felt like? She tried to breathe, but the air wouldn't enter her lungs. She pushed her way through the door at the end of the corridor, stabbed at the elevator button, the initial purpose of her visit to the ninth floor forgotten.

She didn't remember how, but somehow she made it to her room. To her bed. She lay down and closed her eyes. She tried to tune in to the sounds of the trees, but they were too far away. Deep beneath the desert, so far from the forest, she couldn't hear them anymore.

Oh God . . .

She shoved the doubts away.

Jimmy had been right. She needed to rest. That was all.

Chapter 37

It was silent in the barn. Samuel could hear the wind stirring the branches of the trees beyond the walls, and, every now and then, he would hear what he was convinced were footsteps outside. As a kid he might have imagined bears or mountain lions, coyotes or even mythical beasts. Monsters in the woods. Creatures from the fairy tales their mother used to tell them. But now he knew the worst monsters didn't walk on all fours, and he was convinced they would come back for him. So he sat there, desperate to leave this place but paralysed with fear.

Come on, Sam, he whispered to himself. *You can do this. You have to do this.*

Samuel and the other workers had been asleep in their bunks when the first gunshots had rung out. They'd ventured out and Samuel had immediately run up to the house, where he'd found Nancy emerging from the front door.

'Where's Lana?' Samuel asked her. 'Is she back?'

'No. There's no sign of Lorenzo either. Come with me, into the house. We'll find somewhere for you to hide.'

But he hesitated. Lana had risked so much, put herself in so much danger, to find him. He couldn't just leave her. He had to see if she was okay.

Ignoring Nancy's pleading, he jogged down towards the border between the farms. There were other workers standing around, wondering what in the hell was going on.

And then the night turned to hell around him.

Chaos and gunshots and screams. People Samuel had never seen before came running out of the trees, and then more people behind them, shouting, shooting. A woman fell face down in the dirt and Samuel's instinct was to run and help her, but there was another burst of gunfire close by. Another scream.

He turned and ran towards the house.

As he neared the hoop houses, Nancy came walking towards him. She was holding a rifle.

'Nobody comes onto my farm.'

'No, you were right, we should hide—'

His words were cut off by a shot. The crack of another rifle.

Nancy collapsed to the ground.

'No! Nancy!' Samuel threw himself down in the dirt beside her. Her eyes were still open but she was gone.

A man strode out of the darkness, holding the rifle that had killed Nancy, heading straight towards Samuel but looking around, taking it all in. He paused to shoot one of the other workers who was trying to flee into the barn, then stood still to rack another round into the chamber. Samuel sprang to get to his feet and sprinted towards the nearest hoop house. Behind him, he heard someone call out to the man with the rifle: 'Jimmy, I'll check the house.'

He paused by the hoop house. It would offer no protection. There was a barn just behind there that was used for storage. He put his head down, convinced he would be brought down at any moment, and ran towards it. It only took a minute to reach but it felt like an hour. He pushed open the door and ran inside, hiding behind some large metal storage tanks.

In the near distance, he heard the *pop-pop* of gunshots. Someone, a man, cried out in pain. More shots.

Footsteps coming towards the barn.

A male voice saying, 'Better check in here.'

'I'll do it,' said the other man. 'You stay out here in case anyone runs out.'

Samuel looked around, desperate. An empty fertiliser sack lay on the ground just beyond the tank. He crawled across the floor, grabbed the sack and wriggled into it, feet first. He contorted himself so it just covered his head and he was able to hold the opening shut with one hand pressed against the top of his skull.

He lay still.

The footsteps crossed the barn floor, then came back again. They stopped. Samuel tried not to breathe. He thought about Lana and his mother. And he thought about Elizabeth. Remembered kissing her, lying in the grass beside the murder house. All that kissing. He thought about the time he had climbed the tree and carved their initials. He wanted to live so he could see her, kiss her, again. But if the man found him, shot him, he wanted to die with a happy picture inside his head.

He closed his eyes and stayed motionless.

'Clear in here,' he heard the man say.

It was a long time after the man's footsteps had receded before Samuel dared to wriggle out from the sack.

ϖ

He stayed in the barn until well after the sun came up.

It was quiet outside now. Birds calling out to one another in the treetops. Samuel looked down and saw there was blood on his T-shirt. Nancy's. He made his way past the hoop houses, and walked towards the main house, hoping he'd find help there, that someone had survived.

It was empty. He drank water from the faucet and knelt to pray on the kitchen floor.

He tried to decide what to do. He needed to get off this mountain, find civilisation. But almost as soon as he had started walking towards the gate, he stopped.

What if there were other people like him on the other farm? Hiding, too terrified to come out?

He had to see.

He headed for the trees that bordered the two farms. There were flies everywhere, but Nancy's body and the others that had fallen on Sugar Magnolia Farm had been removed. He didn't know if the people who'd done this had taken them away or simply dragged them out of sight. After a little while, he came to a chain-link fence and found a spot where it had been cut. He squeezed through and continued until he reached a clearing. There was a barn across the way and he made his way towards it. He looked inside and saw a mass of flies. Bodies piled up.

He staggered outside and vomited noisily into the grass, then began to make his way back towards the fence, convinced he was the only survivor, feeling like he ought to turn around, check in that barn to see if Lana's body was in that pile. But he couldn't bear it. Didn't want to see her corpse.

He stopped and threw up again, cried out in anguish.

And someone in the near distance shouted, 'Hey!'

He stood motionless.

'Hey! Is there someone up there? I need help.'

Up there?

It was a woman's voice.

'I'm over here,' she called. 'Over the cliff.'

He looked around, then saw the spot she must have been talking about, and ran over. He peered over the edge. And there, clinging to a ledge, gazing up at him, was Lana.

ω

He found a length of rope in the barn and tied one end to a tree near the cliff edge. Lana was about fifteen feet down, crouched on a shallow ledge and holding on to a gnarled tree that jutted out from the cliff face. Looking at the drop beneath her gave Samuel vertigo. Later, Lana would explain that the ledge had started out half as large again, but when she'd slammed onto it some of it had fallen away beneath her, crashing down into the brush below and leaving her dangling in space from the tree until she managed to fight her way onto what was left of the ledge.

It took thirty minutes for Lana to climb back up, trying to find footholds, every muscle in her arms straining as she gripped the rope. Samuel leaned over, encouraging her, looking for places for her to put her feet. Finally, he took her hand and helped her with the last heave, pulling her over the lip of the cliff, and then she sat on the ground, shaking from the exertion, while Samuel told her all the things he'd seen. Her palms were burned raw from the rope and she was covered in bruises and scrapes, but she insisted she was fine. Hungry and thirsty, but fine.

'God saved us,' he said.

He led her into the barn and, with her hand covering her nose, she looked at the pile of bodies, examining their faces. Samuel knew who she was looking for.

'They must have taken Aidan,' Lana said, with a mixture of relief and fear, when she'd finished and they'd gone back out into the fresh air.

'Can we go to the police now? Or the FBI? I can't hide any-more. Can't keep secrets.'

'Yeah. We can. But we need to know where they've taken him.'

'Any ideas?'

'No. But I think we both know someone who might know.'

It took Samuel a few seconds to realise who she meant. 'Mayor Hood?'

They walked through the trees, back through the fence, and kept going until they reached the house. There were no cars. No trucks. Shannon and her men must have taken them. They went inside and Lana drank thirstily from the tap.

'Maybe if we walk down to the road, we can hitch a ride,' Samuel suggested, when she had finished and they were back outside.

'I think we can do better than that.' She pointed. 'Wanna ride a quad bike?'

Chapter 38

Aidan paced the tiny room, convinced he now knew what it felt like to be a prisoner on death row whose time was almost up. Every flicker, every shadow, convinced him that an army of fat, hairy spiders was going to emerge. He had never thought of himself as arachnophobic, but then he'd only had to contend with pathetic British spiders, and their equally puny Seattle equivalents, up to this point. He realised, though, that the real danger here didn't come from the tarantulas or whatever they were. He was far more likely to be killed by Cody, Jimmy or Shannon herself.

He wasn't sure why they hadn't murdered him already. He guessed it was so she could question him, find out who he'd spoken to, whether there were any loose ends she needed to tie up. If anyone was going to come looking for him.

How long would his parents wait before they contacted the authorities? With their family history, not long. But Aidan figured it would take a lot longer for anyone in America to actually try to find him. And even if they did, what were the chances of them finding this place?

Zero.

During the hours since Jimmy had brought him here, he had examined every inch of wall and ceiling, inspected the lock on the door over and over again, searched the room for something he could use as a weapon. There was nothing. An empty plastic bottle. The foam inside the thin mattress. He laughed darkly. He would hardly be able to brain someone with a foam-filled Shastina Spring bottle.

He sat on the mattress, back against the wall, watching the crack the spider had crawled through. He thought about Lana – the way her arms had windmilled as Cody had shoved her over the edge of the cliff, the cry that had come as she fell – and he pinched the bridge of his nose to stop the tears from coming. Now was not the time for more grief or despair; that could come later.

He had to find Scarlett.

If she was still alive.

He went to the door and hammered on it, shouting, 'I want to talk to Shannon!'

'*Hello?*'

He looked around. For a moment he wasn't sure if he was hallucinating.

'Hey. Aidan?' An Australian voice.

It was coming through a small vent low on the wall. He had spent ten minutes on his knees beside it earlier, seeing if he could tug the cover free, and had concluded that even if he could remove it, the space would hardly be big enough to get an arm through, let alone his body.

He scrambled across the room and dropped to his hands and knees beside the vent. 'Hello?'

'Aidan? It's me. Cameron. Are you all right?'

'I'm not sure how to answer that.'

Cameron grunted. 'I'm in the laundry room. There's an old-fashioned mangle in here. I think that's what it's called.'

'What's going on out there?' Aidan asked.

'All of us from the farm have been given jobs,' Cameron said. 'In the kitchen. Cleaning. I'm on laundry duty today. Trying to work out how to use this stupid thing.'

'Everyone from the farm?'

'Yeah. Except Kristin. We don't know what happened to her.'

'Shannon hasn't told you?' Aidan said. 'She calls this place the Cradle. I'm guessing there's a . . . what would you call it – a maternity suite somewhere. Kristin will be there, along with God knows how many other women. Shannon is planning to use them to repopulate the earth.'

Cameron didn't speak for a moment. 'You know,' he said eventually, 'I'm not even that shocked. The amount of crazy stuff I've heard people talk about since I came to the States . . . I knew Shannon was extreme when I signed up. I *wanted* to join something extreme. People who could really see the urgency. The freaking *emergency*. After they sent us to the farm I thought the whole thing was a trick – a set-up to hand us over to those assholes. I'm actually kind of pleased, in a sick way, to find out that Shannon really does believe the world is dying.'

Aidan listened, a little impatient.

'There was a meeting earlier,' Cameron said. 'An assembly. Shannon talked a lot about wildfires, floods, plague sweeping across the earth. It was a pretty inspired performance.'

'And how did everyone react?'

Cameron sighed. 'There was a lot of crying. Praying too. Shannon went around the crowd talking to everyone, hugging them. Most of the people from the Ranch are acting like she's the Messiah.'

Aidan nodded to himself. He wasn't surprised these people were predisposed to believe her talk of a climate apocalypse; they had been predicting it, waiting for it, all their lives, and God knew there was no shortage of science to back it up. These were the young people whose heads were full of stats about melting ice caps and deforestation and rising temperatures, and they'd been whipped into a frenzy by years of wildfires and crazy weather and the never-ceasing arguments between them and the climate-change deniers – two entrenched armies in a polarised world. They believed it so strongly that they had been willing to wave goodbye to their friends and families and dedicate their lives to saving the planet. As Cameron had just said, they'd wanted to join something extreme.

'What about the people from the farm?' Aidan asked.

'Most of them are worn down to next to nothing. They're just glad to be free of Moses. We all talked about the other place like it was the worst, but it's a hell of a lot better here than on the farm.'

'If you're not being forced to have babies to save humanity.'

Cameron grunted again. 'Shannon's convinced most people that she didn't know what was going on at Moses's place – that as soon as she found out, she staged a rescue, made him pay. She's showing around photos of Moses's dead body like it's a trophy. She's making herself out to be a liberator and they're keeping a close eye on the few of us who know the truth, like me.' He paused. 'Maybe I could persuade one or two of them that Shannon's full of shit. But the rest of them . . . I guess she's leading up to telling everyone about the baby thing. Maybe she's going to ask for more volunteers. I mean, how many people do you need so we don't end up with an inbred population?' He paused. 'Jesus, I'm talking like it's actually going to happen.'

He was silent for a few seconds.

'You should go,' Aidan said. 'If they catch you talking to me . . .'

'Yeah. I know. But I have to tell you something. There's going to be another assembly tomorrow morning. Shannon told us. She started going on about how there was an enemy in the camp.'

'An enemy.' It took Aidan a couple of beats. 'Me?'

'Yeah. She says there's evidence you work for one of the big oil corporations, that you've been working to sabotage what she's doing.'

'*What?*'

'She says there's going to be a trial in the morning. And that if you're found guilty . . .'

'They'll execute me.'

'Sorry,' said Cameron.

It was clever of Shannon, Aidan supposed. This so-called trial in Shannon's kangaroo court would help bond the others. A common enemy and a show of strength. That was why she had kept him alive. He was a sacrificial lamb. He looked down at his hand and saw that it was shaking. His mouth had gone dry. Any hope that Shannon might keep him alive had gone.

'I'm sorry,' Cameron said again. 'I thought I should warn you.'

It was hard for Aidan to keep the tremor out of his voice. 'Do you know what time this trial is taking place tomorrow?'

'Early. Eight in the morning.'

'And . . . and what time is it now?'

'Just after nine p.m.'

So he had eleven hours left.

'Are you able to remove the vent cover from your side?' Aidan asked. 'Maybe if you could get it off you could pass something through that I could use as a weapon.'

'Hang on.' He heard Cameron pulling at it, grunting with the effort. 'It won't move. I'm sorry, man. They're going to start wondering where I am.'

'Okay. Forget that. What about keys to this room?'

'Jimmy has them.'

'Of course.'

'Aidan, I'm so sorry but I'm going to have to go. I'll try to talk to some of the others, tell them they're going to be expected to have babies. Maybe some of the true believers would take that in stride, but there have to be others who'll be blown away by the concept. Maybe if we protest at the trial—'

'It's okay,' Aidan said, sinking onto his mattress. 'I guess I'll see you tomorrow.'

But there was no response. Cameron had already gone.

Chapter 39

Shannon dreamed that she had been buried alive. She pounded at the lid of the coffin, scratched at it until her fingernails bled, screamed for help. All around her she could sense tree roots, but they were black, dead. And then she realised there was something inside the coffin with her. Something fat and furry with sharp teeth, nosing at her face, trying to work its way into her mouth.

She was awoken by a knock on the door.

She got out of the bed, groggy with something that felt like jet lag, and called out, 'Wait.'

She put a robe on and opened the door. Jimmy strode in.

'What time is it?' she asked, realising with a strange jolt that she had no idea if it was morning, afternoon or night. She had come to lie down after the assembly, where she had drawn on her last reserves of strength to give what had been a blistering performance. What time was that? She had no idea.

'It's just after ten,' Jimmy said.

'At night? Why are you waking me up at this time?'

He looked surprised. 'You asked me to come, remember? To talk about plans for the trial in the morning. I've been knocking for a long time.'

'Oh. Yeah.'

She was still trying to wake up, the nightmare lingering. That sense that she had been buried. The silence in her head that was usually filled with whispering; the language of the trees.

'Sit down,' she told him, trying to get a grip. She realised she was sweaty, her heart beating too fast. Still half asleep, she looked for a window to open, then realised that, of course, there were no windows here. The plans to install screens that would replicate a view of the outside had come to nothing, so all she had was a print showing Lake Tahoe. She breathed deeply.

Jimmy perched on the edge of the couch, studying her closely.

'Are you okay?' he asked. He was looking at her like she was crazy.

'Has Cody gone to Eaglewood?'

'Yup. Waiting to hear back from him.'

'What about the fire reports? From above?'

She expected him to say it was happening. That the wildfires were spreading, that hurricanes were approaching the East Coast, heatwaves and earthquakes in the Pacific. Riots across Europe. The apocalypse. The end.

But he said, 'Sounds like they got control of the fires down south. That sand fire I told you about is still burning, but it all seems calm.'

She stared at him. 'Are you sure?'

He shrugged. 'Unless they're all lying on the radio.'

That must be it. Of course they would be hiding it. The president and his cabinet were probably heading to their own bunkers now. Billionaires would be riding private jets to New Zealand. It was coming. It had to be coming.

She tugged at the neck of her robe. 'Why is it so hot in here? There's no air.'

'I think it's fine.'

Suddenly, she couldn't bear the sight of him anymore.

'Get out. Leave me alone.'

She felt dizzy. The walls were closing in. She really needed air. A window.

'Shannon, are you sure you're okay?'

Angrily, she waved his concern away. 'I. Am. Fine. I just need to sleep, uninterrupted.'

'Well, I'm sorry I disturbed you.'

He stood up. Was he smirking? Yes, he was smirking at her. Mocking her. Giving her that look he'd given her when she first met him – like she was naive, wet behind the ears. Just a girl.

'You're still here?' she half screamed. 'Go! Get out! I'll see you tomorrow at the trial.'

He finally left and Shannon crawled back onto her bed, pulling the sheet over herself. She fought back tears of self-pity. This was what her life had been building to. The day she had prepared for all these years. It wasn't supposed to be like this.

Still, she thought, as she burrowed towards sleep, executing Faith in front of her disciples – no hesitation; a swift, sure demonstration of her power, her willingness to do what must be done to protect what they'd built and all they would become – would make her feel better.

Chapter 40

It took hours to get to Lake Shastina on the quad bike, with Lana driving as fast as she dared along the quiet forest roads, and Samuel riding shotgun. At first it was kind of exhilarating, and she was happy to be moving again after the night and morning spent on the cliff ledge. The wind in her face as she rode the quad reminded her she was alive, that she hadn't died of thirst or exposure. She suspected that the trauma of the past few days would come back to bite her soon, and being shoved over that cliff by Cody – that asshole Cody – would be up there on the list of things that haunted her, beaten into top place only by the horror of shooting Sergeant Giglio. Right now, though, she was focused fully on the present. Finding where they had taken Aidan.

They reached Eaglewood. Samuel, holding on to her back, hadn't spoken on the journey.

She pulled over just inside the boundaries of the town. She had no idea what time it was. Sometime around 10 p.m., she guessed.

'I'm taking you home,' she said.

'No, I can't, I'm coming with—'

She cut him off. 'No, Samuel. I'm not putting you in any more danger. Do you know what it's been like for Mom?' She couldn't help but laugh. 'She's going to get a terrible shock when you turn up on the doorstep.'

He didn't argue. He clearly wanted to go home.

'You should come back too. Call the police. Let *them* deal with it now.'

'I can't. They'll be too slow. But I'll call them as soon as I've spoken to Hood and got the location of wherever they've taken Aidan.'

'Promise?'

'I promise.'

Five minutes later they pulled up outside the trailer park. She wanted to escort him to the front door, but she knew that if their mom saw her she would never let her leave. It was a shame she wasn't going to get to see her mom's face, though. The shock and relief; the joy and tears.

Samuel disembarked, and Lana pulled him into a hug, kissing his cheeks.

'I'll see you later. Okay?'

'What about Elizabeth? Can I call her?'

Lana sighed. 'Just go and see Mom.' She ruffled his hair. 'Love you, little brother.'

Then she sped away, the quad bike's engine buzzing angrily, still feeling faintly ridiculous on this exposed vehicle. As she turned the corner, she looked over her shoulder and saw Samuel illuminated by streetlights, crossing the road. Going home.

ϖ

Lana drove the quad bike up the steep path, desperately thirsty and hungry again. Like hers, the quad's fuel tank was almost empty. *Running on fumes*, she thought. *I'm running on my last fucking fumes.*

She marched up to the door and hammered on it with her fist.

The housekeeper answered. Yolanda.

'I need to see the mayor,' Lana said.

'He's not home.'

'Okay,' said Lana. 'Whatever.' And she pushed her way past.

'Hey,' Yolanda called, following her. 'I told you, there's no one here.'

Lana stopped and looked around. 'Bullshit. Where is he?'

'Yolanda?' a voice called from a nearby room. 'What's going on?'

Lana marched off in the direction of the voice and strode into a kitchen. Mayor Hood was standing by a massive refrigerator, its door open.

'What the hell are you doing here?'

'Mr Hood, I'm so sorry—' Yolanda tried to grab hold of Lana but Lana shrugged her off.

'Making dinner, are you?' Lana asked, taking a seat at the island that dominated the centre of the room. 'I'll take whatever's in the works. Oh, and by the way, I know everything, so if you want your housekeeper here to also know about Shannon Reinhardt and the deep shit you've got yourself into, just keep on gawking at me.'

Mayor Hood closed the refrigerator door.

'It's okay, Yolanda,' he said, gesturing for his housekeeper to make herself scarce.

Lana got up and went over to the sink, filling a glass with water and gulping it down, then doing it again.

'Am I going to have to fix my own food too?' she asked. 'Holy shit. I guess this is what it's like when you've got servants, huh? You forget how to do anything for yourself.'

Hood stared at her like he couldn't quite believe what he was about to do, then he took a slab of cheese and some lunch meat out of the fridge and proceeded to construct a sandwich. His hands shook as he did it.

She grabbed it from him and took a huge bite. She groaned with pleasure. 'That's better. What kind of cheese is this? I like it.' She swallowed. 'The only reason I haven't grabbed one of those knives and held it to your throat is that you saved Samuel. I thank you for that. He's safe at home now.'

The mayor's eyes widened. 'You've been to Nancy's?'

She told him everything, as succinctly as she could. He fixed himself a glass of Scotch while she talked. He made a *want one?* gesture, and though the temptation was almost overwhelming she forced herself to say no. When she got to the part about Nancy being killed, he poured himself another shot and downed it.

'I should never . . .' He trailed off.

'No, you shouldn't. What the hell were you thinking?'

'I needed the money. Everyone thinks I'm loaded because I live in this house, but you should see my mortgage. Shastina Spring is barely profitable. Shannon promised to help rebuild Eaglewood.'

'Give your construction company plenty of work, you mean?'

He filled his glass yet again. 'It wasn't just that. I genuinely love this town. I've lived here all my life and I wanted to make it special again. I took the money she paid me for her big project and put it into rectifying all the damage—'

Before he could finish, Yolanda appeared in the doorway. She seemed nervous. 'Mayor, there's someone else here to see you.'

A shadow appeared behind her, darkening the doorway, and Lana caught a glimpse of a looming figure.

Cody.

'Fuck,' she hissed, and she leapt off the stool, grabbed Hood and pulled him down behind the kitchen island.

'What the hell are you—' Hood demanded.

A gunshot cut him off. Crouched behind the island, Lana couldn't see what had happened, but the *thud* told her everything. Cody had shot Yolanda.

Hood looked at Lana with panic in his eyes.

'Do you have a gun?' Lana whispered.

He whispered back: 'Upstairs. In the drawer beside my bed.'

'Hey, Mayor Hood,' said Cody, from the other side of the broad island. Lana heard him sniff, then the faint sound of a glass being put down on the surface. He had drunk some of the Scotch. 'Whoa, that's good. You never shared any of the good shit with me when I worked for you. You never shared nothing.'

Lana realised Cody hadn't seen her. Didn't know she was there. Still alive. She gestured for Hood to reply to Cody, and at the same time looked around for a weapon. The knife block was on the counter on the other side of the kitchen, but Cody would shoot her in the back if she went for it. She couldn't see anything useful within reach.

'What's the problem, Cody?' said Mayor Hood, the words sounding like they were getting stuck in his throat.

'Oh, there's no problem. Just solutions.'

'Is Shannon with you?'

There was the sound of more liquid being poured into a glass. Then the smacking of lips. 'Nope, Shannon's back at the Cradle.'

The Cradle? Lana mouthed the words to the mayor, who shook his head, like: *Don't ask.*

'Gotta say, I'm impressed. It's an awesome place. You know they're aiming to repopulate the planet? Got all these super-hot babes down there and, guess what, they need studs to knock them up.' He chuckled. 'There's this one chick called Kristin. We're gonna make beautiful babies together. You remember Lana Carrera? It's kind of a shame she ain't there. I always wanted to tap that little bitch.'

Oh, how Lana wished she had a gun. If she was going to die, that was bad enough. But to be killed by a misogynistic prick like Cody? She remembered how he used to look at her at school – like a lizard regarding a fly it was hoping to have for dinner.

Cody went on. 'Shannon's crazy as a motherfucker, though. I mean, the end of the world? Hell, everyone with any sense knows climate change isn't even real. The world ain't about to stop turning. She's cold as ice, though. You shoulda seen her when we caught Darryl Moses. She got me to put down all the crack whores they had locked up there. Cold as *ice*, man. Guess I'm lucky she likes me. Probably wants a piece of old Cody herself.'

Lana had never heard Cody string so many words together. Why was he here? What was his errand? Bring the mayor with him to Shannon, or just kill him? She crawled a little way to the left and peered around the corner of the island. She could see Cody's boots. Whatever he was up to, he didn't seem in any great hurry. She heard the glug of Scotch coming out of the bottle and the smell of smoke as he lit a cigarette.

'It's a shame Elizabeth ain't here. She'd fit in perfect at the Cradle. Coulda squeezed out a little Cody or two.'

Lana shook her head sharply at the mayor, urging him not to react. But his face had gone red.

'How old is she, Mayor?' Jimmy went on. 'Sixteen? Seventeen? Just the age I like 'em. I mean, it's a shame she's not a virgin, but Lord oh Lord, her titties are—'

The mayor stood up.

'I'm gonna rip your head off,' Hood said. 'And then I'm gonna—'

Cody shot him.

Hood cried out in pain and fell. He was at the other end of the island, just his legs visible from where Lana was crouched. They were twitching, kicking out. She heard Cody take a step towards him.

The path between Lana's position and the kitchen door was clear.

She ran.

Cody whirled round. 'What the hell? *Lana?*'

She leaped over the prone Yolanda and didn't look back. She bounced off the door frame and used the momentum to propel her towards the central staircase in the hallway. Cody finally emerged from the shock of seeing her and a shot popped, a bullet smashing into the banister beside her.

'Lana!' he roared. 'Get your ass back here, bitch!' He let out a happy whoop and came pounding after her.

She didn't look back – just kept ascending the stairs, two at a time, ignoring the pain in her bruised legs. Another shot rang out, the bullet blasting a hole in a family portrait on the mezzanine level.

She needed to find the mayor's bedroom. His gun.

She reached the next floor and looked left and right. She could hear Cody starting up the stairs. He'd be here in seconds. There was a heavy ceramic vase on a side table. She picked it up and leaned over the banister. There he was, just below her, giggling to himself as he climbed.

'Hey!' she yelled.

Cody looked up and she dropped it, aiming at his head. He lurched back, lost his balance and tumbled loudly down the stairs. She was already on the move when she heard him hit the bottom and swear loudly. Still functional, dammit. She'd bought a few seconds, anyway.

She tore along the hallway, pushing and pulling open doors. A bathroom. A closet. At the end of the hallway, just before the bend, was a room that was clearly Elizabeth's. Lana could hear Cody coming up the stairs again. As soon as he reached the top, she'd be directly in his line of fire.

She made a snap decision and went into Elizabeth's room, looking around wildly for a weapon. There was a pair of scissors in a pot on the desk but they were too blunt. She picked up a snow globe from a shelf but it was too light.

'La–na,' she heard from down the hall, in a singsong voice. 'I'm so happy you're still alive.'

He was taking his time, opening and closing the same doors she had. She could picture him, with that greasy blond hair, that shit-eating grin.

'You probably don't even know how long I've wanted you. Why would you? Little Queen Bee. You know what I'm gonna do? I'm gonna take you back to the Cradle with me. We can make beautiful babies together.'

The temptation to shout *What, with your pencil dick?* was almost overwhelming.

She looked up and saw, on a higher shelf, a bronze trophy in the shape of a microphone. She reached up and took it down, testing it in her hands. *GLEE CLUB 2016*, it read. The base was square and weighty. She held it at the microphone end and waited on the other side of the door.

'Hey, Lana, where aaaaare you?' He was right outside. 'Come out here and show me that beautiful ass.'

She pictured the moment he had shoved her off that cliff. Replayed the vile words that had oozed from his lips in the kitchen. She knew she ought to be scared. He was a murderer. Without a conscience. And he was the one holding a gun.

But she had survived so much already.

She was better than him. Better in every way.

And she wanted him dead. She'd *make* him dead.

When he shoved the door open wide and started inside, she was already swinging the base of the trophy at him. She drove it into his grinning face, twisting it so the sharp corner struck him between the eyes. It made a hollow, meaty sound.

He cried out and clutched his face with both hands.

She followed up with a kick to the balls so hard she heard a squelch. He screamed and dropped to his hands and knees. She stamped on his hand as hard as she could – he screamed again – and kicked him in the face. A crunch as his nose shattered.

Then she scooped up the gun he'd dropped and pointed it at his head as he clutched his streaming nose, rocking back on his heels to look up at her.

'Where's the Cradle?' she demanded. 'Where is it?'

He took his hands away from his face. Blood streamed down from between his eyes. He smiled, and the blood ran from his lips onto his teeth.

She jabbed the gun towards him, her finger on the trigger. '*Where is it?*'

He smirked at her.

She shot him in the thigh. He cried out and clutched his leg, blood pumping through his fingers.

'Tell me where it is or I'll—'

He made a grab for her legs. She stepped back, almost tripping, and he lurched sideways and picked up the trophy that she'd dropped when she picked up the gun. With a cry of fury, he swung it towards her.

She leapt backwards, dodging it. He pulled it back, preparing to swing it again.

She shot him in the face.

Lana leaned against the wall, panting, exhausted. Blood and brains were spattered across the floor.

Cody was dead, and that was a wonderful thing. But now she would never know where the Cradle was.

Chapter 41

Shannon had the dream again. This time, she was sealed in a crypt, surrounded by corpses. Her belly was swollen and she realised, in the dream, that she was nine months pregnant – ripe, ready to give birth. Up above, beneath a warm summer sky, there was a carnival happening: children danced barefoot in the streets and fireworks painted the night. She was in labour, and she banged on the door of the crypt, pleading for help. Cody was beside her, but his face was a scorched hole, half his head missing, bits of bone and brain exposed to the air, flies crawling in and out of what remained of his skull.

'Come on, honey,' he said, encouraging her in a rasping voice. 'Push. It's time to meet our baby.'

And she lay down and felt it coming, trying to force its way out of her. Something black and wet, with strong muscles and sharp teeth.

Cody said, 'I can see the head. I can see the claws. That's it, Shannon. Push. *Push*.'

She woke up gasping and leapt out of bed, and rushed over to the window, desperate for air, for light, but it wasn't a real window, it was a picture. A stupid goddamn *picture*.

She ripped it from the wall and, with a yell, tore it in two.

She tried to calm down, to push the images from her head. She showered but the water was cold, the flow weak. She tried yoga, attempting a kriya that had helped her before, but it was no good. She could feel the weight of all the concrete and steel and earth above and around her, and it was like being back in the nightmare, like there was something inside her, the trembling of her belly caused by the monster she was carrying. Drying herself, she saw something large and hairy move in the corner of the room, scuttling into the shadows, and she drew back, trying to breathe.

Oh God.

What have I done?

She'd never spent a prolonged period in a confined space like this before. Most of her life had been spent out in the open – from the sprawling town where she'd grown up, to the Ranch, via all the open spaces of Central and South America. She'd spent her life without walls around her. She hadn't even thought about what it would be like living underground. How it would feel like she was being crushed – that there was not enough air or light or space.

You'll get used to it, she told herself. *You'll have to.*

But right now, right this second, she had to get out of here.

It was slightly better in the corridor – less enclosed – but not much. She needed real air. Oxygen. Sunlight.

How do you think you're going to get through five years *of this?* said the voice in her head. *You can't even handle twenty-four hours.*

She told it to shut up, still muttering to herself when the elevator doors opened and she found herself face to face with Jimmy.

He held the door for her and she got in. Again, he was giving her that curious look.

'You still want to do it first thing tomorrow?' he asked.

'It?'

He stared at her. 'Faith's execution. I guess you still want to go ahead, right?'

She rubbed her face. 'Of course. I just need . . . Is Cody back?' As she said his name, the image of the nightmare version of Cody came to her. The missing face. The pink, exposed brain.

'No. No word from him.'

'Oh God.' The dream was real. Cody was dead. She knew it. 'Shannon?'

It wasn't Cody's death that upset her. He was just hired muscle. She felt no warmth towards him, no sadness that he was dead, in the same way she felt no warmth towards Jimmy or, well, *anyone* these days. But she couldn't shake the image from her dream, the fact that she had *known* about Cody, and the way it was mixed up with the dream that she was giving birth to a monster. It all seemed like an omen. A very bad omen.

What have I done?

'What's the matter with you?' Jimmy asked.

She snapped out of her reverie. 'What?'

'You've seemed completely different since we got here. I don't get it. This is what you've always wanted, Shannon. Yeah, okay, it's not finished. It's not as luxurious as you'd like. But this is it.'

She could hardly breathe. The elevator was ascending, and all she could think about was the warmth of the sun outside. The taste of the air. Outside, she would be able to hear the whispering of the trees again – even here, in the middle of the desert. She would be able to shake off the horrific image of Cody's ruined face and the sense that there was a monster growing in her belly, waiting to push its way out.

'Earth to Shannon. Hello?'

She wheeled around on him and grabbed hold of the front of his shirt. 'The fire reports. What's happening?'

He grasped her hands, freed himself from them, gently pushed her away. 'Nothing. They're all under control. And it's been raining overnight, across the state. The fires are going out.'

The edges of her vision were going dark and the rest was turning red. The walls of the elevator were closing in. She could see Cody in the corner. Blood and bone and brain. A fat tarantula squatted on his shoulder.

'I've made a mistake.'

She said it to herself, not intending Jimmy to hear, but she must have said it louder than she'd meant to because he said, 'You're kidding me. You're telling me this *now*? What do you want to do, huh? Go back to the Ranch?'

She nodded and he barked out a laugh. 'It's a bit late for that, Shannon. After we left that pile of bodies at the farm? What do you think is gonna happen? We're going to have the whole fucking state of California looking for us.' He grabbed hold of her arms and began to shake her. 'We are *stuck* here now, Shannon. And you'd better snap out of—'

'Get your hands off me!'

She screamed it in his face and he released her, took a step back. At the same moment, the elevator came to a halt and the doors slid open.

'I need to breathe,' she said.

All she cared about was seeing the sky, the sand, the clouds. She would feel better after that. Jimmy was right: this was what she had always wanted. It was too late to back out now. They had to carry on with the plan, even if the apocalypse was delayed. She could move her room closer to the surface. Take regular trips to the outside. It would be fine.

So yes, carry on with the plan. Starting with Faith's execution. But only after she'd filled her lungs with fresh air and felt the sun on her face.

Jimmy was still in the elevator, looking out at her, pressing the button to hold the doors open.

'Stop looking at me like that!' she yelled. 'Or do you want to join Faith? You want to die too?'

He shook his head and let go of the button, muttering to himself. The elevator doors slid shut.

Chapter 42

Aidan paced the little room, his cell, trying to figure out a plan. They had agreed to bring him a final breakfast. Perhaps, as Jimmy or whoever handed him the plate or tray, he could strike him in the face with it. Would there be a knife or fork? No, surely they wouldn't be that stupid.

It was more likely that he was going to have to wait until he was out of this room. He wasn't going to overpower anyone. And there were fourteen floors and how many soldiers between him and the surface, anyway? What did that leave?

This was going to be a show trial. He'd have the ear of the crowd, presumably. His only, minuscule hope was to try to appeal to them. Persuade them, somehow, that Shannon was lying. Tell them about the breeding programme. It might shock them into action. Cameron would be in the crowd, maybe Kristin too, if she was allowed out of the maternity suite. And what about all the other people Aidan had freed, at least temporarily, from the farm? Cameron said they were beaten, weak, but surely they weren't all so brainwashed that they couldn't see through this insanity?

He heard the key turn in the lock and Jimmy came in, a gun in his left hand. No sign of Aidan's last breakfast.

Jimmy seemed amused by something. Aidan's impending death, no doubt. Aidan was trying to work out if there was any way he could fight – perhaps he could strike Jimmy's weakened, bandaged right hand – when Jimmy reached behind his own back and produced a second gun, a black pistol.

He held it out to him, butt first.

Aidan held his hands up, palms out. 'What's this?'

'Take it,' Jimmy said.

'What, so you've got an excuse to shoot me right here?'

Jimmy chuckled. 'Think, Faith. Would I need an excuse? Take the goddamn gun, all right?'

Again, Aidan had no choice. As soon as Aidan was holding the gun, Jimmy turned and left the cell, leaving the door open.

For a moment, Aidan was too stunned to move. Was this a trap? It had to be. But what other option did he have? Tentatively, he peered out of the room.

Jimmy was already halfway along the corridor towards the elevator.

'What are you doing?' Aidan called after him. It *had* to be a trap. A test of some kind.

Jimmy stopped walking and turned around. 'I'm getting out of here,' he said. 'And you're going to help me.'

'What?'

'I could try to persuade the guards that Shannon has lost it, that they should listen to me, but I don't think they'd buy it. They're loyal to her. Hell, *I* was loyal to her. We're going to have to shoot our way out, and it'll be easier if there are two of us.'

'Hold on. What do you mean, "Shannon has lost it"? Did she ever have it?'

That made Jimmy laugh. 'An excellent point. You know, when she came to find me after her time in the jungle, her vision, I was tapped *out*. I'd had it. I'd spent so long fighting the fight, you know? My whole goddamn adult life. I'd been in Brazil for two years by that point, putting my life on the line every freaking day – and were things getting better? More of the rainforest was being cleared by the minute. The planet wasn't just warming, it was starting to sizzle. More and more extreme weather events. More species going extinct every day. Every *hour*. We were wasting our goddamn time.'

'And what? Shannon had a plan?'

'Not just a plan. She was on fire, man, with, like, an honest-to-God *mission*. She lit me up like I didn't think I'd ever get lit up again. So I followed her. It was crazy, but *good* crazy. *Necessary* crazy. I bought into it and I did everything I could to help her.'

He rubbed a hand, hard, across his face, and released a hollow, self-amazed laugh.

'And now? You know those cults who yell about the end of the world, the end is nigh, it's going to happen tomorrow . . . and then the planet keeps turning and they say, "Oh sorry, we got it wrong, the apocalypse is *next* June?" That's Shannon. And the decisions she's been making. Sending us into that stinking weed farm, risking all these lives just so she could get her revenge on Darryl Moses. Fucking madness. Even keeping you alive, so she could look big in front of everyone, show them how strong and merciless she is with this bullshit show trial.' He took off his cowboy hat and scratched his scalp. 'I guess you can say I've puked up the Kool-Aid. I'm going back to Brazil. I left a woman there. A good woman. I think it's time I retired.'

He walked on and Aidan hurried after him. He wasn't going to argue, even if there was a small part of him that still worried this might be a trap.

'There's only one way out,' Jimmy said as they approached the elevator. 'The same way we came in.'

'I assume it's guarded?'

'Yeah. Three guys.'

Jimmy pressed the button to call the elevator and they waited for it to arrive.

When the doors opened, it was, blessedly, empty. 'What about the others?' Aidan asked, as they got in.

'What others?'

'All the other people here! We can't leave everyone.'

Jimmy shook his head. 'I don't know. Once we get out of here and I've skedaddled, you can call the cops. Whatever. I don't give a shit. I'll be long gone.'

'What about Scarlett?'

Jimmy smiled.

'What are you smiling at? She's here, isn't she?'

'Yeah,' Jimmy said. 'She's here.' This time he laughed, presumably at the look on Aidan's face.

'Where? Where is she?'

'Where do you think? She's in the maternity suite.'

Jimmy moved to push the button that would take them up to the ground level. Aidan stepped in the way.

'Take me to her. I'm not leaving here without her.'

'Get out of the way, Faith.'

'No. You want my help getting out of here? Take me to Scarlett first. She's coming with us.'

Jimmy narrowed his eyes and muttered something to himself. Then he exhaled. 'All right. I guess it'll be fun to see her reaction when she sees you. I'm pretty sure Shannon hasn't told her you're here. She was going to do the big *ta-dah* moment this morning.'

'At my execution?'

Jimmy pressed the button for the ninth level and they travelled the short distance upwards in silence. It was a struggle for Aidan to remain calm. Scarlett was here. *She was actually here*. He was about to see her. He imagined their mum and dad's faces when he told them. Pictured himself flying home to England with Scarlett beside him. Saw them walking through the door of their old home, where they had grown up. The nightmare of the past two years behind them. His guilt finally assuaged. Everything okay, at last, at last.

'Here we are,' said Jimmy. 'Ninth floor. Ladies' sundries, maternity wear. Please watch your step, sir.'

He sniggered at himself as the doors slid open.

A man in a black boiler suit stared at them. One of the guards Aidan had seen when they'd arrived here.

'Hey, man,' Jimmy said, as cool as anything.

The guard looked at him, then at Aidan. 'What's this?' he said.

'Taking the prisoner to the assembly hall,' Jimmy said. 'For the trial.'

'So what are you doing down here?'

Jimmy feigned confusion. 'Crap. I pressed the wrong button. I know. I'm a dumbass.'

The guard glared at him. 'Maybe I should help you escort him,' he said, looking at Aidan as if he was beneath contempt.

'Sure. Thanks.'

The guard entered the elevator. He stood facing Aidan, with his back to Jimmy. 'I'm looking forward to seeing this guy die,' he said.

'Yeah, me too,' said Jimmy, and he lashed out, as quick as a scorpion, cracking the guard's skull with the butt of his gun. The guard dropped and, while Aidan stared, Jimmy stooped and lifted the semi-automatic rifle from the guard's arms. 'This will be useful. Hold the elevator open, would you?'

While Aidan did so, Jimmy dragged the guard out of the elevator and opened the door of what turned out to be a storage closet. Aidan helped him pull the guard inside and Jimmy locked him in, pocketing the key.

'This way,' Jimmy said.

Aidan hurried along the corridor after Jimmy, clutching the pistol Jimmy had given him with palms that were slick with sweat. He paused for a moment to familiarise himself with the weapon – found the safety, practised flipping it off – then took a deep breath and gathered himself. This was it. Again, he pictured his parents' faces when he told them the news. The joy. But before that, he would see Scarlett's face. Two years older than when she'd stayed with him in Seattle. Not a child anymore, but not quite an adult. What had she been through over the past two years? Had she suffered? Was she scared? And what had happened in that clearing last week? Had she discovered her fate as one of Shannon's 'chosen ones', and tried to run? It must be that.

They passed a nursery, with toys and stuffed animals stacked up neatly around a floor covered with rubber mats. The next room was for storage: diapers and large tins of powdered baby milk. A couple of doors along was a large room containing a pair of what looked like hospital beds. Unlike the rest of the bunker, these rooms were clean, freshly painted. They were still claustrophobic, the lack of natural light giving them an abandoned, creepy air, but there were no cracks in the walls, no stink of mouse droppings or spiders hiding in the shadows. Shannon had clearly given her maternity suite priority. But where were the women?

They turned a corner and found a door.

'I'm going to wait here and keep watch,' Jimmy said. 'In case Shannon or one of the guards comes. She's in room fourteen.'

With his heart pounding, Aidan peeked through the frosted-glass panel and saw another empty corridor. He tried the door handle. Unlocked. He opened it slowly and went through.

A woman wearing a white boiler suit came around the corner. She saw him and the gun in his hand, and dropped the pile of towels she had been carrying, bracing herself to run. Aidan saw a box on the wall a few feet further down the corridor behind her. It looked like an emergency alarm.

'I'll shoot!' he yelled, raising the gun.

The woman, with her back to him, froze.

'Put your arms in the air.'

He marched up to her and went past so he was facing her and standing between her and the alarm.

'What's your name?' he said.

She glared at him. 'Madison.'

'I'm here for my sister. Scarlett. She's in room fourteen.'

Madison's eyes darted towards the alarm on the wall.

'Don't even think about it,' Aidan said. 'Take me to room fourteen.'

Her attitude – that of a grumpy shopworker being bothered by a demanding customer – almost made Aidan laugh. She took a bunch of keys off her belt and found the one she needed. Aidan kept his gun trained on her, and his body between her and the alarm, and escorted her along the corridor.

They reached room fourteen. Madison fumbled with the key in the lock and, finally, it turned. She pushed the door open and stepped through. He followed her in, not allowing himself to focus on the form lying on the bed, facing away from him, until he'd taken the key and locked the door behind him so Madison couldn't get out and raise the alarm.

This was it.

The moment he'd waited for, the last two years.

The moment he would be reunited with his sister.

'Scarlett?' he said to the red-haired woman on the bed. His voice cracked as he spoke. A large part of him still thought this might be a trick, that Jimmy had been lying, that Francesca had made a mistake. That when the woman on the bed turned over she would look similar to Scarlett but not be her. It would be a stranger and he would be no closer to finding his sister.

The woman rolled over to face him. There was the little birth-mark on her upper lip. The gap between her teeth, the same as his.

'Aidan?' she said, sitting up. '*Aidan?*'

It was her.

ϖ

Scarlett sat on the edge of the bed, staring at him, and he stood there, frozen, just staring back. She looked, as he'd expected, older. She had always looked older than her age, and now, at seventeen, if he hadn't known her he would have guessed she was in her early twenties. She looked fit and healthy, no sign of physical mistreatment. He guessed Shannon needed to keep her 'chosen ones' in peak condition. She was wearing what looked like yoga pants, and loose cotton clothes. There was a book open beside her: a philosophy primer.

He rushed over and, at the same time, she got off the bed. He flung his arms around her, pulled her into a hug, aware that he was probably holding her too tight, but he had to know she was real, flesh and blood. His sister. He had found her. It took all his self-control not to cry with relief.

He wasn't sure how long passed before he felt her palms on his chest, gently pushing him away. He stepped back, still marvelling at her.

'What . . .' she began. 'I can't believe . . . What are you doing here?'

'I'll tell you everything,' he said, aware that Jimmy was waiting for them. 'But we have to get out of here.'

'What?'

'I've come for you. To take you home. To . . . save you.'

She was blinking at him, puzzled. 'Save me?'

He took hold of her hand.

304

'I know what Shannon wants you to do. I know how crazy she is. Jimmy's seen it too, at last, and he's waiting out there. We're going to fight our way out of this place.'

She blinked at him again. Did she not know what he was talking about? Was she not aware of her fate yet? He wondered if Shannon kept the women drugged, maybe stoned. He peered into Scarlett's eyes, but her pupils didn't appear to be dilated.

'How did you find me?' she asked. 'Wait, have you joined? Are you—'

He cut her off. 'No. A woman named Francesca saw you – God, it was only a few days ago – running across a clearing.'

'A woman? Wait, was she on a train?'

'Yes! You saw her too? It was so lucky. So crazy! If she hadn't seen you being chased, if she hadn't recognised you, I would never have—'

It was her turn to cut him off.

'What are you talking about?' she asked.

'The woman on the train. Francesca. She saw you being chased across the clearing near Eaglewood. I assume it was Jimmy and he caught you. Did you find out what they were intending for you here? You don't need to worry about it anymore. But we need to leave. Now.' He tried to tug her towards the door but she wouldn't budge.

'Scarlett . . .'

She laughed.

'What is it?'

'Oh Aidan,' she said, pulling her hand away. 'Big brother. I remember the woman. Staring out at me like she'd seen a ghost. But I wasn't being chased.'

Aidan could only say, 'You were.'

'No, I wasn't. I was *chasing*.'

Chapter 43

It was her time at last. After two years at the Ranch, Shannon had told Scarlett that she was finally being sent to the other place, to fulfil her destiny. She was being sent to the Cradle, where she would live in luxury, with her own room – 'The largest we have,' Shannon had told her – and a midwife to look after her. Everyone at the Ranch had a job, but Scarlett knew she had the most important job of all. She was going to be a mother. As the planet died, Scarlett would be one of the Eves, bringing life and hope and a future. A better future. A future in which their children would be raised to take care of the planet, to nurse it back to health, to start again from scratch.

It was an honour. The greatest honour of all.

She had known from the moment she met her that Shannon was going to change her life. It had been on her first day in Seattle, at the protest. It had been so exciting. Revelatory – that was the word. Seeing the protestors, the belief in their eyes, the placards they waved with such passion, she had known instantly that she needed to be part of it. Being vegan and nagging her parents to recycle was nowhere near enough. It didn't matter how many petitions she signed or tweets she sent, her efforts achieved nothing. She needed to do more.

Being caught up in such a scene on her very first day in America had felt like fate. And then she had become separated from Aidan, and while she waited for him to find her, gazing in awe at the drama around her, a woman had approached her, looking at her with such naked admiration that Scarlett had felt raw and exposed.

'You,' the woman had said. 'I've seen you.'

Scarlett hadn't been able to respond, and then the woman had laughed. 'Sorry, you must think I'm crazy but . . . that hair, that face. I feel like I know you. I'm Shannon Reinhardt.'

She had handed Scarlett a card with a phone number on it. 'You want to do something, don't you?'

Scarlett nodded.

'WhatsApp me using that number. I'll explain everything.' Before going, she had taken Scarlett's hands in hers and said, 'Please don't be afraid. We need to save the earth. We can't be timid.'

Seconds after Shannon Reinhardt had vanished, Aidan had appeared. And though she loved her brother, he didn't understand her.

Nobody had ever understood her.

But Scarlett had known Shannon would.

Now, she sat in the back of the van with the other two women, Jenny and Taylor. Jenny was a quiet, mousy girl who seemed so shy around Scarlett that her voice trembled when Scarlett spoke to her. Taylor was more confident: a skinny brunette who had been an athletics champ at high school and who wanted everyone to know about it. Up front were Jimmy and Frank.

They had been driving for several hours and Taylor had barely stopped talking that whole time. Speculating about where they were going. Where they would be sent. What their mission would be. Taylor longed to be taken to Brazil, to do what Jimmy had once done, fighting to save the Amazon. She was sure they were being taken somewhere like Eureka, where they would be picked up in a boat and transported to their destination.

Scarlett had nodded and played along. Shannon had explained everything to her. That Taylor and Jenny had different roles than hers. Their destiny was to work, to help raise funds for the great cause. It was easy work, Shannon had said. Fun work. The camaraderie between the recruits on the farm made it more like summer camp than anything approaching labour. But it was important that Scarlett didn't share this information. The other women might not understand.

The van slowed and stopped.

'What's going on?' Scarlett asked, leaning forward to talk to Jimmy and Frank.

'Frank's gotta take a leak,' Jimmy replied. 'Any of you need the bathroom, now's a good time. This is our one and only stop.'

He opened the back doors of the van and let them out.

Taylor and Jenny climbed out first, then Scarlett. It was still dark, not quite dawn, and the only lights were those from the van. She was disappointed to see that they were on the side of a main road that cut through the forest.

'Hey, I thought you might be taking us to the murder house again. Giving Taylor and Jenny the tour.'

Jimmy smiled. 'We haven't got time. Not today.'

'Murder house?' Taylor asked. Jenny had gone a little way into the trees, presumably to go to the toilet. Frank was already pissing noisily against a trunk, not caring if anyone saw.

'It's this awesome place near here,' Scarlett said. 'Last time, Jimmy took me and the others there to show us around. It's supposed to be haunted. This prepper guy went bonkers and—'

Taylor cut her off. 'Last time? You mean you've done this before?'

Jimmy gave Scarlett a look, like: *You shouldn't have said that.* Nobody was supposed to know that Scarlett had been allowed to ride with the men a couple of times, as a special treat. It was her reward for being Shannon's favourite, the one who was earmarked to be the first mother.

'I was meant to be going into the field,' Scarlett said, making it up on the spot. 'But I got sick, had to be taken back. I've had to wait another year for my chance.'

Was it her imagination, or did Taylor seem suspicious?

'So are you going to tell us where you're taking us?' Taylor asked Jimmy.

'It's a surprise.'

'Go on. We can't be that far away now.'

'Sorry,' he said, lighting a cigarette, the orange glow revealing . . . what? Distaste? Scarlett had always got the impression Jimmy didn't enjoy these excursions, that he saw them as a necessary evil.

She took a few steps away, ensuring the smoke wasn't blowing towards her. She couldn't risk being contaminated. It was one of the reasons why she'd been chosen to be the first mother. She had never smoked, taken drugs or drunk alcohol, and she'd been vegan since she was eleven. The doctor at the Ranch had said she was the 'healthiest specimen he'd ever seen', which made her glow with pride.

'Come on, Jimmy, don't be an asshole,' Taylor said. 'Tell us.'

Scarlett knew why Taylor could never be one of the mothers. She had a dirty mouth. She was disobedient. She didn't deserve it.

'I can't tell you,' Jimmy said, exhaling smoke, 'just in case we get intercepted and someone quizzes you. It's better for you not to know.'

'This is bullshit,' said Taylor. 'This whole thing about Scarlett here getting sick last time sounds like a lie too. You were obviously making that up, Scarlett.'

'No I wasn't.'

'Come off it. You're always up at the big house with Shannon. I bet you know where we're going. It's Brazil, isn't it?'

Scarlett didn't respond. She looked to Jimmy for help.

'Let's get back in the van,' he said.

'Uh-uh. Not till Shannon's pet here tells me where we're going. Oh God, please don't tell me you're taking us to LA. I've got a lot of friends there and I can't—'

'You're not going to LA,' Jimmy said.

'Not San Francisco?'

'Jesus wept,' Jimmy said, throwing his cigarette to the ground and stubbing it out beneath his boot. 'No wonder—'

He stopped himself.

'No wonder what?'

'Nothing.'

They were all silent for a few seconds. Scarlett studied Taylor's face in the dim light. She could almost see her brain whirring away.

'All right, let's get going,' Jimmy said.

Frank climbed back into the driver's seat and Jenny got into the back of the van, but Taylor hesitated.

'I still need to pee,' she said.

Above them, the sky was beginning to lighten. Just a shade. Scarlett could feel it. The world beginning to stir from sleep, preparing to wake up.

'You've had your chance,' Jimmy said.

'But I really need to go. If you don't let me go now I'm going to complain all the way there.'

He swore, then said, 'Fine. Be quick.'

Taylor gave Scarlett a look, then stepped off the road.

As the sky continued to lighten, the air taking on a greyish-purple tinge, Scarlett could see Taylor's silhouette among the trees.

'You shouldn't have mentioned the murder house,' Jimmy said.

'I'm sorry.'

He sighed. 'It's fine. But we really ought to get going.'

They both looked towards Taylor.

She wasn't there. And then Scarlett heard crashing, the sound of branches shaking, footsteps crunching.

She bolted into the cedars, directly towards the noise. Jimmy followed but he was older, slower, his lungs damaged by years of smoking. Scarlett had sharp eyes, even in low light, and she caught a glimpse of Taylor running away from her.

'Taylor,' she called. 'Come back. What are you doing?'

There was no response except for the sound of scuffling and branches being shoved aside. Scarlett could see them moving, waving in a helpful line as though bent on pinpointing where Taylor was headed. With the air around her growing lighter by the second, Scarlett ran as fast as she could, darting between tree trunks, aware of Jimmy panting and complaining behind her.

Suddenly, she emerged into a clearing. Long grass. Rocks strewn about. Dawn was breaking, the sky turning orange and pink. The birds were waking up, filling the forest with their chorus. And, running away across the clearing, was Taylor.

'Wait!' Scarlett called. She didn't know what punishment Jimmy would mete out to Taylor, but Scarlett knew it wouldn't be pleasant. She felt no sympathy, though. Taylor was a loudmouth, a troublemaker. She didn't deserve to be one of the survivors.

Scarlett increased her pace, watching as Taylor passed the centre of the clearing.

As, a moment later, a train came thundering out of the forest.

Taylor froze, goggling at the train, but didn't stay still for long: she kept running, crossed over the track to the far side just before the train roared between them. Scarlett kept going too, nearing the track, the train right in front of her, just metres away.

A face stared out at her. A woman. Old, wide-eyed. Palms pressed against the window.

Scarlett couldn't help but stare back as she ran. She sensed movement behind her and stole a glance over her shoulder, saw Jimmy emerge from the trees. He had lost his cowboy hat somewhere along the way.

Scarlett's foot hit a rock. She fell, and the impact knocked the breath from her. Before she knew it, Jimmy was there, hauling her to her feet. The train rattled past and disappeared from view, swallowed by the forest.

Scarlett didn't hesitate. She ran on, immediately putting distance between herself and Jimmy, who had paused to catch his breath. Taylor had stopped to look back at the train and seemed to be frozen, until she saw Scarlett coming towards her again. Taylor turned to run but only managed a few steps before she cried out. This time she had tripped herself, and she didn't get up again. Her hands went to her ankle.

'Oh Taylor,' Scarlett said, fighting for breath after she'd crossed the train tracks and reached her. 'That was a silly thing to do.'

They both looked up to see Jimmy holding his gun, jogging towards them. He was clearly furious, holding his side like he had a stitch.

'It isn't right,' Taylor said, panting with fear and pain. 'Whatever they're doing, wherever they're taking us, it isn't right.' She held out a hand. 'Scarlett, please. Help me.'

'I'm sorry,' Scarlett said, as Jimmy reached them, and she turned away so she didn't have to see.

But there was no shot.

'Come on,' Jimmy said. 'We're taking her to the farm. Darryl Moses is gonna love her. I'm going to suggest he takes her straight to his freaking joy house. What she deserves.'

'What's the joy house?' Scarlett asked.

He didn't reply, and Scarlett never found out. She guessed it was some kind of entertainment venue. Maybe a bar or something.

Together, they escorted the weeping Taylor across the clearing, through the woods and back to the van.

Chapter 44

'I *want* to be here, Aidan,' Scarlett said. 'It's a privilege. It's where I'm meant to be. Shannon saw me in one of her visions. Isn't that amazing? The moment she saw me at that protest in Seattle, she recognised me.'

He couldn't believe what he was hearing.

'I'm going to be the first mother,' she said.

He stood up. 'Oh my God. You're not . . . ?'

'Pregnant?' She laughed. 'Not yet. To be honest, I was expecting to be here for longer before everyone else showed up. I'm still waiting for Shannon to tell me who she's chosen for me.'

He went to grab her hand again but she snatched it away.

'Scarlett, we can talk about this later, but we need to get out of here.'

'No!' The smile she had been wearing slipped away. 'You think you can just show up here and start bossing me around? You were always trying to tell me what to do, ever since I was a little kid. You were the same when I came to Seattle.'

'But Scarlett. This is insane. The world isn't ending. You've been brainwashed.'

She sneered at him.

'You can't tell her what to do.'

He turned. Madison was standing there with her arms crossed.

There was a banging on the door. Jimmy. 'What the hell's going on?' he shouted.

Aidan was in a daze. He unlocked the door automatically. Jimmy nodded a greeting to Scarlett.

'Tell her,' Aidan said, pointing a finger at Scarlett. His heart was thumping and he felt sick. This couldn't be happening. 'She thinks it's all true. She's talking about being the "first mother" or something insane.'

Scarlett's lip curled. 'You never believed in anything.'

Jimmy took Aidan's elbow. 'You've seen her. You know she's safe. As deluded as Shannon, but safe. We have to go. Now.'

'Deluded?' Scarlett said.

Jimmy waved a hand at her. 'You'll figure it out. It took me long enough to see the light but, Hallelujah, I've seen it, and if you don't come with me this second, Aidan, I'm going on my own.'

'No. I can't leave her.' He turned back to his sister. 'I came here to save you.'

'How many times do I have to tell you? I don't need saving.'

'Please. Scarlett. You have to listen to me. Shannon is wrong. There's no apocalypse. And she doesn't even have enough of you for her crazy plan.'

'He's right,' said Jimmy.

Scarlett's eyes flashed with rage. 'You're a traitor. I'm going to make sure Shannon casts you out, so you burn with the rest of them.'

'Whatever,' Jimmy said. 'Aidan, I'm going.' He pointed his pistol at Madison. 'Stay here.'

He strode from the room.

'Wait,' Aidan called. He could hardly think straight. He couldn't leave here without her. That would be insane. He went into the doorway to see how far Jimmy had gone – not far – and was about to turn, determined to persuade Scarlett to come with him, when he felt hands on his back, a violent shove, and he lurched forward into the corridor.

The door to room fourteen slammed shut behind him.

He tried the handle. Scarlett and Madison had locked it from the inside. He hammered at the door and Scarlett yelled, 'Leave me alone!'

Jimmy was still in the corridor. 'Come *on*. You can send the Feds back for her. This is your last chance, man, because I'm *gone*.'

Still Aidan couldn't move. There was nothing to do *but* follow Jimmy. He wasn't going to get Scarlett out of this place unless he managed to bust down that door and physically carry her out of here. She was too far gone. Jimmy was right. Once Aidan had escaped he could send the police or the FBI here to get everyone out, including Scarlett. Yet Aidan couldn't take the first step away from the door.

Until Jimmy shrugged and walked off.

It was seeing his back – the back of the man who represented his best, his only, hope of getting Scarlett out of this place alive – that turned the switch that set him in motion away from his sister.

He'd started running to catch up when a woman's voice called 'Hey!' from behind a different door. Aidan paused.

'Aidan? It's Kristin. Don't go without me.'

Up ahead, Jimmy had stopped and was looking back at him incredulously. '*Now* what?'

'We need to break this door down. She can help us.'

Muttering swear words, Jimmy stalked back to Aidan. After ordering him to stand behind him and calling to Kristin to stay away from the door, he stood at an angle to the door and fired at the lock. The explosion made Aidan's ears ring but, a moment later, the door opened and Kristin emerged.

'Come on,' Aidan said. 'We're leaving.'

'Wait,' said Kristin. 'What about the other women?'

'Leave them,' Jimmy snapped. 'Most of them are as far gone as Scarlett. You can come back for them later.'

'Scarlett?' said Kristin. 'She's here?'

Aidan didn't have a chance to reply because the air was filled with the shriek of an alarm. The gunshot must have alerted the guards. They were probably on their way right now.

Jimmy jogged off down the corridor.

Aidan took one last rueful look back towards room fourteen. Shannon had done it to her: taken a malleable, idealistic girl and moulded her. Warped her. He couldn't blame Scarlett. And he was sure she would come around eventually. She would need help. Therapy. And he would be there for her, whatever it took.

But only if they made it out alive.

Aidan, Jimmy and Kristin went through a door to the stairwell. 'I assume this goes all the way to the top?' Aidan said, looking up the stairs.

'Yep. Follow me.' Jimmy began to climb.

Kristin took a deep breath and didn't move. She seemed scared now.

'Are you sure you want to do this?' Aidan asked. 'To come with me? You can wait in your room if you prefer.'

'I'm sure. I can't stay here a second longer.'

Jimmy was already halfway up the stairs. Aidan wondered what was happening. Maybe the alarm would do them a favour. Guards would be on their way to the ninth level. Perhaps Shannon was too.

They started up the stairs after Jimmy. Aidan wished Kristin had a gun so they could cover both directions, up and down. Each time they reached a new floor, he ducked and waited. The alarm continued to blare. But no guards came. Jimmy had vanished. So much for doing this together.

Aidan was out of breath by the time they reached the floor below ground level. The stairs ended at a set of double doors.

Kristin peered through the glass. She gestured for Aidan to follow her and they went through into a small annex that contained nothing but a couple of dumpsters on wheels. The smell of garbage and old food hung in the air. Some metal steps led up from the far side of the room.

The dumpsters were full of old food and packaging.

'Those steps must lead up to the kitchen,' she said.

They hurried up the metal steps, Aidan first, then Kristin. They reached the top and Aidan opened the door slowly, bringing his finger to his lips.

He went through into the kitchen.

There were five people in the room. Most of them turned as the door opened to stare at the new arrivals. One of them was Cameron, who seemed stunned but excited to see them. Aidan recognised the others from the back of the van that had brought them here from the farm.

And, crouched by the door, gun in hand, was Jimmy.

Jimmy looked over his shoulder and said, 'Faith.' Aidan went over and crouched beside him.

'There are guards out there. I'm not sure how many.'

'They don't know you're in here?'

'I don't think so. But I've got an idea.' Jimmy beckoned to Cameron. 'Hey. You. Want to get out of here?'

'Well, yeah.'

'Good. They know you. Go take a look outside, then come back and tell us who's out there. Got it?'

Cameron said yes.

'Any of you holler or make a fuss,' Jimmy said to the others in the kitchen, 'and I'll shoot you in the face. Understand?'

Cameron went out. He came back after a few seconds.

'There's a guy by the elevator with his gun trained on the doors. He looks kind of confused.'

'Anyone else?' Jimmy asked.

'Yeah. There's a guard by the inner doors too. The ones that lead out to the hangar.'

Jimmy motioned for the others to come closer. 'I want one of you to run out there. Act panicked. Tell them Faith is in here and that he's waving a knife around.'

'I'll do it,' said Kristin. She went to move towards the doors, but Jimmy grabbed her arm.

'You're not going to rat me out, are you?'

'Don't be a dick, Jimmy,' she said.

Chapter 45

Aidan took a deep breath, checked the safety on his gun and waited for Jimmy to give him the nod. Then the two of them took up positions either side of the door.

Kristin left the room.

'I've been talking to people,' Cameron said to Aidan. 'The ones from the farm, trying to persuade them Shannon's lying—'

He was drowned out by Kristin, screaming out an unintelligible torrent of words.

The first guard came running into the kitchen. Jimmy shot him in the head and he went down – revealing the second guard, right behind him, swivelling towards Jimmy as the first guard fell.

Jimmy rolled as the gun fired and blasted the wall behind him. 'Do it!' he yelled to Aidan.

Aidan had never shot a live target before. He'd only fired a gun for the first time two days ago. The scene played out in slow motion: the guard's head turning towards him, the widening of his eyes, his gun coming up, Jimmy yelling, voice deep and distorted.

Aidan fired.

The man went down.

Aidan stood there for a second, stunned. He'd killed someone. Staring down at the two bodies on the floor, he felt very little but numb shock. He knelt beside the second guard, putting his gun on the floor, and checked for a pulse. The guy was dead. Aidan stayed beside him for a moment. His ears rang. His chest hurt. All that was keeping him going was adrenaline.

Jimmy, however, was all motion. He had run from the room. Aidan shook himself from his state of shock and followed, just in time to see Jimmy press the switch on the wall to release the door that led out to the hangar.

It didn't open.

'Goddammit.'

There was a number pad beneath the switch.

'You don't know the code?' Aidan said, arriving beside Jimmy.

'Only Shannon knows it. Maybe the guards.'

'Who we just killed.'

'Yeah.'

Aidan studied the pad. They were close. So close.

'Maybe there's an override,' Aidan said. 'Maybe if we shut off the power?'

'The generator's in the basement. I think there's a backup too, and I don't even know where that is.'

'Can we break it down?' Aidan asked, examining the door.

'It's solid steel. The whole place is designed to be impenetrable.'

Kristin and Cameron had joined them, with the others from the kitchen milling around behind them.

'Try Shannon's birthday,' Cameron said.

'How the fuck should I know when her birthday is?' said Jimmy.

'It's December twenty-first,' said Cameron. 'Midwinter. I remember because that was the day I arrived at the Ranch. There was a party. Did you forget?'

'I can barely remember my *own* birthday.'

Aidan punched in the number, remembering to use the American date format. One, two, two, one. Nothing happened.

He tried the British format – two, one, one, two – just in case. Still, the door didn't open.

'I guess that would have been too easy,' he said.

'We need to find Shannon,' said Kristin. 'Make her tell us the code. Where is she?'

Kristin and Cameron ran back towards the kitchen, where the others from the farm stood, and at the same moment the elevator door pinged open and another guard came out, gripping a black pistol. He stopped when he saw the small crowd outside the kitchen.

'Shit,' Jimmy said, and the guard must have heard him because he yelled Jimmy's name.

'Get out of the way!' the guard yelled. 'All of you, get back in the kitchen.'

No one moved.

The guard yelled at the group again, trying to get a clear shot at Jimmy and Aidan, but neither side was able to fire because of the people between them.

'Move out of the goddamn way!' the guard yelled, grabbing at Kristin. She tried to get away but his grip on her arm was too firm. He pulled her against him and pressed the barrel of the pistol against her cheek.

'Lay down your weapons,' he shouted, 'or I'll kill her.'

'I don't give a shit,' yelled Jimmy in response. 'Shoot all of 'em.'

The guard changed tack. He screamed at the remaining group: 'Get out of the way! Move or I'll—'

He fell silent and his knees gave away. He let go of Kristin and slumped to the floor, revealing Cameron standing behind him, a bloody knife that he'd taken from the kitchen in his hand. He must have gone in there while Jimmy and the guard were yelling at each other.

At the same time, the elevator doors pinged open again to reveal around a dozen recruits. Aidan recognised most of them from the farm. The people Cameron had spoken to, trying to persuade them Shannon had been lying. They came swarming out of the elevator into the corridor.

Aidan and Jimmy pushed their way through the chaos. Jimmy knelt beside the fallen guard. He was still breathing.

He stuck his gun in the guard's face.

'What's the code for the door?'

The guard hesitated.

'The code and I'll get you medical help.'

'Seven three four one,' he said, before closing his eyes. Even if Jimmy hadn't been lying about getting a doctor, it was too late for the guard now.

Jimmy jumped up and Aidan followed him back to the door.

'Any idea of the significance?' Aidan asked.

'What am I, a numerologist?' Jimmy replied.

Aidan punched in the numbers and the door opened slowly inwards.

Aidan and Jimmy immediately went through, with the others behind them.

'Huh?' said Jimmy, and Aidan saw it at the same time. The outer doors were already open. Bright light flooded into the hangar. Aidan went over to the exit, getting a proper look outside for the first time. A path led towards a high chain-link fence that appeared to surround the bunker. Beyond that, nothing. An expanse of flat, sun-scorched ground that stretched to low hills on the horizon. Scattered boulders and spiky, dry grass. But why was the outer door already open?

Kristin arrived at Aidan's shoulder. 'What do you think?' he asked.

Her answer was drowned out by a revving engine. Aidan turned to see Jimmy behind the wheel of a truck, which had been parked to the side of the hangar. And he was already driving towards the exit.

'Hey!' Aidan stood in the truck's path, and Jimmy stopped and wound down the window.

'You can't leave without us,' Aidan shouted. 'I need to find a phone so I can call the police.'

Jimmy rolled his eyes. 'Our deal's done, Faith. Take one of the other vehicles. I'm not a freaking Uber.'

And then Jimmy stopped. He had seen something. Aidan turned around to follow his stare.

'Well, look who it is,' Jimmy said.

There was a woman standing on the path, near the open gate in the perimeter fence.

Shannon.

She was looking in the other direction, face turned up towards the sun, seemingly oblivious to everything that was going on behind her.

Jimmy was laughing now, a dark brand of laughter that raised the hairs on the back of Aidan's neck, and he revved the truck's engine. 'Get out of my way, Faith,' Jimmy called down to him.

'What are you going to do to her?'

'What the hell do you care?' When Aidan didn't move, Jimmy pointed his gun at him. 'Listen. Don't be thinking I *like* you, Faith. We helped each other get out and that's where it ends. If you don't move, I *will* shoot you.'

Aidan had no choice. He stepped out of the path of the truck and Jimmy revved the engine again.

This time, Shannon must have heard it. She turned. From this distance, Aidan couldn't make out her features. As the truck shot through the exit doors, Jimmy leaning out of the window with his pistol in his left hand, steering with his bandaged right, she ran through the gate.

Despite everything Shannon had done – he saw a flash of Lana, falling from the cliff, Shannon standing nearby with a little smile on her face; she had taken Scarlett from him and brainwashed her

– Aidan didn't want to see her gunned down by Jimmy. He wanted her to face justice. To spend the rest of her life in jail. Answer for what she'd done.

He told Kristin to stay where she was – 'Try to keep these people back' – and ran after the truck, which had already followed Shannon through the gate, gaining on her fast.

Shannon turned and put her hands in the air. As Aidan reached the gate, Jimmy stopped the truck and hopped out, keeping the gun trained on Shannon. He walked slowly towards her.

'Get on your knees!' Jimmy shouted. 'Do it!'

Shannon hesitated for only a moment before sinking to the ground, lowering her hands.

'Wait!' yelled Aidan. He sprinted, the sun beating down on him, convinced he would hear another shot at any moment. His heart and lungs hurt. When he reached the truck, Shannon was still on the ground on her knees, and Jimmy was standing over her, his pistol pointed at her head, breathing heavily, seemingly torn. There was still, apparently, some vestige of loyalty or love inside him. Something that stopped him from putting a bullet in Shannon's head.

'Take the truck and go,' Aidan panted. 'Leave her to me.'

Jimmy squinted at him. 'You're gonna kill her?'

'I don't care what you do to me,' Shannon said, in a distant, dreamy voice. 'I'm free now. I can hear them whispering to me again. And if it's not me who saves this—'

'Shut up!' Jimmy screamed. He took a half-step closer to her. 'I ought to bury you here. Make you spend the rest of eternity underground. You've made me waste years of my life.'

She smiled. 'You followed me willingly. And the mission isn't over yet, Jimmy. Maybe I was wrong about this place. Wrong about the time. But the end is coming. Can't you feel it?'

He wasn't listening. He was gazing into the distance.

'Shit,' he said.

Aidan followed his gaze, not sure what had made Jimmy swear, and then he saw it.

On the horizon, emerging through the curtain of the shimmering heat haze, came a police car. Then another. And another.

Jimmy ran towards his truck. He got in, slammed the door behind him. The truck took off across the rocky desert floor, in the opposite direction to the cops, leaving Aidan alone with Shannon.

The cop cars were getting closer. One of them peeled off to pursue the truck. Aidan turned to see Shannon's former recruits, all the young men and women who had believed in her, gathering by the fence, watching. Shannon followed his gaze, then looked back at the approaching cars, the plumes of dust rising from beneath their wheels.

Shannon fell forward, pressing her forehead to the earth. The men and women behind the fence stared at her, some confused, some sneering; one or two were weeping.

Aidan couldn't bear to look at her anymore. He was exhausted. He slumped to the rocky ground and his chin dipped to his chest. The sun beat down on the back of his neck. He had come all this way, seen things he had never dreamed of, done things he would have hardly imagined possible. He had killed a man. He had met someone unlike anyone he had ever met before, then watched her die. He hadn't even had time to process it yet – Lana's death – but he knew it would hit him soon, and hit him hard. And then there was Scarlett, locked in a room with a head full of mad beliefs.

But you found her, said a little voice in his ear. *You actually found her.*

He knelt in the desert dirt, and soon the engines of the police cars became audible. Moments later, they were pulling up just a few metres away from him, and doors were opening and slamming. He still didn't look up.

Not until a shadow fell over him and a familiar voice said, 'There's no need to kneel, Aidan. I'm Lana Carrera, not Queen Elizabeth.'

Chapter 46

The Feds had made Aidan stay in California for a week after the events at the Cradle, interviewing him repeatedly about everything he'd seen and found out. They were pissed that he and Lana hadn't called them after Giglio was killed, and gave him a stern lecture about 'taking the law into your own hands' and 'trying to be some kind of hero'. He tried to explain he wasn't trying to be a hero. He'd just wanted to find his sister. For a few days, he was worried they might charge him with something – obstructing justice, not reporting a serious crime – but in the end they let him go.

Before he left the police station in Barstow, which the FBI were using as a base while they carried out their investigation, he said, 'What's going to happen to Shannon?'

The lead agent, a tough guy with cropped grey hair, folded his arms and said, 'Murder. Abduction. Fraud. The list is almost as long as that bunker is deep.'

'Will I need to be a witness at the trial?'

'I doubt it will get that far,' said the agent. 'Her lawyer's already talking about making a deal. Shannon has information about a lot of organisations we're highly interested in.'

'Other eco-terrorist groups? Wait. What are you saying? She might get away with all this? End up in witness protection or something?'

'No comment,' said the agent.

Jimmy definitely wouldn't face trial. The police had pursued him for twenty minutes before their cars had surrounded his truck. In a silent part of the Mojave, witnessed only by lizards, Jimmy had refused to surrender.

Jimmy had helped Aidan escape. For a brief time, they'd been allies. But when Aidan heard that Jimmy was dead, he wasn't sorry.

ω

Aidan left the police station and found Lana at the motel, sitting out front in the shade. She had a bottle of water in front of her. She had already told him that the Feds had told her it was fine to go home, and she would be taking a rental back to Eaglewood that evening.

Aidan sat opposite her and picked up the bottle, checking the label. Evian.

'Not Shastina Spring?'

She smiled.

It had been Lana who had alerted the authorities and told them where in the Mojave to find the Cradle. Because when she'd gone downstairs, she'd found Mayor Hood was still breathing. Just. She'd called an ambulance, and while they waited for it, he'd come to for just long enough to tell her where to find the address. The map coordinates were in a protected file on his computer.

'The password?' she'd asked.

'Elizabeth,' he'd said, before slipping back into unconsciousness. The housekeeper, Yolanda, had been alive too. She and her employer were in hospital now, expected to make full recoveries. Hood was under police guard, and apparently Elizabeth was there too.

'Samuel and Elizabeth had a big reunion yesterday,' Lana said now. 'Apparently my mom even let her stay over.'

'Young love.'

'It's a beautiful thing.'

Aidan met Lana's eye and he held her gaze. Lana smiled in a way that told him she was thinking the same thing he was. Remembering what had been happening in her motel room every night since they'd been reunited. Aidan felt her skin against his, saw her eyes in the half-light of the room, her hair spread out on the pillow.

'I need to get going soon, or I've got no hope of making it back by dark,' she said. 'Hey, what is it? You knew I was heading back today, didn't you?'

'Yeah. Yeah, of course.'

He'd been hoping, foolishly, that she might delay her return. That they could stay here, in this little bubble of time, before they had to return to normal life, for a little longer. A day or two.

She reached across the table and squeezed his hand. 'Aidan. This week has been – well, I think you know how it's been. You're going back to England for a while, though, right? We both need to spend time with our families.' She smiled. 'But we'll always have Barstow.'

'Not to mention Birches Rock, Fortuna and the murder house.'

'Good times, baby.'

The plan was for Aidan to take Scarlett back to the UK, to their parents, once the Feds had finished interviewing her. Aidan had already spoken to his cat-sitter, who had promised to keep feeding and taking care of Frosty. Aidan would stay in England as long as he was needed before heading back to Seattle, his cat and his job. Lana was going to do something similar, spending time in Eaglewood with Samuel and their mother before going back to DC. Family came first. It always came first.

He squeezed her hand. 'I'm so pleased you're not dead.'

That cracked her up. 'Me too, Aidan. Me too. Hey, what's wrong? Don't go all abandoned puppy dog on me, please.'

Now he laughed. 'I'm not. I promise. I was thinking about Scarlett, that's all. You know the cops had to drag her out of her room, kicking and screaming?'

'You said.'

'She hates me. Says I've ruined everything. You know, she really believed everything Shannon fed her.'

'She'll come around. She's been brainwashed. That kind of thing can take a long time to get over. It's going to be traumatic for her. But she's a survivor, Aidan, and she's got you. She'll be fine.'

'I hope so.'

They lapsed into silence. It was warm out here, a soft breeze blowing across the terrace. In the distance, the quiet drone of cars heading down Route 66. It was a trip Aidan had always wanted to take, driving from coast to coast, and although he didn't mention it now, he thought maybe someday it might happen. Not Route 66, but another route east to Washington. He was sure his and Lana's story wasn't over yet.

'Well,' she said, standing up. 'I guess this is it.'

'For now.'

She smiled. 'For now.'

He stepped into her arms and they embraced, holding each other for a long time. Aidan didn't want to let go.

'Are you sure you don't want to stay for another night?'

She laughed, kissed him quickly then stepped away. 'Oh God. Don't tempt me.'

He watched her go, walking across to her rental car. When she reached it she stopped and waved, then climbed in. Soon she was driving away, exiting the parking lot, heading north, and then she turned a corner, leaving nothing behind but the empty road.

Aidan sighed and was about to head back to his room when his phone – the new one he'd bought in town this week – pinged with a text message. It was from the FBI agent who'd interviewed him.

Scarlett is free to leave. Someone is bringing her to your motel now.

Aidan was about to reply when he saw the three dots to indicate the agent was typing something else.

Keep your eye on her, the second message read.

Aidan went back to his room and waited for Scarlett.

It was time to go home.

Epilogue

Scarlett hated being on the plane. She gripped the armrests and closed her eyes, chewing a piece of gum in a vain attempt to stop her ears from popping. All she could picture was how much nitrogen oxide and sulphur dioxide was being pumped into the atmosphere. As the plane ascended through the clouds, she looked around her at all the people in this metal tube, fiddling with their headphones, poking at the screens in front of them, and she wondered if any of them realised their days were numbered. That every action they took, every plane they boarded, every car journey they went on, every animal they ate, hastened their demise.

The end was coming.

She couldn't hear them all the way up here, but the trees whispered it to her.

'You okay?' Aidan asked. 'Do you need anything?'

She gave him her sweetest smile and said, 'I'm fine, thanks.'

He looked relieved. Since they'd been reunited, she'd noticed him watching everything she did. It was infuriating, but it allowed her to practise. Shannon and Jimmy had taught her this: that if, for whatever reason, she found herself out in the world again, she would need to wear camouflage.

'You have to fit in,' Jimmy had said. 'No one wants to be lectured about environmental destruction. And no one wants to hear that their home is about to burn down around them.'

'They think we're crazy,' Shannon had added. 'What they don't realise is that we're the sane ones. We're the ones who know the truth.'

Okay, so Shannon had got the dates wrong. There had been no all-consuming fire. No continent-drowning tsunami, no great extinction event. The world was still turning, people were still getting on planes and driving their cars and going to work. Having babies, eating McDonald's, staring at their phones.

But it didn't mean the day wasn't coming.

The seat-belt sign turned off and Scarlett got up and made her way along the aisle to the bathroom. Inside, she looked at herself in the mirror, brushed her hair with her fingers. She looked pale. A week underground followed by the days in Barstow had made her skin sallow.

At the building the FBI had used to interview everyone, Scarlett had seen a number of the other recruits moving in and out of rooms, all accompanied by agents. Miranda had been there, and a few of the other women from the maternity suite. She had seen Frank too, who had been driving the van the night Taylor had tried to escape. Scarlett had asked about Taylor, feigning concern, and the agent had told her she was in hospital. Shannon had brought her from the brothel on the farm, concealed beneath a blanket in the back of a truck, and locked her in a room somewhere in the Cradle. Scarlett wasn't sure what Shannon's plans for Taylor had been, but she wouldn't have been surprised if, in the end, she'd ended up becoming one of the mothers.

If Taylor hadn't run, if that old woman hadn't seen Scarlett from the train and alerted Aidan . . . A lot of this was her fault.

But it wasn't Taylor that Scarlett was most interested in right now. Shannon had been in that building too, in a heavily guarded room at the end of one of the corridors. Scarlett had been able to sense her.

On Scarlett's last morning there, the agent had escorted her from her room, having told her she was free to go, and at the same moment Shannon had been brought out of her room.

She had been in handcuffs, surrounded by agents and uniformed cops. She looked dirty and dishevelled. Her head hung down. But when she saw Scarlett she lifted her chin and the colour came back into her face. She met Scarlett's eye. Nodded.

And in that moment, Scarlett knew. They would be together again.

If Aidan was right, if Shannon had done a deal with the Feds, it might not be too long. She knew that Shannon would reach out to her, tell her where to find her. And in a few months, Scarlett would be an adult. She'd be able to go wherever she liked, do whatever she wanted. Her parents and Aidan wouldn't be able to stop her.

And when they were together again, they could start to rebuild. Start a new Ranch. Make a plan that didn't involve hiding out underground. Avoid scumbags like Darryl Moses and weak men like Jimmy.

She washed her hands, splashed water on her face and went back to her seat, smiling at Aidan before sitting down.

'So,' she said brightly, 'I haven't watched a movie for about two years. What good ones have I missed?'

And as he helped her negotiate the guide on the entertainment screen, recommending several vacuous pieces of fluff that she had no interest in, she kept smiling, kept pretending. This was how it was going to be for a while. Pretending. Wearing camouflage. Listening to the trees, to the wind, to the sea and the sky and the earth.

Waiting for the fires.

Acknowledgements

Thank you for reading *No Place To Run*. Whether you're a first-time reader of my books or a loyal veteran, I hope you enjoyed it. You can let me know by emailing mark@markedwardsauthor.com. I love hearing from readers and always respond. Alternatively, you could join my Facebook community (@markedwardsauthor) or send me a tweet @mredwards.

No Place To Run had a long gestation period. I started writing it in 2019 and worked on the opening chapters on a research trip to Seattle, Oregon and Northern California in October of that year, accompanied by my friend and fellow author Ed James. We took the *Coast Starlight* to Klamath Falls then drove into California, stopping at the gloriously named Weed and the New Age paradise of Mount Shasta. I came home inspired and excited to finish the book. That winter, as bushfires raged in Australia, the climate themes of the book felt more relevant and urgent than ever.

Then the pandemic happened. My children were sent home from school. The streets were deserted and I found myself doom-scrolling and home-schooling instead of writing. Work on this book stalled and, unable to get back into it, I set it aside and wrote something else instead (last year's *The Hollows*).

But as we emerged from the first wave or two (or three?) of the pandemic, my thoughts returned to the book you've just read. I had left Aidan in the fictional town of Eaglewood, neither of us knowing what had happened to Scarlett. I am not the kind of author who starts out knowing how his stories will end – it's a journey of discovery for me too – and I needed to find out the truth about whether Francesca really had seen Scarlett. So I came back to this book with renewed energy.

A number of people helped me with this endeavour. First, I'd like to thank the aforementioned Ed James for accompanying me on the trip and for providing several hair-raising moments which will no doubt form the basis of one or two future horror stories.

Lisa Harrison did invaluable research into environmental activism and filled her head with terrifying stories about what might happen to our planet if we don't get our collective act together.

My agent, Madeleine Milburn, read the early drafts of this book and provided incisive feedback. Then my editors, David Downing and Victoria Oundjian, helped me rip it up and reassemble it. They put me through hell, but it was all worth it.

My good friend Colin Scott helped me brainstorm titles and pointed out that perhaps I shouldn't call my fictional town Cougar Creek.

Sarah Shaw at Amazon made me feel so welcome in Seattle and introduced me to her lovely dog, Moose. Thanks to both of you!

A number of my regular readers volunteered to have their names used for characters in this book. I must point out that these characters are purely fictional and bear no resemblance to their namesakes. They are: Christopher Hood, Paige Caldaralo, Bethany Caron, Kristin Fox, Tom Stretton, Richelle Heard, Michael Giglio (his surname anyway!) and Zach Van Beekum. Thank you all for your evergreen enthusiasm.

The biggest thank you goes as always to my wife, Sara, who is full of brilliant ideas, as well as to my children and the rest of my family. It's been a hard couple of years, but we made it through.

The following books helped me with the background of this novel: *The Uninhabitable Earth* by David Wallace-Wells; *This is Not a Drill: An Extinction Rebellion Handbook*; *Notes From an Apocalypse* by Mark O'Connell; and *Bunker: What It Takes to Survive the Apocalypse* by Bradley Garrett.

Finally, thanks again, to you – yes, you – for reading. There are a billion books in the world. Thanks for choosing mine.

Mark Edwards
www.markedwardsauthor.com

Free *Short Sharp Shockers* Box Set

Join Mark Edwards' Readers Club and get a free collection of four stories, including *Wish You Dead*, *Kissing Games*, *Consenting Adults* and *Guardian Angel*.

You will also receive exclusive news and regular giveaways.

Get it now at www.markedwardsauthor.com/free.

About the Author

Mark Edwards writes psychological thrillers in which scary things happen to ordinary people.

He has sold 4 million books since his first novel, *The Magpies*, was published in 2013, and has topped the bestseller lists numerous times. His other novels include *Follow You Home*, *The Retreat*, *In Her Shadow*, *Because She Loves Me*, *The Hollows* and *Here to Stay*. He has also co-authored six books with Louise Voss.

Originally from Hastings in East Sussex, Mark now lives in Wolverhampton with his wife, their children and two cats.

Mark loves hearing from readers and can be contacted through his website, www.markedwardsauthor.com, or you can find him on Facebook (@markedwardsauthor), Twitter (@mredwards) and Instagram (@markedwardsauthor).